RORY O'MORE

RORY O'MORE

A NATIONAL ROMANCE

Samuel Lover

NONSUCH

First published 1837
Copyright © in this edition 2006
Nonsuch Publishing Limited

Nonsuch Publishing Limited
The Mill, Brimscombe Port, Stroud, Gloucestershire, GL5 2QG
www.nonsuch-publishing.com

Nonsuch Publishing is an imprint of Tempus Publishing Group

For comments or suggestions, please email the editor of this series at
classics@tempus-publishing.com

British Library Cataloguing in Publication Data.
A catalogue record for this book is available from the British Library.

ISBN 1-84588-202-4
ISBN-13 (from January 2007) 978-1-84588-202-0

Typesetting and origination by Nonsuch Publishing Limited
Printed in Great Britain by Oaklands Book Services Limited

Contents

INTRODUCTION TO THE MODERN EDITION

An Irishman's heart is nothing but his imagination.

George Bernard Shaw, *John Bull's Other Island*

William Butler Yeats famously held that the symbol of Irish art should be that of the cracked looking-glass, reflecting, if you will, how Irish art is continually informed and defined by the fact that it is simply not English. Implicit in this is the fact that so much of the art and literature of this nation is bound up with the question of what it means to be Irish at all. Such a search to establish a separate identity of one's own is an artistic pattern repeated in almost all post-colonial literature, from V.S. Naipaul's depictions of Trinidad to Jean Rhys' reflections on the stark and beautiful hills of Dominica. The rugged plains of Samuel Lover's Ireland may be less exotic, and are certainly less volcanic, but not only is the nature of his writing bound up with such questions, the subject of *Rory O'More* is that very struggle for independence itself.

In 1791 Theobald Wolfe Tone, whom Professor Declan Kiberd of University College Dublin describes as a 'coachmaker's son turned Jacobin and rebel', helped to found the Society of the United Irishmen, an association which sought to 'unite Catholics, Protestants and Dissenter' in the cause of parliamentary reform.

Though explicitly diverse, these groups allowed themselves to be drawn together by their common exclusion from the ruling Protestant ascendancy. The desired reforms, however, proved unforthcoming through peaceful means, and the United Irishmen, fired by the events of the French Revolution of 1789, turned their gaze from reformation to revolt. The aim, as Tone saw it, was now to sever entirely the connection with England, 'the never failing source of all our political evils', and to do so by force.

While the numbers associated with this movement swelled to over 100,000, these men were largely untrained and would be hard-pressed to overturn the organised might of the British Army. Consequently, Tone saw the best hope for Ireland as coming from the French, against whom the English had been officially at war since Louis XVI's execution. Agents were dispatched to England and Ireland to see how seeds of insurrection might flourish, but it was felt that an outright invasion of Ireland by sea might yield the best results. General Louis Lazare Hoche, a man of humble roots who eventually rose by a circuitous route involving more than one charge of treason to become the French Minister for War, was chosen to lead the mission. Tone accompanied the force of 15,000 French soldiers, who set sail in 1796. The invasion was not a success. While they managed to elude the Royal Navy, poor weather and poor seamanship conspired to prevent the force from landing on Irish shores.

Tone referred to the aborted invasion as 'England's luckiest escape since the Armada', but what actually resulted from it was a brutal campaign of repression and coercion by the British forces, who sought to quell the clamour of the dissidents through house burning, torture and murder. Sectarian division lay just beneath the surface of the rebel unity, particularly in Ulster, and this fact did not escape the attention of the Establishment. Brigadier C.E. Knox, in a letter to General Lake, wrote, 'I hope to increase the animosity between Orangemen and United Irishmen. Upon that depends the safety of the centre counties of the North.' While such a strategy may have a left a dubious legacy, it seemed to produce the desired effect, as the movement became riven by internal conflict. The Catholic Church in Ireland had by now already been co-opted to the support of the Crown by the foundation of Maynooth Seminary College. Raids soon began throughout the country in an effort to root out the rebel leadership, sparking a pre-emptive rising in County Tipperary, which in turn sparked the imposition of martial law. Little option remained to the rebels but to act before all opportunity was lost.

And so act they did. The rising was set for 23 May 1798, to begin in Dublin, with the surrounding counties to rise in support. The Dublin rising imploded before fighting began, however, thwarted from the outset by informers. The surrounding counties rose as planned, the greatest success coming in Wexford, until the Battle of Vinegar Hill on 21 June saw the British forces regain control of the region. The French did eventually land on the west coast in August, where, together with the local rebels they prompted the 'Castlebar Races' – so named for the speed of the retreat of the British forces – before being eventually defeated. October saw Tone attempt to land with a French force in Donegal, but they were intercepted by the Navy. Tone was sentenced to be hung as a traitor rather than as a soldier, to which fate he objected, and which he avoided in the end by killing himself.

The rebellion was marked mostly by the atrocities committed throughout, of which both sides were guilty. It was followed by a period known as 'the great silence', in which people feared to speak of what had happened at all. The Act of Union of 1801 was the official response of the Crown, drawing the two countries closer together under the Parliament in London.

Rory O'More, first published in novel form in 1837, takes up the tale at the point at which an agent of the French, Horace de Lacy, has just arrived in Ireland. He had already explored the possibilities of spreading dissention in London but, rather than recruits to his cause, he found there a people corrupted by luxury, reflecting that 'the Londoner will endure the abuses of his time, because he enjoys from them a temporary benefit, and even upholds the very tyranny of which he himself will be the last to suffer.'

In Ireland, De Lacy is thrown together with Rory, the eponymous hero of Lover's tale, and their story begins to unfold. Set against the tumultuous backdrop of the times, this fictionalised account of very real events was an instant success for its author. Beginning life as a ballad, and drawing the name of its hero from a character in the Rising of 1641, after whom a bridge over the River Liffey is named, *Rory O'More* struck a dramatic chord with the reading public. It was quickly adapted for the stage, where it ran at the Adelphi in London for 100 nights and, in doing so, sealed Samuel Lover's reputation as a writer of the very first degree.

I

The cottage of Rory O'More, with scenery, machinery, dresses, and decorations.

IN A RETIRED DISTRICT OF the south of Ireland, near some wild hills and a romantic river, a small by-road led to a quiet spot, where, at the end of a little lane, or *boreen*, which was sheltered by some hazel-hedges, stood a cottage which in England would have been considered a poor habitation, but in Ireland was absolutely comfortable, when contrasted with the wretched hovels that most of her peasantry are doomed to dwell in. The walls were only built of mud, but then the doorway and such windows as the cabin had were formed of cut stone, as was the chimney, which last convenience is of rare occurrence in Irish cabins, a hole in the roof generally serving instead. The windows were not glazed, it is true, but we must not expect too much gentility on this point; and though the light may not be let in as much as it is the intention of such openings to do, yet if the wind be kept out the Irish peasant may be thankful. A piece of board—or, as Pat says, a wooden pane of glass—may occupy one square, while its neighbour may be brown paper, ornamented inside, perhaps, with a ballad setting forth how

'A sailor coorted a farmer's daughther
That lived convaynient to the Isle of Man,'

or, maybe, with a print of Saint Patrick banishing the *sarpents*—or the
Virgin Mary in flaring colours, that one might take for

> 'The king's daughter a come to town,
> With a red petticoat and a green gownd.'

But though the windows were not glazed, and there was not a
boarded floor in the house, yet it was a snug cottage. Its earthen floors
were clean and dry, its thatched roof was sound : the dresser in the
principal room was well furnished with delf; there were two or three
chairs and a good many three-legged stools—a spinning-wheel, that
sure sign of peace and good conduct—more than one iron pot—more
than one bed, and one of those four-posted, with printed calico curtains
of a most resplendent pattern: there was a looking-glass, too, in the
best bedroom, with only one corner broken off and only three cracks
in the middle; and that further damage might not be done to this most
valuable piece of furniture—most valuable I say, for there was a pretty
girl in the house who wanted it every Sunday morning to see that her
bonnet was put on becomingly before she went to chapel—that no
further damage might be done, I say, this inimitable looking-glass was
imbedded in the wall with a framework of mortar round it, tastefully
ornamented with cross bars, done by the adventurous hand of Rory
O'More himself, who had a genius for handling a trowel. This came to
him by inheritance, for his father had been a mason; which accounts
for the cut-stone door-way, windows, and chimney of the cottage,
that Rory's father had built for himself. But when I say Rory had a
genius for handling a trowel, I do not mean to say he followed the
trade of his father—he did not—it was a gift of nature which Rory
left quite unencumbered by any trammels of art; for as for line and
rule, these were beneath Rory's consideration; this the setting of the
glass proved—for there was no attempt at either the perpendicular, the
horizontal, or the plane; and from the last being wanting, the various
portions of the glass presented different angles, so that it reflected a
very distorted image of every object, and your face, if you would
believe the glass, was as crooked as a ram's horn—which I take to be

the best of all comparisons for crookedness. Mary O'More, however, though as innocent a girl as any in the country, did *not* believe that her face was *very* crooked: it was poor Rory who principally suffered, for he was continually giving himself most uncharitable gashes in shaving, which Rory attributed to the razor, when in fact it was the glass was in fault; for when he fancied he was going to smooth his upper lip, the chances were that he was making an assault on his nose, or cutting a slice off his chin.

But this glass has taken up a great deal too much time—which, after all, is not uncommon: when people get before a glass, they are very likely to linger there longer than they ought.

But I need not go on describing any more about the cottage—nobody wants an inventory of its furniture, and I am neither an auctioneer nor a bailiff's keeper. I have said Rory's father was a mason. Now his mother was a widow—argal (as the grave-digger hath it), his father was dead. Poor O'More, after laying stones all his life, at last had a stone laid over him; and Rory, with filial piety, carved a crucifix upon it surmounted by the letters I.H.S. and underneath this inscription:

'Pray for the sowl of Rory O'More; Requiescat in pace.'

This inscription was Rory's first effort in sepulchral sculpture, and, from his inexperience in the art, it presented a ludicrous appearance: for, from the importance Rory attached to his father's soul—or, as he had it, *sowl*—he wished to make the word particularly conspicuous; but, in doing this, he cut the letters so large hat he did not leave himself room to finish the word, and it became divided—the word *requiescat* became also divided: the inscription, therefore stood as follows:—

You were thus called on to pray for the Sow in one corner, while the Cat was conspicuous in the other.

Such was Rory's first attempt in this way, and though the work has often made others smile, poor Rory's tears had moistened every letter of it, and this humble tombstone was garlanded with as much affection as the more costly ones of modern Père-la-Chaise: and though there were none who could read who did not laugh at the absurdity, yet they regarded Rory's feelings too much to let him be a witness of such mirth. Indeed, Rory would have resented with indignation the attempt to make the grave of his father the subject of laughter; for in no country is the hallowed reverence for father and mother more observed than in Ireland.

Besides, Rory was not a little proud of his name. He was taught to believe there was good blood in his veins, and that he was descended from the O'Mores of Leinster. Then, an old school master in the district, whose pupil Rory had been, was constantly recounting to him the glorious deeds of his progenitors—or, as he called them, his 'owld anshim anshisthers in the owld anshim times'—and how he should never disgrace himself by doing a *dirty turn*; 'Not that I ever seen the laste sign iv it in you, *ma bouchal*—but there's no knowin'. And sure the divil's busy wid us sometimes, and dales in timtayshins, and lays snares for us all, as one av you'd snare a hare or ketch sparrows in a thrap; and who can tell the minit that he might be layin' salt on your tail onknowst to you, if you worn't smart?—and therefore be always mindful of your anshisters, that wor of the highest blood in Ireland, and in one of the highest places in it too, Dunamaise—I mane the rock of Dunamaise, and no less. And there is where Rory O'More, King of Leinster, lived in glory time out o' mind and the Lords of the Pale daren't touch him—and pale enough he made them often, I go bail;—and there he was—like an aigle on his rock, and the dirty English afeard o' their lives to go within miles iv him, and he shut up his castle as stout as a ram.'

In such rhodomontade used Phelim O'Flanagan to flourish away, and delight the ears of Rory and Mary, and the widow no less. Phelim was a great character: he wore a scratch wig that had been built somewhere about the year One, and from its appearance might justify the notion that Phelim's wig-box was a dripping-pan. He had a pair of spectacles, which held their place upon his nose by taking a strong grip of it, producing thereby a snuffling pronunciation, increased by his taking of snuff: indeed, so closely was his proboscis embraced by this primitive pair of spectacles, that he could not have his pinch of snuff without taking them off, as they completely blockaded the passage. They were always stuck low down on his nose, so that he could see over them when he wished it, and this he did for all distant objects; while for reading he was obliged to throw his head back to bring his eyes to bear through the glasses; and this, forcing the rear of his wig downwards on the collar of his coat, shoved it forward on his forehead and stripped the back of his pate: in the former case, his eyes were as round as an owl's; and in the other, closed nearly into the expression of disdain, or at least of great consequence. His coat was of grey frieze, and his nether garment of buckskin, equalling the polish of his wig, and surpassing that of his shoes, which indeed were not polished, except on Sunday, or such occasions as the priest of the parish was expected to pay his school a visit—and then the polish was produced by the brogues being *greased*, so that the resemblance to the wig was more perfect. Stockings he had, after a sort; that is to say, he had woollen cases for his legs, but there were not any feet to them: they were stuffed into the shoe to make believe, and the deceit was tolerably well executed in from, where Phelim had

them under his eye; but, like Achilles, he was vulnerable in the heel—
indeed, worse off than that renowned hero, for he had only one heel
unprotected, while poor Phelim had both. On Monday, Tuesday, and
Wednesday, Phelim had a shirt—you saw he had, but towards the latter
end of the week, from the closely buttoned coat, and the ambuscade of
a spotted handkerchief round his neck, there was ground for suspicion
that the shirt was under the process of washing, that it might be ready
for service on Sunday; when, at mass, Phelim's shirt was always at its
freshest.

There was a paramount reason, to be sure, why Phelim sported a clean
shirt in chapel on Sunday: he officiated as clerk during the service—as
it would be said amongst the peasantry, he 'sarved mass'; and in such a
post of honour personal decency is indispensable. In this service he was
assisted by a couple of boys, who were the head of his school, and enjoyed
great immunities in consequence. In the first place they were supposed,
from virtue of the dignity to which they were advanced, to understand
more Latin than any of the rest of the boys; and from the necessity of
their being decently clad, they were of course the sons of the most
comfortable farmers in the district, who could afford the luxury of shoes
and stockings to their children, to enable them to act as *acolytes*. The boys
themselves seemed to like the thing well enough, as their frequent passing
and repassing behind the priest at the altar, with various genuflexions, gave
them a position of importance before the neighbours that was gratifying;
and they seemed to be equally pleased up to one point, and to proceed in
perfect harmony until the ringing of a little bell, and that was the signal
for a fight between them. When I say fight, I do not mean that they boxed
each other before (or rather behind) the priest, but to all intents and
purposes there was a struggle who should get the bell, as that seemed the
grand triumph of the day; and the little bell certainly had a busy time of
it, for the boy that had it seemed endued with a prodigious accession of
devotion; and as he bent himself to the very earth, he rattled the bell till it
seemed choking with its superabundant vibration; while the Christianity
of his brother acolyte seemed to suffer in proportion to the piety of his
rival, for he did not bow half so low, and was looking with a sidelong eye
and sulky mouth at his victorious coadjutor.

As for Phelim, his post of honour was robing and unrobing the priest before the altar; for in the humble little chapel where all this was wont to occur there was no vestry—the priest was habited in his vestments in the presence of his congregation. But Phelim's grand triumph seemed to be assisting his clergy in sprinkling the flock with holy water. This was done by means of a large sprinkling-brush, which the priest dipped from time to time in a vessel of holy water which Phelim held, and waving it to the right and left, cast it over the multitude. For this purpose, at a certain period, the little gate of a small area railed round the altar was opened, and forth stepped the priest, followed by Phelim bearing the holy water. Now it happened that the vessel which held it was no other than a bucket. I do not mean this irreverently, for holy water would be as holy in a bucket as in a golden urn; but, God forgive me! I could not help thinking it rather queer to see Phelim bearing this great bucket of water, with a countenance indicative of the utmost pride and importance, following the priest, who advanced through the crowd, that opened and bowed before him as his reverence ever and anon turned round, popped his sprinkling-brush into the water, and slashed it about right and left over his flock, that courted the shower, and were the happier the more they were wet. Poor people! if it made them happy, where was the harm of it? A man is not considered unworthy of the blessings of the constitution of great Britain by getting wet to the skin in the pelting rain of the equinox; and I cannot, nor ever could see, why a few drops of holy water should exclude him.—But hang philosophy! what has it to do with a novel?

Phelim, like a great many other hedge-schoolmasters, held his rank in the Church of Rome from his being able to mumble some scraps of Latin, which, being the only language his Sable Majesty does not understand, is therefore the one selected for the celebration of the mass. How a prince of his importance could be so deficient in his education may well create surprise, particularly as he is so constant an inmate of our universities.

Phelim's Latin, to be sure, could scarcely 'shame the d—l,' though certainly it might have puzzled him. It was a barbarous jargon, and but for knowing the phrases he meant to say, no one could comprehend him. *Spiritu tuo* was from his mouth, 'Sperchew chew ô,' and so on.

Nevertheless, it was not in chapel alone that Phelim sported his Latin—nor in his school either, where, for an additional twopence a week, he inducted his scholars into the mysteries of the classics (and mysteries might they well be called)—but even in his social intercourse he was fond of playing the pedant and astonishing the vulgar; and as poaching piscators throw medicated crumbs into the water where they fish, so Phelim flung about his morsels of Latin to catch *his* gudgeons. Derivations were his forte; and, after elucidating something in that line, he always said, 'Derry wather!' and took snuff with an air of sublimity.   Or, if he overcame an antagonist in an argument, which was seldom the case, because few dared to engage with him—but, when any individual was rash enough to encounter Phelim, he always slaughtered him with big words, and instead of addressing his opponent, he would turn to the company present and say, 'Now I'll make yiz all sinsible to a demonstheration;' and then, after he had held them suspended in wonder for a few minutes at the jumble of hard words which neither he nor they understood, he would look round the circle with a patronising air, saying, 'You persaive—Q. E. D. what *was* to be demonstherated!'

This always finished the argument in the letter, but not in the spirit for Phelim, though he secured silence, did not produce persuasion: his adversary often kept his own opinion, but kept it a secret too, *as long as Phelim was present;* 'for how,' as they themselves said when his back was turned, 'could it be expected for them to argufy with him when he took to *discoorsin'* them out o' their common sense?—and the hoighth o' fine language it sartainly was—*but sure it wouldn't stand to raison.'* How many a speech in higher places is worthy of the same commentary!

Perhaps I have lingered too long in detailing these peculiarities of Phelim; but he was such an original that a sketch of him was too great a temptation to be resisted: besides, as he is about to appear immediately I wished the reader to have some idea of the sort of person he was.

The evening was closing as Phelim O'Flanagan strolled up the *boreen* leading to the widow O'More's cottage. On reaching the house, he saw the widow sitting at the door knitting.

'God save you, Mrs. O'More!' said Phelim.

'God save you kindly!' answered the widow.

'Faith, then, it's yourself is the industherous woman, Mrs. O'More, for it is working you are airly and late and to think of your being at the needles now, and the evenin' closin' in!'

'Oh, I don't call this work,' said the widow; 'it is only jist to have something to do, and not be lost with idleness, that I'm keepin' my hands goin'.'

'And your eyes too, 'faith—God spare them to you.'

'Amin, dear,' said the widow.

'And where is the *colleen*, that she isn't helpin' you?'

'Oh, she's just gone beyant the meadow there, to cut nettles for the chickens—she'll be in in a minit. Won't you sit down, Mr. O'Flanagan?—you'd betther dhraw a sate.'

'I'm taller standin', Mrs. O'More—thank you all the same, ma'am. And where would Rory be?'

'Why, indeed, the Scholar wint out shootin', and Rory wint wid him. It's fond of the sport he is, Mr. O'Flanagan as you know.'

'Thrue for you, ma'am; it's hard if I wouldn't, when I sot over him for five years and betther; and hard it was to keep him undher! for he was always fond o' sport.'

'But not the taste o' vice in him, Phelim dear,' said the mother.

'No, no, Mrs. O'More, by no manes—nothing but heart and fun in him; but not the sign o' mischief. And why wouldn't he like to go a start with the young gintleman a-shootin'?—the dog and the gun is tempting to man ever since the days o' Vargil himself, who says, with great beauty and discrimination, "*Arma virumque cano;*" which manes, "Arms, men, and dogs," which is three things that always goes together since the world began.'

'Think o' that now!' said the widow 'and so Vargo used to go shootin'!'

'Not exactly, Mrs. O'More, my dear: besides, the man's name was not Vargo, but *Vargil*. Vargo, Mrs. O'More, manes the Virgin.'

'God forgi' me!' said the widow; 'is it the blessed Vargin I said wint shootin'?' and she crossed herself.

'No, Mrs. O'More, my dear—by no manes. Vargo means only vargin; which is not blessed without you join it to something else. But Vargil was the man's name; he was a great Roman pote.'

'Oh, the darlin'!' said the widow; 'and was he a Roman?'

'Not as you mane it, Mrs. O'More, my dear: he was not a good Catholic—and more's the pity, and a sore loss to him! But he didn't know betther, for they were lost in darkness in them days, and had not the knowledge of us. But whin I say he was a Roman, I mane he was one of that famous nation—(and tarin' fellows they wor)—*Romani populi*, as we say, his nativity being cast in Mantua, which is a famous port of that country, you persaive, Mrs. O'More.'

Here Mrs. O'More dropped her ball of worsted; and Phelim, not wishing a word of his harangue to be lost, waited till the widow was reseated and in a state of attention again.

'Mantua, I say, Mrs. O'More, a famous port of the *Romani populi*—the port of Mantua—which retains to this day the honour of Vargil's nativity bein' cast in that same place, you persaive, Mrs. O'More?'

'Yis, yis, Mr. O'Flanagan, I'm mindin' you, sir. Oh, what a power o' larnin' you have! Well, well, but it's wondherful and sure I never heerd afore of any one bein' born in a portmantia.'

'Oh! ho, ho, ho! Mrs. O'More! No, my dear ma'am,' said Phelim laughing, 'I didn't say he was born in a portmantia: I said the port of Mantua, which was a territorial possession, or domain, as I may say, of the *Romani populi*, where Vargil had his nativity cast—that is to say, was born.'

'Dear, dear! what knowledge you have, Mr. O'Flanagan!—and no wondher you'd laugh at me! But sure, no wondher at the same time, when I thought you wor talkin' of a portmantia that I *would* wondher at a child bein' sent into the world in that manner.'

'Quite nath'ral, Mrs. O'More, my dear—quite nath'ral,' said Phelim.

'But, can you tell me—'

'To be sure I can,' said Phelim: 'what is it?'

'I mane, *would* you tell me, Mr. O'Flanagan, is that the place portmantias come from?'

'Why, indeed, Mrs. O'More, it is likely, from the derrywation, that it is; but, you see, these is small thrifles of histhory that is not worth the while o' great min to notice; and by reason o' that same we are left to our own conjectures in sitch matters.'

'Dear, dear! Well—but, sir, did that gintleman you were talkin' about go a shootin'—that Mr. Varjuice?—'

'Vargil, Mrs. O'More—Var-gil,' said Phelim with authority.

'I beg his pard'n, and yours, sir.'

'No offince, Mrs. O'More. Why, ma'am, as for goin' shootin', he did not—and for various raisons: guns was scarce in thim times, and gunpowdher was not in vogue, but was, by all accounts, atthributed to Friar Bacon posteriorly.'

'Oh, the dirty divils!' said the widow, 'to fry their bacon with gunpowdher!—that bates all I ever heerd.'

Phelim could not help laughing outright at the widow's mistake, and was about to explain, but she was a little annoyed at being laughed at, and Rory O'More and the Scholar, as he was called, having returned at the moment, she took the opportunity of retiring into the house, and left Phelim and his explanation and the sportsmen all together.

II

Showing how a journey may be performed on a gridiron without going as far as St. Laurence.

THE ARRIVAL OF RORY O'MORE and the Scholar having put an end to the colloquy of the Widow and Phelim O'Flanagan, the reader may as well be informed, during the pause, who the person is already designated under the title of 'the Scholar.'

It was some weeks before the opening of our story that Rory O'More had gone to Dublin, for the transaction of some business connected with the lease of the little farm of the widow—if the few acres she held might be dignified with that name. There was only some very subordinate person on the spot to whom any communication on the subject could be made; for the agent, following the example of the lord of the soil, was an absentee from the property as well as his employer;—the landlord residing principally in London, though deriving most of his income from Ireland, and the agent living in Dublin, making half-yearly visits to the tenantry, who never saw his face until he came to ask them for their rents. As it happened that it was in the six months' interregnum that the widow wished to arrange about her lease, she sent her son to Dublin for the purpose—'For what's the use,' said she, 'of talking to that fellow that's down here, who can never give you a straight answer, but goes on with his gosther, and says he'll write about it, and will have word for you next time;

and so keeps you goin' hither and thither, and all the time the thing is just where it was before, and never comes to anything?—So, Rory, dear, in God's name go off yourself and see the agint in Dublin, and get the rights of the thing out of his own mouth.' So Rory set out for Dublin, not without plenty of cautions from his mother to take care of himself in the town, for she heard it was the 'dickens' own place; and I'm told they're sich rogues there, that if you sleep with your mouth open, they'll stale the teeth out o' your head.'

'Faix, and maybe they'd find me like a weasel asleep,' answered Rory—'asleep with my eyes open: and if they have such a fancy for my teeth, maybe it's in the shape of a bite they'd get them.' For Rory had no small notion of his own sagacity.

The wonders of Dublin gave Rory, on his return, wide field for descanting upon, and made his hearers wonder in turn. But this is not the time nor place to touch an such matters. Suffice it here to say, Rory transacted his business in Dublin satisfactorily; and having done so, he mounted his outside place on one of the coaches from town, and found himself beside a slight, pale, but rather handsome young gentleman, perfectly free from anything of that repulsive bearing which sometimes too forcibly marks the distinction between the ranks of parties that may chance to meet in such promiscuous society as that which a public conveyance huddles together. He was perfectly accommodating to his fellow-travellers while they were shaking themselves down into their places, and on the journey he conversed freely with Rory on such subjects as the passing occurrences of the road suggested. This unaffected conduct won him ready esteem and liking from his humble neighbour, as in such cases it never fails to do: but its effect was heightened by the contrast which another passenger afforded, who seemed to consider it a great degradation to have a person in Rory's condition placed beside him; and he spoke in an offensive tone of remark to the person seated at the other side, and quite loud enough to be heard, of the assurance of the lower orders, and how hard it was to make low fellows understand how to keep their distance. To all this, Rory, with a great deal of tact, never made any reply, and to a casual observer would have seemed not to notice it; but to the searching eye of his pale companion, there was the quick and momentary quiver of indignation on the peasant's lip, and the compression of brow that denotes pain and anger, the more acute from their being concealed. But an occasion soon offered for this insolent and ill-bred fellow to make an open aggression upon Rory, which our hero returned with interest. After one of the stoppages on the road for refreshment, the passengers resumed their places, and the last to make his reappearance was this bashaw. On getting up to his seat, he said, 'Where's my coat?'

To this no one mode any answer, and the question was soon repeated in a louder tone: 'Where's my coat?'

'Your coat, is it, sir?' said the coachman.

'Yes—my coat; do you know anything of it?'

'No, sir,' said the coachman; 'maybe you took it into the house with you.'

'No, I did not: I left it on the coach. And, by-the-bye,' said he, looking at Rory, 'you were the only person who did not quit the coach—did *you* take it?'

'Take *what*?' said Rory, with a peculiar emphasis and intonation on the *what*.

'My coat,' said the other, with extreme effromery.

'I've a coat o' my own,' said Rory, with great composure.

'That's not an answer to my question,' said the other.

'I think you ought to be glad to get so quiet an answer,' said Rory.

'I think so too,' said the pale traveller.

'I did not address my conversation to you sir,' said the swaggering gentleman.

'If you did, sir, you should have been lying in the middle of the road now,' was the taunting rejoinder.

At this moment, a waiter made his appearance at the door of the inn, bearing the missing coat on his arm; and handing it up to the other, he said, 'You left this behind you in the parlour, sir.'

The effect was what any one must anticipate: indignant eyes were turned on all sides upon the person making so wanton an agression, and he himself seemed to stagger under the evidence against him. He scarcely knew what to do. After much stammering and hemming and hawing, he took the coat from the waiter, and turning to Rory, said, 'I see—I forgot—I thought that I left it on the coach;—but—a—I see, 'twas a mistake.'

'Oh, make no apologies,' said Rory; 'we were both undher a mistake.'

'How both?' said the Don.

'Why sir,' said Rory, 'you mistuk me for a thief, and I mistuk you for a gintleman.'

The swaggerer could not rally against the laugh this bitter repartee made against him, and he was effectually silenced for the rest of the journey.

Indeed, the conversation soon slackened on all sides, for it began to rain: and it may be remarked, that under such circumstances travellers wrap up their minds and bodies at the same time; and once a man draws his nose inside the collar of his great-coat, it must be something much above the average of stage-coach pleasantry which will make him poke it out again—and spirits invariably fall as umbrellas rise.

But neither great-coats nor umbrellas were long proof against the torrents that soon fell, for these were not the days of macintosh and indiarubber.

Have you ever remarked, that on a sudden dash of rain the coachman immediately begins to whip his horses? So it was on the present occasion; and the more it rained, the faster he drove. Splash they went through thick and thin, as if velocity could have done them any good; and the rain, one might have thought, was vying with the coachman—for the faster he drove, the faster it seemed to rain.

At last the passengers seated on the top began to feel their seats invaded by the flood that deluged the roof of the coach, just as they entered a town where there was change of horses to be made. The moment the coach stopped, Rory O'More jumped off, and said to the coachman, 'I'll be back with you before you go;—but don't start before I come;' and away he ran down the town.

'Faix, that's a sure way of being back before I go!' said the driver: 'but you'd betther not delay, my buck, or it's behind I'll lave you.'

While change was being made, the passengers endeavoured to procure wads of straw to sit upon, for the wet became more and more inconvenient; and at last all was ready for starting, and Rory had not yet returned. The horn was blown, and the coachman's patience was just worn out, when Rory hove in sight, splashing his way through the middle of the street, flourishing two gridirons over his head.

'Here I am,' said he, panting and nearly exhausted: "faith, I'd a brave run for it!'

'Why, thin, what the dickens do you want here with gridiron?' said the coachman.

'Oh, never mind,' said Rory; 'jist give me a wisp o' sthraw, and God bless you,' said he to one of the helpers who was standing by; and having got it, he scrambled up the coach, and said to his pale friend, 'Now, sir, we'll be comfortable.'

'I don't see much likelihood of it,' said his fellow-traveller.

'Why, look what I've got for you,' said Rory.

'Oh, that straw will soon be sopped with rain, and then we'll be as badly off as before.'

'But it's not on sthraw I'm depindin',' said Rory; 'look at this!' and he brandished one of the gridirons.

'I have heard of stopping the tide with a pitchfork,' said the traveller, smiling, 'but never of keeping out rain with a gridiron.'

'Faith, thin, I'll show you how to do that same,' said Rory. 'Here—sit up—clap this gridiron *undher you*, and you'll be *undher wather* no longer. Stop, sir, stay a minit—don't sit down on the bare bars and be makin' a beefstake o' yourself; here's a wisp o' sthraw to put betune you and the cowld iron—and not a dhryer sate in all Ireland than the same gridiron.'

The young traveller obeyed, and while he admired the ingenuity, could not help laughing at the whimsicality of the contrivance.

'You see I've another for myself,' said Rory, seating himself in a similar manner on his second gridiron: 'and now,' added he, 'as far as the sates is consarned, it may rain till doomsday.'

Away went the coach again; and for some time after resuming the journey, the young traveller was revolving the oddity of the foregoing incident, in his mind, and led by his train of thought to the consideration of national characteristics, he came to the conclusion that an Irishman was the only man under the sun who could have hit upon so strange an expedient for relieving them from their difficulty. He was struck not only by the originality of the design and the promptness of the execution, but also by the good-nature of his companion in thinking of him on the occasion. After these conclusions had passed through his own mind, he turned to Rory, and said:—

'What was it made you think of a gridiron?'

'Why, thin, I'll tell you,' said Rory. 'I promised my mother to bring a present to the priest from Dublin, and I could not make up my mind rightly what to get all the time I was there. I thought of a pair o' top-boots; for indeed, his reverence's is none of the best; and only you *know* them to be top-boots, you would not *take* them to be top-boots, bekase the bottoms has been put in so often that the tops is wore out intirely, and is no more like top-boots than my brogues. So I wint to a shop in Dublin, and pick'ed out the purtiest pair o' top-boots I could see;—whin I say purty, I don't mane a flourishin' "taarin" pair, but sitch as was fit for a priest, a respectable pair o' boots; and with that, I pulled out my good money to pay for thim, when jist at that minit, remembering the thricks o' the town, I bethought o' myself, and says I, "I suppose these are the right thing?" says I to the man.—"You can thry them," says he.—"How can I thry them?" says I.—"Pull them on you," says he.—"Throth, an' I'd be sorry," says I, "to take sitch a liberty with thim," says I.—"Why, aren't you goin' to ware thim?" says he.—"Is it me?" says I. "Me ware top-boots? Do you think it's takin' lave of my sinses I am?" says I.—"Then what do you want to buy them for?" says he.—"For his reverence, Father Kinshela," says I. "Are they the right sort for him?"—"How should I know?" says he.—"You're a purty boot-maker," says I, "not to know how to make a priest's boot!"—"How do I know his size?" says he.—"Oh, don't be comin' off that a-way," says I. "There's no sitch great differ betune priests and other min?"'

'I think you were very right there,' said the pale traveller.

'To be sure, sir,' said Rory; 'and it was only jist a *come off* for his own ignorance'—"Tell me his size," says the fellow, "and I'll fit him."—"He's betune five and six fute," says I.—"Most men are," says he, laughin' at me. He was an impidint fellow. "It's not the five, nor six, but his *two* feet I want to know the size of," says he. So I persaived he was jeerin' me, and says I, "Why, thin, you disrespectful vagabone o' the world, you Dublin jackeen! do you mane to insinivate that Father Kinshela ever wint barefutted in his life, that I could know the size of his fut," says I; and with that I threw the boots in his face. "Take that," says I, "you dirty thief o' the world! you impidint vagabone o' the world! you ignorant citizen o' the world!" And with that I left the place.'

The traveller laughed outright at the absurdity of Rory's expectation that well-fitting boots for all persons were to be made by intuition.

"Faith, I thought it would plaze you,' said Rory. 'Don't you think I sarved him right?'

'You astonished him,' I dare say.

'I'll engage I did. Wanting to humbug me that way, taking me for a nath'ral bekase I came from the counthry!'

'Oh, I am not sure of that,' said the traveller. 'It is their usual practice to take measure of their customers.'

'Is it, thin?'

'It really is.'

'See that now!' said Rory with an air of triumph. 'You would think that they wor cleverer in the town than in the country; and they ought to be so, by all accounts;—but in the regard of what I towld you, you see, we're before them intirely.'

'How so?' said the traveller.

'Arrah! bekase they never throuble people in the counthry at all wit takin' their measure; but you jist go to a fair, and bring your fut along with you, and somebody else dhrives a cartful o' brogues into the place, and there you sarve yourself; and so the man gets his money and you get your shoes, and every one's plazed. Now, isn't that betther than sitch botches as thim in Dublin that must have the measure, and keep you waitin'; while in the counthry there's no delay in life, but it's jist down with your money and off with your brogues!'

'On with your brogues, you mean?' said the traveller.

'No, indeed, now!' said Rory; 'you're out there. Sure we wouldn' be so wasteful as to put on a bran new pair o' brogues to go licken the road home?—no, in throth; we keep them for the next dance we're goin' to, or maybe to go to chapel of a Sunday.'

'And if you don't put them on, how can you tell they fit you?'

'Oh, they're all alike!'

'But what would you do, when you wanted to go to your dance, if you found your brogues were too small?'

'Oh, that niver happens. They're all fine aisy shoes.'

'Well, but if they prove too easy?'

'That's aisy cured,' said Rory; 'stuff a thrifle o' hay into them, like the Mullingar heifers!'

'Mullingar heifers!' said the traveller, rather surprised by the oddity of the expression.

'Yes, sir,' said Rory; 'did you niver hear of the Mullingar heifers?'

'Never.'

'Why, you see, sir, the women in Westmeath, they say, is thick in the legs, God help them, the craythurs! and so there's a saying again thim, "You're beef to the heels, like a Mullingar heifer."'

'Oh! I perceive.'

'Yes, sir, and it's all on account of what I towld you about the hay.'

'How?' said the traveller.

'Why, there's an owld joke you may take a turn out of, if you like, whin you see a girl that's thick in the fetlock—you call afther her and say, "Young woman!" She turns round, and then says you, "I beg your pardon, ma'am, but I think you're used to wear hay in your shoes." Thin, if she's innocent, she'll ask "Why?"—and thin you'll say, "Bekase the calves has run down your legs to get at it."'

'I see,' said the stranger; 'that is, if she's innocent.'

'Yis, sir—simple I mane; but that seldom happens, for they're commonly up to you, and 'cute enough.'

'Now, in case she's not innocent, as you say?' said the traveller.

'"Faith! maybe it's a sharp answer you'll get thin, or none. It's as like as not she may say, "Thank'ee, young man, *my calf* doesn't like hay, and so you're welkim to it *yourself.*"'

'But all this time,' said the traveller, 'you have not told me of your reasons for getting the gridirons.'

'Oh! wait a bit,' said Rory; 'sure it's that I'm coming to. Where's this I was?'

'You were running down the Mullingar girls' legs,' said the traveller.

'I see you're sharp at an answer yourself, sir,' said Rory. 'But what I mane is, where did I lave off tellin' you about the present for the priest?—wasn't it at the bootmaker's shop?—yes, that was it. Well, sir, on laving the shop, as soon as I came to myself afther the fellow's impidence, I begun to think what was the next best thing I could get for his reverence; and with that, while I was thinkin' about it, I seen a very respectable owld gintleman goin' by, with the most beautiful stick in his hand I ever set my eyes on, and a goolden head to it that was worth its weight in goold; and it gev him such an iligant look altogether, that says I to myself, "It's the very thing for Father Kinshela, if I could get sitch another." And so I wint lookin' about me every shop I seen as I wint by, and at last, in a sthreet they call Dame Sthreet—and, by the same token, I didn't know why they called it Dame Sthreet till I ax'd; and I was towld they called it Dame Sthreet bekase the ladies were so fond o' walkin' there; and lovely craythurs they wor! and I can't b'lieve that the town is such an onwholesome place to live in, for most o' the ladies I seen there had the most beautiful rosy cheeks I ever clapt my eyes upon—and the beautiful rowlin' eyes o' them! Well, it was in Dame Sthreet, as I was sayin', that I kem to a shop where there was a power o' sticks, and so I wint in and looked at thim; and a man in the place kem to me and ax'd me if I wanted a cane. "No," says I, "I don't want a cane; it's a stick I want,' says I. "A cane, you *mane*," says he. "No," says I, "it's a stick"—for I was determined to have no cane, but to stick to the stick. "Here's a nate one," says he. "I don't want a *nate* one," says I, "but a responsible one," says I. "Faith!" says he, "if an Irishman's stick was responsible, it would have a great dale to answer for"—and he laughed a power. I didn't know myself what he meant, but that's what he said.'

'It was because you asked for a responsible stick,' said the traveller.

'And why wouldn't I?' said Rory, 'when it was for his reverence I wanted it? Why wouldn't he have a nice lookin', respectable,[1] responsible stick?'

'Certainly,' said the traveller.

'Well, I picked out one that looked to my likin'—a good substantial stick, with an ivory top to it—for I seen that the goold-headed ones was so dear I couldn't come up to them; and so says I, "Gis me a howld o' that," says I—and I tuk a grip iv it. I never w so surprised in my life. I thought to get a good, brave handful of solid stick, but my dear, it was well it didn't fly out o' my han a'most, it was so light. "Phew!" says I, "what sort of a stick is this?" "I tell you it's not a stick, but a cane," says he. "'Faith! I b'lieve you," says I. "You see how good and light it s," says he. "Think o' that, sir!—to call a stick good and light—as if there could be any good in life in a stick that wasn't heavy, and could sthreck a good blow!"   "Is it jokin' you are?" says I. "Don't you feel it yourself?" says he. "Troth, I can hardly feel it at all," says I. "Sure that's the beauty of it," says he. Think o' the ignorant vagabone!—to call a stick a beauty that was as light a'most as a bulrush!" "And so you can hardly feel it!" says he, grinnin'. "Yis, indeed," says I; "and what's worse, I don't think I could make any one else feel it either." "Oh! you want a stick to bate people with!" says he. "To be sure," says I; "sure that's the use of a stick." "To knock the sinses out o' people!" says he, grinning again. "Sartinly," says I, "if they're saucy"—lookin' hard at him at the same time. "Well, these is only walkin'-sticks," says he. "Throth, you may say *runnin'*-sticks," says I, "for you daren't stand before any one with sich a *thraneen* as that in your fist." "Well, pick out the heaviest o' them you plaze," says he "take your choice." So I wint pokin' and rummagin' among thim, and, if you believe me, there wasn't a stick in their whole shop worth a kick in the shins—divil a one!'

'But why did you require such a heavy stick for the priest?'

'Bekase there is not a man in the parish wants it more!' said Rory.

'Is he so quarrelsome, then?' asked the traveller.

'No, but the greatest o' pacemakers,' said Rory.

'Then what does he want the heavy stick for?'

'For wallopin' his flock, to be sure,' said Rory.

'Walloping!' said the traveller, choking with laughter.

'Oh! you may laugh,' said Rory ; 'but, 'pon my sowl! you wouldn't laugh if you wor undher his hand, for he has a brave heavy one, God bless him and spare him to us!'

'And what is all this walloping for?'

'Why, sir, whin we have a bit of a fight, for fun, or the regular faction one, at the fair, his reverence sometimes hears of it, and comes, av coorse.'

'Good God!' said the traveller in real astonishment, 'does the priest join the battle?'

'No, no, no, sir! I see you're quite a sthranger in the counthry. The priest join it!—Oh! by no manes. But he comes and stops it; and, av coorse, the only way he can stop it, is to ride into thim, and wallop thin all round before him, and disparse thim—scatther thim like chaff before the wind; and it's the best o' sticks he requires for that same.'

'But might he not have his heavy stick on purpose for that service, and make use of a lighter one on other occasions?'

'As for that matther, sir,' said Rory, 'there's no knowin' the minit he might want it, for he is often necessitated to have recoorse to it. It might be, going through the village, the public-house is too full, and in he goes and dhrives thim out. Oh! it would delight your heart to see the style he clears a public-house in, in no time!'

'But wouldn't his speaking to them answer the purpose as well?'

'Oh no! he doesn't like to throw away his discoorse on thim and why should he?—he keeps that for the blessed althar on Sunday, which is a fitter place for it; besides, he does not like to sevare on us.'

'Severe!' said the traveller in surprise; 'why, haven't you said that he thrashes you round on all occasions?'

'Yis, sir; but what o' that?—sure that's nothin' to his tongue—his words is like swoords or razhors, I may say: we're used to a lick of a stick every day, but not to sich language as his reverence sometimes murthers us with whin we displaze him. Oh! it's terible, so it is, to have the weight of his tongue on you! Troth! I'd rather let him bate me from this till to-morrow, than have one angry word from him.'

'I see, then, he must have a heavy stick,' said the traveller.

'To be sure he must, sir, at all times; and that was the raison I was so particular in the shop; and afther spendin' over an hour—would you b'lieve it?—divil a stick I could get in the place fit for a child, much less a man—all poor contimptible things; and so the man I was talkin' to says to me at last, "It's odd that in all these sticks there is not one to plaze you." "You know nothin' about it," says I. "You'd betther be off, and take up no more o' my time," says he. "As for your time," says I, "I'd be sorry to idle anybody; but in the regard of knowin' a stick, I'll give up to no man," says I. "Look at that!" says I, howldin' up my own purty bit o' blackthorn I had in my fist. "Would you compare your owld batther'd stick," says he—(there *was* a few chips out of it, for it is an owld friend, as you may see) would you compare it," says he, "to this?"—howldin' up one of his bulrushes. "By gor," says I, "if you like to thry a turn with me, I'll let you know which is the best!" says I. "You know nothin' about it," says he—"this is the best o' sugar-canes." "By my sowl, thin!" says I, "you'll get no sugar out o' this, I promise you!—but at the same time, the devil a sweeter bit o' timber in the wide world than the same blackthorn—and if you'd like to taste it you may thry." "No," says he; "I'm no happy cure"—(or somethin' he said about cure). "Thin if you're not aisy to cure," says I, "you'd betther not fight;" which is thrue—and some men is unwholesome, and mustn't fight by raison of it—and, indeed, it's a great loss to a man who hasn't flesh that's aisy to hale.'

'I'm sure of it,' said the traveller. 'But about the gridiron?'

'Sure I'm tellin' you about it,' said Rory; 'only I'm not come to it yet. You see,' continued he, 'I was so disgusted with them shopkeepers in Dublin, that my heart was fairly broke with their ignorance, and I seen they knew nothin' at all about what I wanted, and, so I came away without anything for his reverence, though it was on my mind all this day on the road; and comin' through the last town in the middle o' the rain, I thought of a gridiron.'

'A very natural thing to think of in a shower of rain,' said the traveller.

'No, 'twasn't the rain made me think of it—I think it was God put a gridiron in my heart, see that it was a present for the priest I intended;

and when I thought of it, it came into my head, afther, that it would be a fix thing to sit on, for to keep one out of the rain, that it was ruinatin' my cordheroys on the top o' the coach; so I kept my eye out as we dbrove along up the sthreet, and sure enough, what should I see at a shop half way down the town but a gridiron hanging up at the door! and so I went back to get it.'

'But isn't a gridiron an odd present?—hasn't his reverence one already?'

'He had sir, before it was bruk—but that's what I remembered, for I happened to be up at his place one day, sittin' in the kitchen, when Molly was brilin' some mate an it for his reverence; and while she jist turned about to get a pinch o' salt to shake over it, the dog that was in the place made a dart at the gridiron on the fire, and threwn it down, and up he whips the mate, before one of us could stop him. With that Molly whips up the gridiron, and says she, "Bad luck to you, you disrespectful baste! would nothin' sarve you but the priest's dinner?" and she made a crack o' the gridiron at him. "As you have the mate, you shall have the gridiron too," says she; and with that she gave him such a rap on the head with it, that the bars flew out of it and his head went through it, and away he pulled it out of her hands, and ran off with the gridiron hangin' round his neck like a necklace—and he went mad a'nmost with it; for though a kettle to a dog's tail is nath'rel a gridiron round his neck is very surprisin' to him; and away he tatthered over the counthry, till there wasn't a taste o' the gridiron left together.'

'So you thought of supplying its place?' said the traveller.

'Yes, sir,' said Rory. 'I don't think I could do bether.'

'But what did you get two for?' said the traveller.

'Why sir, when I thought of how good a sate it would make, I thought of you at the same time.'

'That was very kind of you,' said the traveller, 'more particularly as I have done nothing to deserve such attention.'

'You'll excuse me there, sir, if you plaze,' said Rory; 'you behaved to me, sir, like a gintleman, and the word of civility is never thrown away.'

'Every gentleman, I hope,' said the traveller, 'would do the same.'

'Every *rale* gintleman, certainly,' said Rory,—'but there's many o' them that *calls* themselves gentlemin that doesn't *do* the like, and its the stiff word they have for us, and the hard word may be—and they think good clothes makes all the differ, jist as if a man hadn't a heart undher a frieze coat.'

'I am sorry to hear it,' said the traveller; 'but I hope such conduct is not common.'

'Troth there's more of it than there ought to be,' said Rory. 'But thim that is the conthrairy is never losers by it—and so by me a you sir—and sure it's a dirty dog I'd be, to see the gintleman beside me sittin' in wet that gave me a share of his paraplew, and the civil word, that is worth more—for the hardest rain only wets the body, but the hard word cuts the heart.'

'I have reason to be obliged to you,' said the traveller; 'and I assure you I am so; but I should like to know what you'll do with the second gridiron.'

'Oh, I'll engage I'll find use for it,' said Rory.

'Why indeed,' said the traveller, 'from the example you have given of your readiness of invention, I should not doubt that you will,—for certainly, you have made, on the present occasion, a most original application of the utensil.'

'Faith, I daar say,' said Rory, 'we are the first mortials wor ever on a gridiron.'

'Since the days of Saint Laurence,' said the traveller.

'Why, used Saint Larrance, God bless him! sit on a gridiron?' said Rory.

'No,' said the traveller; 'but he was broiled upon one.'

'Oh, the thieves o' the world to brile him!—and did they ate him afther, sir?'

'No, no,' said the traveller,—'they *only* broiled him. But I thought you good Catholics all knew about the martyrs?'

'And so we do, sir, mostly;—but I never heerd of Saint Larrance afore; or if I did, I'm disremembered of it.'

'But you *do* know about most of them, you say?'

'Oh! sartinly, sir. Sure I often heerd how Saint Stephen was hunted up and down; which is the raison we begin to hunt always on Saint Stephen's Day.'

'You forget there, too,' said the traveller: 'Saint Stephen was stoned.'

'To be sure, sir—sure I know he was: didn't I say they run after him throwin' stones at him, the blackguards! till they killed him—huntin' him for his life?—Oh, thin! but wasn't it a cruel thing to be a saint in thim haythen times, to be runnin' the world over, the poor marchers, as they might well be called?'

'Yes,' said the traveller; 'those were days of trial to the saints.'

'Faith, I go bail they never gave them any thrial at all,' said Rory, 'but jist murthered them without judge or jury, the vagabones!—though, indeed, for the matther o' that, neither judge or jury will do a man much good while there's false witnesses to be had to swear what they're paid for, and maybe the jury and the judge only too ready to b'lieve them; and maybe a boy is hanged in their own minds before he's put on his thrial at all, unless he has a good friend in some great man who doesn't choose to let him die.'

'Is it possible,' asked the traveller, 'that they manage matters here in this way?'

'To be sure they do, sir; and why wouldn't a gintleman take care of his people if it was plazin' to him?'

'It is the laws and not the gentleman should be held in respect,' said the traveller; 'the poor man's life should never depend upon the rich man's pleasure.'

1. Responsible is always applied by the Irish peasantry in the sense of respectability.

III

A peep into Ireland forty years ago.—Hints for charging juries.—Every landlord his own lawgiver.—Pride of birth.—A jocular prince on foot and a popular peer on horseback.

A TRAIN OF MUSING, ON THE traveller's part, rapidly succeeded his last remark; and as he went jolting along unconsciously over the wretched road, he was mentally floundering through the deep ruts of political speculation, and looking forward, through the warm haze which a young imagination flings round its objects, to that happier time when Ireland should enjoy a loftier position than that implied by what Rory O'More had said. But, alas! instead of this brilliant advent, blood and crime, and all the fiercer passions that degrade human nature, making man more like demon than a human being, were the futurity which Ireland was doomed to experience; and while the enthusiasm of the young traveller looked forward to the heights where his imagination enthroned his country's fortunes, he overlooked and saw not the valley of blood that lay between.

And forty years (almost half a century) have passed away since the young enthusiast indulged in his vision, and still is Ireland the theme of fierce discussion.

It was Rory O'More's remark upon the nature of judicial trials in Ireland that had started the traveller on his train of musing. An Irishman by birth, he had long been absent from his native land, and was not aware of its internal details: and that such a state of feudality as that implied by Rory's observation could exist in Ireland, while England enjoyed the fullest measure of her constitution might well surprise him—but so it was.

The period to which this relates was 1797, when distrust, political prejudice, and religious rancour, were the terrible triumvirate that assumed dominion over men's minds. In such a state of things the temple of justice could scarcely be called a sanctuary, and shelter was to be found rather beneath the mantle of personal influence than under the ermine of the judge. Even to this day, in Ireland, feudal influence is in existence; but forty years ago it superseded the laws of the land.

So much was this the case, that it is worth recording an anecdote of the period which is fact: the names it is unnecessary to give.

A certain instance of brutal assault, causing loss of life, had occurred, so aggravated in its character that the case almost amounted to murder, and the offender, who stood his trial for the offence, it was expected, would be sentenced to transportation, should he escape the forfeiture of his life to the law. The evidence on his trial was clear and convincing, and all attempts at defence had failed, and the persons assembled in the court anticipated a verdict of guilty on the heaviest counts in the indictment. The prosecution and defence had closed, and the judge had nearly summed up the evidence, and was charging the jury directly against the prisoner, when a bustle was perceived in the body of the court. The judge ordered the crier to command silence, and that officer obeyed his commands without producing any effect. The judge was about to direct a second and more peremptory command for silence, when a note was handed up to the bench, and the judge himself, instead of issuing his command for silence, became silent himself, and perused the note with great attention. He pursued his charge to the jury no further, but sent up a small slip of paper to the foreman, who forthwith held some whispered counsel with his brother jurors; and when their heads, that had been huddled together in consultation, separated and they resumed their former positions, the judge then continued his address to them thus:—

'I have endeavoured to point out to you, gentlemen of the jury, the doubts of this case, but I do not think it necessary to proceed any further;—I have such confidence in your discrimination and good sense, that I now leave the case entirely in your hands:—if you are of opinion that *what you have been put in possession of* in the prisoner's favour counter-balances the facts sworn to against him, you will of course acquit him—and any doubts you have, I need not tell you, should be thrown into the scale of mercy. It is the proud pre-eminence, gentlemen, of our criminal laws—laws, gentlemen, which are part and parcel of the glorious constitution that is the wonder and the envy of surrounding nations, that a prisoner is to have the benefit of every doubt; and therefore, if you think proper, of course you will find the prisoner NOT guilty.'

'Certainly, my lord,' said the foreman of the jury, 'we are of your lordship's opinion, and we say NOT GUILTY.'

The fact was, the great man of the district where the crime had been committed, whose serf the prisoner was, had sent up his *compliments* to the judge and jury, stating the prisoner to be a *most useful* person to him, and that he would feel *extremely obliged* if they could acquit him. This ruffian was a sort of bold, sporting, dare-devil character, whose services in breaking-in dogs, and attending his master and his parties on wild mountain-shooting and fishing excursions, were invaluable to the squire, and human life, which this fellow had sacrificed, was nothing in the scale when weighed against the squire's diversion. This will scarcely be credited in the present day; nevertheless, it is a fact.

Another occurrence of the time shows the same disregard of the law; though the case is by no means so bad, inasmuch as the man was only taken up for an offence, but was not tried—he was only rescued to save him that trouble. He had committed some offence which entitled him to a lodging in the county gaol, and was accordingly taken into custody by the proper authorities but, as the county town was too distant to send him to at once, he was heldover to the care of a military detachment that occupied a small village in the neighbourhood. To the little barrack-yard or guard-house of this outpost he was committed but he did not remain there long, for his mountain friends came down in great numbers and carried him off in triumph, having forced the barracks. The moment the colonel of the regiment, a detachment of which occupied the post, received intelligence of the circumstance, he marched the greater part of his men to the place, vowing he would drag the prisoner who had been committed to the care of his troops from the very heart of his mountains, and that neither man, woman, nor child should be spared who dared to protect him from capture. While the colonel, who was an Englishman, was foaming with indignation at this contempt of all order displayed by the Irish, Mr. French waited upon him and asked him to dinner. The English colonel said he would be most happy at any other time, but at present it was impossible;—that if he could, he would neither drink, nor sleep till he had vindicated the laws.

'Pooh, pooh! My dear sir,' said Mr. French, 'it is all very well to talk about the laws in England, but they know nothing about them here.'

'Then it's time, sir, they should be taught,' said the colonel.

'Well, don't be in a hurry, at least, my dear sir,' said Mr. French. 'I assure you the poor people mean no disrespect to the laws; it is in pure ignorance they have made this mistake.'

'Mistake!' said the colonel.

''Pon my soul! nothing more,' said Mr. French; 'and if you think to make them wise at the point of the bayonet, you'll find yourself mistaken; you'll have the whole country in an uproar, and do no good after all; for once these fellows have given you the slip, you might as well go hunt after mountain-goats.'

'But, consistently with my duty, sir—'

'Your duty will keep till to-morrow, colonel dear, and you'll meet three or four other magistrates, as well as me, at my house, who will tell you the same that I have done. You'll be wiser to-morrow, depend upon it:—so come home with me to dinner.'

The colonel, who was a man of deliberation, rode home with Mr. French, who talked him over as they went along: 'You see, my dear sir, how is it possible you should know the people as well as we do? Believe me, every landlord knows his own tenantry best, and we make it a point here never to interfere in that particular. Now, the fellow they took away from your men—'

'Curse them!' said the colonel.

'Keep yourself cool, my dear colonel. That fellow, for instance—now *he* is one of Blake's men: and if Blake *wants* the fellow to be hanged, he'll send him in to you.'

'Send him in!—why, sir, if my regiment could not keep the rascal, what chance has Mr. Blake of making him prisoner?'

'I said nothing, colonel, of making him prisoner: I said, and still say, that if Blake *wants* him to be hanged, he'll *send him in*.'

'Do you mean to say, my good sir, that he'll desire him to come in and be hanged?'

'Precisely.'

'And *will* he come?'

'Most undoubtedly, if Blake desires him.'

The colonel dined with Mr. French that day; the day following the regiment was marched back to head-quarters—and Blake did *not* send in his man to be hanged. So much for feudality!

But the young traveller knew not these facts, and he was awakened from the reverie in which he was indulging by the blowing of a long tin horn, announcing the arrival of the coach at a dirty little town, where it was to stop for the night. It drove up to what was called an hotel, round the door of which, though still raining heavily, a crowd of beggars stood, so thick, that the passengers could hardly press their way through them into the house; an while they were thus struggling for admittance, obstreperous prayers assailed their ears on all sides, in horrid discord and strange variety—for their complaints and their blessings became so jumbled together as to produce a ludicrous effect. There were blind and lame, broken bones, widows and orphans, etc., etc.

'Pity the blind! and may you never see—'

'To-morrow morning won't find me alive if you don't relieve—'

'The guard will give me something, your honour, if you'll only bid him—'

'Be quiet, you devil! and don't taze the gintleman! Sure he has—'

'Three fatherless childher—'

'And broke his two legs—'

'That is stone blind—'

'And met a dhreadful accident!—and sure the house fell on him, and he's lyin' undher it these three weeks without a bit to ate, but—'

'Three fatherless childer and a dissolute widow—'

'Lying on the broad of her back, with nothing on her but—'

'The small-pox, your honour!'

'For heaven's sake! let me pass,' said the young traveller, who had a horror of the small-pox; and pressing through the crowd that environed him into the house, he entered the first room he saw, and suddenly closed the door behind him.

As soon, however, as he recovered his first alarm at the mention of the terrible disease he so much dreaded, he called for the waiter and made inquiries for Rory. Finding he was in the house, he sent him a message to say he would be glad to see him; and on Rory making his appearance, he requested him to be seated, and asked him would he have something to drink?

Rory declined it, until the traveller said that he himself would join him in a potation after their wetting; and when Rory understood that the traveller meant they should sit down together over their glasses, he accepted the offer with modest thankfulness, and expressed his acknowledgment for the honour done him by his travelling companion.

In the course of their conversation the young traveller found, that with all the apparent simplicity of Rory, he was not deficient in intelligence, and that the oddity of the incidents in which he had described himself as being an actor arose more from the novelty of his position in a large city than in any inherent stupidity. He became possessed of his name also, and Rory could not help showing his pride in having one so good; for while he affected to laugh at his proud descent, it was quite clear he had a firm belief in it.

'I suppose, sir, you have heerd tell of one Rory O'More in the owld times?'

'Yes—King of Leinster, you mean.'

'So they say, sir—that he and his people before him wor kings time out o' mind, until bad fortune came to thim and they went to the bad entirely; and the English dhruv thim out, bekaze they had a way of puttin' between people; and while they were squabblin' one with the other, the English used to come in and do them both out—like the owld story of the lawyer and the oysthers. Well, when once they were dhruv out, they went witherin' and dwindlin' down by degrees, and at last they hadn't a fut of land left them, nor even a house over their heads, and so we wore reduced that way, sir.'

'Then you consider yourself the descendant of the O'More?' said the traveller.

'Throth, sir, and they say that we are the owld O'Mores—but sure I laugh at it.'

'But wouldn't you be angry if any one else laughed at it?'

'I dunna but I might,' said Rory, with much ingenuousness.

'And why do *you* laugh at it then?'

'Why, afther all, sir, sure it's quare enough for a man to be talkin' of his great relations that *was* formerly, when at this present he is only a poor workin' man; and if I was ever so much the thrue discindant of Rory O'More, sure I can't forget what I am now.'

'You may be the representative of the house, for all, that,' said the traveller.

'Oh! as for the house,' said Rory, ''pon my sowl! there's a cruel differ there betune us : the right Rory O'More lived in Dunamaise—that was something like a house and I have only a poor cabin to live in.'

'But still you may be the true descendant of the right Rory, as you call him,' said the traveller, who wished to probe the feelings of the peasant on this subject, and discover how far the pride of *birth* could survive loss of *station*: and he was pleased to discover (for he was himself of high descent) that ages of misfortune could not extinguish the fire of a proud race; and he more than ever felt the truth of the observation, that it is only they who have no ancestry to boast of who affect to despise it.

To such as these, or those to whom ancestral *power* as well as name has descended to the many who take no pleasure in tracing to their secret sources the springs of action and feeling in the human mind and heart—it may seem incredible that a poor peasant could retain the pride of birth when all its substantial appendages were gone:—yet so it was.

But it was a pride that was unobtrusive.

Circumstances had modified and moulded it to the necessities of the peasant's station: he was respectful in his demeanour to all whose position in society was better than his own, conscious though he might be of their inferior blood; and while he took off his hat to some wealthy plebeian, he never considered the blood of the O'Mores to be degraded.

The fallen fortunes of his house were not a subject of *personal* regret to him; it was in a *national* point of view they were lamented.

That Ireland had lost her King of Leinster he considered a misfortune; but he never for a moment regretted that he, his heir, as he believed himself to be (and perhaps was), was obliged to eat potatoes and salt.

But of the fair fame of the O'More he was as jealous as their founder, and insult, in the remotest degree, roused the latent feelings of family pride in his bosom. Not the great Rory himself, perched on his castled crag of Dunamaise, could be more jealous of the honour of his house than his humble namesake in his thatched cabin.

The young traveller, it has been already said, took pleasure in making manifest this feeling of our hero; and in doing so, he found that Rory had a provincial as well as personal pride of ancestry. The south, Rory protested, 'bet all Ireland in the regard of high blood.'

'They have good blood in the north, too,' said the traveller.

'Oh, they may have a thrifle of it; but it's not of the *rale* owld sort—nothing to compare with us.'

'Do you forget the O'Neill?' said the traveller.

'Oh, that's good, I don't deny,' said Rory; 'but one swallow makes no summer.'

'But I can count more than one,' said the traveller: 'There's Talbot, De Lacy, Fitzgerald——'

'Oh, murther! murther! sir!—sure *thim* is only invadhers, and not the owld Irish at all. You would never compare *thim* with the O'Mores, the O'Dempsys, the O'Connells, the O'Donaghues, the O'Shaughnessys!'

'Stop, stop!' said the traveller, who did not know to what length this bead-roll of Os might extend; 'you forget that the head of the Fitzgeralds is Duke of Leinster.'

'But O'More was *King* of Leinsther, sir, if you plaze.'

'Very true, Rory; but still the Geraldines are a noble race.'

'Who are *they*, sir?'

'The Fitzgeralds.'

'Oh, the Juke o' Leinsther you mane, is it?'

'Yes,'

''Faith thin, to show you, sir, how little we think o' them down in the south, I'll tell you something that I know is a thruth bekaze I had it from O'Dempsy himself, who played the thrick an the juke, and said the thing to him; for he's a comical blade.'

'Well, what was it?'

'Why, you see, sir, O'Dempsy was comin' home from Dublin, and the money was gettin' *fine-dhrawn* with him, and he wanted to see if he had enough left to pay for the coach home; and, by dad! the change was so scarce that he was obliged to hunt it up in his pocket into the corner, like a contrary cowlt, before he could lay howld of it at all: and when he did get it into the pawm of his fist, it was a'most ashamed to see the light, it looked so contimptible; and my bowld O'Dempsy seen the coach was out o' the question, or even a lift in the canal-boat, and so he put his thrust in Providence, and took a big dhrink that night to strenthin him for the mornin'; and the next day off he set home, with a short stick in his hand and a pair o' good legs undher him; and he met nothin' remarkable until he came to betune Kilcock and Maynooth; and it was thin that he heerd the thramp of horses gallopin' afther him and he turned round and seen three gintlemen comin' up in great style: one o' them, a fine full handsome man, the picthur of a gintleman, and a fine baste undher him, and the gintlemin along with him very nice too; one in particular, a smart nate-made man, with a fine bright eye and a smilin' face, and a green hand kicher round his neck, and a sportin' asy sate on his horse; and Dempsy heerd him say, as they dhrew up jist behind him, 'Look what a fine step that fellow has!' (manin' O'Dempsy; and, indeed, a claner boy isn't in all Ireland than himself, and can walk with any man). So when they came up to him, the small gintleman said, "God save you!" "God save you kindly, sir!" says O'Dempsy. "You don't let the grass grow undher your feet my man," says the gintleman "Nor *corn* neither, sir," says Dempsy. "So I see by the free step you have," says the gintleman, laughin'; and the others laughed too, the full gintleman in particular; and says he, "Well, Ned, you got your answer."

'Now the minit that O'Dempsy heerd the word "Ned," and it bein' in the neighbourhood o' Cartown, which is the Juke o' Leinsther's place, the thought jumped into his head that it was Lord Edward Fitzjaral' was in it; for he always heerd he was small, and handsome, and merry, and that the juke his brother was a fine-lookin' man; and so with that he made cock-sure in his own mind that the full gintleman was the Juke o' Leinsther, and the little one Lord Edward. So hearin' that Lord Edward liked a joke, O'Dempsy never let on to suspect who they wor, and they walked along beside him, and had a great dale o' discoorse and jokin', and the answers passin' betune them as fast as hops.

'At last says the juke (for it was himself), "You're a very merry fellow," says he; "where do you come from?" "From Dublin, sir," says O'Dempsy. "Oh, I know that by the road you're goin'," says the juke; "but I mane, where is your place?" "Faith and I have no place," says O'Dempsy: "I wish I had.' "That's a touch at *you*," says the juke, to the third gintleman,' whoever he was. "But where are you goin' to?" says the juke. "I'm goin' home, sir," says O'Dempsy. "And where are you when you're at home?" says the juke. "Faith, I'm at home everywhere," says O'Dempsy.

'Well, Lord Edward laughed at his brother, seein' he couldn't force a sthraight answer out of O'Dempsy. "Will you tell me thin," says the juke, "which are you—Ulsther, Leinsther, Munsther, or Connaught?" "Leinsther, sir," says O'Dempsy, though it was a lie he was tellin'; but it was on purpose to have a laugh agin the juke, for he was layin' a thrap for him all the time. "You don't spake like a Leinsther man," says the juke. "Oh, the tongue is very desaitful sometimes," says O'Dempsy.

'Lord Edward laughed at his brother agin, and said he'd make no hand of him. "By gor," says Lord Edward, "that fellow would bate Councellor Curran!" "Well, I'll thry him once more," says the juke; and with that, says he to O'Dempsy, "What's your name?" Now that was all O'Dempsy wanted, for to nick him; and so says he, "My name is O'Shaughnessy, sir." "I've cotch you now," says the juke; "you can't be a Leinsther man with that name." "'Faith, I see you're too able for me, sir," says O'Dempsy, laading him on. "Well, Mr. O'Shaughnessy," says the juke, "it's somewhere out of Munsther you come." "No, 'faith, sir," says O'Dempsy, "I am a Leinsther man in airnest; but I see you couldn't be desaived about the name, and so I'll tell you the thruth, and nothin' but the thruth, about it. I am a Leinsther man, but I wint to live in Munsther, and I was obleeged to change my name, bekaze they had no respect for me there with the one I had." "And what *was* your name?" says the juke. "My name was Fitzjarl', sir," says O'Dempsy; "but they thought me only an upstart down in Munsther, so I changed it into O'Shaughnessy." With that the juke and Lord Edward laughed out hearty, and the third gintleman says to the juke, "I think *you've* got *your* hit now." Well, sir, the juke pulled a guinea out of his pocket, and put it into O'Dempsy's hand, and says to him, laughin', "Take that, you merry rascal, and drink my health!" "Long life to *your grace*!" says O'Dempsy, taking off his hat; "*you desarve to be an O'Shaughnessy!*" "More power to you, Paddy!" says Lord Edward, as they put spurs to their horses; and away they powdhered down the road, laughin' like mad.'

The young traveller enjoyed Rory's anecdote excessively, and scarcely knew which to admire most—the impudent waggery of Rory's friend, or the good humour of the Duke of Leinster and Lord Edward Fitzgerald.

After much praise of the latter, and some other strange odds and ends from Rory, the travellers separated for the night.

IV

O N THE FOLLOWING MORNING THE coach resumed its journey, and Rory and the stranger still continued fellow-travellers.

The insolent aggressor upon Rory, as well as the passenger who sat beside him, did not appear; but their places were occupied by a person to whom Rory touched his hat as he took his seat, and another who seemed to be his companion. The latter was decidedly a Scotchman; what the other might be, it was not so easy to decide—perhaps north of England.

He addressed Rory, and expressed surprise at seeing him.

'Troth, and it's just as little I expected to see you, Mr. Scrubbs,' said Rory.

'I was up here on a little business,' said Scrubbs.

'That's what you're always up to, Mr. Scrubbs,' answered Rory.

'And *you're* just as ready for fun, Rory. I suppose it was *that* brought *you* here?'

'No, indeed, sir—it was the coach brought me here yesterday.'

'Ay, ay, there you are at your answers! I suppose it was in Dublin, then you would be?'

'No, indeed, I *would*n't be if I could help it.'

'Well, but you were there?'

'Yes, I was.'

'And what business had you in Dublin?'

'About the lease of the place below.'

'Didn't I tell you I'd see about that when the agent came down?'

'Why, you wor seein' about it so long that I thought it might be out o' sight at last, and so I wint myself to the head agent, and settled it at wanst.'

Scrubbs did not seem well pleased at this information; and silence having ensued in consequence, Rory took from his pocket a newspaper and began to read. For some time Scrubbs cast suspicious glances at the paper, till at last, when Rory turned over its from page and discovered the title of 'The Press,' Scrubbs could no longer remain silent.

'I wonder you're not ashamed,' said Scrubbs.

'Of what?' said Rory.

'To read that paper.'

''Faith, I'd be more ashamed if I couldn't read it!' said Rory.

'Why, it's all sedition, and treason, and blasphemy.'

'What's blasphemy?' said Rory.

''Tis a word,' said the young traveller, 'that some people always join to treason and sedition.'

Scrubbs gave a look askance at the last speaker; but seeing he was a gentleman, and rather better dressed than himself, he made no observation to him, but said in continuance to Rory,

'I always thought you were of the peaceable and well-disposed class, O'More, and I'm sorry to see you read that desperate paper.'

''Faith it's very desperate, sure enough, if it be thrue what they say here, that bank-notes will be soon worth nothin', and won't bring a penny a pound in a snuff-shop.'

'What's that but treason, I'd like to know,' said Scrubbs; 'endeavouring to undermine the government.'

'Sairtainly,' said the Scotchman, 'it is varra bad to destroy the cawnfidence in pooblic creydit.'

'I dare say, sir,' said Rory to the Scotchman, '*you* would rather have bank-notes, than golden guineas?'

'I did na say that,' said the Scotchman drily; 'but bank-notes are a sufficient security.'

'And they say here,' said Rory, 'that we oughtn't to dhrink tay nor coffee, nor take snuff, nor smoke tabacky, nor dhrink whisky.'

'And what do you think of that?' said Scrubbs.

''Faith, I think thim that has no money will follow their advice,' said Rory.

'Ay! but look at the villainous intention—to injure the revenue, or produce a rebellion.'

'You think then,' said the traveller, 'that people must either smell snuff or gunpowder, whether they will or no?'

'I know, sir, they'll have gunpowder enough if it goes to that. We have plenty of loyal men to put down sedition, both militia and yeomanry.'

'Which you can't trust,' said the traveller.

'Do you doubt their loyalty, sir?' said Scrubbs, waxing rather angry.

'It would seem the government does,' said the traveller, 'for whole regiments of yeomanry have been disbanded this year.'

This was a bitter truth to Scrubbs, who, not being able to deny the fact, returned to the charge upon 'The Press.'

'As for that vile paper, they would do right to serve it as "The Northern Star" was served the other day, when the Donegal Militia, God bless them! broke open their office, burnt their papers and broke their printing-presses.'

'What noble and constitutional work for soldiers to be employed upon!' said the traveller. 'I do not wonder, when the cloth is so degraded, that high-minded gentlemen, such as the Duke of Leinster, Lord O'Neil, and Colonel Conolly, resign their regiments.'

This was another bitter fact to which Scrubbs was unable to reply; so, leaving the field in possession of the enemy, he addressed his Scotch friend on some fresh subject, and thus evaded the discussion.

The traveller with Rory, and Scrubbs with the Scotchman, now kept themselves distinct, and the day was passing away slowly enough, the monotony of the road only broken by some occasional remark between Scrubbs and his friend, or the young traveller and Rory: seeming to observe each other with mutual distrust, a restraint was put upon general conversation, and it was only some passing observation on the surrounding scenery that either party would. venture to indulge in.

The day was more than half spent, when they were driving through a fine tract of country, which called forth the Scotchman's admiration.

'A fine kintra, this, Mr. Scrubbs,' said he.

'Yes,' said Scrubbs, ''tis a good sort of country, but not fit to compare with England.'

Rory looked indignantly at him, but said nothing.

'I dinna ken aboot England,' said the Scotchman; 'but this kintra puts me varra much in mind o' my ain.'

'Your kinthry, do you say?' said Rory, with what heroines call 'ineffable contempt.'

'Yes, my kintra.'

'Oh, do you hear this!!' said Rory to the young traveller. 'He's comparin' this counthry to his!!—Why, 'tare an ouns sir,' said Rory to the Scotchman; 'sure you wouldn't be comparin' this lovely fine counthry to Scotland—or sayin' it was like it?'

'Yes, but I would though,' said the Scotchman pertinaciously.

'Why, by the seven blessed candles, you haven't seen a *thistle* for the last tin miles,' said Rory.

The young traveller laughed at Rory's illustration, and the silence and disunion of the two parties increased.

Thus the day wore on uncomfortably enough, and the evening began to close, when a premature stop was put to their journey by the breaking down of the coach.

Fortunately for the passengers, the accident was not one that placed them in any danger. Some of them were *nearly* thrown off, and a lady-passenger who was inside screamed, of course; and the more she was assured that there was no danger, the louder she screamed. In the meanwhile, the passengers jumped off; and the extreme amount of damage to them was that they proceed no further by the coach on their journey, as one of the wheels was broken.

Now, whenever an accident of this kind occurs which is manifestly so bad as to be beyond retrieving, it may be remarked that every one looks at it in all possible ways—under it, and over it, and round it, just as if looking at it could do any good. So were the passengers congregated round the wheel of the coach, all making their remarks.

'It was the nave,' said one.

'No, the spokes,' said another.

'Oh dear, no—the tire,' added a third.

'Most provoking!'

'Scandalous!' said Scrubbs; 'like everything else in this country! The proprietors ought to be prosecuted for having a coach in such a condition.'

'Murther, murther!' said the coachman, who lost his temper at last when the honour of his coach was concerned: 'do you hear this! just as if an accident never happened to a coach before.'

'When people pay their money,' said Scrubbs, 'they have a right to complain.'

'Sairtainly,' said the Scotchman. 'In fact, I thenk the money should be refunded.'

'Arrah! listen to him!' said Rory aside to the stranger.

'How far is the coach from the end of its journey?' said the lady.

''Pon my word, ma'am,' said Rory, 'the coach is at the end of its journey for this day, anyhow.'

'And what are we to do?' said the lady.

'I'd adveyse,' said the Scotchman, 'that we should get post-chaises, and chorge them to the coach propreytors.'

''Faith, that's a fine plan, *if you could get them*,' said Rory.

'Then what *are* we to do?' said the lady, again.

'If you'd be quiet the laste taste, ma'am, if you plaze,' said the coachman, 'we'll conthrive some conthrivance by and by.'

'Why, the night is falling,' said the lady.

'It's time for it,' said Rory.

'My God!' said the lady, 'what odd answers these people give one!'

The horses now became restless, for the wheelers, pulling, and find so much resistance, began to kick, and their example set the leaders going. The coachman and Rory ran to their heads.

'Bad luck to you, you fools!' said Rory to the horses; 'sure it's glad, and not sorry you ought to be, that the dhrag is off o' you; be quite! you garrans, will you!' and he forced them at last into some obedience. 'I tell you what you'll do now,' said he to the coachman: 'jist take off the horses—they'll be quiet enough here, grazing by the side o' the gripe;[1] and you get on one o' them, and pelt away into the town, and come out agin wid a fresh coach.'

'Throth, and it's the best plan, I b'lieve,' said the coachman, 'after all.'

'And must *we* stay here?' said the lady.

'Barrin' you walk, ma'am.'

'And how far might it be to walk?'

''Faith; I don't rightly know,' said the coachman.

'You're a feyne driver,' said the Scotchman, 'not to know the distance on your ain road!'

'I know it well enough whin I'm dhrivin',' said the coachman; 'but how should I know how far it is to walk?'

'Why, you stupid rascal!' said the Scotchman, about to make an elaborate argument to show the coachman the bull he had made—but he was interrupted by Rory.

'Arrah! never mind his prate, Hoolaghan; do what I bid you—away wid you into town!'

'Indeed, I think 'tis the best thing you can do,' said the young traveller.

'And must *we* stay here? Why, 'tis growing dark already, and we may be murdered while you are away.'

'Divil a one 'ill take the throuble to murther yon—don't be in the laste afear'd!' said Rory. 'Up wid you now on the grey, Hoolaghan, your sowl, and powdher away like shot!'

'What's that he's saying, sir, about powder and shot?' said the lady in alarm.

'He's only giving directions to the coachman, madam,' said the young traveller.

'But he said powder and shot! sir. Is there any danger?'

'None in the least, I assure you, madam.'

'The horses 'ill stay quite enough while you're gone,' said Rory; 'here, gi' me your fut—I'll lift you on the baste.' And so saying, Hoolaghan placed his left foot in Rory's right hand; and thus aided, he sprang astride of one of the coach-horses.

'There now,' said Rory, 'you're up! and away wid you! Jist be into the town in no time, and back in less. "That's the cut!" says Cutty when he cut his mother's throat.'

'What's that he's saying, sir, about cutting throats?' said the lady.

'Nothing, madam, I assure you, you need be alarmed at,' said the traveller.

'Indeed, you need not make yourself onaisy, ma'am, in the laste,' said Rory, after he had placed Hoolaghan on horseback. 'It will be all over with you soon now.'

The lady shuddered at the phrase, but spoke not.

'And now, sir,' said Rory to his fellow-traveller, 'It's time we should be thinkin' of ourselves: there's no use you should be loitherin' here until the other coach comes back; for though it's some miles from the town, where, I suppose, you were goin' to, it's not far from this where I must turn off to my own place, which lies acrass the counthry, about two miles or thereaway and if you, sir, wouldn't think it benathe you to come to a poor man's house, sure it's proud I'd be to give your honour a bed; and though it may not be as good as you're used to, still maybe 't will be betther than stoppin' here by the roadside.'

The traveller expressed his thanks to Rory for the kindness of his offer but said that perhaps he could as well walk to the town. To this Rory objected, suggesting the probability of the traveller's losing his way, as he could only be his guide as far as the point where he had to turn towards his own home; besides many other arguments urged on Rory's part with so much heart and cordiality, that he prevailed on his fellow-traveller to accept his proffered hospitality. Selecting a small portmanteau from the luggage, the traveller was about to throw it over his shoulder, when Rory laid hold of it, and insisted on carrying it for him.

'You've your own luggage to carry!' said the traveller.

'Sure, mine is nothin' more than a small bundle—no weight in life.'

'And your gridirons, Rory?'

'By the powers! I was near forgettin' *thim*,' said Rory; 'but sure, thim itself is no weight, and I can carry thim all!'

'Stay a moment,' said the traveller, whose gallantry forbade that he should leave the lady of the party, alarmed as she was, in such a situation, and apparently not regularly protected, without the offer of his services. He approached the coach, into which the lady had retired to avoid the dew that was now falling heavily, and made his offer with becoming courtesy.

'I'm much obliged to you, sir,' said she, 'but I have my husband here.'

'Thank you, sir,' said a miserable-looking little man, who had not uttered a word before; 'I am this lady's husband.' He did not dare to say, 'This lady's my wife.'

The traveller made his bow, and he and his guide, leaving the forlorn coach-passengers on the road, proceeded at a smart pace towards the cottage of Rory O'More.

'Those people, I think, are likely to remain a good while before assistance can reach them,' said the traveller.

''Faith, I'm thinking myself they'll have a good long wait of it,' said Rory; 'and in throth I'm not sorry for some o' thim.'

'Don't you pity that unfortunate woman?'

'Sorra much!' said Rory; 'the screechin' fool, with her shoutin' about her throat bein' cut!—though, indeed, if it was cut itself, it wouldn't be much matther, for all the sinse I heard her spake. Throat cut, indeed! as if the whole counthry was murtherers and moroders. In throth the counthry would be quite (quiet) enough if they'd let us be quite; but it's gallin' and *aggravatin'* us they are at every hand's turn, and puttin' the martial law on us and callin' us bad names, and abusin' our blessed religion.'

'And are the people much dissatisfied at this state of things?'

'Why, I don't see how they could be plazed, sir! And sure, my heart warmed to you whin you gave that dirty Scrubbs his answer to-day; 'faith, he got his fairin' anyhow from you! he had no chance at all with you, sir. Oh, when you silenced him, sure it was butther to my bones!'

'By the by, who is that person?' said the traveller.

'He is a fellow that lives not far from this, sir; they call him the Collecthor.'

'Collector of what?'

'Of everything, 'faith. He collects tithes for the parson, and rints for the agint, and taxes and cess, and all to that; and so he goes by the name of the Collecthor.'

'He's not an Irishman?'

'No, thank God, he's not! Though, indeed, there's some of the Irish bad enough to their own, or worse than sthrangers maybe; but I say, thank God, bekaze there's one blackguard the less belongs to us.'

'Has he been long here?'

'Not to say very long, indeed, considerin' all he has done for himself in the time. I remember, whin he came among us first, it was with some horses—a sort of low stable-helper, a kind of a hanger-on about some officers that was in the town, and thin he was badly off enough. He hadn't as much clothes on him as would scour a spit; and his flesh, the little he had of it, hangin' about him as if it didn't fit him. But he wint to church the first Sunday he was here, and, as Prodestants is scarce, he was welkim to the parson; and so that he mightn't disgrace the congregation, the parson gev him some dacent clothes and thin he got him to do odd jobs for him, one way or another; and so he made himself plazin' somehow to the parson, and got on one step afther another. And the parson noticed him to the squire, and thin the squire gave him a lift, for he it was got him to be collecthor; and now he has a mighty snug house, and a nate farm nigh hand to the parson, though the first place he slep' in, not long ago, whin he came to the town beyant, was in the hayloft of the inn, for they wouldn't dirty the barrack-stables with him.'

'Then the parson is his patron?'

'Not only the parson, but the magisthrits about the place as well, for they know that Squire Ransford notices him.'

'How does he get into the squire's good graces?'

'There was a cast-off lady of the squire's, that was throublesome to him and so he gev some soft discoorse, and hard cash too, I b'lieve to Scrubbs, to make an honest woman of her, and take her off his hands;

and so he did; and now you'll see her goin' in her jantin' car, if you plaze, along wid that mane-spirited dog that tuk another man's lavings, marchin' into church every Sunday as bowld as brass, and wid as many ribbons on her as would set up a thravellin' pedlar.'

'And what does the parson say to all this? Does he countenance the affair?'

'Arrah, what can he do, sir?' said Rory. 'Sure, *he* can't help if she was unproper; and isn't it betther she'd go to her duty than stay a bad as she is? And sure, if she was a sinner, that's the greater the raison why he'd be glad to help her in mendin' her ways; and sure, as she hasn't the luck to be a Roman, it's well for her she's even a Prodestant!'

'That's a very charitable view of the matter on your part,' said the traveller.

'Oh, by dad, sir! you mustn't be too hard on the parson, for he's a dacent man enough. If all the Prodestants was as quite (quiet) as him, we'd never fall out wid thim, for he's a nice aisy man, and is good friends wid Father Kinshela, and both o'them dines together wid the squire whin he's here. And you know, sir, that's hearty!'

'Very indeed,' said the traveller. 'I'm glad to hear it.'

'Scrubbs himself is a nasty fellow; and his *lady* is a *dab*, and nothin' else: but sure the parson can't help that, and I wouldn't expect of him to be too particular on thim, for sure he must be glad to get a Prodestant at all in his church, where they are so scarce. Throth it thust be cowld work there, in a big ramblin' church in the winther, wid so few in it, to be sayin' prayers!'

'You seem to like the parson, I think?' said the traveller.

'Oh, I don't mislike him, sir, for he's civil-spoken, and a hearty man, and he likes huntin' and shootin', and divarshin of all sorts.'

'But do you think that becoming in a clergyman?'

'Oh, you're too hard on the clargy, sir;—why wouldn't they be merry?—sure Father Kinshela himself sometimes takes a dart afther the dogs, whin the squire is down here, as well as the parson.'

'Squire Ransford, then, lives here a good deal?'

'Not a good dale, sir, only by times, whin he comes down to take a start huntin' or shootin', and thin he brings down a power o' company wid him: but unless at that time, the place is like a wildherness, only an ould woman and a couple o' maids to mind the house, and a stable-helper left, or somethin' that way, to watch the place.'

'A single stable-helper! Didn't you tell me he keeps a pack of hounds?'

'Yis, sir; but he doesn't keep up the dogs unless whin he's here himself.'

'How does he manage, then?'

'Why, he gives one couple o' dogs to one tenant, and another couple to another, and so on in that way, while he isn't in the place; and whin he comes back, he gathers thim in again; and so he isn't at the expense of keepin' up the kennel while he's away.'

'What a shabby fellow!' said the traveller.

'Oh! not to say shabby, sir.'

'Why, what else can you call quartering his dogs on his poor tenantry?'

'Oh, for all that he's not shabby; for whin *he is* down here, the company is never out of his house; and they say there's lashings and lavings of everything in it, and the claret flyin' about the place as common as beer, and no stint to any one, I'm towld.'

'That's mere wastefulness and rioting, and cannot in my opinion redeem his shabbiness, for I cannot call it anything else. Can he not feel that when the poor people feed his sporting-dogs, the fruit of their labour is invaded to contribute to his pleasure?'

'Why, if you go to the rights o' the thing, what your honour says is thrue enough; but we wouldn't be too sharp in lookin' at what a gintleman would do—and indeed I don't mislike it myself, as far as that goes, for the couple o' dogs that is left with me I do have a great deal of fun with.'

'How?'

'Huntin' rabbits, sir?'

'They must be nice dogs after that?'

'Divil a harm it does them!—sure it comes nath'ral to the craythurs, and would be cruel to stint them of their divarshin.'

'And do you all hunt rabbits with the dogs left to your care?'

'Every one of us.'

'Then the pack can't be worth a farthing.'

'Why indeed I don't deny they run a little wild now and thin; but sure what would be the use of a whipper-in if the dogs won't a little fractious?'

Rory continued his discourse with the stranger as they proceeded on the road, giving him various information respecting the squire, and the collector, and the parson, in all of which, though Rory did not so intend it, his hearer found deep cause of disapproval of their conduct. Their conversation was now interrupted by the deep baying of dogs; and Rory answered the sound by a cheering whoop, and the calling of the dogs by their names.

'There they are, sir?' said he; 'you see we're jist at home.'

As he spoke, they turned into the little *boreen* already noticed, and two hounds came rushing wildly up the lane and jumped upon Rory with all the testimonials of canine recognition.

'Down, Rattler, you divil, down!—you'll tear the coat av my back. Murther! Sweetlips, don't be kissin' me—down, you brutes!'

And he drove the animals from him, whose furious caresses were more than agreeable.

'Poor things!' said he to the stranger, in a kindly tone 'sure, thin, it's pleasant even to have a dog to welkim one home.'

'More than a dog, Rory, dear,' said a sweet voice from amid the darkness; and the next instant a girl ran up to Rory, and throwing her arms round his neck, kissed him over and over again.

He returned her embrace with affection, and said,

'How is the mother?'

'Hearty, thank God!' said the girl.

'And yourself, Mary dear?'

'Oh, what would ail me?—But tell me, what sort of a place is Dublin?—and how did you like it?—and did you get me the ribbon?'

'It's my sisther, sir,' said Rory to his guest, paying no attention to the numerous questions of Mary, who now for the first time observing the stranger, dropped a short curtsey to him, a said in a subdued voice:

'Your sarvant, sir.'

'Run on, Mary dear, and tell the mother we're comin',' said Rory, accompanying his words with a significant pinch on Mary's elbow, which meant, 'Make the place look as dacent as possible.'

Mary ran hastily forward, fully understanding Rory's telegraphic communication; and when the travellers reached the cottage, they found the mother and Mary in that peculiar state of action which in the polite world is called 'hurry-scurry;' and the dragging of chairs and stools, cramming of things into corners, and slapping about with the ends of aprons, testified their anxiety to receive so unusual a visitor with proper honour.

When they entered, the widow first received her son with the strongest evidence of a mother's affection, kissing him tenderly; and with the reverential appeal to heaven in which the Irish peasantry so much indulge, she said:

'God bless you, alanna, you're welkim home!' She then turned to the stranger, and in that soft accent of her country which so we expresses the gentlest emotions of human nature, she said, in tones that would have almost conveyed her meaning without words, 'You're kindly welkim, sir.'

The stranger expressed his thanks; but, notwithstanding the manifest commotion which his arrival occasioned, he was too polite to see to notice it, and did not, as a vulgar person always does, overload the people with requests not to trouble them *on his account*.

He quietly took a seat; and Rory, with instinctive good-breeding, took another, and continued to discourse with his guest. Now and then, to be sure, he could not help casting his eyes towards his mother, who was busy in all sorts of preparation, and asking:

'Can I help you, mother dear?' But the answer always was:

'No, alanna. Sure you're tired afther your journey; and Mary and myself will do everything; and sure it's glad we are to have you, and proud that the gintleman is come with you, and only hopes he'll put up with what we can do: but sure, if the enthertainment is poor, the welkim is hearty, anyhow.'

The stranger assured her of his sense of her kindness.

'If we knew of your comin', sir, sure we could have had a couple of chickens ready; and if the gintleman would wait a bit, sure it isn't too late yet, and can have a rashir and egg in the mane time.'

'My dear ma'am,' said the stranger, 'pray don't think of chickens to-night: the fact is, I'm very hungry, and I don't know a better thing than a dish of rashers and eggs, which has the great advantage, besides, of being got ready sooner.'

Rashers and eggs were accordingly got ready immediately and while the mother was engaged in the culinary department, Mary spread a coarse but white cloth upon the table, and taking down from a cleanly-scoured dresser some plates of coarse delf, arranged the table for the supper. This the hungry travellers discussed with good appetite and much relish; and after many relays of the savoury viands had vanished rapidly before them, a black bottle of whisky was produced, and some hot punch being made, Rory's guest protested he had eaten one of the best suppers he ever made in his life.

Rory and his mother and sister were lavish in their compliments to the stranger on being so easily pleased, and uttered a profusion of wishes that they had better to offer. This by their guest was pronounced impossible; and when at last the stranger retired to bed, they parted for the night with the highest opinion of each other—he in admiration of their hospitality, and they of his condescension.

Rory then, with his mother and sister, drew round the fire, and, relieved from the presence of a stranger, indulged in that affectionate family gossip which always is the result when one of the circle has returned from a temporary absence. Rory sat on a chair in the middle, his sister on a low stool beside him, with one hand resting on his knee, and her pretty eyes raised to his, in open wonder, only to be exceeded by the more open wonder of her mouth, as Rory told something of what he had seen in Dublin. The widow, on the other side, seated in a low easy chair of plaited straw, looked upon her son with manifest pleasure; and while she led Rory into a digression, by asking him how he managed 'the little business' about the lease, Mary filled up the interval very agreeably by looking with ecstasy at the roll of ribbon which her brother brought her. This was a great delight to Mary: it was no pedlar's trash, no common thing bought at a booth in a fair, but a real downright metropolitan ribbon, 'brought all the way from Dublin to herself.' Wasn't she happy? And maybe she didn't think how she'd astonish them next Sunday at chapel!

Rory told them how he met the stranger he brought home, and of the accident which led to it, and praised him to the skies for his liberality and gentlemanly conduct—swore he was of the right sort, and said he was one for whom a poor man ought to lay down his life. Such was Rory's opinion of the stranger he had met, and who was introduced to the reader in the first chapter under the title of the 'Scholar.' How he acquired this title, will be subsequently seen.

The trio talked on until the embers on the hearth were quite burnt out, and it was at an advanced hour in the morning that they separated and retired to their slumbers, which were sound because their lives were healthful and innocent.

1.   The ditch.

V

Whisky versus small-pox.—Gibberish versus French.—A secret with two handles to it, which our hero and his sister lay hold of.

THE NEXT MORNING THE WIDOW O'More and her son and daughter arose fresh and light-hearted, but not so their guest: he awoke with the burning thirst, intense headache, and deadening sensation of sickness, which are the precursors of fever.

It was early, and from the silence that reigned in the cottage he concluded no one had yet risen.

He endeavoured to sleep, but the effort was vain: he fell but into a confused dozing, filled with broken images, confused recollections, and wild imaginings, from which he started but with an increased sensation of illness upon him; and even when the inhabitants of the cottage rose, they came not near him, wishing to leave him undisturbed after his fatigue.

At length, on his hearing Rory's voice, he exerted his so as to make himself heard; and when Rory entered, he perceived, from the heavy eye and altered countenance of the stranger, that he was unwell.

'God be good to us! what's the matther with you, sir?' said Rory.

'I'm ill, very ill, O'More,' said the stranger languidly.

'Well, don't disturb yourself, sir, and you'll be betther by and by, plaze God!"

'I'm afraid I've caught the small-pox,' said the stranger.

'I hope not, sir don't be thinkin' o' sich things. Sure, how would you get the small-pox?'

'From a beggar in the crowd here last night, when we alighted at the inn. I remember shuddering at the mention of the disease when she spoke of it: and I fear I am infected with what I dread more than anything under the sun.'[1]

'I had betther bring my mother to you, sir,' said Rory, 'for she is very knowledgeable in sickness, and undherstands the *aribs*' (herbs); and with these words he left the room, leaving the poor sick stranger utterly at a loss to know what her knowledge of the *Arabs*, as he took Rory's word to be, could have to do with his illness.

When Rory returned with his mother, she asked the stranger (for so we shall yet continue to call him) how he felt. He told in what manner he was suffering, and she replied by proposing to him to take a glass of whisky. The very name of the thing produced nausea to the sick man, who refused the offer with a shudder.

'See how you thrimble, sir!' said she. 'Indeed, if you b'lieve me, a good big dhrop o' whisky is the best thing you could take.'

'Don't mention it, I beg of you. I fear it is the small-pox I have caught.'

'Plaze God, I hope not!' said the widow: 'but if it is, not a finer thing in the world than a dhrop o' whisky to dhrive it out from your heart.'

Thus she continued to urge the taking of ardent spirits, which, to this hour, in the commencement of every sickness amongst the Irish peasantry, is considered the one thing needful, and for the reason the widow assigned in this case, namely, to 'dhrive it out from the heart.'

The heart is by them considered the vulnerable point in sickness as well as in love; so much so indeed, that no matter what disease they labour under, it is always called an 'impression on the heart.' So well understood does this seem to be amongst them, that even the part affected is not necessary to be named, and the word 'heart' is emitted altogether; and if you ask 'What's the matter with such a one?' the answer is sure to be, 'He's got an impression.'

'Mrs. O'More,' said the stranger, 'I am certain it is the small-pox; and while I may yet be moved, pray let me be conveyed to the neighbouring town, to the inn, and let not your house be visited with the disease and the contagion.'

'Oh, God forbid that I'd do the like, sir, and turn the sick sthranger outside my doors whin it's most he wanted the carin' for—and in an inn too! Oh, what would become of you at all in sich a place, where I wouldn't have a sick dog, much less a gintleman, beholdin' to! Make yourself aisy, sir; and if it's as bad as you think, we'll take care o' you, niver fear.'

'I don't fear,' said the stranger, affected by the widow's kindness : 'but it is not right that you should have this horrid disease under you roof, and all for a stranger.'

'Keep your mind aisy, dear, do,' said the widow:—'sure we're all poor craythers, God help us!—and if we did not help one another in our want and throuble, it's the dark and blake world it would be!—and what would we be Chrishthans for at all, if we hadn't charity in our hearts? I beg your pardon, sir, for sayin' charity to a gintleman—but sure it's not charity I mane at all, only tindherness and compassion. And as for the sickness being undher our roof, my childher, God be praised! is over the small-pox—iv it be it—and had it light—as well as myself: so make your mind aisy, dear, and dhrive it out from your heart with the whisky. Well, well! don't shake your poor head that way; I won't ax you to take it till you like it yourself: but whin there *is* an impression, there's nothin' like dhrivin' it out. So I'll lave you, sir, for a while—and see if you can sleep; and I'll come in again by and by; and if you want anything in the manetime, you can jist thump on the flure with the chair—I have put it convaynient to your hand: and the sooner you can bring yourself to take the sper'ts, the betther. Well, well! I'll say no more—only it's the finest thing in the world, with a clove o' garlic, for worms or fayver, to threw out the venom.' And so, muttering praises on her favourite panacea, she left the room.

The illness of the stranger increased during the day, and in the evening he began to speak incoherently.

The Widow O'More now thought it probably was the small-pox with which her guest was visited, and began to take the most approved measures that were in these days established for the cure of that

terrible disease; that is to say, she stopped every crevice of the room
whereby air could be admitted, opened the door as seldom as possible,
and heaped all the clothes she could on the patient, and gave him hot
drinks to allay the raging thirst that consumed him.

Not content with heaping bed-clothes over the unhappy sufferer,
she got a red cloth cloak and wrapped it tightly round his body; it
being in those days considered that a wrapper of red cloth was of
great virtue.

Let the reader, then, imagine the wretched plight the poor stranger
was reduced to, and what chance of recovery he had from such
treatment.

The fever increased fearfully, and he soon became quite delirious.
During his ravings he imagined the bed in which he lay to be a tent;
for, with national hospitality, he had been placed in the best bed in the
house, with the flaring calico curtains before mentioned.

'Why is this tent square?' said he.

'Whisht, whisht, dear,' said the widow, soothingly.

'But why is it square?—And look here,' said he, seizing the
curtain,—'why is not this white? why is my tent red?—or is it the
blood of the enemy upon it?'

'God help the craythus!' said the widow.

Rory now entered the room; and the stranger started up in the bed
and said,

'*Qui vive?*'

'Sir?' said Rory, rather astonished.

'Ah! c'est mon caporal,' pursued the sick man. '*Caporal, nous avons
vaincu les Anglais!—voilà leur sang;*' and he shook the curtains fiercely.

'Humour him, dear,' said the widow to Rory; 'the craythur's ravin':
purtend you know all about it—that's the best way to soother him.'

'Sure I dunna what he's sayin'—he's muttherin' ghibberish there.'

'Well, do you mutther ghibberish too,' said the widow, and left the
room.

'*Répondez vite, caporal,*' said the invalid.

'Hullabaloo!' shouted Rory.

'*Qu'est-ce que c'est?*'

'Hullabaloo!' cried Rory again.

'*Vous êtes étranger,*' said the poor sufferer; '*tremblez! esclave, tremblez! rendez-vous!*' and he jumped up in bed—'*rendez au drapeau tricolour!*'

'A dhrop o' what?' said Rory.

'*Vive le drapeau tricolor!*' cried De Lacy.

Rory left the room, and told his mother he believed 'the poor gintlmen was callin' for a *dhrop* o' something.' She entered with more hot drink, and asked the sick man to swallow it; 'It'll do you good, dear,' said she.

'Is there anything you'd like betther, sir?' said Rory; 'and if it's to be had I'll get it for you.'

The stranger seemed to be recalled from his raving a moment by the sounds of another language upon his ears; and looking wildly again at Rory, and his mother, and the bed, he said:

'This is not my tent—who are you?—where am I?'—and he flung the bed-clothes down from him;—then seeing the red cloak wrapped round him, he said fiercely, 'Take this accursed cloth from off me,—I'm no slave of the English tyrants;—where's my blue uniform?'

'Lie down, dear, lie down,' said the widow.

'Never! said the sick man,—'we'll never lie down under tyranny!' and he attempted to jump from the bed.

'Rory, dear, howld him,' said the widow,—'howld him, or he'll be out; and if he catches cowld, he's lost.'

Rory now by force held down the sufferer, who struggled violently for a while, but, becoming exhausted, sank back on the bed and groaned aloud:

'Ah! see what my fate is—I'm a prisoner in the hands of the accursed English!'

For some time he now lay quieter, and Mary was left to watch in his chamber while Rory was absent for some drugs his mother sent him or to the neighbouring village.

During her sojourn in the room, Mary often heard the stranger lamenting his fate in a plaintive tone, and calling on a female name in passionate accents. In this state for some days the patient continued his paroxysms of raving being but varieties of lamenting his fate as a prisoner, calling for his blue uniform and invoking a female name.

From the nature of all this raving, Rory and Mary drew each their
own conclusions. Rory, from his knowledge of the stranger's bearing
and opinions before he fell sick, and from the tone of his subsequent
delirium, suspected he was an officer in the French army; and Mary,
from his frequent calling on a female name, had no doubt he was in
love. Now, to the end of time, Mary could never have guessed at the
stranger's profession, nor Rory at the state of his heart: but these are
the delicate shades of difference that exist between the mind of man
and woman. The sympathies of the former are alive to turmoil and
strife; those of the latter, to the gentle workings of our nature: the
finer feelings of a woman vibrate with magic quickness to the smallest
indications of affection; while man, like the war-horse of the Psalmist,
'smelleth the battle afar off.'

Both Rory and Mary were right in their conclusions: the sick
stranger was an officer in the French service, and also was in love.

With respect to the love affair, the tangled business may go
tangling on, as the more tangled such affairs become the better but
of the stranger's name and purposes it is time the reader should be
informed.

1.   He must have caught the disease earlier, as the infection of small pox does
     not exhibit itself so soon. But young gentlemen are not expected to be
     too learned in such matters.

VI

In which a gentleman writes a letter as long as a lady's.

HORACE DE LACY WAS THE stranger's name. Descended from the noble race of De Lacy, one of the original conquerors of Ireland, he inherited all the fire and courage of his ancestors; but now, the descendant of the enslaver became the champion of liberty, and panted with as burning a zeal for the regeneration of his country as his ancestors had done for her subjugation, for Ireland was now his native land, and the remark so often made in the chronicles of England, that the descendants of English settlers in Ireland became more fierce in their rebellion than the natives themselves, was about to be once more verified in the person of Horace de Lacy.

Though an Irishman by birth, he had for some years been resident in France. There he imbibed all the fierce enthusiasm to which the epoch of the French revolution gave birth, and the aspirations for universal liberty which fired his young heart were first directed to his native land. As early as 1794, communications were carried forward between the disaffected in Ireland and the French executive; and Doctor Jackson, one of the agents at that period, was discovered, and would have been hanged, but that he escaped the ignominious death by swallowing poison in the dock, where he died in the face of his accusers and his judges.

The death of Jackson produced a great sensation in Ireland. It made the rapacious and intolerant faction that *then* ruled the country, more insolent; and those who cursed their rule and endeavoured to overthrow it, more cautious.

The result was fearful. Wrong was heaped upon wrong by the oppressor suffered in hopelessness, but *remembered*, by the oppressed. Each new aggression on the one side produced a debt of hatred on the other, and the account was carried on with compound interest.

In 1797, another communication was opened between the disaffected in Ireland and the executive of the French government and De Lacy was one of the agents.

He was an officer in the French army, and volunteered to undertake the dangerous duty of visiting Ireland and England, with a view of ascertaining the probable likelihood of success in a revolutionary movement in the one country, and the state of feeling as regarded a desire of revolution in the other.

In France, at that period, it is singular the total ignorance that existed with relation to the state of the united dominions of Great Britain.

Repeatedly as they had been assured of the certainty of cooperation in a descent upon Ireland, and the futility of any such attempt upon England, nevertheless the absurd scheme was entertained of letting loose some French desperadoes in England, and carrying on a system of *Chouannerie* in that country.

The most active and intelligent of the Irish emissaries, Theobald Wolfe Tone, then resident at Paris, had repeatedly assured the French executive that such a plan was worse than hopeless, but still they were not convinced; and General Clarke, then minister of war, because he bore an Irish name, and was of Irish descent, thinking he must know something of the matter, though he had never set foot in the country, helped to strengthen them in this belief, and notwithstanding all the assurances and arguments of Tone, Clarke would not be satisfied of the truth of such statements without having an emissary of his own to visit the country and report upon it.

De Lacy was the person who volunteered this service; and crossing the Channel in the boat of a smuggler, who knew the coast well, and was in constant habit of communication with both England and

Ireland—but particularly the latter—he had been for some time in London and through the English provinces before he visited Ireland. There he had but recently arrived when Rory O'More met him as a travelling companion; and of the events of his journey since, the reader is in possession.

What impression his observations in England produced, may be seen by the following letter, which was forwarded to France by a sailor on board a vessel which traded between Dublin and France, under Swedish colours, and under the particular patronage of Lord —, then high in the government of Ireland, and the most vindictive enemy of the Liberal party.

It may be asked, why did Lord — permit, much less patronise, this proceeding? It was because the vessel was chartered by a certain merchant to whom he was indebted in large loans of money; and the accommodation thus afforded was partly paid by the exclusive permission of trading with France thus granted by Lord —, whose influence in Ireland was then so paramount, that a word from him was sufficient to guarantee the safety of his friend's ship, by the willing blindness of the commissioners of customs, who always treated this make-believe Swedish vessel with the most exemplary indulgence.

Certain intelligence from France, too, was procured in this way; but while the noble lord and his party thus obtained information, they little dreamed that the same channel was used for the transmission of intelligence between their enemies.

In the packet of information that follows, the reader must not be startled at its high-sounding style the tone of the period was extravagant, particularly in France; and De Lacy was at that age and of that profession which delights in flourishes, whether of trumpets or words.

The packet was addressed to a certain 'Citizen Madgett' at Paris, well known in those days to the Irish Republican party, and to whom General Clarke had desired De Lacy's communications to be made. Its contents ran thus:

'You know with what feelings I left France. I rejoiced there, in common with my fellows, in the triumph that right had achieved

over wrong; in the majesty of human nature overcoming the kings
that would have enslaved her; in the brilliant era of retribution and
resuscitation that more than redeemed the tyranny and suffering that
gave it birth. You know how I hoped, in the warmth of my head and
heart, that the rest of mankind should share in the blessings we had so
dearly purchased with our blood, and that man, freed from the thraldom
of ages, should form but one family; that the prejudices and distinctions
of countries should be forgotten, and regenerated mankind, as one
nation, kneel, Peruvian-like, to the newly-risen sun of their freedom.

'But this glorious dream has been disturbed since I left you. I visited
England with the view of kindling on a thousand altars the fire of
liberty that I bore with me from liberty's own temple but the moral as
well as the natural atmosphere of England is damp and chilly compared
with the country of the vine, and I found myself a disappointed
enthusiast, with few or none to share in my raptures.

'My hymn of liberty was not half so cheering to me as the clank of
John Bull's chains to his own ears (and long enough they are); and a
priest of liberty, like any other priest, cuts a very contemptible figure
without a congregation.

'So, after some little time, seeing the state of affairs stand thus, I began
to look about me with more observation.

"Perhaps," said I to myself, "John Bull is like his own flint-stones, with
fire enough in him, only you must strike him hard;" and so I laid myself
out for observation, and was on the alert for every grievance.

'I was baffled in making any great advances towards my object, and
after some time fruitlessly spent, it struck me that the capital city of
a kingdom is not the place to judge of the real state of a country, or
measure the feelings of the people.

'"Here," said I, "in London, where peers have their palaces, and
merchants their mansions; where wasteful wealth and lavish luxury
deprave the whole community, and blinding the citizen to the real state
of things, make him believe, because he is a sharer in the plunder they
are wasting, that he is a gainer by their extravagance; here is not the
place to hope for the altar of freedom and the rights of regenerated
man to be respected. The Londoner will endure the abuses of his time,

because he enjoys from them a temporary benefit, and even upholds the very tyranny of which he himself will be the last to suffer. But to be the last in suffering is considered a wondrous gain in our contemptible natures. How like men are to children in such matters I remember, at school, how the timid boys hung back from a cup of medicine, or the cold-bath, or punishment, and the wretch who was last drenched with rhubarb, shoved into the river, or flogged, thought himself a clever fellow, and enjoyed a sort of percentage on the suffering that had gone before him. So is it," thought I, "with the Londoner: but I will go into the country, and there, in the interior of England, observe the canker that is at her heart; and while I observe the disease, I will inculcate the remedy."

'With this view, I quitted the capital and visited a village. The lord of the soil (one of the magnificent English baronets) I knew was in the capital at the time, and from his neglected and forsaken tenantry I might hope to hear the murmurs of dissatisfaction and the desire of redress. But in this I was disappointed.

'I wished to see what extent of domain the aristocrat appropriated to his own enjoyment (when he was at home), and walked towards "the Honor," as it is called, in expectation of seeing the shutters closed, and grass growing through the avenues.

'I leaped a fence, and proceeded through a rich field and a piece of beautiful plantation, until I was accosted by a well-dressed peasant, who asked me, somewhat sturdily, what brought me there. I told him I was going to look over the grounds and see the house. He asked me, had I got leave, and how did I get in? On telling him how, he said that crossing the fence was not permitted, and suggested my going back. I said, if the family were at home, I would not have taken the liberty to intrude; but in their absence there could be no offence. "Sir Richard is quite as particular when he is away," was the answer.

'"Is he so very churlish," said I, "as to object to a gentleman crossing his domain when he is away, and when his privacy can not be invaded?" "Oh, whether he's here or not, is no odds," replied the man; "for strangers running in and out of the park would spoil it just as much, whether Sir Richard be here or no."

"'Then he keeps up his park at all times?" said I. "To be sure, sir, he do," said the man, looking at me as if he did not knew whether I was a rogue or a simpleton.

"'And may I not be permitted to walk through the park?'

"Why, Sir, if you get leave of Mr. Lowndes, or Mr. Banks, or the steward or the agent, or—" And on he went, telling me how many people could give me leave, till I interrupted him by saying, 'Why, you have a large establishment here.' "Oh yes, sir," said he; "it's all the same, like, whether Sir Richard be here or no—except that there's not the company at the house."

"'And who may you be?" I inquired. "One of the keepers, sir," "Well," said I, "as I have not time to ask any of the people you have named, perhaps you would be so obliging"—and all the time I kept a telegraphic fumbling of my right hand in my waistcoat pocket—"you would be so obliging as to show me up to the house," and as I finished my query, I slid a half-crown backwards and forwards between my forefinger and thumb. "Why, sir," said the keeper, "as I sees you're a gent'eman"—and he looked, not at me, but at the half-crown—"I cawn't see no objections;" and a transfer of my money and his civility at once was effected.

'My guide led me through a splendid park towards the house: no grass growing through the walks, as I anticipated, but beautifully kept, as if the lord of the soil were present. We reached the house: no closed shutters, but half-open windows, and the curtains from within, caught by the breeze, peeping out to visit the roses that were peeping in to meet them—a sort of flirtation between the elegancies of the interior and exterior.

'On entering the house, I found myself in a square hall, lined throughout with oak. The ceiling was low and divided by richly-carved octagonal frame-work into compartments; the polished floor was also inlaid after the same pattern, and the wainscot elaborately panelled and covered with curious carving. Old suits of armour, cross-bows, bills, partisans, two-handled swords, and other weapons, were distributed around the apartment; and an enormous blood-hound lay stretched upon the floor, basking in the sun, and seemed a suitable tenant of this domestic armoury.

'I strolled through room after room, and an air of habitual wealth prevailed throughout.

'There was an old library, with pieces of buhl furniture, and old ebony seats and chairs, with large down cushions, where one might luxuriate in learning. And this delightful old room looked out on an antique-looking garden, whose closely-cut grass-plots were like velvet, and divided by high hedgerows of yew, cropt as smooth as a wall. Then a large cedar spread his dusky branches so close to the windows as to exclude some portion of the light, and produce that *demi-jour* so suitable to a place of study.

'There were pictures throughout the house, principally portraits, of which the English are *so* fond—some of them very good, sufficiently so to be valuable as works of art. Holbein and Vandyke had immortalised some of the former owners of the Honor; and there they hung in goodly succession, holding a place on the walls of the *château* they had successively been masters of.

'The seal of Time was on all this evidence; here from sire to son had plenty been transmitted, and wealth and comfort were hereditary. There was, withal, such an air of peace and tranquillity about the old place, that it was quite soothing: you could hear through the open casements the rustling of the flowers in the garden, as the warm breeze whispered through them and wafted their fragrance into the library. Could one at such a moment think hopefully of revolution?—where so much comfort existed, there also would exist the love of repose.

'I confess I was overcome by the influence of all I had seen, and convinced that Tone is quite right.

'On quitting the Honor, however, I considered that though the aristocracy might revel in such enjoyments as these, the great mass of the people would be willing to invade a repose that was purchased at the price of their labour and taxation, and a system where the many were sacrificed to the few. "It is not in Allenby Honor I must look," thought I, "but in the village."

'Here, after days of observation, I confess I think the hope of revolutionising England quite absurd. The comforts of the people are generally such, that men with less caution than the English would not risk the loss of them in the hope of speculative blessings.

'Their houses are well built, and so beautifully clean!—but not merely clean—a love of *embellishment* is to be seen: trailing plants perhaps festoon their windows round a bit of trellis, a white curtain peeping from within; there is a neat paling round the house, and flowers within this fence; the cultivation of flowers in the little gardens of the lower orders bespeaks a country in contentment.

'Then the better class of dwelling, with its paved walk leading up from the outer gate through evergreens, and its bright brass knocker and bell-pull, and white steps, that seem as if they had been washed the minute before; the windows so clean, with their Venetian blinds inside and fresh paint without—in short, I could not enumerate a twentieth part of these trifling evidences that go to prove the ease and prosperity of these people.

'Their domestic arrangements keep pace with this outward show. They are universally well found in the essential comforts of life; they have good beds, are well clothed and well fed.

'I saw an old fellow yesterday evening driving his water-cart to the river, and he was as fat and rosy as an alderman: the cart and the water-barrel upon it were nicely painted, and as the little donkey drew it along, the old fellow trudged beside it, comforting himself with the support of a stick. Fancy a peasant with a walking-stick!—do you think that fellow would turn rebel?—never!

'On a little green beside the village some boys were playing at cricket: they had their bats and ball—poverty cannot be here, when peasants can buy the materials of play for their children. Then the children seemed so careful! The coats and hats they had taken off during their exercise were piled in a heap at a distance, and when their game was finished, they dressed themselves with such regularity!—and with what good clothes were they provided!

'This is not the country for revolution!—such is my firm conviction. There are some in England who hail with rapture the dawn of liberty, and wish that its splendour may lighten all nations; but that number is comparatively small, and I cannot wonder at it, after all I have seen. Believe me, there are few men in England like Horne Tooke. By the by, I must tell you a capital thing he said the other day. The conversation ran upon definition and some one said it would be very hard to define what was treason. "Not at all," said Horne Tooke; "it is nothing but *reason* with a *t* to it."—Wasn't it capital?

'To conclude—Tone is right. I repeat it, no hopes can be entertained of revolutionising England.

'I go to Ireland next week; and from all I can learn here, matters promise better for us *there*. I carry this letter with me to Dublin, whence I shall transmit it to you by our *Swedish* friend. You shall hear from me again, immediately that I have made my observations.

'H. D. L.'

Now, bating the flourishes about freedom and regenerated mankind, there is much good sense and shrewd observation in this letter.

It will be perceived, that however great his revolutionary enthusiasm, it did not carry him away into the folly of believing in impossibilities: he saw, and said, that England could not be revolutionised, for her people enjoyed too many comforts to throw them away in a civil war.

This temperate tone is noticed to the reader, to show that De Lacy was a trusty agent in the cause he undertook; that, uninfluenced by his preconceived notions, and in the very teeth of his wishes, he saw England was beyond the reach of revolutionary influence, and pointed out the reasons why.

Let the reader mark the calm and judicious observation of the man, for in due time *another* letter of his will appear, describing the state of Ireland; and the influence of that letter will be the greater by remembering the foregoing one, and bearing in mind that the same man, exercising the same observation, and with the same desire to ascertain the *real* probability of success in a revolutionary movement, is the writer.

The wishes and hopes of the republican were utterly overthrown by the security and prosperity of England, but he found in the misery and misrule of Ireland the ready materials for a country's convulsion.

VII

A man of law and physic.

'He was a man to all the country *dear!*'

D E LACY'S FEVER CONTINUED TO rage, and his ravings to proceed
in their usual course. Two things were in his favour: his fury
at the red cloth obliged the widow O'More to give up *that* hope of
recovering her patient; and all her ingenuity could not induce him
to take whisky, even in the most diluted form.

Sometimes, when the poor sufferer had been calling for drink
for some time, the cunning prescriber would enter with a vessel of
liquid containing a portion of the favourite medicine, and hoping that
the anxiety for any alleviation of thirst would make him swallow it
without examination, she would say,

'Now, dear, here 'tis for you. Dhrink it up at once—dhrink it up
big!'

Poor De Lacy would seize the vessel with avidity, and make a rush
with open mouth upon it; but the moment the presence of whisky
was apparent, he would refuse it. In mere charity, at last, though
without any hope of doing him good, the widow made him some
plain two-milk whey, and this he swallowed with that fierce desire for
drink that the thirst of fever or the Desert only knows.

Rory procured the drugs his mother ordered at the village, and
brought them back to her with all the speed that might be.

What they were it is needless to know, and perhaps the Faculty might or might not be benefited by the knowledge; but as vaccination has triumphed over the terrible plague that then scourged mankind, it is unnecessary to seek what were the nostrum the widow employed in her medical capacity.

'Who do you think did I meet at M'Garry's to-day, whin I wint ther for the physic?' said Rory on his return.

'Arrah, who thin?' said his mother.

'Sweeny!'

'Is it Sweeny?'

'Divil a less!'

'I wondher he isn't ashamed to go to the place, the dirty scut! his father was a 'pottekerry, and he must turn atturney; and instead of follyin' his dacent father's business before him, and attindin' to the 'pottekerryin', it's the 'turneyin' he must be afther—bad luck to him!—and instead of doin' people good, and curin' them of anything might come over thim, he's doin' thim all the harm he can, and laying them without anything over them—not as much as a blanket, much less a house. His father used to cure 'ructions,[1] but he's risin' them; and, as I said before, I wondher he's not ashamed to go into the owld shop, for it ought to remind him that he might be a dacent 'pottekerry, instead of a *skrewging* 'turney, as he is: and more betoken, the dirty little 'turney to set up to be a gintleman, and for that same to change his blessed and holy religion, and turn prod'stant! Oh, the little vagabone!'

Now it will be seen the widow wound up her phillipic against Sweeny by placing the heaviest offence the last;—'He turned prod'stant;'—this was the great crime in the widow's eyes, and indeed in those of most of the people of her class. Sweeny might have robbed all Ireland, and suffered less in their opinion than by the fact of his going to church.

Poor Ireland!—the great question of a man's vice or virtue, fitness or unfitness, talent or stupidity, wisdom or folly, treason or loyalty, was answered in those days by the fact of whether he went to a protestant church or a catholic chapel.

The two sects disliked each other equally; but the protestant born and bred was not half so much loathed as the apostate who renounced the faith of his fathers for 'the flesh-pots of Egypt;' and the Roman Catholics were the more jealous of this defection, because they never had any converts from the protestants in return, and for the best reason in the world—*there was nothing to be made by it.*

Now it was by a process of consecutive reasoning that Sweeny had denounced physic and popery, and. assumed the attorney and ascendency. He gave up the healing art because he saw his father could make nothing of it. How could he? When a population is so poor as not to be able to afford the necessaries of life, they cannot be expected to command the remedies against death: if they cannot buy bread, they will hardly buy physic. So Sweeny the younger turned his attention towards the law, which is an amusement that those who *have* something to lose deal in, and therefore belongs more to the richer classes, or, as *they* call themselves, the *better* classes.

Now as these better (*alias* richer) classes in Ireland were on the side of the protestants, Sweeny thought that conforming to the church as by law established would be a move in his favour, and accordingly he (to use the words of a paragraph in one of the government papers of the day) 'renounced the errors of the Church of Rome, and embraced those of the Church of England.'

He had lived long enough with his father to pick up a few words of apothecary Latin, and these he mixed with a vile jargon of his own, which he imposed on people for medical knowledge and although as ignorant as a horse in every way, he had the impudence to enact the amateur doctor, and give advice gratis in physics to his clients in law.

This dabbling in doctoring permitted him to indulge in a ruling propensity of his nature, which was, curiosity: while he played the doctor, he could play the inquisitor; and by his joint possession of cunning and impudence, it is surprising how he used to ferret out intelligence.

He seldom ventured on giving prescriptions of his own, and to avoid this he always recommended some patent medicine, a supply of which he kept by him to furnish to his friends, and he charged them a handsome profit on the same. He would say:

'My dear ma'am, don't be going to that dreadful M'Garry! You'll ruin your health—your precious health! you can't depend upon his drugs at all: he hasn't them pure—how could he, poor creature! I would give you a recipe if his drugs could be depended upon; but they positively cannot. Suppose now, my dear ma'am—suppose your little nerves get out of order, and I wished to give you something of an *alluviating* nature, I might wish to exhibit a small dose of *hippopotamus*, and most likely he, not having the article in his *cornucopia*, might give you *vox populi*. Now only fancy your swallowing *vox populi* instead of *hippopotamus!* There's no knowing what the consequence might be: perhaps utter prostitution—prostitution of strength I mean—only fancy! I tell you, M'Garry is dangerous; besides, M'Garry keeps the Post-office—and how can a man mind the post and his profession?— or, as the Squire most fassyetiously said the other day, "How can he be at his two posts at once?" Ha, ha! Very good—wasn't it? Capital, *I* think. But, to be serious, M'Garry's dangerous: he'd better throw his physic to the dogs, as the Bard of Devon says, for 'tis fit for no one else. You had better let me send you a little box of pills, and a bottle of that thing I sent you before; they are *patent* medicines, and must be good. You liked the last—didn't you? Tastes rather *strong,* you say; so much the better—make you strong: very nice, though. It is an *expensive* medicine, *rather;* but what o' that in comparison to your precious health? Better than being poisoned with *vox populi.*'

Thus would this impudent and ignorant vagabond talk his vile rubbish to the fools who would let him send them his patent medicines, and charge them in his bill.

When Sweeny saw Rory O'More getting drugs at M'Garry's, he asked him who was ill. Rory, not liking him, and aware of his prying nature, wished for reasons of his own that he should not know for whom they were intended, as he thought it possible the animal might pay a visit to the cottage on the plea of giving advice, and see the stranger, and what would be worse, *hear* him raving too; and Rory's surmises as to the profession of his guest made him anxious that this should not be. He accordingly evaded all the questions of the medical attorney as well as he could, and left him without giving him any information on the subject. But this was quite enough to excite Sweeny's suspicion, and set his curiosity craving; and so he rode out the next day to pay Rory's home a visit, and ferret out the mystery.

On arriving at the house, he hung his horse's bridle-reins over a hook near the door, and bolted into the cottage at once. Rory, his mother, and sister, were all there; therefore, it was a plain case that none of the family were ill.

'Good morrow, widow!' said Sweeny in his politest manner—'glad to see you well, ma'am—and you, Mary O'More—well and hearty;— all well, I see—glad of it. I was afraid some one was sick—saw Rory getting drugs yesterday—just dropt in as I was coming by, to see could I offer any advice: who's sick?'

'Thank you, Mr. Sweeny, I'm obleeged,' said the widow coldly; 'I jist wanted a thrifle of physic, and so Rory wint for it:' and she bustled about, evidently having no inclination to enter into conversation with him, and letting him see that such *was* her intention; but Sweeny was not to be put off so.

'Can I do anything in the way of advice, Mrs. O'More?'

'Yis, indeed, Mr. Sweeny, you can: and I think I'll be goin' over to you to ask about a little bit o' law soon, for I'm having an alteration made in my lase.'

'Yes, yes—certainly—law business—certainly—always ready, Mrs. O'More: but I mean in the medical way—you know I'm skilful in that way, Mrs. O'More—and as there's some one sick here, if I can be of any use, I'll be most happy—most happy, Mrs. O'More.'

The widow saw there was no evading the attorney, and so she said a traveller had been going the road, and was taken ill, and they took him in and put him to bed; but 'it wouldn't signify, plase God! and he'd be well enough in a day or two.'

'If I can be of any use, I'll see him with pleasure.'

'Thank you, sir, but I gave him something myself that I know will do him good—obleeged to you all the same.'

'Is he poor?' said Sweeny.

'I never asked him that,' said the widow reproachfully.

'Of course—of course; but then I mean, you might guess.'

'Guess!' said Rory, who had been eyeing Sweeny all this time with a side-long glance of contempt,—'Guess!—why, thin, tare an ouns! do you think the man's a riddle or a *conundherum*, that we'd be guessin' at him?'

All the time this conversation was going on, Sweeny kept rolling his little grey eyes about him; and at last he spied De Lacy's portmanteau, and approaching it directly, and laying hold of it, he said, 'This is the traveller's portmanteau, I suppose?'

'Well, and what if it is?' said Rory. .

'Oh, nothing—nothing,' said Sweeny, who had turned it over and over to look for a name or initials; but there were none: 'no harm in my asking, I hope?'

'Nor no good, either,' said Rory.

'Only, by this portmanteau, the traveller is a gentleman, I perceive.'

'Well, he's not the worse of that,' said Rory.

'Anything I can do for the gentleman, I'll be most happy,' said Sweeny, who always laid a *gentleman* under obligation if he could.

'Thank you, sir, but he's very comfortable here, I can tell you, and shan't want for anything,' said the widow.

'I've no doubt of that, Mrs. O'More; but if I could see him, perhaps might be able to give some little advice. Is he in that room?' said Sweeny, pointing as he spoke.

'He's asleep and mustn't be disturbed,' said Rory.

Just that moment De Lacy's raving took a noisy turn, and he became audible to Sweeny.

'There,' said Sweeny, 'he's awake—now you can let me go in;' and he vas advancing to the door when Rory stepped between, and said the patient shouldn't be disturbed; at the same time he turned towards his mother, and made a grimace as much as to say, 'Sweeny must not be admitted.'

The widow grinned and blinked her eyes, as much as to say, 'He shall not.'

'You see, Mr. Sweeny,' said she, 'the poor gintleman's ravin', and doesn't like sthrangers.'

'Raving—ho, ho!—fever—dangerous, Mrs. O'More care, take care.'

'I've taken every care, sir.'

'But fever, Mrs. O'More—have you given him *feverescing* drinks?'

'He has all he wants.'

'You should write to his friends, and tell them;—may die, you know; I'll write to them, if you like.'

'And charge six-and-eightpence for it,' said Rory aside.

'Do you know his name?'

'No,' said Rory very short; '*we* didn't ax him any impid'nt questions.'

'Rory, my man, don't be unreasonable—don't be in a passion;— maybe a person of consequence—his friends in a state of suspense.— He's raving: now all you have to do is to open his valise and examine his papers, and find out who he is. I'll do it for you, if you like.'

Rory's rage now burst its bounds. The prying impertinence of Sweeny he bore so long as it merely amounted to his personal annoyance; but when he made the last proposition, Rory opened upon him furiously.

'Why, thin, do you take me for such a mane-sperited dog, that while a sick man was on his back, I'd turn spy and thief, and break open his portmantle and hunt for his saycrets?'

'My dear Rory——'

'Don't dear me!—*Dear* indeed,—'faith! its *chape* you howld me, if you think I'd do sitch a dirty turn,—to bethray the man undher my roof; you ought to be ashamed of yourself!'

'But it's a common practice!'

'A common 'turney's practice maybe,—or a common thief's practice.'

'Hillo, Rory!'

'Oh, to the divil I pitch you and your hillo!—I say, a common thief's practice, again,—to break locks or cut open bags, and pimp and spy;—faugh on the man would do the like! Throth, if I thought there was one dhrop o' blood in my body would consent to it, I'd open my veins till it was out. Oh, murther, murther,—to hear of sich a scheming turn!—If I done such a rogue's thrick I'd howld myself disgraced to the end of my days, and think myself only fit company for Judas.'

Sweeny was dumb-foundered before the torrent of Rory's honest indignation, and was about to make some shuffling reply, when Mary O'More entered the cottage, she having left it a moment before, and said,

'Run, run, Mr. Sweeny! there's your horse has got his head out of the bridle, and is run into the field.'

Now it was Mary herself who had loosened the bridle from the beast, and let him escape, for the purpose of getting rid of their troublesome visitor.

Sweeny cut short his discourse, and darted from the house, pursuing his horse into the field, where he arrived in time to see him rolling over in great glee, much to the benefit of a new saddle.

Sweeny shouted 'murder!' and it was some time before the horse could be caught, even with the assistance of Rory. When he was secured, the saddle was discovered to have been split by the horse's tumbles; and when Sweeny got into his seat, and turned homewards, he saw Mary O'More showing her white teeth in a most undisguised laugh at the result of her trick, which Rory rejoiced in equally.

After De Lacy suffering under dangerous fever for some time, the eruption made its appearance, and he was soon out of danger.

He had no other aid in his illness than that of the widow's simple remedies, which, backed by a good constitution, carried him through, and now quiet and patience were all that he required.

As soon as he recovered his senses, it was some time before he could perfectly understand how he came to be in Rory O'More's cottage; but a few words from his kind host gradually gave the key to memory and he was enabled to recall the circumstances that preceded his illness.

After this he was for some time silent, and then he asked what was the day of the month. On being told, he knit his brow, and seemed to undergo some feelings of disappointment, to which an expression of great anxiety succeeded.

'O'More,' said he at last, 'shut the door. Come close to me; I want to ask you a question, and I charge you, as you hope for salvation, to answer me truly. I know I have been out of my senses, and I suppose I talked a great deal while I was so. Now tell me honestly, did anything remarkable strike you in my raving?'

'Yes, there did, sir,' said Rory, smiling at De Lacy, and looking straight into his eyes with that honest look that honesty alone can give.

There was a soothing influence to De Lacy in the expression of that smile and look, and a peculiar intelligence in them, that showed him Rory knew the drift of his questions, by having fathomed the circumstances of his situation.

'I am sure you guess what I am?' said De Lacy.

'Shouldher arms—whoo!' said Rory, laughing.

De Lacy smiled faintly at Rory's mode of illustrating his knowledge.

'Yon are right,' said De Lacy, 'and you know I'm not a soldier of King George.'

Rory sang, in a low tone,

Viva la, the *French* is coming—
Viva la, our friends is thrue;
Viva la, the French is coming—
What will the poor yeomen do?'

De Lacy nodded assent, and smiled, and after a short pause, said:

'You're a sharp fellow, O'More."

'I've been blunt enough with you, sir.'

'Honest as the sun,' said De Lacy. 'Now tell me, do the women know anything about this?'

'Not a taste; they suspect you no more nor the child unborn: only, Mary says— —'

'What?' said De Lacy, rather alarmed.

'That you're in love, sir—beggin' your pardon.'

'Oh! that's all. Well, she's right too. Why, you're a sharp family altogether.'

'Divil a much sharpness in that,' said Rory 'sure, whin there's the laste taste o' love goin', the wind o' the word is enough for a woman. Oh! let them alone for findin' out the soft side of a man's heart!—the greatest fool o' them all is wise enough in such matthers.'

'O'More,' said De Lacy, after another pause, 'you're a united Irishman.'

Rory smiled.

'Now it's your turn to be sharp.'

'You *are* a united man, then?' said De Lacy.

'To the core of my heart,' replied Rory with energy.

'Then my mind's at ease,' said De Lacy; and he held out his hand to O'More, who gave his in return, and De Lacy shook it warmly.

'God be praised, sir!' said Rory; 'but how does that set your mind at aise?'

'Because you can fulfil a mission for me, Rory, that otherwise must have failed; that is, if you'll undertake it.'

'Undhertake it!—I'd go to the four corners of the earth in a good cause.'

'You're a brave fellow!' said De Lacy.

'But will you tell me, sir,' said Rory, 'is the French comin' in *airnest* to help us?'

'No doubt of it, Rory—and *you* shall be the joyful messenger of their coming by doing the errand I wish for.'

'Oh! but that'll be the proud day for me, your honour!'

'Well, then, there's no time to lose. I asked you the day of the month a few minutes ago, and my heart sank within me when you to me the date; to-morrow I am bound by promise to be in the town of —, where an agent from France is waiting, who bears intelligence to Ireland. It is impossible for me to go; now will you undertake the duty, Rory?'

'With all the veins o' my heart!' said Rory, 'and be proud into the bargain.'

'Go, then,' said De Lacy, 'to the town of —, and there on the quay there's a public-house.'

''Faith there is—and more,' said Rory.

'The public-house I mean bears a very odd sign.'

'I'll be bound I know it,' said Rory, whose national impatience would not wait for De Lacy's directions; 'I'll engage it's the Cow and the Wheelbarrow.'

'No,' said De Lacy, who could not help smiling at the oddness of the combination in Rory's anticipated sign, 'it is not; but one quite as queer: the Cat and Bagpipes.'

'Oh, that's a common sign,' said Rory.

'There are a great many very queer things common in Ireland,' said De Lacy, who even in his present weakened state could not resist his habitual love of remark. 'You are well acquainted, I see, with the town,' he continued.

'Indeed, and I'm not,' said Rory; 'I never was there but wanst, and that happened to be on the quay, by the same token, where I remarked the Cow and the Wheelbarrow, for it's a sign I never seen afore, and is mighty noticeable.'

'But that is *not* the sign of the house you are to go to, remember.'

'Oh, by no manes, sir; the Cat and Bagpipes is my mark.'

'Yes and there about the hour of six in the evening you will see a party of three men.'

'But if there's two parties of three?' said Rory.

'You can distinguish our friends by contriving, in the most natural way you can—I mean so as not to excite observation from any but those who will understand and answer your signal—to say, *One, two, three*, in their hearing; and if those whom I expect you to meet should be there, you will be spoken to by them, and then you must introduce into whatever you say to them these words, *They were very fine ducks*. They will then leave the public-house, and you may trust yourself to follow wherever they lead.'

'Now, how am I to make sure that they are right?' said Rory.

'You have my word for their being trusty,' said De Lacy.

'Oh, sir, sure it's not your word I'd be doubting; but I mane, how am I to make sure that it *is* the right man I spake to?'

'Their noticing your remark will be sufficient; but, as a further assurance, they can return you the united man's signal and grip. Give me your hand,' said De Lacy, and he clasped the extended palm of Rory.

'That's the grip,' said Rory, 'sure enough. Why, thin, how did you come by that, sir?' said Rory; 'tare alive! are the French united Irishmen?'

'Not exactly,' said De Lacy, smiling; 'but the chosen know your signs. Now I've told you all that's requisite for your mission when you give these signs, they whom you'll meet will tell you what it is requisite for me to know, and you can bring me back the intelligence.'

'I've no time to lose,' said Rory; 'I must be off to-morrow by the dawn.'

'Will your mother or sister suspect anything from your absence?'

'Why, sir, the thruth is, neither mother nor sisther ever question me about my incomins or outgoins; though they have, av oorse, observed I was not always reg'lar, and women is sharp enough in sitch matthers; but they suspect something is going on in the counthry; how could they help it? but they know it is in a good cause, and that *they* have no business to meddle with it, and so the fewer questions they ask, they think it is the betther. They know men must do what becomes men; and though the mother and sisther loves me as well as ever a son or a brother was loved in this wide world, they would rather see me do what a man ought to do, and die, than skulk and live undher disgrace.'

De Lacy was touched by this simple expression of the chivalrous feeling which existed throughout this humble family, and, after Rory assuring him he would do his mission, and telling him to '*keep never minding*' to the mother, he took his instructions once more and recommended De Lacy to go to sleep.

It was evening; so Rory bade his guest good-night.

'You won't see me till afther I come back; make yourself aisy, sir. The thing will be done, depend upon that; above all, say nothing to the mother; she'll ask *me* no questions, and I'll tell her no lies.'

With this wise saying, Rory left De Lacy, who soon slept, from the fatigue which the excitement he had just gone through produced.

---

1.   'Ruction signifies a breaking out, a disturbance.

VIII

'Britannia rules the waves.'

IT WAS IN THE GREY of a fine autumnal morning, about a fortnight previously to the scene and time just recorded, that a swift lugger was seen dashing the spray from her beautiful bows as she sailed through a fleet of stately men-of-war that lay in the Texel. The lugger made for the shore, and when close in, dropped her anchor; and her small boat being lowered from her stern, three men entered it, and it was pulled swiftly to the beach. To one who knew not that a craft like the lugger required a numerous crew, it might have been supposed, when those three men left her side, that every living thing had departed from her; for the stillness which prevailed within her was profound. There she lay on the placid water, quiet as the element she floated on, without a sign or a sound to indicate that she was the den of many a daring ruffian.

About noon the boat reapproached the lugger, with two additional persons, and after hailing her, and remaining a few minutes under her quarter, again pushed off, and made for the centre of the fleet, where the flag of Admiral De Winter floated from the mast of the Vryheid,—a splendid seventy-four.

Three persons from the boat went up the side of the admiral's ship, two of whom were admitted to the admiral's cabin; the third, the commander of the lugger, waited on the deck until those he brought from the shore should command his presence below. And, these two were persons, whose names are well known in the eventful history of the period, and on their

heads was the price of blood,—Theobald Wolfe Tone, and Lewines: the
former an exile for some time from his country; and the other, more
recently an envoy from the executive of the disaffected party in Ireland.
Tone had obtained rank in the French army, and was at this moment on
the *état major* of the armament destined for the invasion of the kingdom
of Great Britain; though at what point that invasion might take place
was not yet decided;—it being matter of dispute whether the expedition
should land on the English coast, or in Ireland; whether it should strike
at the vitals of Great Britain, or assail her from the extremities.

General Hoche, who was only second in fame to Bonaparte, was
anxious to do something brilliant, while the fame of his rival's Italian
campaigns made Europe ring with wonder; and as the prevalence of
contrary winds had prevented the expedition sailing for some weeks
for Ireland, he made the daring proposal of landing in Lincolnshire and
marching direct on London.

A year before, his expedition which sailed from Brest for Ireland was
utterly defeated by contrary winds; and as the same element seemed, as
usual, to interpose a providential barrier between England and her foes,
he, with that impatient thought so characteristic of genius, suggested the
idea that as the wind did not blow in favour of the course they wanted
to steer, they should make it subservient to another purpose, descend on
the most open quarter, and trust to the fortune of war; for he burned
that some great achievement of his should prevent his name being
overshadowed by the freshly-springing laurels of Napoleon Bonaparte.

Against this preposterous notion of carrying England by a *coup de
main*, Tone had always argued strenuously; but he found such a singular
ignorance of the state of England, as well as Ireland, to exist amongst the
French, that it was with great difficulty he could make General Hoche
listen to a word against his newly-conceived expedition.

It was, therefore, with great pleasure he had the letter of De Lacy,
bearing so strongly on this point, put into his hands that morning by
the commander of the lugger, and he lost no time in laying it before
the authorities in command of the expedition, to dissuade them from a
course that he knew could be no other than ruinous.

When he and Lewines entered the cabin of the admiral, Generals

Hoche and Daendells were looking over a map of England; and Admiral De Winter, with his second-in-command, Admiral Storey, were exanmining charts of the British Channel and the North Sea.

'You see I've not given it up yet,' said Hoche vivaciously to Tone.

'I perceive you have not, general,' said the latter; 'but I think *this* will decide you:' and he presented to him the letter of De Lacy.

Hoche pounced upon it, and began to devour its contents. He passed rapidly on, till, stopping suddenly, he asked:

'Who is this from?'

Tone informed him it was from an agent of General Clark, who had been commissioned to inquire into the truth of all the statements Tone had made to the Directory.

'I remember,' said Hoche; and he resumed his reading.

A conversation ensued in the mean time between the admirals and the Irish emissaries, until it was interrupted by Hoche exclaiming impatiently.

'*Que diable!* What have carved ceilings and handsome apartments to do with the matter? His oak ceiling is only good for burning! What nonsense!' And he threw down the letter contemptuously.

'Pray, go on, general,' said Tone. 'There is a good deal of detail, certainly, in the communication; but if the writer has been careful and elaborate in his observations, it is only fair to read them all to arrive at a just estimate of his judgment.'

Hoche continued the reading of the letter, and as he proceeded, his face became more thoughtful, he read with deeper attention and when he had finished the perusal, he laid down the letter in silence, as if he had not the heart to say, 'I must give up my expedition,' although he felt it was hopeless.

'You see, general,' said Tone, 'the expedition to Ireland is the only thing.'

'Whenever it can sail there,' said Hoche.

'That may be a month,' said Daendells.

'Or to-morrow,' said Tone.

'This south-westerly wind is blowing as if it had set in for it,' said the admiral, shaking his head, as if he doubted Tone's hopeful anticipation.

'The troops have now been embarked nearly a month,' said General Daendells, 'and though amply provisioned for the *probable* necessities of the expedition, it is impossible their stores can last much longer; and whenever they become exhausted, I doubt how far our government would deem it prudent to advance further supplies.'

'General Daendells,' said Hoche, 'it has appeared to me, lately, that the Batavian republic seems to have a jealousy that her army should be led by a general of France in an affair that promises so much glory, and I should not wonder that much further delay in the sailing of the expedition might prevent this noble undertaking altogether. Now, I would not for the glory of Cæsar that my personal fame should interfere with the great cause of universal freedom; and if you think that your legislative assembly would be more willing to pursue this enterprise if it were under the command of one of its own generals, I will withdraw my pretensions to the command, and give all the chance of the glory to you.'

'You are a noble fellow,' said Daendells, extending his hand to Hoche; 'there may be some truth in what you say, and I shall never forget this act of generosity on your part, for none can deny that you, from your efforts made and disappointments endured in this cause, deserve to reap all the laurels that may be mine in the result. This is the greatest of your conquests,—you have triumphed over your ambition!'

Tone was affected almost to tears—he could scarcely speak but, struggling with his emotion, he said:

'General, my country will never forget this noble conduct on your part. We knew how brave you are, but we did not know how generous!'

'Who brought this letter?' said Hoche, wishing to turn the conversation.

'De Welskein, the smuggler,' said Tone; 'and he wishes to know whether he may promise speedy aid to the sufferers in Ireland, for they are beginning to be impatient of it.'

'The moment the wind permits, they shall have succour,' said Daendells. 'Is it not so, admiral?' said he to De Winter.

'Certainly,' answered the admiral 'Is the smuggler on board?' added he, addressing Tone.

'Yes, admiral.'

'Then I wish to speak to him;' and the smuggler was ordered into the admiral's presence.

De Welskein was a Frenchman, though bearing a Dutch name: he was one of the many desperate characters that the French revolution produced. A fellow of loose habits and desperate fortunes, he took to smuggling, as the readiest mode of indulging the one and repairing the other; he had also a love of *finesse*, and a spirit of intrigue, that this sort of life enabled him to indulge in; and he was the most active of the agents in carrying on intelligence between France and Ireland at that period;—not that he cared for the Irish, not that he had a moral sensibility within him to desire the liberation of the veriest slave,—but that it gave him an opportunity to smuggle and intrigue.

Many a turbulent spirit in Ireland who longed for an outbreak of rebellion, and who looked to France for aid, courted Monsieur de Welskein as an emissary from the land of promise, and he made them, through this hold upon them, more ready instruments in his smuggling speculations.

Deficient though De Welskein was in any moral appreciation of the beauty of freedom, he babbled in the jargon of his time about it, and shouted '*Vive la liberté!*' because his *liberté* meant the absence of all restraint, human or divine; and he had a sort of confused notion that a revolution was glorious, and that it was the business of tbe *grande nation* to revolutionise the world in general, but Ireland in particular, because it gave him a good opportunity for smuggling brandy and tobacco.

There was a species of melodramatic fancy about the fellow, too—a propensity for romance and adventure, that his connection with Ireland gratified.

Besides, it indulged his vanity, as, in his present situation, Monsieur Eugene St. Foix de Welskein was no small personage in his opinion: he rhodomontaded about the *fate of empires* and the *destinies of nations*, as if he were a sucking Jupiter, or one of the French Directory.

His names too were a source of rejoicing to him: Eugene St. Foix. The former he inherited from his father; the latter was the maiden name of his mother, who was a washerwoman. De Welskein he did not much like; so that his companions, when they wished to vex him, called him by his surname, while in moments of friendship they addressed him as Eugene; but when they courted him, the heroic title of St. Foix was the one they preferred. To be sure, they sometimes called him, behind his back, *Sans foi*; but in his presence he was fond of having his courage celebrated under the name of *Sans Peur*: so that *St. Foix sans peur* was a flattering address sometimes made to him:—but though St. Foix was certainly *sans peur*, he was not *sans reproche*.

When De Welskein entered the cabin, Admiral De Winter asked him, had he seen the English fleet?

He answered, that he had passed them in the night.

'Then you could not count the number of their ships?' said the adiniral.

'I was sufficiently near in the morning to see them,' said the smuggler, 'and I think they are eighteen sail.'

'Eighteen!—are you sure?'

'I think, eighteen; I'm almost sure.'

'Frigates, or line-of-battle?'

'Most line-of-battle.'

'I see he has observed them,' said the admiral, 'for I could perceive, even from the harbour, with a glass, that they were all line-of-battle:—but I could only make out fifteen; they must have been reinforced. Some of their ships were in mutiny at the Nore; perhaps the mutiny has been suppressed, and that accounts for the increase of numbers.'

'That's unlucky,' said Tone.

'How unlucky, sir?' said Storey.

'As long as our fleet had a superiority, there was a chance we could force our passage; but—'

'Sir,' said Storey, 'you mistake very much if you think we would shrink from contending with an equal, or even superior, number of the enemy. I wish for nothing better than to be broadside to broadside with them.'

This was the bravado of the man who, in about a month after, deserted De Winter in his engagement with that identical fleet, and literally *ran away* with his division of the Dutch force from the enemy he vaunted himself so eager to engage.—So much for braggarts!

'Pardon me, admiral,' said Tone; 'I hope neither you nor Admiral De

Winter'—and he bowed deferentially to that gallant officer, as if it were to him rather than to Storey he apologised—'I hope you do not suppose me so unworthy as to undervalue the bravery of the Dutch navy, at the same time that I consider it a matter of importance we should reach Ireland without an engagement, as by that means our force will be undiminished; and I wish that the army landed should be as large as possible, for the affair will be the sooner decided, and thus an effusion of blood will be spared—and I wish from my heart that in my poor country as little blood as possible may be shed.'

'Bah!' said Hoche; *'you can't make omelettes without breaking of eggs.'*

'Adjutant-general,' said De Winter to Tone, 'I do not misapprehend you: there is no denying that the English are a brave enemy, and Admiral Duncan is a gallant and able officer. I shall not seek an encounter with him until I land your expedition,—but I shall certainly not *shun* it.'

Thus spoke the man of true courage, who fought his ships gallantly in the subsequent action, even after the defection of the braggart who deserted him.

Tone tapped General Hoche on the shoulder, and led him apart for a few words in private; the door being open that led to the stern gallery, they walked forth, and Tone began an energetic address, requesting the general to dissuade the admiral as much as possible from an engagement with the English fleet.

'Let the troops be landed in Ireland,' said he: 'on the land you are invincible, as the English are on the seas. Fate seems to have given to them the dominion of the ocean. Mark me—my words are prophetic— so sure as this fleet shall engage the English, so surely shall it be beaten!'

'De Winter is an able officer,' said Hoche.

'He is,' said Tone, 'and a brave man, I am certain, from his moderate manner; while I doubt very much the courage of that flourishing gentleman. But have we not the example of repeated engagements to show us that Great Britain is an overmatch for every nation on the seas? and it makes my blood boil to think that while her fleets are freely manned by Irishmen, the land that gives them birth groans beneath her oppression. Ireland helps to gather laurels for Britain's brows, but not a leaf of the chaplet is given to her; she shares in winning the victories that enrich and aggrandise the Queen of the Ocean, but is allowed no portion of the fame or the prosperity.'

'Be not thus agitated,' said Hoche soothingly, touched by the fierce enthusiasm with which Tone uttered the latter part of his address: 'when once this armament lands in Ireland, there is an end of Great Britain's domination.'

'Ay, *when* it lands,' said Tone, with a voice in which impatience and hopelessness were strangely blended. 'Oh!' said he, stretching out his hands to the expanse of sea and sky before him—'Oh! ye elements—ye mysterious agents of heaven! why do ye interpose your potent shield of air and foam between England and her foes? You blasted the Armada of Spain; I saw you scatter the ships of France at Bantry; and now this gallant fleet, with fifteen thousand chosen men, who burn for the liberation of my country, is chained here by an adverse wind for whole month! Ireland, my country, I fear you are doomed!'

His hand dropped to his side, his head sank on his chest, and he stood with his eyes fixed on the ground.

'Rally, than, rally!' said Hoche, slapping him on the shoulder: 'why, Adjutant-General, I have never seen you thus before!'

'Whenever I think of the fate of that unhappy country, it breaks my heart! But I've done:—only, for God's sake, General Hoche, dissuade them from a sea-fight; we are ruined if they attempt it.'

Hoche and Tone now re-entered the cabin. They found De Winter and Daendells giving instructions to the smuggler. De Winter desired him to put himself in the way of the English fleet, and give them some false information.

It was planned that De Welskein should pass the English squadron in the night, and towards morning sail back again, as if he came up Channel, and tell the English admiral that he saw a French fleet at the Channel's mouth; this might give him an idea that the Brest fleet had got out to sea, which would serve to divide his attention, and possibly draw him farther off the coast, and leave a passage from the Texel more open, in case the wind should change so as to favour such a movement.

General Daendells told him to assure the Irish of speedy succour, for that fifteen thousand men were embarked for that service, and only waited a fair wind to sail. A few lines to De Lacy, from Hoche, was all the writing the smuggler bore, and he left the ship on his mission.

Such were the plans that were proposed; such were the promises made. What was the result?

The wind continued foul a fortnight longer; in all, six weeks. The provisions for so large a number of troops, as well as seamen, became exhausted; the troops were relanded; the expedition to Ireland was given up—and England again was spared the danger of a formidable invasion into a disaffected portion of her kingdom.

The night the troops were disembarked Tone went to his tent with a heavy heart: the next morning he saw the pennants of the fleet turned towards England.

The breeze which the day before would have made his blood dance, had he felt it on the deck of the Vryheid, now only made his heart sick; he stood on the beach like one possessed.

After remaining motionless for some minutes, he stamped fiercely, clenched his teeth, struck his forehead with his hand, and walked rapidly away; but ere he descended a slight declivity that shut out the bay, he turned round and cast a look of despair towards his country.

Thus ended the second expedition undertaken for the invasion of Ireland: and the gallant Hoche, within a month after, was no more—cut off in his prime of manhood and career of glory by the hand of the assassin![1]

And what was the fate of the fleet?

Admiral De Winter, the October following, sailed from the Texel, met the English squadron under Admiral Duncan, and fought like a hero—but Storey deserted him. De Winter, nevertheless, maintained a fierce engagement against superior numbers but the prophecy of Tone was fulfilled; after a well-contested fight, the Dutch struck their colours, and the flag of England again floated triumphantly over the seas.

---

1.   Hoche's life was attempted more than once. His death was attributed to slow poison.

IX

The pretty girl milking her cow.

'I saw a young damsel,—'twas Noreen:—
Her ringlets did carelessly flow.
Oh! how I adore you, *ma vourneen,*
Ma colleen dhas crutheen na mbho.'

Rory O'More left his cottage at an early hour the morning after his conversation with De Lacy. For a few miles he followed the by-road that led from his house, and then struck into a path through some fields, for the purpose of making the high-road which was the direct way to the place of his destination.

As he was walking briskly on, looking neither to the right nor the left, but quite absorbed in the contemplation of the business he had undertaken, his attention was suddenly arrested by hearing one of those quaint and sportive melodies of his country sung by a sweet voice.

Rory paused—he recognised the tones that had so often made his heart thrill with pleasure,—and running up the gentle hill before him, he beheld, as he topped the summit, on the other side of the hillock, seated under the shade of a hawthorn hedge, a beautiful peasant girl, whose song proceeded merrily while she was milking her cows.

Kathleen Regan was sitting with her back towards the point whence Rory approached, so that he was enabled, unperceived by her, to gaze with pleasure on her sweet figure and listen to her sportive song.

'There's a lad that I know; and I know that he
Speaks softly to me,
The *cushla-ma-chree!*
He's the pride of my heart, and he loves me well;
But who the lad is, I'm not going to tell.

'He's as straight as a rush, and as bright as the stream
That around it doth gleam,—
Oh! of him how I dream!
I'm as high as his shoulder—the way that I know
Is, he caught me one day, just my measure to show.

'He whisper'd a question one day in my ear
When he breathed it, oh dear!
How I trembled with fear!
What the question he ask'd was, I need not confess;
But the answer I gave to the question was, "Yes."

'His eyes they are bright, and they looked so kind
When I was inclined
To speak my mind!
And his breath is so sweet—oh, the rose's is less!
And how I found it out,—why I leave you to guess.'

The scene was one to excite the imagination and charm the senses of one less keen to such pleasures than Rory. He could catch the soft scent of the morning breath of the cows, vieing in fragrance with the woodbine that was peeping through the hedge at the same time that he could hear the sweet voice of the girl he loved, and see her bright ringlets curl down her graceful neck and beautifully-rounded shoulders.

He watched her for some moments in silent admiration, and then, stealing softly behind her and suddenly uttering 'Wow!' the girl started, and in her moment of surprise Rory caught her in his arms and snatched a kiss. A hearty box on his ear followed the salute, with the exclamation of,

'You divil! how dar you!'

'I *lave you to guess*,' said Rory, laughing.

'You're mighty impident, so you are, Rory.'

'Arrah! how could I help it, Kathleen darlin'?' said Rory, with a look of admiration that would have softened the anger of even a more cruel beauty than Kathleen;—a look that appealed more strongly to the self-love of the woman than the liberty taken had startled her modesty.

'You're very impident, so you are,' said Kathleen, settling her hair, that had been tossed into a most becoming confusion over her face in the struggle.

'You often towld me that before,' said Rory.

'It does not do you much good, thin,' said Kathleen. 'You *hear* me, but you don't *heed* me.'

'Why, if you go to that, how can I help myself. Sure you might as well keep the ducks from the wather, or the bees from the flowers, as my heart from you, Kathleen.'

'Now, Rory, lave off!'

'By this light, Kathleen!'

'Now don't be goin' on, Rory!'

'There's not a girl—'

'Now, don't be makin' a fool o' yourself and me too,' said Kathleen.

'If makin' you my own would be to make a fool of you, thin, it's a fool I'd make you, sure enough,' said Rory.

'Rory,' said Kathleen rather sadly, 'don't be talkin' this way to me,—it's good for neither of us.'

'Kathleen darling!' said Rory, 'what's the matther with you?' and he approached her and gently took her hand.

'Nothing,' said she, 'nothing,—only it's foolishness.'

'Don't call honest love, foolishness, Kathleen dear. Sure, why would we have hearts in our bodies if we didn't love? Sure, our hearts would be no use at all without we wur fond of one another. Arrah! What's the matter with you, Kathleen?'

'I must go home, Rory;—let me go, Rory dear,' said she with a touching tone of sadness on the *dear*, as she strove to disengage from her waist the hand that Rory had stolen round it.

'No, I won't let you go, Kathleen, *ma vourneen*,' said Rory, with passion and pathos, as he held her closer in his embrace. 'Now or never, Kathleen, I must have your answer. You are the girl that is, and ever was, in the very core of my heart, and I'll never love another but yourself. Don't be afraid that I'll change; I'm young, but I'm thrue: the blessed sun that sees us both this minit is not thruer: and he's a witness to what I say to you now, Kathleen *asthore*, that you're the pulse o' my heart, and I'll never rest aisy till you're my wife.'

Kathleen could not speak. She trembled while Rory made his last address to her; her lip quivered as he proceeded; two big tear-drops sprang to her eyes, and hung on their long dark lashes, when he called her 'pulse of his heart'; but when he named the holy name of wife, she fell upon his neck and burst into a violent flood of tears.

Rory felt this was a proof of his being beloved; but it was not the way in which, from Kathleen's sportive nature, he thought it likely she would accept a husband to whom there was no objection; and while he soothed the sobbing of the agitated girl, he wondered what could be the cause of her violent emotion. When she became calm, he said:

'Kathleen dear, don't be vexed with me if I took you too sudden:— you know I'm none of the coolest, and so forgive me, jewel! I'll say no more to you now;—only give me an answer at your own good time, my darling.'

Kathleen wiped the tears from her eyes, and said:

'No, Rory dear: you've been plain with me, and I'll be plain with you. As for myself—' she looked up in his eyes, and their soft and confiding expression, and the gentle pressure of the hand that accompanied the look, told more than the words could have done which her maiden modesty forbade her utter.

'You love me, then;' said Rory, with delighted energy; and he pressed her to his heart, while she yielded her lips to the pressure of a kiss which the fire of pure love had refined from the dross of passion.

'Oh, Rory,—but my brother Shan?'

'Well, what o' that?' said Rory.

'Oh, you know,—you know,' said Kathleen mournfully.

'Yis, Mary didn't take to him; but sure that's no rayson.'

'Oh! you don't know him!'

'We've been rather cool, to be sure, since, but I never put coolness between me and him; and if my sister couldn't like him, sure that's no rayson to put between you and me.'

'Oh, Rory, Shan is very dark; and I'm afeard.'

'But why should *he* prevent our comin' together? Sure, isn't there your mother?'

'Oh, but she's afeared of him, and— —'

'But how do you know he would make objections?'

The poor girl blushed scarlet, as she said:

'Why, to tell you the thruth, Rory, and it's no matther now that you know it, afther what's passed between us this morning but Shan suspected I liked you, and he warned me agen it, and swore a bitter oath, that if ever I'd think of you, he'd— —'

'What?' said Rory.

'Curse me,' said Kathleen; and she shuddered as the said it.

'God forgive him!' said Rory solemnly. 'But never mind, Kathleen; I'll meet him, and I'll spake him fair, and tell him the thruth. And when I spake to him like a man, he can't be less of a man, and he wouldn't be of so dark a heart to keep spite agen me because my sisther didn't love him.'

'It's the kind and generous heart you have, Rory ; but I'm afeard it be no use at all events, don't be in a hurry about it; wait a bit, and maybe when he comes across some other girl that will wane his heart from the old love, he may be aisier about it; but at this present, Rory dear, don't purtend that you love me, nor let on what you said to me this morning.'

'It's hard to hide what's in the heart,' said Rory; 'for even if the tongue doesn't bethray you, it may peep out of your eyes.'

'But we shan't meet often,' said Kathleen; 'so there will be the less danger of that.'

'That's hard too,' said Rory. 'But, Kathleen, will you—' he could not finish the sentence, but Kathleen caught his meaning and said,

'You ouldn't say the words, Rory,—you were going to say, will I be thrue to you? Oh, Rory dear! I have given you my heart, because I couldn't help it, and I trust to you that you have given me yours; and, oh! don't take it away from me! I must hide my love for a time. I'll hide it as a miser would hide his gold; and oh, Rory! don't let me find the treasure gone when I may venture to show it to the day.'

'Kathleen darling! while there's life in my heart, it is you are the queen of it.'

'Go now,' said Kathleen; 'go,—don't stay longer here; I wouldn't have you seen for the king's ransom.'

'May the heavens bless and keep you!' said Rory; 'one more kiss, my own—own girl;' and clasping her in his arms, they bade each other farewell.

Rory hurried on with a rapid step that accorded with the tumult of his feelings, and was soon lost to Kathleen's sight.

She looked after him while he remained within view, and then resumed her occupation; but it was in silence. The sportive song had ceased—the light-heartedness of the girl had passed away even with the consciousness of a deeper pleasure.

Her task ended, she took up her pail, and went her way homewards, but not with the elastic step with which she had trodden the wild flowers on her outgoing.

When Rory gained the high-road, he pursued his way mechanically towards the place of his destination, without a thought of the immediate business he had in hand. His brain was in a whirl, and his heart in a blaze; and love and Kathleen Regan were the objects of his thoughts, and not conspiracies and his mysterious guest.

His approach to the town, however, reminded him of the object of his mission, and he proceeded at the appointed hour to the public-house indicated by De Lacy.

It was market-day in the town, so that the public-house was more crowded than on ordinary occasions; and Rory, when he entered, saw many persons engaged in drinking porter and whisky, but mostly the latter. He cast his eyes about to see if such a group as he was instructed to look for was there, and more than one party of three was present; he therefore had to exercise his sagacity in selecting which of the groups was the one to test by his signal,—and he was not long in deciding.

It was at the further end of the room, where a small square window admitted as much light as could find its way through some panes of greenish glass with bulls' eyes in the middle of them, covered with dust, that three men were seated at a dirty table where a congregation of flies were finishing a pot of porter.

The aspect of one of the men struck Rory to be 'outlandish,' as he would have said himself, and the quick and restless twinkle of his dark eye spoke of a more southern climate.

To this group Rory approached, and looking round, as it were to see where he should sit, he asked permission of the party to take share of their box—for the room was divided into such compartments. They made room for him; and he, taking up the empty quart pot on whose dregs the flies were regaling, knocked loudly with it on the table and started the buzzing nuisances from their banquet, and being driven from their pewter palace, they alighted on the various little pools and meandering streams of various liquids that stood upon the filthy table, which seemed to be left to them as a sort of patrimony, as the fallen dates are to the wanderers in the East. The tender-hearted *sthreel* who was the Hebe of the house would not have robbed the poor flies of their feast for the world, by wiping the table. Charity is a great virtue

This dirty handmaiden came in answer to Rory's thumping of the quart-pot on the board.

'Loose were her tresses seen,
    Her zone unbound.'

Her foot was unsandalled, too; in short, she was, as Rory remarked to his neighbour beside him, 'loose and careless like the leg of a pot.'

'What do yiz want?' says Hebe.

'Something to dhrink,' says Rory.

'Is it a pot, a pint, or a crapper?' says Hebe.

'I'll jist take the cobwebs out o' my throat with a pint first,' says Rory.

'I'll sarve you immadiently,' says Hebe, who took up the quart, and to save time she threw out the dregs of the liquor it had contained on the floor, and then held it up inverted in a most graceful manner, that it might drain itself clean for the next custom so that her course might be tracked up and down the room by the drippings of the various vessels, and thus she, 'did her *spiriting* gently, dropping odours, dropping wine,' ale, and sper'ts.

She returned soon with a pint of porter to Rory, who took out a shilling to pay for it.

'I'll throuble you for the change, my dear,' said he.

Off she went again to get the change, and after some time again returned, bearing two quarts of porter in one hand, and a jug of punch hanging between the forefinger and thumb of the other, while a small roll of tobacco and a parcel of halfpence were clutched in the remaining fingers. The liquids and the tobacco she deposited before a party that sat in a box opposite to Rory, and then, advancing to him, she flopped the halfpence down on the table before him, and putting her hand to her mouth, pulled out of it piece of tin which she was pleased to call sixpence, and sticking it on the top of the halfpence, she said, 'There's your change, sir.'

'It's a tinker you have to make change for you, I b'lieve,' said Rory.

'How is it a tinker?'

'Oh, I wouldn't take that piece of tin from you for the world,' said Rory, 'you might want it to stop a hole in a saucepan, and maybe it's coming afther me you'd be for it.'

'I'd be long sorry to folly you,' said the damsel, saucily, and turning away.

'See, young woman,' said Rory—'don't be in sitch a hurry if you plaze—I gave you a good hog,[1] and I throuble you for a good taisther.'

'I haven't a betther to give you, sir—barrin' halfpence.'

'Well, I'm noways proud, so the halfpence will do for me: good copper is better than bad silver, any day.'

The state of the silver currency in Ireland at this period was disgraceful—so bad, that it left the public almost at the mercy of the coiners. When the Warwickshire Militia went to Ireland, many of the privates, having been workmen in Birmingham, were very smart hands at the practice, and many stories are current of their doings in this line. Amongst others, it is stated that a party of these men in a public-house offered some bad money for what they had drunk; but the publican being on his guard, as their habits in this way were becoming notorious, refused several shillings one after another. The soldier who offered them said the dealer in liquor was over-particular; but he retorted, that they were so well known for their tricks, it was necessary to be cautious. 'Well,' said the soldier at last, here then, since nothing else will do;' and he threw down another coin, and a very good-looking one it was. The landlord examined it for a while, but at last it was rejected. 'What!' said the soldier, 'nor not *that* neither.' 'No,' said the landlord. So a good shilling was obliged to be produced at last, and as the party left the house, the discomfited hero was heard to say, 'Well, I never know'd *one o' Tom's make* to miss before.'

The girl brought back Rory the value of the sixpence in copper—or rather, much more than its value; and then Rory commenced reckoning his change, which was the means he had decided on for throwing out his signal. So, spreading the halfpence before him, he began—

'One, two, three—there's some sense in good halfpence; one, two, three—jist as if I was to rob you of your tin, my good girl; one, two, three!—phoo! murdher! I'm mixin' them all.'

'Arrah! will you never be done reckonin' them!' said Hebe impatiently; 'one ud think 'twas a hundher poun' you wor' countin,' let alone change of a hog. I'm thinkin', it's no great credit to your schoolmasther you are.'

'Fair and aisy goes far in a day,' said Rory, again commencing to count his change.

'One, two, three;' and while he spoke, he looked at the dark-eyed man, in whose face he fancied he caught something of an expression of intelligence of his meaning, and then he proceeded with his reckoning and dismissed the girl.

One of the men now addressed him and said:

'You are particular in counting your change.'

'Yes, indeed I am,' said Rory, 'and I'll tell you the reason why because I lost some money the other day by not being particular in that same, when I was buying some ducks.'

The dark-eyed man looked very sharply on Rory as he proceeded.

'To be sure, I didn't mind the loss much, for the ducks was worth the money. *They wor very fine ducks.*'

A still keener glance from the dark-eyed man followed Rory's last words, and he rose immediately and left the public-house; his two companions did so likewise, and Rory lost no time in following them. On reaching the door, he saw them standing together a few paces removed from the house, and on seeing him appear they walked down the quay until they arrived at a corner, where looking back to see that he followed, they turned up the street. Rory tracked them, and at another turn the same practice was observed by his conductors, whom he continued to follow, dodging them through many an intricate winding, until arriving at a very narrow alley, they turned for the last time, and when Rory reached the spot, he perceived them about half-way up the passage standing at the mouth of a cellar; and the moment he appeared they all suddenly descended. He followed fast upon them, and going down a steep and broken stair, entered a low door, which was closed the moment he had passed it, and he found himself in total darkness.

1. The shilling and sixpence were called by the lower orders 'hog' and 'tester.'

X

In which Rory hears and sees more than he bargained for, and finds in the conclusion the truth of the proverb, that providence never shuts one door without opening another.

WHILE SPOTS OF RED AND green were dancing before Rory's eyes by his sudden immersion from light into darkness, a voice close beside him said,

'Very glaad to see you.'

'God spare you your eyesight !' said Rory; 'I wish I could return the compliment to you.'

Rory heard a low laugh in another tone, and then the former voice spoke again:

'Whaat! you no glad to see me?'

''Faith, I would be very glad to see you; but how can I see you in the dark?'

'Ho! ho! I see, you fonee feylow—ha, ha!'

'Strek a light;' said another voice.

'Wait a minit—I'm gettin' the tendher-box,' was the answer.

The foreign voice again said, addressing Rory,

'You air wailcome.'

'Thank you kindly,' said Rory; 'give us your fist.'

'Vaut you say?'

'Give us your fist.'

'He's biddin' you shake hands wid him,' said a voice that had not yet spoken; and Rory thought it was one he should know, though where he had heard it he could not remember.

'Oh!' said the foreigner, '*donnez-moi la main.*'

'No, I dunna any man,' said Rory.

'Bah! shek han' wis me!' said the voice.

Rory now stretched out his hand, and encountered an extended palm which grasped his and exchanged with him the grip of the United Irishman.

This satisfied Rory all was right, and he now waited with patience for the light. The sound of a flint and steel, followed by a shower of sparks, showed that the process of illumination was going forward; the tinder soon became ignited, and the sharp sound of blowing was soon followed by the lighting of a match—and the first face that its lurid glare fell upon was that of Shan Regan.

Rory started: he was the last person he expected to meet, and certainly the last he could have wished to see in that place. A coolness for some time had existed between them, as the reader already knows; and though Rory fully intended to do all in his power remove it, and to meet Regan for that purpose as often as he could, yet on such an occasion as the present he could have wished him absent. His presence there, it is true, showed him to be engaged in the same cause as Rory, and one at the first glance might suppose that this would have facilitated a reconciliation between them; but on closer examination we shall find this not to be the ease. In all conspiracies where men are linked together in a cause whose penalty is death, private friendship is desirable amongst its members, at least in its early stages, where fidelity is essential to its existence. Personal foes may fight side by side in the same cause when once a conspiracy arrives at its outbreak; but in its secret preparatory councils, a man recoils from the contact of any but a friend.

It was the consciousness of this fact, perhaps, that led to the ingenious construction of the plan by which the heads of the Society of United Irishmen contrived to organise a great portion of Ireland. The system was this: There was a chief committee of twelve; each of these twelve was the head of another twelve, but between each knot of twelve there was no acquaintance—they were totally distinct from each other; so that an extensive ramification of union existed in parties of twelve, each obeying its own superior, through whom, alone, all commands and plans were conveyed. Each knot was thus a little band of friends, and from their distinctness, the secret was the more likely to be kept. It will be seen that by this means the head committee organised one hundred and forty-four members, whose knots of twelve each being multiplied, gives a force of twenty thousand seven hundred and odd men, and their multiplied dozens would produce nearly two hundred and forty-nine thousand: thus, at three removes from the focus of the system, a powerful force was at a moment's command, within whose several knots private friend ship as well as the common cause was a source of union and fidelity. It was only in the higher grades of the confederation that private signals existed. In the inferior classes, each dozen only knew their own circle; so that to whatever extent the system might be spread, each of the subordinate actors was intimate with no more than twelve persons, which tended at once to give greater personal security, and to prevent also a premature explosion of the conspiracy.

This brief sketch of the system is given, to account for Rory not knowing Regan to be a United man, although living in the same district. Regan belonged to another circle; and it was from very different desires that he was of the association, and with a very different set that he was leagued. Rory became a United Irishman from other and better motives than Regan. However erroneous those motives might have been, they had their origin in a generous nature; wild notions of the independence of his country were uppermost in the mind of Rory, while the mere love of licence was the incentive to Regan. During that terrible period of Ireland's history, some of the insurgents were pure, however mistaken enthusiasts; while there were others whose love of turbulence was their only motive. Of the latter class was Regan: he had inherited from his father a comfortable farm, but his love of debasing amusements—such as cock-fighting, etc., the frequency of his visits to public-houses, aud his attachment to disorderly company, had led him from the wholesome pursuits that would have made him good and prosperous, to become improvident and embarrassed.

It is strange that whenever this takes place, a man mostly becomes an idler: the very fact which should warn him of his danger, and make him exert himself the more, generally operates in the contrary way. He gives himself up as it were to ruin, and seeks in dissipation forgetfulness of the past and disregard of the future. This state of things lasts as long as there is anything left to support him; and when all is lost, he is then fit for every sort of violence or meanness; he must be either a beggar or a desperado.

It was in the middle stage that Regan fell in with De Welskein. They were just the men for each other:—Regan was the head of a disorderly set of fellows, who were ready and active agents in assisting the Frenchman in his smuggling; and, in return, the brandy and tobacco, and merry-makings of the smuggler were ample temptations and rewards for Regan. The debauched orgies of the cellar, where Rory now found himself for the first time, were familiar to the unfortunate victim of idleness, bad company and lawless desires.

Though he was often absent from home and neglected his husbandry, he still retained his farm; but his payments of rent became irregular, his farming stock grew less by degrees; a cow, a sheep, a pig, was obliged now and then to be sacrificed to supply his riotous propensities, and his poor mother and sister saw with sorrow their comforts lessening around them: but they complained not, for they dreaded the fierce tempter of Shan Dhu, or Black John, as he was called. It was not only the diminution of his worldly substance they lamented, but they felt that the most respectable of their neighbours, one by one, dropped off from their acquaintance with them; and this, to the sensitive nature of the Irish peasant, cuts deeper than even want. Want, they are familiar with; they see it on every side, and they can bear it with patience: but the social virtues flourish amongst them in the midst of barrenness, like the palms in the desert.

Amongst the friendships which had decayed was that of the O'Mores. The widow loved her daughter too well to give her to a disorderly though a comparatively wealthy peasant, as Shan Regan was when he asked Mary O'More for his wife; and Mary herself had an intuitive dislike for all that was gross, which revolted from Regan's brutal nature.

Rory, though he knew him not as a friend at any period,—for the men were too unlike each other ever to have associated closely,—yet always had recognised him as an old acquaintance whenever they met; but he never sought his company—for Rory, though as full of fun, as fond of mirth, and loving his glass, his joke, and a pretty girl, as much *as every Irishman ought to do*, yet he reverenced the decencies of life too much to be a drunkard, a buffoon, or a debauchee. His acquaintance with Regan might have gone on, as far as Rory was concerned, just the same, quite uninfluenced by his sister's refusal; but not so with the rejected one. He considered the part Mary had taken, as a family affront: his pride (such as it was) was wounded more than his heart; or rather, it was his love for himself, and not for the girl, that suffered most. So he made a feud of the business, and included Rory amongst his foes. To this he was the more inclined, as he suspected Conolly, who was a sworn friend of O'More's, to be his rival.

From all these circumstances, it is no wonder that Rory was startled at seeing Regan at such a time: but as he could not help himself, he determined to affect composure, which he was the better able to accomplish, as he had time to recover from his surprise before his presence was manifest to Regan. The scene that had occurred in the morning, too, rendered him the more anxious to conciliate, and with a sincere wish to overcome the coolness that Regan had lately observed towards him, he advanced to him with open hand and greeted him kindly. It was obvious, from the expression that passed over Regan's face, that the meeting was quite as startling and disagreeable to him as it had been to Rory, who continued still, however, the offer of his hand, and repeated his words of kindly recognition. A cold reply was all that followed, though the hand was accepted: but there was no sympathy in the contact; the touch of friendship was wanting,—that touch whose sensation is so undefinable, but so well understood,—that natural freemasonry which springs from and is recognised by the heart.

As soon as the light was struck, a lamp was lighted in a ship-lantern that hung from the low roof of the cellar over a coarse table, round which benches of a rude construction were placed. Another person as well as Regan was present in addition to the three Rory had followed from the public-house; and this man seemed more familiar with De Welskein then any of the others and sometimes addressed him in French. Round the cellar were some coils of rope; a couple of hammocks were hung in one corner; two or three kegs and some rolls of tobacco were stowed away under a truckle-bed in another quarter of the den; and in a rude cupboard, coarse trenchers and drinking-cans were jumbled together, with some stone jars of a foreign aspect. After some hustle, pipes and tobacco were laid on the table, the stone bottles and the drinking-vessels were taken from the cupboard, and De Welskein invited Rory to sit down beside him.

'Combe, you sair—seet down—here someting for you to dreenk—not nastee, like pobelick-house, bote goot—ha, ha! No doretee portere, bote brandee—ver goot and nussing to pay.'

All the men sat down, and sending the stone jars from man to man, the cans were charged with brandy, slightly diluted with water from a black pitcher; pipes were lighted, smoking and drinking commenced, and while a desultory conversation was kept up among the rest of the party, De Welskein questioned Rory as to the cause of his being the messenger to him. Rory made him acquainted with De Lacy's illness, and the circumstances that led to his being his guest; in all of which communication the person who spoke French assisted in making De Welskein and Rory intelligible to each other. This was no very easy matter sometimes; the Frenchman's English bothering Rory uncommonly, as his name did also. However, as it was necessary he should drink to the founder of the feast, he was obliged to make an offer at his name, and so he boldly took his can of grog in his hand and with his best bow said—

'Here's to your good health, Mr. Wilkison.'

A laugh followed at Rory's expense, in which the Frenchman only half joined, for it has already been noticed that his name was matter of anxiety to him; so soon as the laugh had subsided, he said—

'No, no! not dat my nem;—De Welskein.'

'I beg your pardon, sir—but would you say that agin, if you plaze?'

The Frenchman now slowly and distinctly pronounced his name, giving the *w* the sound of the *v,* which it assumes in Dutch names, and repeated—'De-vel-skeen.'

'Thank you, sir,' says Rory,—'I ax your pardon, and again I say, Here is to your good health, Mr. Devilskin.'

A roar of laughter followed this mistake of Rory's, and all swore that that was the best name of all the others he enjoyed; but the Frenchman did not like it, and said impatiently, using his own language, as a foreigner generally does when he becomes excited—

'*Non, non, non, mon ami!*—Devilskeen!—*non; c'est "Poil-de-diabel!"*— *Sacré—quel nom!—"Poil-de-diable!"* you say not dat.—Pierre,' said he, addressing his friend who spoke French, '*faites-lui comprendre mon nom—pas De Welskein, parceque c'est trop difficile, mais St. Foix.*'

'*Ou, Sans-peur,*' said Pierre.

The Frenchmnn nodded assent and said, '*Bon.*' The compliment appeased him.

Pierre now told Rory to address De Welskein by the favourite name of *Sans-peur;* but this was as difficult to Rory as the other, and the nearest approach he could make to it was 'Scamper.' This he varied, sometimes into 'Sampler,' or 'Sandpaper,' as luck would have it.

While the drinking and smoking proceeded, De Welskein told Rory of the intended expedition from the Texel: and when he had given him all the verbal instruction he thought requisite, he entrusted him with the letter to De Lacy from General Hoche.

'Tare an' ouns!' said Rory; 'is it the rale Gineral!' for Hoche's name and reputation were well known in Ireland.

'*Oui,*' said De Welskein.

'What do you mane by *we*?—It's not us at all I'm axin' about; but I want to know, is this letther from the rale Gineral?'

'Certanlee!—*oui.*'

'Augh! what is he sayin' *we* for?' said Rory, turning to Pierre, who was grinning at Rory's mistakes and the Frenchman's impatience.

'He means, yes,' said Pierre: '*oui* means yes.'

'Oh! I ax your pardon, Mr. Sandpaper;—then this is the rale Gineral's letther!—Oh! to think that I'd ever see the proud day that I'd have a letther of Gineral Hoche's in my fist!' and he kissed it with rapture.

The Frenchman cried , *Sacré!*' and laughed at his enthusiasm; and Rory proceeded—

'And will we see the Gineral here, Mr. Scraper?'

'Me fraid no!' said De Welskein; and he shook his head mysteriously and made a grimace.

'What do you mane?' said Rory.

'Me fraid he die.'

'Is it Gineral Hoche die?—arrah, an' what would he die for?'

'Me tsinks he get vaut you call gunstump.'

'Gun—*what?*'

'He as got de gunstump in him.'

'God keep us!' says Rory,—'think o' that! And where is it in him, sir?'

'Inside, into his boddee.'

'Oh! murdher, my poor fellow! to have the stump of a gun stickin' in him!'

'No, no, de gun not stick in him—you mistek: it is vaut I vood say, dat he has de ticklehine.'

'What is it he says about ticklin'?' said Rory to Pierre, who only grinned and enjoyed the mutual mistakes of the Frenchman and the Paddy.

'*Mal à la poitrine,*' said De Welskein.

'That's thrue, 'faith,' said Rory. 'if he's so bad as that, his only dipindince is in the *Padhereens,* sure enough.'

Peter (or Pierre) now laughed outright at Rory's blunder, which must be explained. *Padhereens* is the name the Irish give to their beads, upon which they count the number of *Paters* (or Pathers) they repeat, and hence the name *Padhereens;* and Rory very naturally came to the conclusion, that if a man was at the point of death, which Rory conceived to be most likely when he had the '*stump of a gun stickin' in him,*' the best thing he could do would be to say his prayers.

De Welskein saw there was a mystification going forward; so he said to Pierre,

'*Expliquez donc!*'

'What he says is,' said Pierre, 'that the General has a consumption.'

'Ah! I forgess de *terminaison;*—gunstumpsion,—yais, dat is raight!— gunstumpsion.'

'Oh, murdher!' said Rory: 'if we had him here, we would cure him initirely.'

'*Comment?*' said the Frenchman.

'Oh, it's common enough in this counthry, indeed,' said Rory. 'The finest thing in the world for consumption is goat's milk, made into whey.'

'Ah, yais,—ghost's milk ver goot.'

'*Goat's* milk, I say,' says Rory.

'Yais, yais, I oonderstan','said the Frenchman with great complacency: 'Ghost's milk.'

''Faith it's ghost's milk he'll be takin', I'm afeard, sure enough,' said Pierre laughing at De Welskein's mistake.

'Oh, murdher!' said Rory, 'and is Gineral Hoche goin' to die? Oh, thin, that is the murdher!'[1]

So, Rory in the idiom of his language, unintentionally expressed what was in fact the fate of the gallant Hoche.

A tap at the door of the cellar announced a fresh arrival; and after some signals given, the door was opened and some other men entered, and, at short intervals after, a few girls. Some of the latter were good-looking, though with a certain expression of boldness and recklessness that Rory did not admire. Rory had enough of imagination and sentiment to render the society of the softer sex always matter of delight to him; but there was something in the manner of these girls he did not like.

'You see,' said De Welskein, 'de leddees mek visite to me.'

'Yis, sir,' said Rory, who did not know how, very well, to answer this appeal.

'But you no dreenk.'

'Thank you, sir, I doin' very well.'

'You no like brandee?'

''Faith, it's iligant stuff it is! But you know, Mr. Sandpaper, that enough is as good as a faist.'

'If you no like brandee, give you wine.'

Rory refused the offer; but one of the girls addressed De Welskein, and thanking him for his offer, said, 'if he'd make a big jug o' the nice thing he gave them the other night?'

Pierre explained to him that some of the ladies would like negus, because they thought it genteel.

'Ah ' said the Frenchman, 'yais, my dear, *certainement,* you moste have your leetle niggers: vouds you like to have some nutmarks een it?'

'What do you say, Mr. Whelpskin?' said the girl, simpering.

'Vouds you like nutmarks?'

Pierre came to the rescue.

'He says, would you like to have your jug o' negus made with nutmegs? my darling.'

'Any way Mr. Whelpskin plazes.'

'So it's not too *wake,*' says another.

'A dash o' sper'ts through it will make it livelier, sir,' said the most audacious of the party. And accordingly a large jug of niggers, with nutmarks *and* the dash o' sper'ts, was made. A fiddler, in some time, made his appearance; and after the *first* jug of niggers had been demolished, a dance was set on foot. One of the ladies asked Rory to 'stan up on the flure,' which, of course, Rory did, and exerted himself to the utmost to do credit to his dancing-master. In short, Rory, though he did not like the party, had intuitively too much *savoir vivre* to let any repugnance he might entertain be manifested. He drank, to be sure, sparingly; and after the niggers was introduced, he took no more brandy-and-water: he smoked an occasional pipe, and danced 'like anything,' but he kept himself clear of intoxication, though he had drunk enough to produce exhilaration. Dance after dance succeeded; and Rory displayed so much elasticity of limb, that it excited the admiration even of De Welskein. One of Rory' partners seemed much taken with him; and after a certain jig they had executed, much to their mutual honour and the admiration of the beholders, the fair *danseuse* sat beside him so close, as not to admit of any doubt that she *rather* admired him. A cessation to the dancing now took place, and brandy-and-water and niggers *ad infinitum* was the order of the day—or rather the night. A song was next called for from the girl who sat beside Rory; and after a proper quantity of hemming and hawing, and protestations that she was very hoarse, she sang with a good voice, whose natural sweetness seemed to have been rendered coarse by exposure to the weather, the following song:

Oh! if all the young maidens was blackbirds and thrishes,
Oh! it all the young maidens was blackbirds and thrishes,
Oh! if all the young maidens was blackbirds and thrishes,
Its then the young men would be batin' the bushes.

Oh! If all the young maidens was ducks in the wather,
Oh! if all the young maidens was ducks in the wather,
Oh! if all the young maidens was ducks in the wather,
It's then the young men would jump in and swim afther.

Oh! if all the young maidens was birds on a mountain,
Oh! if all the young maidens was birds on a mountain,
Oh! if all the young maidens was birds on a mountain,
It's then the young man would get guns and go grousin'.

If the maidens was all throat and salmon so lively,
If the maidens was all throut and salmon so lively,
If the maidens was all throut and salmon so lively,
Oh! the divil a man would ate mate on a Friday.

Loud applause followed this charming lyric, during the singing of which the damsel cast sundry sly glances at Rory, who could not mistake that she was making love to him. Rory was a handsome fellow, and was as conscious as most handsome fellows are, that there is a certain readiness on the part of the softer sex to be affected by good looks—but this rather open manifestation of it embarrassed him. To repel a woman was what his nature would not permit him to do; yet to yield to the species of temptation that was offered to him was what his heart forbade.

The revel had proceeded now for some hours, and great licence was exhibited on the part of all. Rory's partner still clung to him with a degree of seductiveness that might have influenced him at another time; but now the unholy spell was powerless. He had that morning won the plighted troth of his Kathleen, and the bare thought of being faithless to her was profanation. He thought of her sweet song, even in defiance of the scraping of the tipsy fiddler, who still stimulated the drunken party to stagger through the dance and above the reeking streams of punch and tobacco rose the sweet odour of the breath of the cows and the morning flowers to his memory the recollection was his salvation.

Oh, what *earthly* influence can so fortify the heart of man against the seductions of vice as the love of a virtuous woman!

Let us pursue this scene no further: suffice it to say, their brutal revelry had so far overcome the party, that of all present, Rory O'More and his partner only were thoroughly conscious of what was going forward. When Rory saw that there was none to oppose his retiring, he drew the bolt of the door to depart: his tempting partner made a last appeal to induce him to stay, and even threw her arms round his neck and kissed him.

Rory's manhood rebelled for a moment, but the thought of Kathleen came over him, and in as soothing a tone as he could command he said—'Don't blame me; I've a sweetheart that trusts to me, and I mustn't deceive the innocent girl!'

The words 'innocent girl' seemed to go through the heart of the woman like a pistol-shot. She withdrew her arms from Rory's neck, and hiding her flushed face in her hands, burst into tears, and throwing herself on a bench, sobbed as though her heart would break.

Rory looked on her with pity; but, fearing to trust himself to so softening an influence as a woman's weeping, he rushed up the broken steps of the cellar, and ran down the narrow alley until he had turned its corner. He then paused a moment, to endeavour to remember the way he had come, which had been so intricate, that under the exciting circumstances in which he had been led to the place and was leaving it, it cannot be wondered his recollection was rather misty; so, taking the turn which chance suggested when he ran from the alley, he threaded some lonely lanes, treading as stealthily as his haste would permit:—for an occasional gleam of light through a cracked shutter or the chink of a door betokened that some of the inhabitants of this ill-conditioned quarter were still watchers; and from the specimen he had seen of the company it afforded, he had no wish to encounter any more of its inmates. The sensation of a freer atmosphere than that of the confined closes he had been traversing now came upon hin and indicated the vicinity of a more open space; and facing the current of air that streamed up the lane, he soon arrived in what appeared to him to be the high street of the town. Here all was empty, dark, and silent, except for the splashing of the rain from the spouts of the houses, and Rory was obliged again to pause, for he knew not which way to turn, as he had made his way from the alley by a route different from that by which he entered, and he was consequently in a street he had never seen before, in a town to which he was a stranger.

He stood for some minutes, unmindful of the torrent of rain that was falling, quite absorbed in the consideration of what he should do. It was late, and he doubted whether at such an hour he would be likely to get admittance to a place of abode for the night; he he did not know where to find it; and it struck him that the only course left him was to make the best of his way out of the town, and proceed homewards. This, to be sure, was a heavy task to impose on himself, for he had not taken any rest since he left his own house; he had traversed a considerable tract of country, and to go over the same ground again without the intervention of sleep was what even so active a fellow as Rory O'More did not relish the contemplation of. Therefore the decision he came to at last was to leave the matter to chance;—if in his pass through the town he saw any place that promised him shelter to ask for it; and if not, to start direct for home.

His resolve being taken, he wrapped his frieze-coat about him—for he now noticed that it did rain rather heavily—and walked at a smart pace up the length of street that lay before him. He had not proceeded far when the fall of many footsteps attracted his attention; and from the heavy and measured tread, it was plain that a party of soldiers was in his neighbourhood. He stopped and held his breath; the party was evidently getting nearer; he had no right to be abroad at that hour, for the curfew law had been revived of late. He thought of the letter he had in his possession, and death to himself, and discovery of the plot, flashed upon his imagination. To tear the letter suggested itself to him; but then, it might contain intelligence of importance: to preserve it therefore was desirable; yet to have it found, destruction. What was to be done?

Listening intently to ascertain the quarter whence the footsteps approached, he was soon sensible that the party advanced from the point towards which he was moving: therefore trusting to the darkness of the night and the lightness of his heels, Rory turned about, and with that peculiar agility of step so characteristic of his countrymen, he ran lightly down the street. As he advanced towards the end of it, he perceived there was a wider space beyond it; and knowing the shade of the houses favoured his escape, and still hearing the footsteps following him, he dreaded that the moment he should emerge from the street into the open space, he should be seen. While this thought occurred to him, he perceived, a few steps in advance of him, a large old-fashioned projecting porch, whose clumsy columns and deep recess suggested at once the idea of concealment; so, turning sharply up two or three steps, he became ensconced in the door-way, drawing himself up closely behind one of the columns.

As the footsteps advanced, Rory could hear the rattling of fire-arms mingling with the heavy tramp of the men. His anxiety was at its height when he saw the party just before the door. 'Another instant,' thought he, 'and the danger's past!' when, to his consternation, the sudden exclamation of '*Halt!*' brought the file of men to a dead standstill within a few feet of his place of concealment. He now thought it was all over with him: he expected to be dragged from his hiding-place every instant, brought before the military authorities, and the letter he bore about him being inevitably found, hanged at the drum-head for a rebel. He heard some mysterious mutterings of the corporal, and immediately after, the clattering of a couple of bayonets,—he fancied them already in his body. But still he remained unmolested, though the file of men yet stood before him;—Rory scarcely dared to respire.

It happened that this house within whose porch he had taken refuge was inhabited by the colonel of the regiment then quartered in the town. It stood at the corner of an open and irregular space, called 'the Green,' where some houses were scattered round a piece of dirty grass, and geese and pigs used to promenade during the day, and the belles of the town in the evening, to hear the band play, and let the officers stare them out of countenance. The barrack lay at the upper end of the street; but the quarters were so indifferent, that the colonel preferred taking up his residence in this house, which was removed from the barrack, it is true; but, to increase his security, which the suspicious nature of the times rendered it necessary, in his opinion, to look after, he had two sentinels stationed there; conducing not only to his safety, but to his consequence, of which the colonel was not a little vain. The narrowness of the foot-way before the house would have rendered entry-boxes inconvenient in front,—therefore they were placed round the corner; and it was while the corporal was employed in relieving the guard at the flank of the house, that the file of soldiers remained before the porch.

This was for some minutes—for everybody knows that such matters must be conducted with that system and solemnity so necessary to the good of the service.

To relieve the guard, the corporal marches up one of his men to face the sentinel on duty. These two make a rattle with their firelocks and hold them in a transverse position, which looks pretty; then they advance to each other with two long strides, and stick their faces close together, to the manifest danger of flattening their noses, the corporal standing by all the time, as if to see that they should not bite each other: another slap on their firelocks to rattle them; then the new-comer goes over to the sentry-box, and the other takes his place: then the corporal utters some mysterious grumblings—such as 'Haw!' 'Who?' the men throw their transverse muskets upon their arms, as if they were going to join them: another grunt from the corporal—the relieved sentinel joins the main body, the corporal puts himself at their head, gives another mysterious growl, and tramp, tramp, they go, again to perform the same interesting and intellectual ceremony at another sentry-box, until, having finished his rounds, the corporal marches back into the guard-honse twelve wet men, in lieu of twelve dry ones that he took out.

While all this 'pomp and circumstance of glorious war' was going forward, Rory was in agony. No image is insufficient to express the state of excitement his impatient nature underwent during the interval, which he thought an age: a bee in a bottle, a schoolboy in his master's apple-tree, or a hen on a hot griddle, are but faint figures of speech for the purpose. Well was it for Rory that the rain continued to fall so copiously!—the soldiers buried their faces deeply inside the collars of their coats, and cast not a glance towards the porch. Thus, the very inclemency of the night was propitious to the refugee, who was startled once more, however, for a moment, by the return the corporal, which caused a movement amongst the men. 'They see me now,' thought Rory to himself, and his heart sank when he heard the words 'Fall in.'

'Oh, murdher!' thought Rory: 'if they come in, I'm lost.'

They did not 'come in,' however, and after another growl from the corporal, which was unintelligible, the blessed sound of 'March!' fell on Rory's ear with something of the same sensation that the announcement of a reprieve produces on a prisoner in the condemned cell; and he saw the file execute a 'right-about-face,' and go the way whence they came. Every successive tramp that increased the distance between Rory and the soldiers took a ton weight off his heart, and as the receding footsteps of the men faded into distance he breathed freely again.

As soon as the silence was perfectly restored, Rory thought of emerging from his place of retreat. Had he been a person conversant with the relieving of guards, he would have guessed that some such matter must have been the cause of the scene just recorded; but living a rural life, as he did, such martial mysteries were unknown to him, and while he congratulated himself on being free from danger and contemplated a retreat, he little dreamt that at the flank of the house under whose porch he stood, a pair of sentinels were on guard. So, when there was no sound to indicate that any one save himself was on the watch (for, it being still raining, the sentries on the flank kept most religiously bound within their sentry-boxes—and small blame to them!) Rory thought he had better be off, and ventured to withdraw his body from the small space between the column and the wall into which he had miraculously jammed himself: but in the doing of this he was obliged, as it were, to jerk himself out, and by some unlucky chance, either in getting himself in or out, the cape of his coat caught in a bell-pull, and in the effort to free himself he felt he was laid hold of by the shoulder, and heard at the same instant of time the sound of a bell. Those who have felt what it is to be in nervous situations will not wonder that Rory's heart jumped as he felt himself caught, and heard at the same moment a sound whose very purpose is to awake attention. And it was *such* a bell;—none of your trifling tinklers, none of your little whipper-snapper sort of bells; not like the bark of a Blenheim, but the bay of a watch-dog; not like a muffin-merchant's, but a dustman's; not merely made to call Molly upstairs,—but one of your deep-mouthed devils, doomed to destroy the repose of half a street;—in short,

'—a *dreadful* bell,
To fright the isle from its propriety.'

Rory stood aghast! Had the metal that composed this 'infernal machine' been molten and cast down his throat, it could not have astonished him more, besides, it seemed as if it would never have done ringing. We hear great complaints in our days of bell-hangers; but those of old, to judge from the case in question, must have been prime hands,—for on it went, ding, ding ding, as if it really had a pleasure in ringing. Whether it was the specific gravity of the monster that produced so much vivacity in the spring on which it was suspended, or the superior skill of former bell-hangers, may remain a matter of dispute to the curious; but the fact that resulted (and facts are all we have to do with) is, that ere the bell had ceased its villainous vibrations, Rory heard a window raised above his head, and the demand of 'Who's there?' in no very gracious voice.

Rory kept profoundly quiet.

'Who's there?' was again snarled out.

Rory looked up from the shelter of the porch, and saw a head and a nightcap protruded from the window: he was as quiet as a mouse.

'Sentry!' was the next word Rory heard, given in a most authoritative tone.

A gust of wind and a dash of rain whirled round the corner, which must have convinced the colonel (for it was he who was calling from the window) that his voice could not have reached the sentinels in the teeth of the blast which blew his nightcap off his head and dashed it into Rory's face.

Rory was nearly knocked down,—for the smallest thing upsets us when we are alarmed.

'Sentry!' was shouted louder than before.

The soldiers answered the summons. The colonel asked who rang the bell:—the sentries did not know.

'You have been asleep!' said the colonel.

'No, your honour,' said the sentry, 'we couldn't; the guard has been but just relieved!'

'Have you seen no one passing?'

'No, your honour,—no one passed at this side; and we marched down the other street not five minutes ago, and not a living soul was seen.'

'Then what could have rung the bell?'

''Twas only a mistake, sir,' said Rory, whose excitement had been wound to such intensity, that his eagerness to satisfy the question overlooked the consequence to his personal safety in the sound of his voice being heard; but the instant he had spoken, he said to himself, 'The d—l cut the tongue out of you, Rory!'

Fortunately the gusts of wind and splashing of rain tendered all sounds, and the points whence they came, uncertain. Nevertheless, the colonel looked towards the porch; but seeing no one, he said to the sentry, 'What's that you said about a mistake?'

'No, your honour, I don't mistake,' said the sentry, who was equally uncertain with the colonel if any third person had spoken, and fancied he had been charged with making a mistake.

'Didn't you say something of a mistake? asked the colonel in one of the pauses of the storm.

'No, your honour,' said the sentry.

Just at this moment, when Rory was thinking if he hadn't better make a run for it at once, he heard the bolt of the door behind him gently drawn, and the instant after, a pluck at his coat, and a whispered 'Come in,' made him turn round. He saw the door stand ajar, and a hand beckon him forward, at the same moment that the voice of the colonel from the window said, 'See if there's any one hiding in the porch.'

Rory slipped inside the hall-door, which was softly closed as the sentry walked up the steps.

'There's no one here, your honour,' said the sentry.

'Push the door,' said the colonel.

The sentry did so; but the door had been fastened on the inside.

1.   This expression means 'that is the pity.'

XI

Shows that one half of the world does not know how the other half lives; and also, that soft words can bend hard iron, though they do not butter parsnips.

VERY MUCH ABOUT THE TIME that Rory O'More rushed from the cellar and endeavoured to make his way out of the town, there was an old tinker, driving an ass before him, making his way into it. From the rudely-constructed *straddle* of the sorry animal, three or four rusty old kettles, and a budget containing the implements of the tinker's trade, depended; but the *straddle* was worth more than it looked good for,—for the tinker had so contrived the panels of the lumbering affair, that a convenient space was left within for stowing away tobacco, which he bought from Monsieur de Welskein, and sold at a handsome profit to the peasantry during his wanderings among them—for they could get none so good or so cheap through the legitimate channel: besides, they were glad to give a helping hand to the old tinker, whose poverty and shrewdness commanded at once their pity and their fear.

It may seem strange to class these two feelings together—but they often exist. They say 'Pity is akin to love;'—but it is equally true that 'Love is related to fear;'—and thus, perhaps, a sort of collateral relationship may be established between them.

I should not have made any observation on this, but that I do not remember seeing it remarked elsewhere; and when one advances anything new, it is common even to oneself to be startled at it, and a desire is at once engendered to make it manifest that one has not committed an absurdity.

Now, I remember well, when a child, that I was often horrified by the presence of a certain old and disgusting beggarman; yet I constantly gave him alms. There was something in that old man I dreaded; and yet I remember, even to this day, I pitied him. To be sure, the virtue of charity had been early instilled into my mind by one who now, I trust, in heaven enjoys the reward of her goodness; and so gracious and winning is the habit of doing charity's holy offices, that even to the innocent child, on whom neither want nor reason can have impressed the value of the virtue he is taught, there is something pleasant in the timorous dropping of a halfpenny from its pure and dimpled fingers into the soiled and withered palm of age as if heaven had preordained that no weakness or antipathy of our nature should interfere with the sacred duty;—a duty so sacred that even our Lord himself made its beauty the theme of a parable, and reproved the intolerant Jew with the mild precept of 'Go thou and do likewise.'

Solomon, for that was the tinker's name, was pitied and feared; for he seemed to be poor, and was known to be penetrating. He had a prying temper and a tenacious memory. The former led him to a knowledge of the circumstances of most of the people of all classes in the country where he made his rounds, and the latter treasured up the information. Thus the past and present were alike familiar to him; and from these, his natural acuteness was often enabled to presage the future.

Such a power, in the uncalculating community amongst whom he moved, gave him a reputation little short of witchcraft. He was called 'a mighty knowledgable man,'—and 'knowledge is power;' and where did human power ever exist, that its influence has not been dreaded and its possession abused. This was fully exemplified in the case of the old tinker,—he was feared, not loved, by the peasantry; and yet, though no one liked him, there were, from a dread of offending, all the demonstrations of civility shown him that love would have procured. The tinker was quite aware of the position he held, and of its cause; and his bitterness (for he was bitter) enjoyed the triumph of forcing these pretended testimonies of affection, and he laughed at this perjury of the heart. 'Hypocrisy is the homage that vice pays to virtue.' How often is a smile the tribute that fear pays to power!

Nevertheless, with this dread—it may almost be said, dislike—that he inspired, he was pitied, from his apparent wretched and desolate condition. Home he had none, nor living thing with whom he held continued companionship, except the poor ass he drove, whose food was a nibble by the road-side, unless when it was bestowed by the same friendly hand that gave food to his master—for Solomon never paid for anything except what he traded on. The love of money ruled him with a power stronger than that by which he ruled his fellow-men; and though he possessed the superior acuteness that governed intelligent creatures, he was himself the senseless slave of an inanimate metal. He was a miser,—a miser in the fullest sense of the word; not loving money for the sake of what money can procure, but loving it for its own sake—worshipping the mere thing: to him a guinea was a god. To such a wretch, to starve was easier than to pay; therefore he never tasted food except when it was given to him; and even on these terms he seldom wanted, for he laid the country under contribution, from the kitchen of the squire to the peasant's pot of potatoes. With all this, he was stealthy and roguish as a fox, tortuous and treacherous as a snake,—secret, cold and greedy as the grave.

Yet, with the characteristic touch of fun that pervades everything Irish, this hateful old miscreant had a comical name bestowed on him;—he was called 'Sawdhering Solomon,' from his profession of tinker; and this was the name he commonly went by, though sometimes it was changed for 'Solomon Sly.' Neither of these names was meant, of course, to reach *his* ears but he was made cognisant of them by means of the little boys, who hated him openly, and who shouted the name after him when they were quite sure of being out of the reach of the old tinker's crooked stick: and sometimes the urchins ventured so far even as to throw stones or clods at him, when they had the ambuscade of a hedge and the intervention of a ditch to screen and protect them. On these occasions, Solomon might get a whack on the back from a stone, or have a dry clod judiciously lobbed under his ear, powdering his wig with all the breaking particles of earth that did not run down between his clothes and his back. Then would he turn round to strike with his stick but the retiring laugh and footsteps of children at the other side of the hedge were all that were manifest to Solomon: and then would the old vagabond grin and shake his stick with the expression of a fiend, and utter horrible curses on the thoughtless urchin. And though the provocation was unjustifiable, it is true, yet there is something abhorrent in the idea of age cursing childhood, particularly as the vindictive old tinker used to curse.

It was about the time that Rory O'More was leaving the cellar, that Solomon, I say, was making his way into the town, at whose outskirts he made a detour from the high road and drove his ass up a little lane, at the end of which there was a small *haggart*,[1] whose fence was only a low wall of loose stones and some furze-bushes. Solomon very coolly abstracted some stones, pulled away some of the furze, and made a way for his ass to enter the haggart, where, placing him between two small stacks of hay, he procured shelter and provender for the poor brute. He then lifted the straddle and his old kettles from the ass's back, aud withdrew from the premises, carrying his goods to some distance, where, under a hedge, he let them lie; and marking the spot well, he proceeded alone to the town, and made for the cellar of the smuggler.

It was only in his capacity of smuggler that De Welskein held any communication with the tinker. Solomon, though he guessed that an extensive conspiracy was on foot, yet, wise as he was, he did not know any individual engaged in it, for none would trust him to belong to the Union, and those engaged in it kept the secret inviolate,— singularly so, indeed, for in all the thousands who had sworn, there was but *one* found to betray, and *he* entered the confederation for the very purpose.

When the unfortunate girl whom Rory had left sobbing in the cellar had recovered her outbreak of grief, she arose from the bench on which she had flung herself in her passion of tears, and the feeling that had possessed her heart changed from lawless love to bitter hate—for

'Hell has no fury like a woman scorn'd'—

and cursing the man that had made her feel such degradation, she
quitted the den of riot and iniquity, leaving the beastly revellers sunk
in besotted slumber. When Solomon, therefore, reached the cellar and
tapped stealthily at the door, he received no answer. On knocking again
more loudly, the door yielded to his touch, and pushing it gently open,
he looked cautiously into the cellar. He saw a dim lamp, over-turned
drinking-vessels, and prostrate figures, and heard the heavy snoring of
drunken sleep. He advanced noiselessly, and looked carefully about and
when he found that deep and real slumber reigned around him, he
cast about his searching eyes, and his heart (if he had such a thing) was
gladdened at the thought of being a gainer by the universal swinishness
in which his friends were buried. He stole softly over to the truckle-bed
under which the tobacco was hid, and going on all-fours, he looked to
see if there was a roll of it within easy reach—for the legs of one of the
sleepers hung over the side and made a sort of barrier.

He crawled nearer, and, with the aid of his crooked stick, abstracted
a parcel of the precious weed from its place of concealment; and then,
with the stealthiness of a cat, he stole back to the door which he
closed gently after him, and retreated with his booty.

Now, it was to buy tobacco that the tinker had made his visit to De
Welkstein; and he chuckled at the thought of getting the merchandise
without the transfer of coin, and hugged the roll of tobacco to his
heart with the passion of a lover. To re-cram the panel of his ass's
straddle, and depart after his exploit, was Solomon's first intention as
he sneaked back towards the haggart where his ass was committing
robbery also; but another idea arose, and he slackened his pace while
he conned it over, and on second toughts he considered it more
advisable to make his visit to De Welskein, as it was about the period
that worthy knew he had intended calling, and if the abstracted
tobacco should be missed, his unusual absence might direct suspicion
against him, as it was some time since Solomon had made a purchase,
and De Welskein knew that tobacco was what Solomon could not do
without. Therefore, instead of going back to the haggart, he went to

a neighbouring lane where he knew the forge of a blacksmith stood, and poking and scraping out with his stick and hands a hole out of a heap of cinders and ashes that stood near the door, he concealed the treasure beneath it and returned to the cellar. He knocked again, lest any of its inmates might have awoke in the interval; and finding all as silent as before, he entered, and approaching De Welskein, he shook him by the shoulder till he roused him and said:

'One ud think you had nothing to be afeard iv, when you sleep with the door open.'

De Welskein rubbed his eyes, stared up at Solomon, uttered a great many '*Sacrés,*' and '*Diables,*' and proceeded to awake the rest of the party and demand the cause of the door being open. They were all bewildered, being still half-drunk; but after much blustering and swearing, Rory O'More at last was missed, and also the girl with whom he had been dancing. This was conclusive evidence of how the circumstance had occurred, and De Welskein's rage and abuse of Rory were furious. Regan, too, threw in his word of censure; and, amongst them all, poor Rory had more foul words applied to him than he ever had before in the same space of time.

'Who is that you're blessin', all o' yiz?' said Solomon.

'That scatther-brained swaggerer, Rory O'More,' said Regan.

'Rory O'More!' said Soloman who knew Rory's habits were not likely to lead him into the disorderly set;—'why, what brought *him* here?' and he looked sharply at De Welskein, as much as to say, 'There's a mystery.'

'Why, sare! if you go for dat moche, what for *you* come here?—ha!'

'Oh, you know yourself, munseer,' said Solomon, 'what brings *me* here; but—'

'Well, sare,' said De Welskein, interrupting him, 'and *me* know whas bring de osser gentlemans too: das nuff for me—nussing to you.'

'Oh, don't be onaisy,' said Solomon coolly—'I don't want to smoke your saycrets.'

'No, G— d—n! you old rog! you not smok me, you razzer smok my tabac.'

Solomon looked towards the Frenchman, to see if there was any meaning in his eye when he spoke of *his tobacco*; but he saw his secret was safe. The Frenchman proceeded—'Dere! you seet down you—old rog—*vieux chaudronnier de campagne*—seet down, smoke your tabac and dreenk, and never mind nussing else!'

Solomon did as he was desired; he took a pipe and mixed a stiff glass of brandy-and-water, after tossing off a couple of glasses pure, to warm his heart, as he said himself, 'afther the cruel wettin' he got.'

'Warm his heart indeed!' said one of the men aside: ''faith all the sper'ts in Ireland, and all the turf in the Bog of Allen wouldn't warm it.'

De Welskein took Regan aside, and expressed great displeasure against Rory for leaving him without saying where De Lacy was to be found; but Regan set him at rest on that subject by telling him he knew Rory's place of abode, and would conduct him to it if he liked. This consoled the Frenchman, and he again laid down to sleep, requesting more care might be taken about the door. Solomon continued to smoke and drink until the approach of dawn, when the man called Pierre let him out of the cellar, and he went back to the haggart, having made the best bargain he could for some tobacco, and getting his pocket-pistol, as he called a tolerably capacious tin flask, filled with brandy as a bonus for his '*taking sitch a power o' tabakky from them*,' as he said himself; and equivoke gave poignancy to the pleasure of his theft.

When he got back to the haggart, he abstracted his ass from the haystack, which the ass seemed loath to quit, and before retiring, the little beast made a last desperate plunge into the hay, and dragged away so large a mouthful, that it trailed after him all the way from the stack to the gap where Solomon now led him out, and the poor innocent haystack looked very much in the condition of a hot loaf out of which Master Tommy has had his wicked will.

Solomon replaced the stones and the furze-bush, and led off his ass to the hedge where the straddle was secreted; there he stuffed it with the *purchased* tobacco (the stolen roll still lay where the tinker had concealed it), and mounting his wallet and his kettles on the back of the ass, he drove him away from the field as soon as sunrise permitted him lawfully to appear on the road.

What did he do then?

He had the impudence to march up the lane that led to the haggart, driving his ass before him and crying loudly, 'Pots, pans, and kittles to mind.' The ass turned a longing look towards the haggart, and a whack from Solomon's stick was required to remind him that tinkers' asses must not eat hay by daylight. Solomon now approached the dwelling to which the plundered haggart was attached, and found the family awake and doing: the man went out to work, and the woman, in answer to Solomon's request to know 'if there *was* any pots, pans, and kittles to mind,' produced a certain tin saucepan with a demand to know 'what would he take to repair it? not that it wanted it much,' she said, 'only, divil take it! it put out the fire always when it was put on, but didn't *lake* a grate dale at all'

'Why, tares an' ouns, woman,' cried Solomon, holding up the vessel between him and the sky, 'there's a hole in it you could dhrive a coach thro'.'

'Arrah, be aisy!' says the woman.

'Look at it yourself,' says Solomon, letting the saucepan down.

A little child now popped his finger through the hole, and waggling it backwards and forwards, said, 'Look, mammy!' and grinned as if he had done a very clever thing.

The mother gave him a box on the ear, calling him 'a divil' at the same time, and sent him yelping away.

''Faith that's a 'cute child!' said Solomon, giving a horrid smile; 'he'd make an iligant tinker, he sees a hole in a pot so well.'

'The meddlin' cur!' said the mother. 'Well, what'll you put a bit o' sawdher an it for?'

'A bit o' sawdher indeed!' said Solomon. 'Oh, 'faith, it's a piece o' tin I must insart into it.'

'Divil an insart,' says the woman, 'you'll insart my saucepan, my good man! Sawdher is all it wants—jist a weeshee taste o' sawdher.'

'Cock you up with my sawdher indeed!' said Solomon; 'why, 'twould take more than all the sawdher I have to stop it. Sure, sawdher is as dear as tin; and rawzin's riz.'

'Arrah, why would rawzin be riz?'

'There was sitch a power o' fiddlers to be at the fair next week that they bought all the rawzin up.'

'Ah, go 'long wid you!'

'It's thruth I'm tellin' you.'

'Well, what will you take for the saucepan?'

'I'll mind it for fourpince.'

'Fourpince! Oh, where do you expec' to go when you die? Fourpince indeed! I'll give you tupp'ns.'

'Couldn't,' says Solomon, shaking his head and going to drive away the ass.

'Well, what will you say?' said the woman.

'Well, see now,' said Solomon, 'I'm tired with thravelling a'most all night, and I'm wantin' rest; and indeed I'd be glad to sit down, if it was only to rest, let alone doin' a job and airnin' a thrifle; and indeed I want it bad, for the times is hard; and, so God bless you, if you'll jist throw in a thrifle o' brequest into the bargain, and gi' me tupp'ns ha'pny, I'll make the saucepan as good as new.'

'Well, I wouldn't be hard wid you, my poor man, and so you may do it.'

So down sat the tinker and opened his budget; and his iron was heated and his 'sawdher' produced, not forgetting the 'rawzin that was 'riz'; and bits of old tin were produced from his budget, into which the children looked with the most profound curiosity, endeavouring to fathom the depth of its mysterious treasures. Other bits of tin dazzled their longing eyes, and a great shears seemed placed there to guard the invaluable store from plunder. Solomon cut and rasped and hammered away, and rubbing his hot soldering-iron upon his powdered rosin and solder, he raised so great a smoke and so bad a smell, that the children looked on him as some wonderful conjuror; and as they saw the bright streaks that his implement produced wherever it was rubbed, their delight was profound.

When the man of the house returned to breakfast, he saw Solomon seated at the door mending the leaky vessel, and his children standing round him in wonder, and as soon as the job was done, Solomon was called in to breakfast.

'What do you think?' said the husband to the wife.

'What?' said she.

'That blackguard calf got over the wall o' the haggart again last night and made a holy show o' the hay-stack.'

'Oh, don't tell me so!' said the wife.

'Luck to the lie in it!' said the husband.

Solomon kept eating his breakfast with the most profound indifference until the husband and wife had exhausted their eloquence, and then he said:

'Them cawves is great rogues.'

'The divil run a-huntin' with him for a calf! Oh, wait 'till the next time I ketch him!'

'Poor thing, poor thing!' said Solomon, tenderly. 'Sure, it's nath'ral they'd ate!'

''Faith, he may be contint with his good grass, I think,' said the man.

'Thrue for you—thrue for you,' said Solomon quietly: 'but it's remarkable how bowld some o' them cawves is.'

Breakfast was finished—the job paid for—the wallet replaced on the ass amid the observation and regret of all the children, who watched the old tinker and saw him depart with sorrow as he drove his ass down the lane, after getting a job and begging a breakfast from the man he had robbed overnight.

Solomon now proceeded to the town, and went to the forge beside which he had deposited the tobacco. Here he had a plausible pretext to go, for the shoes of the ass wanted to be looked to. On his arrival at the forge, the smith was unoccupied, so there was more time to spare for Solomon to make as hard a bargain as he could for the execution of the job.

'Maybe you could let me make an exchange wid you? and if you would have anything in the tinkerin' line to do, sure I'd do it for nothin' for you, if you'd do the ass for nothin'.'

'Not a pot, nor pan, nor kittle have I,' said the blacksmith; 'I'm a bachelor, and intind to stay so.'

In the meantime he began to examine the ass's shoes; and the tobacco with which the straddle was lined being so near his nose, the smith began to snuff, and said at last, 'Where the dickins is the tabakky?'

Solomon, who caught the sound of the first sniff the smith had given, saw directly how matters stood, and hastened to the rescue: he got close beside the ass, and to the smith's inquiry he said:

'It's here in my pocket, and mighty fine tabakky it is!—see, I got a bargain o' some from a friend a while agon, and—but don't mintion it—if you like I'll share the bargain wid you, to the value of a new set o' shoes for the baste.'

'Gor! that ud be a power o' tabakky!' said the smith.

'But it's iligant tabakky,' said Solomon. Pulling from his pocket several yards of the material, wound into a close ball, and popping it under the smith's nose, he said, 'What do you think o' that, yer sowl?'

'Faix, that *is* tarein' tabakky, sure enough!' was the delighted smith's reply.

'Well, what do you say to a new set o' shoes for the baste?' said Solomon.

'I dunna,' was the undecided answer.

'You know you'll have the owld shoes in.'

'To be sure I will,' said the smith, 'sure that's only nath'ral but what good is a little ass's shoes?'

'Oh, shoes is shoes,' said Solomon.

'Why, tare alive! they are worn as thin as a sixpence.'

''Deed that is thrue,' said Solomon, 'for the last set he had an him was from the finest smith in Ireland: they wore powerful.'

'Arrah, who's that?' said the workman, piqued at the mention of the finest smith in Ireland, he himself not being the person meant.

'Why, would it be but Brian Branagan?' said Solomon, who well knew that Brian Branagan was the rival of the man who stood before him, and living in the adjoining lane, but who had never made shoes for the tinker's ass in his life.

This was a master-touch of Solomon—the smith bristled directly for the palm of superiority.

'Why, thin, is it Branagan you say is the finest smith in Ireland?'

'Yis,' said Solomon very quietly.

'Troth then, it's little you know about it. Branagan indeed! The divil a bigger botch ever dhruv a nail than the same Branagan: he is a smith!!'

'Oh! I don't purtend to know indeed,' said Solomon, with an affected air of not wishing to offend, at the same time laying hold of the halter of the ass. 'But he's good enough for me, anyhow good mornin' kindly to you,' said he, going.

This was too much for the smith.

'Come back here, I tell you! it's I that'll show you what a set o' shoes is: Branagan indeed!'

'Well, will you take what I said?' said Solomon, affecting not to care much whether the smith did or not.

'Yis, yis, but never say the word Branagan to me!' Here he laid hold of his pincers, knife, and hammer, and began to knock off the points of the nail from each hoof, and pull off the ass's shoes—every drag he gave, which was with great vigour, accompanied by a 'hugh,' and the exclamation of 'Branagan indeed!!'

'Hadn' I better take off the sthraddle?' said Soloman.

'Ay, off wid it,' said the smith.

So Solomon took off the highly-perfumed straddle that was so near betraying him, and then, filling the smith's pipe, and his own too, with some of the tobacco which he had sold to the smith, he commenced puffing away vigorously, that the smell of the lighted weed might prevent the perfume of the dry being noticed.

While the smith was engaged in shoeing the ass inside the forge, Solomon had time to disengage the roll of stolen tobacco from the heap of cinders where he had concealed it, and hiding it in one of his old kettles, he was quite at ease, and blew the bellows for the smith while he heated the iron, or looked over him at work with an air of delight, saying, as the smith rasped up and finished his work, 'Well, but thim is the rale iligant shoes!'

'You'll never talk o' Branagan agin, will you, afther *that!*' said the smith.

'Throth, an' I won't,' said Solomon; 'and sure it's only an owld fool I was, up to this present time, in thinkin' the like but the owldher we grow, the more we larn. Sure, it's a grate loss to me I didn't know you sooner!'

'Well, it's never too late to mend,' said the smith.

'Thrue for you,' said Solomon; 'nor to *make*, aither.' And, so saying, he filled his pipe again from the smith's tobacco, and wishing him good-morning, off he went, having secured his plunder, and getting a new set of shoes on his ass; so that he was now ready for a long and prosperous round, through his usual beat.

The smith idled the rest of that day, smoking at his new stock of 'bakky,' drinking to quench his thirst, and filling up the intervals by snapping his fingers and crying, '*That* for Branagan!'

1.   Hay-yard.

XII

'In the dark all cats are grey.'—*Rory becomes possessed of an important secret, and discloses one in exchange.*

WHEN RORY O'MORE WAS ADMITTED to the safe side of the door, he felt the pressure of a hand upon his arm, which he interpreted into the meaning of 'be quiet;' and as it was Rory's own opinion that, in his present circumstances, it was the best thing he could do, he acquiesced. One thing, however, he was sure of—that it was a woman who admitted him to the house, for he felt the sof breathing of one of the gentle sex upon his cheek as he stood motionless by the door beside his benefactress, while they heard a few words passing between the colonel and the sentinel, until the latter descended the steps.

Immediately after, Rory heard the woman say gently, 'Come down, darlin'!' and holding the hand that was laid upon his arm, he followed his conductress as softly as he could. They soon began to descend some stairs, and before they had reached the bottom of the flight, the sound of a bolt being drawn was heard up stairs, and Rory's friend said, in a suppressed voice of terror,

'Oh, murdher! there's the colonel comin' down! you must hide in the coalhole. Make haste, for the love o' God, or I'm a ruined woman!—here, here!' and she dragged Rory along while she spoke. 'Get in there as far as ever you can, and hide yourself, or I dunna what will become of the pair of us!'

At the same time, she opened a door and pushed Rory inside of it. He heard her footsteps retreat lightly and rapidly. 'More opening of doors,' said Rory to himself as he scrambled over some cod and slack, holding his arms extended to save his nose from fracture; and he found the coal-vault extensive, for it was some time before he was stopped by a wall. As soon as he went as far as he could go, he crouched down, keeping his face however turned towards the point whence he entered, and he soon heard the descending footsteps of the person he was taught to believe was the colonel. The footsteps seemed to ramble over a great space of flagged apartments, and various doors squeaked on their hinges as they were opened and shut in succession by the invisible perambulant. At last Rory saw the glimmer of a light, which got stronger by degrees, until the door of the cellar opened, and then he saw a Don Quixote sort of a man, with a candle in one hand and a drawn sword in the other, poke his head in a the door of the cellar, and holding the candle a yard before him say, 'Is there any one here?'

Rory knew better than to make any answer this time, and having thrown the tail of his coat over his head, leaving only a small peep-hole for his eyes, he remained undistinguishable amidst the surrounding gloom; for the vault was so deep, the candle so dim, the colonel so short-sighted, and Rory crouched so low, that he quite defied observation. Despite his dangerous situation, however, it was as much as Rory could do not to laugh; for the colonel, with his long face, long candle, long body, long arms, long sword, long legs, and short shirt, cut so ridiculous a figure, that a man of more solid mood than Rory might have been provoked to mirth. However, by good luck, Rory did not laugh, though the colonel, *à la* Don Quixote, continued to open his goggle eyes on the gloom before him; but he was startled from his fixed observation by hearing a slip amongst the coal, which drew forth a still fiercer demand of 'Who's there?'—Upon the summons, Rory perceived, between him and the light, a great cat cautiously crawl to the summit of the heap of coal, and, with a tail bristling to the size of a sweeping brush, make a desperate rush down the acclivity and dart between the colonel's legs. The man of war actually jumped with alarm at the suddenness of the surprise, and, as if ashamed of being so frightened at such a cause, muttered spitefully, 'D—n the cat!' He now retired from the cellar, and went to wake (as he thought) the woman-servant who let Rory in, and whose sleeping apartment was in the basement story. Rory heard him cry, 'Betty!'—no answer. 'Betty!' again—still silence preserved. 'Betty!' still louder than before;—Rory heard a snort and a growl as if from a suddenly awakened person.

'Who's that?' said a female voice.

'Your master; have you heard any noise in the house?'

'Noise, sir?'

'Yes, noise—have you heard any?'

'No, sir: I have been in bed, sir, and asleep these three hours. I hope there's nothing the matther, sir?' said Betty with very honest seeming.

'I have been disturbed,' said the colonel; 'and I thought robbers had got into the house. I certainly heard a noise,'

'Oh, I dar say, sir,' said Betty; ''twas nothing, but the cat: he's mighty throublesome and lively, that cat is—and I forget to shut him up sometimes—and I'm afeard he has been disturbing you, sir. Oh dear, but I'm sorry!'

This was a good guess of Betty's: for the colonel having seen a cat, now retired, and Rory was once more left in darkness. And now that the immediate chance of discovery was removed, he began to conjecture by what extraordinary means he was let into a house to which he was an utter stranger, at the moment he needed it most, and by a woman of whom he knew no more than the man in the moon: her name was Betty—that was all the knowledge he arrived at—and that he only knew from hearing the colonel address her.

After the lapse of half-an-hour, Rory heard the name of 'Darby' whispered at the door of the cellar.

In equally gentle tone, he barely ventured to say, rather huskily, 'Iss.'

'Come out, darlin'; take care you don't rowl down any of the big lumps o' coal.'

Rory, profiting by the caution, got out with as little noise as possible and coming in contact with his female guide, he was led into an apartment, the door of which was very cautiously locked by the woman.

'Now we may spake more at our aise,' said she. 'How are you, darlin'?'

'Indeed I'm throubled with a mighty bad cowld,' said Rory, who thought this the best thing he could say whereby to account for the husky tone in which he spoke, that his natural voice might not betray the mistake which had so far favoured him.

'Oh, but your voice is gone intirely, Darby darlin'!' says the woman: 'but here's somethin' to comfort you, *agra;* here'—and she led him to where a chair and table stood—'here, sit down and ate your supper; there's an iligant piece o' roast beef, and a jug of beautiful beer, I kept sly for you. If you like, I'll light a candle for you.'

'Oh, by no manes!' said Rory; 'it's betther not; as the house was alarmed the light might be bad.'

'No,—it's not that so much, but I'm afeard o' the noise of sthrikin' the flint.'

'Don't think of it, Betty dear,' grumbled Rory.

'Lord! how your voice is althered!'

'Indeed I'm chokin' with the cowld— hegh! Hegh! Oh murdher!'

'Ate a bit, and it'll do you good. I'm grieved you haven't a light, darlin'; 'twould be sitch a comfort to you.'

'I don't miss it in the laste, Betty; I can find the way to my mouth in the dark.'

And so saying, Rory began to eat his supper, which was most acceptable to him for two reasons: first, he was hungry and in the next place, the occupation accounted for his silence, which it was so desirable to preserve.

'But, you villain! what did you ring that theivin' bell for?'

''Twas a mistake, darlin'—hegh! hegh! hegh! Oh! this cowld is chokin' me.'

'Don't disthress yourself talkin', Darby, dear; relieve yourself with the mate and the dhrink.'

Rory obeyed.

'I run up the minit I heard the bell; and, sure, wasn't it the hoighth o' good luck that I got you in before the colonel kem down! Oh, he'd murdher me, I'm sure, if he thought how it was! But, afther all, Darby jewel, what harm is there in an honest woman havin' her husband to come see her?—sure it's nath'ral.'

'To be sure, Betty jewel,' said Rory, who now perceived that he was mistaken by Betty for her husband; and Rory's inventive imagination set to work in fancying what a dilemma he should be in, in case the real husband might arrive. In the meantime, however, he fortified his patience and resolution with the beef and beer, which did great credit to the colonel's larder and cellar.

'But you're not atein', Darby dear,' said Betty.

'No, but I'm dhrinkin',' said Rory.

'Much good to your heart, jewel! But, tell me, how is Johnny?'

Now, who the deuce Johnny was, Rory could not tell; but supposing, from the diminutive form of the name, it might be her child, he thought it better to please her with a favourable answer; so he said:

'Johnny's very well.'

'Thank God!' said Betty. 'He's a fine craythur: how well he got over it!'

'Iligant!' said Rory, who wondered what it was Johnny had got over.

'And how is the hives?' said Betty.

'They're all where they wor,' said Rory, who did not dream of any other hives than beehives; while Betty meant the cutaneous eruption that 'Johnny' was suffering under.

'And has none of them disappeared?' said Betty.

'Oh! no,' said Rory; 'we take great care o' thim.'

'Do, darlin' do;—keep 'em from cowld.'

'Oh yis; we put sthraw over them,' said Rory.

'Sthraw!' said Betty; 'why, thin, is it takin' lave o' your sinses you are, Darby? Is it sthraw on the hives!'

'Sartinly; sure the bees likes it.'

'Bees!' said Betty; 'arrah, what bees?'

'Why, the bees in the hives,' said Rory.

'Arrah, man, don't be going on with your humbuggin'; you know I'm axing about the child very well, and you must go on with your thricks about beehives. I hate humbuggin', so I do, Darby,—and you know I do; and you will be goin' on, all I do say.'

Rory saw here was some mistake; and to stop Betty, he said:

'Whisht, whisht!'

'What is it?' said Betty.

'Don't talk so much, or maybe they'll hear uz.'

Betty was silent for some time; but as perfect stillness seemed to reign in the house, she returned to the charge on the hives.

'But tell me is the hives all out?'

'Av coorse,' said Rory.

'And do they look well?'

'Mighty pur indeed,' said Rory; 'and there'll be a power o' honey in them, I'm sure.'

Betty now gave him a box on the ear, saying, 'Devil sweep you! you will be humbuggin', so you will. You cruel brute can't you make fun of anything but the poor child that is lyin' undher the hives?'

'Sure, I tell you the child is well and hearty; and isn't that enough?' said Rory.

'And it's only jokin' you wor?' said Betty.

'To be sure,' aid Rory; 'you ought to know my ways by this time.— This is mighty fine beef!'

'But 'deed an 'deed, *is* Johnny——'

'Bad luck to the word more I'll say!' said Rory, affecting an angry silence.

Betty now changed her ground, and thought a bit of scandal confided to Darby would amuse him; so she began to tell him that, suppose the colonel *should* find out she brought her husband into the house, he had no right to complain, for at all events it *was* her own husband, and nobody else.

Rory chuckled at her confidence.

'Not all as one,' said Betty, 'as him—with another man's wife! Purty goin's on.'

'Do you tell me so?' said Rory.

'I found it all out, so he'd better say nothin' to me, or I could desthroy him. Not that she's a bit worse than ever she was; but if the collecthor knew it—'

Rory cocked his ears. 'is it Scrubbs you mane?'

'Who else?' said Betty.

'And his wife?' said Rory.

'—Is come over on a visit, *by the way*—but I know what I know.'

'How long ago?' said Rory.

'Since you were here last,' said Betty.

'That's a long time,' thought Rory to himself.

'Scrubbs went to town last week, and over comes madam—on a visit. Av coorse she'll go back when she expects her nate man home. But it sarves him right!—what could he expec' when he tuk up with the likes of her, the dirty cur!'

Betty went on for some time in this strain, venting the vials of her wrath on the colonel and Mrs. Scrubbs; and Rory did not interrupt her, for he was glad the more she talked, as it relieved him from the difficulty of remaining concealed under her questions. After exhausting her news and her abuse, she began to ask Rory more questions, to all of which he replied by the exclamation of 'Whisht,' protesting at the same time he was afraid to speak for fear of discovery by the colonel. At last, when Betty found he had cleared the dish and emptied the jug, she said:

'You had bether come to bed now, darlin'.'

This was a poser, and Rory said 'Whisht,' again.

'Come to bed, jewel—you'll be more comfortabler there than sittin' here in the cowld, and we can talk without any fear o' bein' heerd, with our heads undher the blankets.'

'I can't bear my head undher the blankets,' said Rory.

'That's newly come to you, thin,' said Betty.

'That is since this cowld,' said Rory, recovering himself: 'it chokes me, this cowld does.'

'There's not a finer thing in the world for a cowld than to go to bed,' said Betty.

'But the cowld rises in my throat to that degree when I lie down,' said Rory, 'that it smothers me.'

'Maybe 'twould be betther to-night, darlin',' said Betty.

'I'd rather sit up,' said Rory.

'You'll be lost with the cowld,' said Betty, 'and no fire in the grate.'

Rory found Betty was determined to have matters her own way, and began to get puzzled how he should avoid this difficulty, and the only chance of escape he saw open to him, was to request the tender and confiding Betty to prepare herself for a 'grate saycret' he had to tell her, and that she would promise, when he informed her of it, not to be too much surprised. Betty protested to preserve the most philosophic composure.

'You won't screech?' said Rory.

'What would I screech for?' said Betty.

'It's mithghty surprisin',' said Rory.

'Arrah, don't keep me waitin', but let me have it at wanst,' said Betty, eagerly.

'Now, 'darlin' take it aisy,' said Rory, 'for you must know—'

'What?' said Betty.

'I'm not Darby,' said Rory.

Betty scarcely suppressed a scream.

'You villain!' said she.

'I'm not a villain, aither,' said Rory.

'What brought you here at all?'

'Yourself,' said Rory: 'sure, wasn't it yourself pulled me inside the hall-door?'

'But, sure, I thought it was Darby was in it.'

'Well, and haven't I been honest enough to tell you I'm not Darby, at last, when it might have been throublesome to your conscience, Betty?'

'Ay,' said the woman, 'there's more o' your roguery; Betty, too!—how did you make out my name, you divil's limb?'

'A way o' my own, Betty.'

'Oh, a purty rogue you are, I go bail—throth, it's not the first house you got into, I dare say, nor the first poor woman you enthrapped, you midnight desaiver—and takin' up my name too.'

'Well, I haven't taken *away* your name any how; so don't be so fractious.'

'Arrah, but how do I know but you will.'

'Well, it's time enough to cry when you're hurt, Betty,—keep yourself cool now—there's no harm done.'

'No harm indeed! Curse your impidence!—No harm! Why, how do I know but it's a robber you are, maybe? Faith I b'lieve I'd best rise the house and own this thing to the colonel.'

'Betty dear,' said Rory very quietly;' 'have a little wit in your anger, *agra!* think o' your *characther*, Betty.'

'Oh my character, my character, sure enough it's ruined for ever! Oh, what'll I do!' And she was going to cry and make a fool of herself when Rory reminded her that crying would do no good.

'The curse o' Crum'll an you: what brought you nigh the place at all? and who are you?'

'No matther who I am, but I tell you what is the best thing you can do: jist let me stay quietly in the house until the dawn, and thin let me out unknownst.'

'Oh, I darn't, I darn't,' said Betty. 'Sure if you wor seen quittin' the place, 'twould be the ruin o' me.'

'By dad! I must quit it some time or other,' said Rory: 'and sure if you let me out now itself, maybe the colonel will hear the door opening; or even if he doesn't, sure the sojers is now on the watch, and would catch me.'

'Oh, you mustn't go out by the front,' said Betty: 'I'll let you out into the garden at the back, and you must get over the wall, for here you mustn't stay—that's tee-totally out o' the question.'

'Well, anything for a quiet life,' said Rory; 'do what you plaze with me: but I think, as I am here, you might as well let me sit up here till towards mornin'.'

'No, no, no!' said Betty, in great tribulation. 'Who knows but Darby might come and then what in the wide world would I do?'

'You should keep him out,' said Rory.

'Out, indeed!' said Betty,—'keep Darby out! Sure, he'd suspec' somethin' wasn't right, for he's as jealous as a turkey-cock, and he'd murdher me if he thought how it was. Oh, what brought you here at all?'

At this moment, some pebbles were thrown against the area window.

'Oh, by this and that,' said Betty, 'there he is.—Oh, what'll become o' me?'

'Tut! woman alive,' said Rory, who endeavoured to make her attend, for she became almost confounded by the difficulty of her situation and was clapping her hands and uttering a volley of Ohs,—'Tut! woman, don't be clappin' your hands like a washer-womam and makin' an uproar, but jist let me out smart into the garden and I'll get over the wall, as you towld me.'

Betty seemed aroused to action by Rory's suggestion, and now led hin to a back window, which she opened carefully; and telling Rory to get out softly, she handed him a chair, and then followed herself. She conducted him then to the end of the garden, and placing the chair close to the wall, she held it firmly, while Rory got upon the back rail, which enabled him to lay his hands on the top of the brickwork, and he soon scrambled up and dropped himself on the outside. On his landing, he ran as fast and lightly as he could from the quarter where the sentinels were placed, and so far escaped unobserved, and continued in a straight line up a narrow street that opened from one of the corners of the green. Here he paused a while before deciding which way he should proceed; for, in the hurry of leaving the house, he never thought of asking Betty which was the way to go. Rory took the first turn out of this street that chance suggested, and was getting on famously, as he thought; but while in the very act of congratulating himself on his wonderful deliverance from the soldiers he turned another corner, a was scarcely round it, when a startling 'Who's there?' was uttered a few paces ahead of him, and the rattling of a firelock accompanied the challenge.

Rory saw the game was up, and that after all his former luck, it was his fate to become a prisoner; so he approached the point whence he was challenged, and said, 'A friend,'

'Advance and give the countersign,' said the sentinel, emerging from a sentry box.

'I haven't sitch a thing about me, sir,' said Rory.

XIII

In which Rory remembers the old saying of
'put that in your pipe and smoke it.'

WHEN RORY COULD NOT GIVE the countersign nor produce a pass, the sentinel told him he was his prisoner, and must remain in his custody until the guard should be relieved; to which Rory made not the least objection.

To all the soldier's questions as to where he had been and what brought him out at that hour of the night, Rory gave ready but evasive answers, until, the first moment of surprise being past, he had to to invent such replies as would least embarrass him in any subsequent examination he might undergo; and was so far successful, that the soldier believed him to be a peasant who was abroad at that hour through his own ignorance.

Rory now thought of General Hoche's letter, and began to feel uneasy at the possession of such a document. Under the *surveillance* of the sentinel he could not well manage to tear it; and even if he had, it being found near the spot, would prove a suspicious circumstance against him. In this dilemma, an ingenious thought occurred to him. Stooping, as it were to rub his leg, he soiled his fingers with the mud upon his shoes, and then introducing his hand into the pocket which held the letter, he dabbled it with the dirt to take off its look of freshness, and doubled it together in narrow folds, so as to resemble those billets of paper which the Irish peasantry so commonly stick in their hats for the purpose of lighting their pipes. This, the thin texture

of the foreign paper enabled him the better to do; and Rory then
stuck the dangerous document into his hatband, where he trusted to
its remaining without exciting suspicion.

In about half an hour the guard was relieved, and Rory was handed
over to the patrol, who marched him into the guard-house of the
barrack, up to whose very walls it was his ill-luck to have directed
his steps on leaving the colonel's house. Rory entered the place of
durance with the greatest composure, and began talking to the soldiers
with the most admirable *nonchalance.*

'Faix, I'm glad I had the luck to fall in with you!' said he, 'for I didn't
know where in the world to go; and here I am undher a good roof,
with a fine fire in the place.'

The soldiers did not attend to him much, but crowded round the
fire, while the sergeant went to make his report to the officer of the
guard that a prisoner had been brought in.

The officer happened to be a very raw ensign, who having late
joined, and being moreover by nature a consequential coxcomb, was
fond of giving himself all the airs in which a position of authority
could permit him to indulge, much to his own personal delight and
the good of his Majesty's service.

When the sergeant had announced his own presence before his
superior officer by the respectful enunciation of 'Plaze your honour,'
he stood as upright as his own halberd—and he had just about as
much brains,—with his arms and hands stuck straight and close to his
side, until the ensign thought fit to lift his gooseberry eyes from the
novel he was reading. When he vouchsafed to look at the sergeant, he
said, 'Whet's your business?'

'The pattherowl, your honour, has tuk a presner.'

'Where did they make the arrest?'

'The rest, your honour? there's no more o' them, your honour.'

'I say, where did they capture him?'

'Oh! they did nothing to him, your honour, until they have your
honour's ordhers.'

'Confound you! I say where did they take him in?'

'They have tuk him into the guard-house, your honour.'

'You horrid individual! I mean, where was he found?'

'In the sthreet, your honour.'

'You beast! What street?'

'Butthermilk-street, your honour.'

'Near the barrack?'

'Yis, your honour.'

'Has he any accomplices?'

'We have not searched him yet, your honour.'

'Confound you!—I mean, was he in company?'

'Yis, your honour; he says he was in company, but they turned him out, your honour.'

'Then he was alone?'

'Yis, your honour.'

'Have you searched him?'

'No, your honour.'

'Demneetion, sir! You should always search a prisoner the first thing—you don't know but a prisoner may have concealed arms or treasonable papers on his person. Search him directly.'

'Yis, your honour,' said the sergeant, raising his arm like the handle of a pump, and when he had it at full length, doubling it up from his elbow till his hand, as flat as a fish-knife, touched his head: then deliberately reversing all these motions until his arm was back again at his side, he turned on his heel, and was leaving the room, when the ensign, calling him back again, said, with an air of great authority,

'I never expect to hear of such a gross breach of discipline and neglect of duty again; never report a prisoner in my presence without being able to answer all such important questions as I have been asking you; and for this purpose let your first duty be always to search him directly. Go, now, and report to me again when the person of this prisoner has undergone rigid inspection. Retire!'

'Yis, your honour,' said the serjeant, repeating his salute with his usual solemnity, and stalking from the room into the guard-house.

Now, the room where the officer sat was a small apartment partitioned off the guard-house; and Rory, whose ears were open, heard every word of the officer's magniloquence and the serjeant's stupidity; and so soon as he heard the order about searching, and the words 'treasonable papers,' he thought that to let the letter remain in existence would be only running an unnecessary risk; so he very deliberately approached the fire, and having taken Hoche's letter from his hatband, he spoke to some soldiers who were sitting round the hearth all unmindful of what was going forward between the officer and the serjeant, and, handing them the letter twisted up in the form of a match for lighting a pipe, he said,

'I beg your pardon for being so throublesome, gintlemnen, but would you oblige me to light this taste of paper for me to kindle my pipe? for indeed it's mighty cowld, and I'm lost with the wet.'

One of the soldiers did as he required; for the request was so natural, and Rory's manner so cool, that no suspicion was awakened of the importance of the document on whose destruction Rory's life or death depended, and the lighted paper was handed him over the shoulders of the party that enclosed the fire, and Rory lighted his pipe with a self-possession that would have do honour to an American Indian. From the wetting the letter had sustained while exposed in Rory's hat, it burned slowly; so, when he heard the serjeant coming from the officer's room, and his feigned match not yet consumed, he leaned over the back of the soldier who had obliged him, and saying, 'Thank you kind sir,' he threw the remainder of the paper into the fire, just as the serjeant returned to execute the ensign's order.

The search instituted upon Rory's person produced no evidence against him. When it was over, he sat down and smoked his pipe very contentedly. In a few minutes another prisoner made his appearance, when a second party, who had been relieving guard, came in. This man was making loud protestations that he was not the person the soldiers took him for; but his declarations to this effect seemed to produce no belief on the part of the guard.

'I wonder you were not afraid to come to the place again, after having escaped once before,' said one of the sentinels who brought him in.

'I tell you again, I never was there before,' said the man.

'Bother!' said the sentinel, 'you won't do an old soldier that way.'

'By this and that,' said the prisoner.

'Whisht, whisht!' said the soldier; 'sure we were looking for you before; however, you contrived to give us the slip.'

'I gave you no slip,' said the prisoner; 'I tell you again, 'twas the first time I was there.'

'Fudge!' said the soldier: 'how did the bell ring?'

'Divil a bell I rung,' said the man.

Rory understood in an instant how this mystification took place: he suspected at once this must be Darby, who had thrown the pebbles that startled Betty so much; and, while he laughed in his sleeve at the poor husband being mistaken for the person who had disturbed the colonel's house, he continued to smoke his pipe with apparent indifference to all that was going forward, and did not as much as look up at the prisoner. It was absurd and whimsical enough, certainly, that Betty should first have mistaken him for Darby, and then that Darby should be mistaken by the soldiers for him. Darby still continued to protest his innocence of any previous approach to the house; but the soldiers could not be persuaded out of their senses, as they themselves said; and so the affair concluded by Darby being desired to sit down beside his fellow-prisoner.

Rory now looked at him, to see what sort of a bargain Betty had made in a husband, and, to his surprise, he beheld one of the men he had seen in the cellar. A momentary look of recognition passed between them, and then they withdrew their eyes, lest the bystanders should notice their intelligence.

'Where will the adventures of this night end!' thought Rory to himself.

But all adventures must have an end at last, and this chapter of Rory's accidents came to a close next morning; in the meantime, however, Rory stretched himself on the guard-bed when he had finished his pipe, and slept soundly. It may be wondered at that he could sleep under such exciting circumstances, and still in a perilous situation; but when we remember all the fatigues he had gone through the preceding day, it does not seem extraordinary that sleep should have favoured one like Rory, who was always full of hope, and did not know what fear meant.

XIV

In which it appears that one man's sin may prove another man's salvation.

IN THE MORNING HE WAS awoke by a prodigious drumming; and various other drummings, and fifings, and trumpetings, &c., went forward, with paradings and such military formula: these being finished, Rory and Darby were conducted from the guard-house, and led into the presence of the colonel, whom Rory recognised for his coal-hole acquaintance of the preceding night.

Rory, on being questioned as to what brought him into the streets at such an hour, said that he was a stranger in the town; that it being market-day, he went with some 'boys' to have some drink, and that he became drowsy and fell asleep in a public house that subsequently he was awoke, and that he then saw other people in the room; that a quarrel arose; that they did not seem to like his company, and 'at last,' said Rory, ' they gave me a hint to go.'

'What hint did they give you?' said the colonel.

'They kicked me down stairs, your honour,' said Rory.

A laugh followed Rory's exposition of what a hint was, and he thought it in his favour; for when serious charges and inquiries are going forward, Momus is the best counsel a prisoner can retain.

'That's rather a strong hint,' said the colonel.

'I thought so myself, your honour,' said Rory; 'and so when they kicked me down stairs, I suspected it was time to go.'

'But, my good fellow,' said the colonel, noticing Rory's fine proportions and bold eye, though Rory endeavoured to look as innocent it as he could, 'I don't think you seem like a fellow that would take such a hint quietly.'

'Why, your honour, I'm behowlden to you for your good opinion and indeed it's thrue, I'm proud to say; but what could I do agin a dozen? I offered to bate them all round singly; but they would not listen to rayson, and so they shoved me outside the door; and there I was in the sthreet, knowin' no more than the child unborn where to turn, or where to go look for a bed.'

'I'll have the keeper of that public-house punished for having it open at such an hour.—Where is it?'

'Indeed and I don't know,' said Rory.

The colonel looked incredulous. He questioned Rory more closely, who fenced very ingeniously; but still the suspicions of the colonel were excited, and he said at last,

'Your account of yourself, my good fellow, is rather confused.'

'No wondher, your honour, when I was dhrunk all the time.'

'That won't do,' said the colonel, who continued in a severe tone,— 'I suspect you're a deep fellow, sir, and know more than you choose to tell, and therefore I'll hand you over to the serjeant.—here serjeant.' That functionary advanced. 'Serjeant,' said the colonel, 'take this fellow to the halberds,—the drummers give him a dozen, and see if that will refresh his memory.'

Rory's heart almost burst with indignation at the thought of the degradation, and he became first as red as crimson and then as pale as death with rage.

'Ha!' said the colonel, seeming to enjoy the pallor his threat had produced, and which he mistook for fear,—'we'll see, my fine fellow, what you think of the hints the drummers will give you!'

In an instant Rory's invention came to his aid; and though, could he have indulged his desire, he would have had the colonel placed before him on equal terms, and could have plucked out his tyrannous heart for the degradation he would inflict on him, still he kept down his rising wrath, and let finesse accomplish what he knew force could never achieve; so, with as much calmness as he could muster, he said,

'I'd be sorry, sir, to put the serjeant to so much throuble; and, if you'll be good enough to clear the room, I'll tell you something you'd like to know, sir.'

'You may tell it out before all,' said the colonel.

'Plaze your honour,' said Rory, who now had recovered his self-command, and enjoyed the thought of foiling cruelty by craft,—'your honour, it's something you wouldn't be *plazed* every one should hear.'

'How shouldn't I be pleased? There's nothing you can tell, fellow, that I should care if the whole world knew.'

'Av coorse not, your honour,' said Rory, with affected reverence; 'but at the same time, if you b'lieve me, sir, it will be betther for no one but *yourself* to know of it.'

'Clear the room, then,' said he to the serjeant. 'You may remain, Mr. Daw.' This was said to the ensign who was officer of the guard.

'No one but yourself, if you plaze, your honour,' said Rory.

The colonel at first imagined that this was some desperate fellow who had concealed arms about him, and meant to take his life; but remembering he had been searched in the guard-house, his personal security no longer was matter of question, and there was a certain meaning that Rory threw into his manner which influenced him to grant the prisoner's request to be alone with him.

'Well, what's this wonderful secret you've to tell!' said the colonel when they were alone.

'Why, sir,' said Rory, affecting great embarrassment, and rubbing his hand up and down the table before which he stood, as if he were ashamed of what he had to communicate, 'I'm loath to tell you a'most, sir, begging your honour's pardon but—'

'Quick, sir, quick!' said the colonel impatiently.

'It's all thrue what I towld you, sir, about bein' a sthranger in the town, and comin' over jist to—'

'The fact, sirrah!' said the colonel,—'the fact—tell me what's this secret of yours.'

'Yis, your honour, that's what I want to *insense* your honour about.'

'You'd incense any one with your delay, fellow. Come to the fact, I tell you—What's this secret?'

Rory fixed his eyes on the colonel while he proceeded.

'You see, sir—I beg your honour's pardon, and hope you won't be offinded with me—but in the regard of Misther—' and he lowered his voice to a mysterious pitch.

'Who?' said the colonel, on whom Ray had his eye fixed like a hawk.

'Mister *Scrubbs*, sir,' said Rory.

The colonel winced: Rory saw he had

"Tented him to the quick;'

and now he felt the game was in his hands.

'What of him?' said the colonel, recovering himself, but yet with a very altered tone of voice to that in which he had hitherto pursued his interrogatories.

'Why, sir, your honour—you'll excuse, me, I hope,—aud wouldn't offind your honour for the world,—but I thought it best not to mention anything about it while the people was here, becaze people is curious sometimes and might be makin' their remark; and I thought I could betther give your honour a hint when nobody would be the wiser of it.'

'I'm not any wiser myself of it yet,' said the colonel.

'No, of coorse, your honour, seein' I was loath to mention the thing a'most for fear of your honour thinkin' I was takin' a liberty; but the misthiss—*Missis* Scrubbs I mane, your honour—' and Rory here stuck his eyes into the colonel again.

'Well,' said the colonel.

'I knew she was over here with a *frind*, your honour, and I knew that she did not expec' the masther down—the collector, I mane.'

'Well,' said the colonel.

'And I thought it best to tell her that I heerd the masther is comin' down to-morrow, and av coorse *your honour knows* he would not be plazed if the misthiss wasn't in the place, and might *suspect*, or the like. I hope your honour is not offended?'

The emphasis on '*your honour knows*' and '*suspect*' was accompanied by sly smiles and winks, and significant nods; and the colonel saw clearly that Rory was possessed of the knowledge of his intrigue with Mrs. Scrubbs, and that the best thing he could do was to make him his friend; so he said very gently,

'Offended! my good fellow, not at all. And so you came over to tell your mistress?'

'I thought it best, sir; for indeed she is a pleasant lady, and I wouldn't for the world that she'd get into throuble, nor your honour aither.'

'Well, here is something to drink my health.'

'Oh, your honour, sure I wouldn't.'

'I insist upon it,' said the colonel, forcing five guineas into Rory's hand, who did all in his power not to take them: for, though he hesitated not to execute this man to save his life, he did not like receiving money on a false pretence.

'Indeed, thin, I never intended to take money, nor to tell your honour of it at all—only the misthiss, but for the quare accident that brought me before your honour.'

'I'm glad I've seen you,' said the colonel, 'to reward your fidelity to your mistress: she shall be home before to-morrow.'

'Throth, then I pity her to be obleeged to lave so iligant a gintleman.'

'Hush!' said the colonel.

'Mum!' said Rory, winking and laying his finger on his nose: 'but sure you're the divil among the women, colonel!'

The colonel was pleased at the compliment paid to his gallantry; and merely saying to Rory, 'Be discreet,' he called in the persons who were waiting in wonder outside to know what important communication had been going forward.

'This man is free,' said the colonel; 'I'm quite satisfied with his explanations. And, serjeant, take him with you to the adjutant's office, and let him have a pass.'

This was a bit of finesse on the colonel's part, to make it appear that it was on public, not private grounds, he gave Rory his freedom; for at this period a pass from a commanding officer empowered the bearer to go unmolested at all hours, and was entrusted only to emissaries or known friends of government.

The colonel was so thrown off his guard by Rory's *ruse de guerre*, that he never asked his name; so Rory obtained his pass without being known, and then turned his face homeward. As he rattled along the road, high in spirits, as men always are when they have conquered difficulties, his head was in a whirl at the retrospect of the various adventures which had befallen him within four-and-twenty hours.

'First, I meet French missionaries' (he meant emissaries, but no matter), then I get all the news o' what's goin' on that will astonish the world,—then I get a *rale* letther from Gineral Hoche—Ah! there's the murdher!—the letter's gone. Bad cess to it! why couldn't I conthrive to keep it? But no matther—afther all, it might be worse, sure; if 'twas found I'd be hanged.—Not that I'd care so much for that, as the thing being *blown*.—Indeed, I might have been hanged maybe, afther all; only I knew about the colonel's purty doings.—Well, well,—to think that the sins of one woman should save the life of another man! But that's the will o' God and the blessed Vargin.—And to think I should not only get home safe, but have five goolden guineas in my pocket into the bargain!—Throth, Rory, luck's on your side, my boy!'

Now, it was not merely luck was on Rory's side, for he turned all the accidents to good account which would have been thrown away on a fool; and this, after all, is what makes the difference, in ninety-nine cases out of every hundred, between a lucky and an unlucky man. The unlucky man often plays life's game with good cards and loses; while the lucky man plays the same game with bad ones, and wins. Circumstances are the rulers of the weak;—they are but the instruments of the wise.

XV

Being a mixture of romance and reality.

THE INTEREST WHICH DE LACY felt on Rory's return, in listening to the important intelligence he brought, was mingled with amusement at the adventurous way in which he had conducted the enterprise. The loss of the letter he did not much regard, as the most valuable information it could have conveyed was in his possession, namely, the preparation of the extensive armament for the invasion of the island: and, under the circumstances, he not only did not blame Rory for the mishap, but gave him great credit for his courage and intelligence; for Rory had communicated to him every particular of his adventures. De Lacy blamed De Welskein for holding the unlicensed communion Rory described in his cellar, and assured O'More he was not aware that such was the smuggler's practice when he sent him on his mission.

'You don't imagine, Rory, that I would countenance nor be the companion of such ruffians?'

'To be sure you wouldn't, sir,' said Rory; 'and I hope you don't think I'd suppose such a thing.'

'No; but as you were sent there by me, I wish you to understand—'

'Oh, sir, I don't mind such a thrifle,' said Rory.

'I don't think it a trifle,' said De Lacy.

'But sure, if it was you was there, of coorse he wouldn't have done the like by you, sir.'

'He dare not, the rascal but that's not enough, he shouldn't have treated my agent so: but, to be sure, in these affairs one must not be too particular. They say poverty makes men acquainted with strange bedfellows; and revolutions must do the same thing.'

Yet, much as De Lacy strove to reconcile the thing to his feelings, his delicacy revolted at the scene of brutal debauch that Rory, a pure-hearted peasant, was made the witness and partly the partaker of. De Lacy was in every way an enthusiast: he believed in that high standard of human virtue which could sacrifice all for virtue's sake; his love of liberty was pure,—unstained by one unholy motive, and however munch he might be blamed by those who thought the cause in which he was engaged unjustifiable, or even flagitious, his motives at least were high and noble; they might be called mistaken, but not unworthy.

And of all worldly things did De Lacy think with as high a tone of feeling, and as deep a confidence in humanity. His profession as a soldier, his present exploit as a patriot, and his love as a man, were all undertaken and pursued with a feeling belonging rather to the age of chivalry than the time in which he lived. Or it might be perhaps more truly said, belonging to his own particular period of existence,—that glorious spring-time when every leaf of life is green, and the autumn of experience has not laid the withering tint of distrust upon one. The age of chivalry, did I say? Oh! every young and noble heart has its own age of chivalry!

De Lacy's love has been once mentioned before—at least glanced at and it may be as well to give some slight notion of that event, so interesting in most people's lives. Not that De Lacy's love has much to do with the events about to be recorded but as it will be necessary to touch upon it perhaps elsewhere, the reader may just be given a peep into the affair; besides, it will help to exhibit the refined nature of De Lacy's mind.

He had left behind him in Paris a girl to whom he was deeply attached, and by whom he believed himself to be ardently beloved. But Adèle Verbigny was unworthy of such a love as De Lacy', inasmuch as she could not understand it. Love was with her a necessity: she thought it quite indispensable that every young lady should have a lover; and if that lover was a hero, so much the better. Now, De Lacy happened to be a handsome fellow and a soldier; and when he volunteered to under take the dangerous mission to Ireland, she was charmed, because that her *Horace* should be the 'saviour of a nation,' &c., &c., she considered a triumph to herself. So, babbling in the exaggerated jargon of the feverish time in which she spoke, she said she offered up the hopes of her heart, &c. upon the altar of Freedom &c., and desired him to go and disenthral his native land from the yoke of tyranny, &c., and return crowned with laurels to enjoy her love, &c.

De Lacy believed the little Parisian felt all she said, and loved her better than ever. While he was yet uncertain of the moment of his departure, he received a peremptory summons from the Directory to start immediately with a government courier to the coast. He hastened to the house of his Adèle to take a tender farewell. Her mother met him as he entered the apartment

'Hush,' said she; 'Adèle sleeps.'

'I have not a moment to wait,' said De Lacy; 'I'm summoned on the instant to depart.'

'You see she sleeps,' said the mother: 'she cried so much last night at the separation of the lovers in the play, that she was quite overcome. Her nerves have been shattered all day, and she went asleep just now on the sofa to restore herself.'

'Sweet soul!' said De Lacy—'poor Adèle! if she wept at a fictitious separation, what would she suffer at a real one! I will not wake her— no—mine be the pain of parting. Tell her,' said he tenderly, and he looked at the sleeping girl while he spoke to her mother,— 'tell her I go to fulfil my duty to my country. I will return with its blessings and the laurels of victory to lay at her feet, and then I shall be worthy of her.' He knelt to kiss her, but paused. 'No,' he said, 'I might awake her: this is all I shall take,' and he gently drew a flower from the folds of her dress,—''tis a type of her beauty, her sweetness, and her innocence!' He then rose and hurried to depart. 'Farewell, mother,' said he,—'permit me to call you so,—and tell Adèle why I would not wake her; and will she not love me the better when she knows how much I renounced in relinquishing the parting charm of a kiss and a blessing from her own bright lips!' He could trust himself to say no more, and he rushed from the house.

Adèle's mother was rather astonished, for the refinement of feeling that had prompted De Lacy was quite unintelligible to her; and, as she snuffed the candles when he left the room, she said, '*Ma foi, que cet home-là est drôle!*'

The ravings of De Lacy during his dangerous illness had been divided between the recollection of Adèle and anticipation of the intended revolutionary struggle. On his recovery, however, his mind reverted more pleasurably to the former subject than the latter; for, to his enfeebled nerves, love was a theme more congenial than war.

In such a frame of mind it was that De Lacy sat in his bedroom, a few days after his recovery, with some papers lying before him, and his eyes resting on the flower he had taken from the bosom of Adèle the night he had parted from her. He thought of the circumstances of that parting; and as the sleeping girl was recalled to his fancy, his heart went through all the emotions of that parting again, through the influence of an imagination always vivid, but now rendered more delicately sensitive through the agency of that susceptibility of nerve which the languor succeeding a severe illness produces, and the fulness of his heart and the excitement of his fancy found vent in recording his farewell and the emotions of that moment in verse; and, dedicating to his Adèle the inspiration of his muse, he wrote the following:—

SONG

I

Sleep, my love—sleep, my love,
Wake not to weep, my love,
Though thy sweet eyes are all hidden from me:
Why shouldst thou waken to sorrows like mine, love,
While thou may'st, in dreaming, taste pleasure divine, love?
For blest are the visions of slumbers like mine, love—
So sleep thee, nor know who says 'Farewell to thee!'

II

Sleep, my love—sleep, my love,
Wake not to weep, my love,
Though thy sweet eyes are all hidden from me:
Hard 'tis to part without one look of kindness,
Yet sleep more resembles fond love in its blindness,
And thy look would enchain me again: I find less
Of pain to say, 'Farewell, sweet slumb'rer, to thee!'

Thus, in writing and reading,—for De Lacy had a few choice books with him,—some days were passed; but his strength began to return, and he was soon able to walk abroad. In his rambles, a book was mostly his companion; and it was the frequency of his being observed by the country people in the act of reading that he obtained the name of the 'Scholar,' for so he became universally called by the peasants, who liked him for his courteous manner, and the freedom with which he conversed with them. Who and what he was, they did not care; but not so little Sweeny and Scrubbs, who used to exchange mutual 'wonders' with each other as to 'What the deuce he could be?—What brought him there?—What he was about?' &c. &c.; and the conclusion they always arrived at was, both shaking their heads very significantly, and saying, 'Very odd!' De Lacy avoided the village in his walks. In the first place, the retirement of the quiet banks of the river, or the wildness of the hills above it, were more congenial to his temper; and secondly, he wished to keep himself beyond the range of observation as much as possible. With reading and sketching, and making short excursions into the adjacent country, his days passed pleasantly enough, while all the time he was taking note of what he saw and heard; for though the expected assistance from the Texel, of which he was in daily hopes of receiving intelligence, rendered it unnecessary to write to General Clarke on the subject, as the blow he expected would be struck without any urgency on his part, yet his own anxiety to acquire a knowledge of the internal state of the country stimulated his inquiries. Old Phelim, the schoolmaster, was often questioned on such matters; and his oddity amused, while his information satisfied, De Lacy.

It might be supposed by the general reader that, engaged in such a cause as De Lacy had then was, an introduction to the parish priest would have been held desirable; but it was not so—far from it. De Lacy, in common with all the leaders of the political movement then going forward in Ireland desired to shun by every possible means any contact with the priesthood. The results of the French Revolution had given the alarm to the clergy of all denominations; and the Irish Roman Catholic priests, so far from countenancing the introduction of revolutionary principles into Ireland, had refused absolution to 'The Defenders,' a political union formed amongst the lower orders of the *Catholic* Irish, to protect themselves from the aggressions of the 'Peep-o'-day Boys, who were Protestants and Presbyterians. The dominant party in Ireland have endeavoured to propagate the belief that the rebellion of 1798 was of religious origin, and put in practice for the murder of all the Protestants in Ireland; but what is the fact? The society of United Irishmen was first established in the North of Ireland, where the majority of the population was Protestant and Presbyterian. It was by *Protestants and Presbyterians* the society was founded, and Protestants and Presbyterians were its principal leaders. So, to credit the Orange account of the affair, we must believe that the Protestants originated the ingenious device of organising a revolution to murder themselves

The truth is, the revolution then contemplated was *purely political*. When the repeated calls for reform in the Irish parliament and a repeal of the penal laws against Catholics were refused till disappointuient grew into despair, then, and not till then, did the people coalesce to take by force what they had vainly sought by petition. The Catholics, from the very nature of their religion, its feudal character, and its habits of slavish subjection, would never have dared to rebel. It was the stern Presbyterians, reformers by descent, that organised the movement to relieve Ireland from the political degradation in which she then was prostrated, and long oppression at last roused the Roman Catholics to make common cause with them.

These facts I mention, lest it might be considered inconsistent that De Lacy should not have been in league with Father Kinshela, who so far

from countenancing the influence of Frenchmen in Ireland, considered
the Gallic revolution and all its emissaries to be quite as pestilential as
they were deemed to be by the staunchest Protestants in the land.

XVI

*An 'Irish' fair with only 'one' fight in it.—De Welskein's metamorphoses.—
Learned pigs.—Roasted ducks.—Love and murder, &c., &c.*

DE LACY BEEN FOR SOME days in expectation of going to a
neighbouring fair, which has the reputation of being a scene of
great merriment in Ireland, and a very characteristic thing; and as he
had not witnessed such a meeting, his curiosity was not a little excited.
It was agreed that he and Rory, as well as his sister, with her suitor
Conolly,—who, by the way, was not a favoured, though a devoted
lover,—should form a party, to which Phelim O'Flanagan begged to
be added, and the request was granted.

'You must not expect, though,' said Rory, addressing De Lacy, 'that
we'll have as much fun as usual; for, you see, the people being more
united, they won't fight as much as they do in common, and the
factions is laid down by common consint until matthers get smooth
again;—and when we have justice and happiness among us once more,
why thin we can enjoy our private battles according to the good owld
fashion.'

'That's the thing that surprises me,' said De Lacy,—'why you are so
fond of factions. You are good-humoured and pleasant fellows enough
individually; but when a set of you get together, you scarcely ever part
without fighting.'

'Why, you see, sir,' said Phelim, 'it is the nature of man to be
disputaarious in their various degrees,—kings for kingdoms—scholars

for argument—and so on; and the disputariousness of human nathur is as like to brake out about which barony is the best ball–players or hurlers, as if Roosia vindicated Proosia, or Proosia vindicated Roosia: for you know, sir, being a scholar, that the vindicativeness of nations to aitch other is no more than the vindicativeness of the human heart, which is as demonstherated in a parish, or a barony, or a townland, or the like, as in the more circumscribed circle of an impire or a principalatine, all as one as a circle is a circle, whatever the size of it may be, from a platther up to a cartwheel. Q. E. D. What *was* to be demonstherated!' and Phelim took snuff, as usual.

'Admirably demonstrated indeed!' said De Lacy, maintaining his gravity; 'but, if the matter in dispute be ball-playing or wrestling, would not the surest method of settling the business be, to play an equal match of either of the given games, instead of beating each other?'

'Arrah, what else do we do?' said Rory.

'You always fight, instead.'

'But how can we help that? Sure, we always *do* challenge each other to play a match of ball or hurling, and thin, in the coorse of play, one man gives a false ball, or another cuts it, and thin there's a dispute about it; or in hurlin', the same way, in the hate of the game, maybe the fellow before you is jist goin' to have the ball all to himself, and you afther him, hot foot, what can you do but give him a thrip? and away he goes head over heels, and if he's not disabled, there's a chance he loses his timper, and comes to thrip you,—when, maybe he is not so necessitated to thrip *you* as *you* wor to thrip *him*, and that doesn't stand to rayson in *your* opinion, and maybe you can't help givin' him a clip o' the hurl, and down *he* goes; and thin, maybe, one o' *his* barony sees that, and doesn't think it raysonable, and slaps at *you*,—and so on it goes like fire among flax, and the play turns into a fight in no time; and, indeed, in the long-run we find 'tis the best way of arguin' the point,—for there might be some fractious sperits would dispute about the fairness o' *this* play, or the fairness o' *that* play, and that it was an accident settled the game; but when it comes rale fightin', there can be no words about it,—for, you see, when you dhrive every mother's son o' them before you, and fairly leather them out o' the field, *there can be no mistake about it.*'

'But does not that produce bad blood amongst you?' said De Lacy.

'By no manes,' said Rory; 'why should it?   Sure, haven't they the chance of wollopin' us the next time?'

'And that perpetuates the dispute,' said De Lacy.

'To be sure,' said Rory; 'that's the fun of it. Oh, it would only be a cowardly thing to be always fightin' a party you were sure to bate!— there would be an end of the glory intirely.'

'All party,' thought De Lacy, 'is like Rory's game of hurling those who are *out* endeavour to trip up those who are in,—and, in conclusion, the only game left is to *leather them out of the field*; when there can be no mistake about it.'

It was the next day following Rory's and Phelim's eloquent, lucid, and reasonable exposition of the necessity and propriety of party fights, that the fair was holden, and the party, as already named, started for the scene of amusement:—Conolly having the honour of being gentleman in waiting on Mary O'More, handing her over stiles, &c.; Phelim and Rory bearing De Lacy company.

On arriving at the scene of action, they found the fair tolerably 'throng,' as the phrase is in Ireland, and the moment they were well on the ground, Conolly commenced the series of gallantries which every aspirant to a pretty girl's favour goes through on a fair-day, by buying a large stock of gingerbread cakes, which appear to have been made of brown paper and treacle, and apples to match, and requesting the whole party, including De Lacy, who was most politely solicited, to partake of the feast. Now, when people are at fairs, it is a point of honour to eat and drink, and see all that you can,—in short, till you can eat, and drink, and see no more; and all the party present, except De Lacy, seemed determined their honour should not be called in question. The cake and apple stands were generally formed by the common car of the country being backed into whatever position it could take up on the fair-ground; and the horse being unyoked, a forked pole of sufficient strength was stuck in the ground, and the backband of the car being deposited between the prongs, it at once

obtained support; after which some *wattles* (long supple boughs) being
bent over the vehicle, a quilt was thrown across these rustic rafters to
form an awning, and the cakes and apples were spread on some sacks,
perhaps, or something equally coarse,—anything, in short, to cover the
bare boards of the car, that probably carried a load of sand or earth,
or something not so agreeable, the day before, and was now at once
converted into a cake-shop. In one corner of the concern, a glass and
a black bottle, with *something in it*, were to be seen and under the car,
from the middle of a bundle of straw, you might perceive the muzzle
of a large jar protruding, whence the black bottle could be replenished
as occasion required.

Booths were erected for the accommodation of those who chose to
dance, and drink to refresh themselves; and both these amusements,—
that is to say, dancing and drinking,—seemed to be the staple
commodities of the fair, even at an early hour; but the dancing tents
were not in their full glory till much later in the day.

There was throwing for gingerbread, and other amusements
incidental to such scenes; but nothing very stirring in this line seemed
as yet to have set in. So the party strolled on through the crowd; Rory
remarking to De Lacy as they went, that he told him there would be
little or no fun—'And you see how quiet they are,' said Rory.

'God save you, Phelim,' said a well-dressed peasant.

'God save you kindly,' answered Phelim.

'How does the gossoons do without you, Phelim, agra?'

'Oh, I gev the craythurs a holiday,' said Phelim. 'I don't like to be
too hard on them. Exercise is good for the gossoons when they are at
college, for larnin' lies heavy on the stomach.'

'Thrue for you, Phelim. Not that I know much about larnin': but I
know you mustn't break the heart of a young cowlt.'

And so saying, off Phelim's friend went.

They now approached a portion of the fair where sales of cattle
were going forward.

'How is the bastes goin'?' said Rory to a farmer.

'Indeed, it's back they be goin',' said the farmer: 'there's no prices at
all here—that is, for bastes; but I hear pigs is lively.'

'What's thim I see up on the hill?' said Rory. 'Is it sojers?'

'No less,' said the farmer; 'though, indeed, they might save themselves the throuble,—they kem here to watch us; but there won't be a blow sthruck to-day.'

'Thrue for you,' said Rory; and so they parted.

They next approached a show-box, where an exhibition of Punch and Judy seemed to give great amusement. That interesting domestic history was about halfway through when our hero and his party arrived; and Rory had been telling in a hasty manner to Mary the nature of Punch's adventures as they approached 'Make haste now,' said Rory, 'for it's bether nor a play. I seen a play when I was in Dublin; but Punch and Judy is worth two of it. Run! run! there he is goin' to kill his wife and child, the comical owld blackguard!'

They arrived in time to witness the death of Mrs. Punch and the child, and then the doctor was sent for. The doctor made his appearance; and Punch, after his legitimate squeak, began—

'Docta-w-r!'—'Sare?' said the doctor.

'Can you cure my wife?'—

'Yes, sare.'

'What will you give her?'

'Some *ghost's* milk.'

Rory started. 'By all that's good, that's himself!' said he.

'Why is it a rale docthor?' said Mary.

'No, no,' said Rory. 'I was only—' he paused, and withdrawing from Mary, he beckoned De Lacy from the group, and said, 'That's Mr. Devilskin that's there,' pointing to the show-box.

'Where?' said De Lacy.

'There' said Rory, pointing again; 'inside the show-box. I'd take my oath it's him. I thought I knew his voice at first; but I'd sware to the *ghost milk.*'

'I want to see him,' said De Lacy, 'and am glad of this chance meeting. We must watch an opportunity to speak to him when the show is over.'

While they were waiting for this, a group of horsemen approached the show, and Rory amongst them saw Squire Ransford, the parson,

Sweeny, and Scrubbs; the latter engaged in conversation with 'the colonel'—he who had given Rory his freedom and his pass. Rory saw there was nothing for it but to retreat, as, if he were seen, his whole finesse about Mrs. Scrubbs would be blown, he would get into trouble, and his name be in the colonel's possession, who, it will be remembered, had never, in his hurry to dismiss our hero, asked who he was. Therefore, screening himself behind De Lacy, he told him how matters stood, and taking Mary and Conolly with him, he left De Lacy with Phelim for a guide.

'If we don't meet again in the fair,' said Rory, 'we must only wait till we go home;' and he retired rapidly from the spot unobserved by the horsemen who had caused his sudden retreat. Appointing then a place of rendezvous with Mary and Conolly, Rory left them, and they returned to witness the finale of Punch and Judy.

Rory pushed his way through the principal row of booths, where the dancing and drinking were going on prosperously, and entering that under whose sign his appointed meeting with his sister and her cavalier was to take place, he sat down, and calling for a small portion of drink, refreshed himself, intending when that was over to rest himself with the dancing. While he sat, he perceived Regan and Kathleen enter at the farther end of the booth, and his heart boundad at the sight of the girl he loved but his joy was damped at the thought that in her brother's presence he had better not approach her. To his unspeakable joy, however, he saw Regan depart, leaving Kathleen, after speaking a few words to her; and when he was some seconds gone, Rory moved towards the girl of his heart gaily, and, as her head was turned away, he proposed surprising her by his presence; so approaching unobserved, he tapped her smartly on the shoulder, and had his most winning smile ready to meet her when she should turn. When she did turn, instead of the flush of joy which Rory anticipated, a deadly paleness and a look of reserve were on the countenance of Kathleen, and Rory's blood ran cold to his heart.

'What's the matther, Kathleen dear?' said Rory.

Kathleen could not answer.

'What *is* the matther?—for God's sake, tell me!' said Rory impressively for he saw by the girl's manner that an unfavourable impression had been made upon her as regarded him.

'Rory,' said Kathleen, with that reproachful tone which an offended woman only can assume—'Rory,' said she, 'need you ask me?'

'What have I done, Kathleen jewel?'

'Oh, Rory! so soon to desaive and think light o' me!'

'Me, Kathleen!—by all that's good—'

'Whisht, Rory—whist!—swaring won't make it betther.'

'But what is it, Kathleen?'

'Oh, Rory! don't be so desaitful. You know you've wronged me!'

'By this blessed light! I never wronged you, Kathleen!'

There was something bearing such inherent evidence of sincerity in Rory' manner, that Kathleen hesitated for a moment, and looked inquiringly into his face; but suddenly withdrawing her eyes and dropping her voice, she said, 'I'd willingly b'lieve you, Rory—but—'

'But what?' said Rory.

'I don't like to accuse you, but you know—' again she paused.

'What?' said Rory, inipatiently.

'The cellar,' said Kathleen.

The word was enough. With all that magic rapidity of thought which instantaneously links a chain of circumstances together Rory saw that his conduct in De Welskein's cellar had been misrepresented; and when he remembered how the girl he had danced with had fastened herself upon him, he could not but see that circumstances might be made to bear hard against him in the opinion of the woman he was courting—he was silenced by Kathleen's one word—and she, mistaking his silence for guilt, was rising to leave the booth, when Rory, taking her hand and pressing it closely, said,

'Kathleen, you wrong me; I know what you mane, but—'

'Let go *my* hand,' said Kathleen. 'You had betther look for the hand of the *lady* you like so much; I b'lieve you can find her in the fair;' and she again made an effort to go, but Rory still detained her.

'Kathleen,' said he, 'it is only Shan Dhu could tell you this, and I did not think he had so black a heart; for, by this light—'

'Whist!' said Kathleen, in terror, 'lave me, lave me; Shan is coming back—I see him.'

'Well, promise to meet me till I clear myself to you.'

'Rory, don't be sthriving to desaive a poor girl—go, I tell you.'

'I won't go, unless you promise?'

'If you've any pity for me go; Shan is close by.'

'Promise!' said Rory, impressively.

'I will, then,' said Kathleen, faintly.

'Meet me by the rath, near the bridge,' said Rory, 'to-morrow evening. God bless you Kathleen, and never b'lieve I have the heart base enough to wrong you!'

So saying, he kissed her hand passionately before she could withdraw it, and slipping out through an opening in the side of the booth, he left it without being perceived by Regan. Poor Rory was heart-sick at the thought of Kathleen's coldness, and he looked forward with the impatience and longing of a child for the morrow's evening, which he hoped would serve to chase every doubt from her mind. While he was moving through the crowd, his attention was attracted by a party of mummers, who were parading up and down on a platform, in dirty rags sprinkled with rusty spangles, and amongst them he recognised the girl that had been so sweet on him in the cellar; he then remembered Kathleen's saying, 'I b'lieve you can find her in the fair,' and the thought struck him that Regan might have even pointed out the flourishing damsel before him as his paramour, and Rory's shame was increased, for, with her ruddled cheeks, short petticoats, and shabby finery, she was a most disgusting object, though rather a fine girl. While Rory looked at her, he fancied he caught her eye; and its brazen glare was for a moment darkened by a demoniac expression, and instantly withdrawn. He wished more and more for the evening of the morrow. On he went through the main chain of tents, but seeing the squire and colonel approaching again, he took a short turn round one of the booths and avoided them; and, making a detour, he returned to the place where he had appointed Mary and Conolly to meet him, and there he found them waiting. Joining company, they commenced another ramble through the fair, and at length reached a booth whence there proceeded much laughter, and at the door of which a bespangled buffoon was inviting the people to enter and see time wonderful conjuror who could tell fortunes on cards and cure all sorts of diseases. This promised much diversion, and the laughter continuing to appeal to the curiosity of those outside, a fresh party, including our hero, his sister, and her admirer, entered. Here they saw a man in a bag-wig and cocked hat, laced coat and ruffles, performing various sleight tricks with cards, and other feats of legerdemain; and after making his beholders' eyes the size of saucers with wonder, and their mouths of equal capacity, he proceeded to offer for sale various nostrums for the cure of diseases; amongst others, he produced one which he protested most solemnly was superior to *ghost's milk*.

'Devilskin again!' said Rory to himself; 'devilskin, sure enough!—more than the skin, by my sowl, for I think he's the d—l himself!'

Here was another metamorphose of the Frenchman. He was in his glory: he had a stall in the fair, in good hands, for the sale of tobacco, and he was masquerading it and making money in another quarter; a French agent in the middle of the fair, where the army were lookers-on to see that no mischief was going forward;—this was his glory, the intrigue and romance delighted him.

Rory left the booth—he did not wish to meet De Welskein's eye: not that he feared him—he could not tell very well himself the precise cause of his dislike to be recognised by the smuggler; but there was an undefined feeling about Rory, that rather shrunk from having anything to do with one who seemed invested with mysterious power.

He awaited outside the booth the egress of his sister and Conolly who suggested that it was time to get something for dinner. To this Rory assented;   for, notwithstanding that his meeting with Kathleen had damped his enjoyment, his appetite was of too keen and hale a nature to be influenced by a frown from his mistress, as those of more refined lovers are said to be.

'Not that I'm very hungry,' said Rory.

''Faith, then I am,' said Conolly; 'for exceptin' five or six dozen o' gingerbread and a score of apples or so, between us, Mary and I have not tasted anything to signify.'

'You were drinking my health very often, too,' said Mary.

'Phoo,—what signifies three or four quarts o' porther!'

While we leave this hungry party looking for their dinner, let us return to De Lacy and Phelim, whom we left opposite De Welskein's show-box.

De Lacy took his opportunity of speaking to the smuggler, whom he followed by a signal to a booth; and leaving Phelim standing outside by De Welskein's desire, he entered the booth, and a rude curtain was drawn across the orifice by which they came in. De Lacy now found himself in a small canvas apartment, from which, through the division in another curtain, he saw into a large space beyond the sentry-box sort of place in which he stood.

'Dis my teatre,' said De Welskein.

'What do you want a theatre for?'

'To 'muse myself—blind de vulgare—mak romaunce—*J'aime les aventures, vous savez, monsieur.*'

'I thought, smuggling——'

'Sare!' said De Welskein with dignity.

'I mean, your mercantile pursuits would have given you enough of employment.'

'*Bah!—bagatelle!*—everboddée can be *marchand*;—bote for *les intrigues*——'

'That requires a man of genius,' said De Lacy.

'Ah!—b'leeve so, indeet,' said De Welskein, with great self-complacency.

'But then your political mission, is not that enough to fill up any spare time you can withhold from your mercantile pursuits?'

'Yais—*c'est vrai—ordinairement*—for most peepel;—but me—love *intrigue*—romaunce—ha! ha!—besise—more hard for discover to *certen persun*. Dis day, marchand—to-mawrow, Ponshe an' Joodee—now me shange agen.'

Here he threw off his coat, and proceeded to take out of a canvas bag that lay under some straw in a corner, the laced coat and cocked-hat, wig, etc., in which Rory subsequently saw him attired.

'Now, me go play Doctair Duck.'

'What character is that?' said De Lacy.

'Quaak, quaak, quaak,' said De Welskein, with a spirit and vivacious expression worthy of the comedy for which his country is so famous.

De Lacy laughed.—'And do you get fees?'

'Certanlee:—no fee, no docteur, sell leetle peels—cure everyting—better dan *ghost's milk*.   Besise,' said he, pulling cards from his pocket, 'here more ting—hocus-pocus—poots card in fool's pauket—ha! ha!—mak dem stare—tink me de divil.'

'They're not far out,' thought De Lacy.

De Welskein having completed his attire, painted his face, rubbed burnt cork on his eyebrows, and shaken flour into his wig, he held some short conversation on the state of affairs over the water; and De Lacy, thinking it better not to remain too long in such company, brought his conference to a close as soon as possible; and after telling De Welskein where he could find him, he drew the ragged curtain, and emerged from the tiring-room of the adventurer.   Having rejoined Phelim, he asked him what was to be done next, for he determined to let Phelim do the honours of the fair.

'I hear there is a pig in the fair, sir,' said the cicerone.

'I've seen some hundreds already,' said De Lacy.

'Oh, you're very smart on me now,' said Phelim, 'and take me up short; but the pig I mane is a larned pig.'

'Indeed! where is he to be seen?'

'Somewhere up here, I hear. Now I'd like to see that above all things; for though I know to my cost that some childhre is no bether than pigs, either in manners nor intellex, I have yet to be *insensed* how a pig can be equal to a Chrishthan.'

They soon came within hearing of a fellow who was roaring at the top of his voice,—

'Walk in! walk in! walk in, ladies and gintlemen; here is the wondherful larned pig that knows the five quarters o' the world, and more;—together with his A. B. C. and apperceeand—and goes through his alphibhit backwards; together with addishin, substhracshin, multiplicashin, and divishin:—knows numerashin, minshurashin, navigashin, and *botherashin*—'

Here the crowd always laughed.

—'Together with varrious accomplishmints too numerous to be minshind,—smokes tabakky and tells cunnundherums.'

'Oh! do you hear the lies he's tellin'?' said Phelim; 'sure no pig could do the like, barring one pig that is minshind in anshint histery.'

'I don't remember that pig, Phelim,' said De Lacy.

'Pig—maylius!' said Phelim, bursting in triumph at having caught De Lacy in one of his old and favourite jokes.

De Lacy could not help laughing at the poor old man's whimsical conceit; and complimenting him on his wit, he proposed to Phelim that they should see if what was promised of the pig were true.

'Impossible!' said Phelim; 'it's only throwing away money.'

'We'll see, at all events,' said De Lacy, who paying sixpence, which was twopence more than was required for two admissions, he and the schoolmaster walked up a low step-ladder, which led to the place of exhibition, deafened, as they passed the crier, by his vociferating, 'Step up, ladies! jist goin' to begin. Step up, step up—all for tuppince—only tuppince; the larned pig, only tuppince for minsurashin, miditashin, contimplashin, navigashin, and *baw*-therashin!'

When the company had been collected in sufficient quantity, a shrewd-looking fellow, fantastically dressed, led in a pig by a string which was fastened to a ring in the animal's nose.

The pig ascended a circular platform, in the middle of which a pole was placed, and round the circle were several holes cut.

'Now, ladies and gintlemin,' said the showman, 'this is the larned pig, that is perfect masther of various branches of idicashin: and first and foremost, he will show you his knowledge of the five quarthers o' the world, aiqual to Captain Cook that purformed the circumlocution of the globe. Excuse me, ladies, till I give him his insthrucshins.'

Here he put his mouth to the pig's ear, and the pig grunted.

'He says he is happy to have the honour of your company, ladies.'

Here the showman was encouraged by a laugh from the spectators, who, all being willing to be pleased, laughed at a trifle.

'What did he say to him, do you think?' said Phelim to De Lacy confidentially.

'I suppose he gave him a pig's whisper,' said De Lacy.

'Good, sir, good,' said Phelim; 'by dad! you're always ready—a pig's whisper!—well, I'll never forget that!'

The showman now laid four pieces of card, with the names of the four quarters of the world written upon them, over four holes on the opposite parts of the circle, and said:

'Now, ladies, which o' the five quarters o' the world shall this wondherful scholar show you?—Europe, Asia, Afrikay, or Amerikay?'

'Amerikay, if you plaze, sir,' said a woman, who blushed excessively at hearing the sound of her own voice in public.

'Sartinly, ma'am. Show the lady Amerikay, sir.'

The animal now got a pull of the string, and he began poking his nose round the circle, and at last stopped at the quarter named, and shoved the card from over the hole.

Great applause followed, and the showman rewarded the pig by giving him an acorn. De Lacy saw at once how the trick was done; but to Phelim's question of 'Arrah, how did he do that?' he made no reply for the present.

The showman was about to remove the cards, when Phelim interrupted him:

'You said, sir, you'd show the five quarthers o' the world by manes o' your pig; and indeed if he knows five quarthers, it's more than I know.'

'To be sure he knows more than you know,' said the showman.

A burst of merriment followed this hit; for many of the spectators knew Phelim, and that a pig should be said to know more than he did, delighted them. When the laugh subsided Phelim continued:

'Maybe you don't know, my good fellow, that you are addhressing a Philomath?'

'A wat?'

'A philomath, sir.'

The showman now turned to the pig, and putting his mouth to his ear, as before, said:

'Can you tell me what is a filly-mat?'

The pig grunted again.

'He says, a filly-mat is a grumblin' owld fellow.' Another laugh against Phelim succeeded the showman's buffoonery, whose practised effrontery was too much for Phelim. Phelim, however, was too used to triumph to give in so easily, particularly in the presence of so many who knew him; and rallying once more, he said:

'Well, if there *is* a fifth quarter o' the world, will you be so good to tell the *other brute* there to show it.'

Phelim had the laugh on his side now. A laugh is a main point of argument with Paddy; and whoever has the last laugh, has the best of the battle in Ireland.

The showman waited till the laugh was lulled, and then addressing the pig, he said:

'Will you tell that ignorant owld fill-pot what the fifth quarter of the world is?'

The pig commenced rubbing himself against the upright stick that stood in the middle of the circle, much to the merriment the crowd.

'There!' said the showman triumphantly.

'Is that what you call answerin' the problem I have propounded?' said Phelim, who thought he had vanquished his man, and got magniloquent in consequence. 'I propound to yiz all—'

'If you were poundin' from this till to-morrow, you're nothing but a *bosthoon,*' said the showman.

Phelim absolutely staggered at the degrading epithet of *bosthoon* being applied to a *philomath*. The showman continued:

'Sure, if you worn't an owld bogie, you'd see that the pig was pointin' out to you the fifth quarter o' the world; but the fact is, *you* don't know that there is sitch a thing as the fifth quarter; but,' said he, making a flourishing appeal to his audience, 'ladies and gintlemin, you see the baste has pointed out to your comprehinshin the fifth quarter of the terrestorial globe, which is the North Pole!'

Phelim uttered an indignant 'Oh!' but his exclamation was drowned in the vociferous plaudits of the multitude.

'Lave the place! lave the place!' said Phelim to De Lacy, bursting with rage but De Lacy did not like to lose the fun, and thought Phelim more diverting than the pig.

'Stay,' said De Lacy; 'you'll expose his ignorance yet.'

Thus tempted, Phelim remained, maintaining a sulky silence, and watching for an opportunity of annihilating the pig and the showman.

The fellow put his pig through some alphabetical manoeuvres upon the same principle that the quarters of the globe had been pointed out, though the trick was unperceived by the spectators, who still continued to be delighted.

'Now, ladies and gintlemin,' said the proprietor of the pig, 'this divartin' baste will go through his alphabit backwards.'

'Maybe he could say the Lord's prayer backwards?' said Phelim, wishing to be severe.

'That would rise the d——l, as every fool knows,' said the showman, 'and that would not be agreeable to the company; otherwise he could do it aisy.'

'Hurrup, Solomon!' continued he, addressing the pig;—'(He is called Solomon, ladies; he is so wise;) go through your alphibit bakwars.'

Upon this the pig mode a retrograde movement round the circle, the showman exclaiming, when he had finished,

'That's doin' it backwards, I think!'

The people were tickled with the quibble, but Phelim said,

'That's only a *thrick.*'

'Well, it's *my* thrick, anyhow,' said the showman with readiness. 'You haven't won a thrick yet.'

Phelim was floored again.

By a similar quibble, the animal went through his multiplication table. A board, with a multiplication table upon it, had a swinging door hung in the middle; and this being placed before the pig, he went through it.

Some of the spectators asked to see the pig 'smoke tabakky,' as one of the things promised.

'He would with pleasure, ladies, but he bruk his pipe in the last exhibishin and there is not one convaynient,' was the answer 'but, what is much more curious, he will answer connundherums. Tell me, sir,' said he, addressing the pig, 'what does the ladies say when they are angry with their husbands?'

The pig grunted furiously.

This was the triumph of the day; the men laughed outrageously, and even the women could not help joining; and a jolly-looking fellow in front cried out,

'By the powers, Molly, that's as like you as two pays!'

Another shout followed this sally.

'Now, sir,' aid the showman, 'what does the girls say when the boys is coaxin' them?'

The pig gave a prolonged squeel.

It was now the young men's turn to laugh, and many a pinched elbow of a pretty girl, at the moment, caused a chorus to the pig's squeel. This was the finale; the pig retired amidst the plaudits of 'an admiring audience,' who made their exit down the step-ladder, to give place to others who were waiting to go up.

Phelim was silent for some time after he left the booth, but at last broke out with,

'That fellow's a humbugger!'

'That's his business,' said De Lacy, 'and therefore you can't give him higher praise than to say he *is* a humbugger.'

'And is that what you call praise?' said Phelim in offended wonder, for he thought De Lacy would have sided with his wounded dignity.

'Certainly,' said De Lacy. 'Every man to his calling.'

'But is it respectable to be humbuggin' people?'

'Oh, that's quite another question, Phelim; I'll say nothing for the respectability; but didn't you perceive the trick by which he makes the pig point out any letter or part of the world he's desired?'

'Not I—how could I?'

'Well, I'll tell you. You perceived there were holes cut round the circular platform, and that a card was always laid over a hole?'

'Yis, I did,' said Phelim.

'Well, you perceived also, that whenever the pig did a trick effectively, his master gave him an acorn?'

'He gave him something, but I didn't know it was an acorn.'

'You know this is the time of their falling, and there is nothing of which pigs are so fond.'

'And do you mane to say, sir, that if you feed a pig on acorns, you'll tache him to spell, and larn him jography?'

'No,' said De Lacy, smiling; 'but I mean, that an acorn was the pig's reward; but he would not have got the reward if he had not *found out the acorns*. Do you see the trick now?'

'Why, thin, indeed, to say the thruth, I only persaive it afther a manner like—that is, not complate.'

'Well, I'll show it to you *complate*, then,' said De Lacy, who enjoyed the hesitation that Phelim evinced to acknowledge that the showman's trick was beyond him.

'You saw every card was placed over a hole?'

'Yis.'

'And that when the pig came to the right card, he began to poke it with his snout?'

'Yis.'

'And can't you guess why?'

'No.'

'It was because his master had a plate of acorns attached to a stick, which he always placed under the hole the card was over; and so the pig went smelling round the circle till he came to the acorns.'

'Tare an ouns! what a chate!' said Phelim.

'If the pig made a mistake, he got no acorn; when he found out the right hole, he was rewarded.'

'Oh, the vagabone! to make the people think that a pig could be taught to know his letthers, and jography, and, afther all, it's only the *nathur* of the brute baste is in it!'

'And did you expect any more?'

'To be sure I did,' said the poor simple Phelim; 'and, what's worse, the people will b'lieve it, and they'll say *I* can't do as much with a Christhan child as that vagabone can with a pig. Why, it's enough to ruin all the schoolmasters in Ireland! I'll go back and expose the villain.'

'No, no, Phelim, you wouldn't do that?'

'Why wouldn't I? Isn't it a common forgery on people's undherstan'in's?' And De Lacy was obliged to lay his hand on the indignant philomath's arm to restrain him.

'Phelim,' aid De Lacy, 'you don't know but that poor fellow has a wife and children to support; and if his humbugging, as you call it, is turned into bread and milk for his little ones, you wouldn't be the cause of making them feel hunger?'

'God forbid, sir!' said Phelim feelingly, his pride giving place to his humanity. 'Bread and milk, indeed! Oh, thin, if it's but potatoes and salt he can airn in such a good cause, may the Lord prosper him!'

It is time to return to Rory and *his* party, whom we left looking for their dinner. But to obtain this, they found no such easy matter. They inquired at various booths without success, for the day was further spent than they imagined, and the viands consumed.

Rory had been so absorbed between anxiety on account of Kathleen, and wonder at De Welskein's Protean powers, that the day had passed over without his being conscious of it; and the various shows kept the attention of Conolly and Mary so much on the stretch, that they were equally unmindful of the flight of time, and, as Mary herself said, "Faith, the day went over like an hour, a'most.'

They sought the long entrenchment of sunken fires over which pots full of beef and cabbage had been 'busy bilin'' when last they passed that way. The fires were there, 'tis true, and so were the pots, but no beef and cabbage: the solids had been demolished, and the huge iron pots had given place to kettles, where water was 'kept continually bilin'' for the manufacture of punch. What was to be done? At this hour dinner was manifestly a scarce thing, and this fact increased their appetites; and even Rory himself, in spite of love and Kathleen, began to feel the inward man making appeals to his common sense. While things were in this state, Rory saw a brace of ducks dangling from a string, roasting before a fire at the end of one of the booths, and a girl very busy in attending the culinary process. Rory's invention was immediately at work; and his love of fun, joined to his desire for dinner, at once suggested the notion of his making himself master of the ducks.

So, desiring Conolly and his sister to secure a seat as near as they could to where the birds were in preparation, he spoke to the landlady of the booth, and asked could they have dinner. She said they had nothing but a little cold beef.

'Well, that same,' said Rory.

So plates were laid, and knives and forks provided, and the half-warm and ragged remains of some very bad beef were placed before Rory and his party.

'That'll do,' said Rory, who, having thus contrived to get the plates, &c., set about securing the ducks. So, feigning an excuse, he said to his party, 'Don't begin till Jack comes to us; he'll be here by-an'-by:' and then, turning to the girl who was cooking the ducks, he kept up a conversation with her, and made her laugh so often, that he got into her good graces, and she fancied him the pleasantest fellow in the world. At last, Rory, when he thought the birds wore nearly done, said to her, seeing that her face was very dewy from her occupation,

'I b'lieve it's roasting thim ducks you are?'

''Faith, it's thim that's roastin' me, you mane,' said the girl.

'It's dhry work, I'm thinkin',' said Rory.

'Thrue for you,' said the girl, 'and no one to offer me a dhrink.'

'Suppose I'd give you a dhrink?' said Rory.

'Long life to you!' said the girl, looking up at him, and wiping dow her face with a back stroke of her red hand.

'Well, you must do something for me,' said Rory, 'and I'll give you a pot o' porther.'

'God bless you!' said the girl.

'Jist run down, thin, to Tinn Donoghue's stan'in',—it's at the far end o' the sthreet,—and get me a ha'p'orth o' snuff, for I'm lost with a cowld in my head that I got through a hole in my hat.'

'Go 'long wid you!' said the girl, giving the ducks a twirl.

'It's thruth I'm tellin' you,' said Rory.

'Oh! I daren't lave the ducks,' said she.

'Oh!' said Rory, in an insinuating tone, 'jist slip out here through the slit in the tint, and I'll take charge o' them till you come back. Here's a hog for you,—and you may keep the change for yourself.'

The 'hog' was too much for the girl's prudence: off she started to Tim Donoghue's; and she wasn't ten steps from the place, when Rory had the pair of ducks on the dish before his party, and, as Rory himself said in telling the story after, 'the sorrow long they wor in making jommethry of the same ducks.'

When the girl came back and saw the skeletons of the birds in tempting plumpness before the fire, she, in the Conolly, 'screeched a thousand murdhers, and riz the tint.'

'Oh! the ducks, the ducks!' cried the girl.

'Oh! you baggage, are they spylte?' said Mrs. Molloy, the landlady, rushing to the spot on hearing the uproar.

'No, indeed, ma'am,' said Rory very quietly, picking the bones of one of them at the same time; 'they are not spylte, for they *wor* as fine ducks as ever I put a tooth in.'

'Oh, God be good to me!' said the woman, with a look of despair; 'is it ating Mr. Regan's wild ducks you are?'

Now this 'took Rory aback,' as sailors say. He would rather that he had not hit upon Regan's ducks for his frolic: but, as chance had so ruled it, he determined to follow up his joke: so he answered,

'In throth, ma'am, I didn't know whose ducks they wor; and as for their being *wild*, I never found it out; and, 'pon my conscience, I think they are a'most as good as if they wor tame.'

'But they wor Mr. Regan's ducks!'

'I didn't know that, ma'am; I supposed they wor yours; and when I kem to your tint for enthertainment, I thought I had a right to whatever ateables was in it, as well as another.'

'Oh! what'll Mr. Regan say?'

'He'll say what he has to say for himself,' said Regan, who, on hearing that *his* ducks had been taken by Rory O'More, became exceedingly wroth, and swaggered up to the scene of action. On his arrival *there*, he saw Conolly sitting beside Mary O'More, and this, as Rory said when speaking of the affair after, 'roused the divil in him;' so, changing his attack, which was intended for Rory, upon Conolly, he said, addressing the latter in a menacing tone,

'How dar you take *my* ducks?'

Conolly was in the act of rising, when Rory laid his hand on his shoulder, and said, 'Sit down—this is no affair of yours.'

In doing this, Rory was actuated by a double motive. In the first place, had the quarrel been established between Conolly and Regan, he knew that his sister's name would be mixed up with it, and his intuitive sense of delicacy recoiled at the thought of Mary's name being connected with a brawl at a fair; secondly, in point of fact he was the person who had committed the act complained of—and Rory was not the man to let another fight his battle. So, turning to Regan, he said,

'It was I tuk the ducks, Shan—Conolly had nothing to do with it; and if I have disappointed you of your dinner, I'm sorry for it,—I hope that's satisfaction enough. And for you, Mrs. Molloy, I beg your pardon if I tuk what I had no right to, and all I can do is to pay you for the ducks.' And he offered her his hand full of silver to take the price from.

'Take your money out o' that!' said Regan fiercely, accompanying the words with a shove that scattered Rory's shillings over the table and the ground. 'The ducks were not Mrs. Molloy's ducks, but mine, and I don't want to be paid for what I didn't intend to sell;—and all I've to say is, that I recommend you not to make away with anything belonging to me for the future.'

There as an emphasis on 'belonging to me' that Rory felt was meant to allude to Kathleen; but that was not so offensive as the phrase 'make away,'—which being a common form of parlance in Ireland for anything that is illegally taken, roused Rory's indignation.

'Regan,' said he, 'what I did, I did in a joke; and I have said in good temper, and with a hope of making friends, all that ought to satisfy man that *wished* to be a friend; and if afther that you *wish* to make a quarrel of it, and *mane* to throw an affront on me, I tell you Regan, it's what I won't take from you.'

'I wish you had been as particular about my ducks,' said Regan, walking off.

'If I tuk your ducks, Regan, I won't take your impidince,' said Rory, disengaging himself from behind the table.

Mary attempted to stop him, but Conolly prevented her, knowing the fatal consequences of a man being hampered with a woman in a fray. 'The best thing you can do,' said he, 'is to lave his hands loose, for he'll have need o' them soon.' Then, handing over Mary to the care of an elderly man, he said, 'Just take care o' the colleen while I see fair play;' and he was at Rory's side in an instant.

There was no time to spare, for Regan turned round at Rory's last word and said:

'Did you say impidince to me?'

'I did,' aid Rory.

The words were no sooner uttered than Regan made a tremendous blow at him; but rage and liquor (for he had been drinking) had deprived him of his usual power in such matters, and Rory easily warded his blow, and returned one so well planted, that Regan measured his length on the floor of the booth.

He rose again, and two or three of his cronies rallied round him, while Conolly and the lovers of fair play saw that nothing foul should befall Rory.

From the fury and intoxication of Regan, the fight was a short one. After his first fall, Rory requested that his opponent's friends would 'take him away, as he wasn't fit to fight;' but this only increased Regan's rage, and he rushed again upon his man. But it was an easy conquest for Rory, though Regan was superior in years and strength; and the end of the affair was, as Conolly and Rory's friends spread far and wide over the country in relating the affair, 'That Rory O'More gave Regan the length and breadth of as fine a licking as ever be got in his life.'

XVII

A moonlight meeting; with one too many.

FROM THE PRESENCE OF THE military at the fair, and the existence of the curfew-law at the period, it became doubly necessary that the people assembled should disperse in good time, and take their homeward way.

De Lacy particularly felt the necessity of this, for, circumstanced as he was, to put himself within reach of military-law would have been madness; so he and Phelim left the fair much earlier than Rory and his party, for the 'small scrimmage' after dinner had occasioned some delay. It is not immediately after a man has 'settled the hash' of his enemy, that he can coolly take up his hat (that is, if he has the good luck not to have lost it in the fight), and pay his tavern bill and depart in peace. The decencies of social life must be observed: he must adjust his ruffled attire, sit down to show his presence of mind, and take a drink to quench his thirst—for fighting is thirsty work. Then, as in the case of Rory, one must not be so uncivil as to turn one's back on the congratulations of one's friends; and there were many who congratulated Rory, for Regan was a quarrelsome fellow, and what, in fighting parlance, is called a 'troublesome customer;' and such a man to get a thrashing where it was least expected, excited great satisfaction, and numerous were the shakings of hands, slaps on the shoulder, and exclamations of admiration, that Rory had bestowed upon him, and several fresh tumblers were called for to drink 'his health, *and more power to his elbow.*'

'Long life to you, your sowl!' was said to him on all sides—'Musha health and power to you, Rory, my boy but you done the thing complate. Divil a purtier bit o' fight myself seen this many a day. Och! but you have the owld blood o' the O'Mores in you, *ma bouchal*!'

When he could escape from these congratulations, Rory, with his sister and Conolly, made the best of their way home. There was not much said on the way: Mary saw that jealousy on Regan's part had been the real cause of his savage conduct, and therefore she, with a woman's tact, wished the subject of the quarrel to be as little discussed as possible. This partly influenced Rory, too; but with him there was a more powerful cause of silence. The events of the day one by one were recalled to his memory; and when he remembered all that had passed between him and Kathleen, he more and more regretted his fight with her brother, and feared it might prove an additional obstacle to the course of his 'true love,' which did not seem to be a bit more likely to run smoother than it was wont to do in Shakspeare's days; and so he trudged on in silence, anticipating the appointed meeting of the morrow, and thinking all he should say to his Kathleen to assure her of his truth.

Conolly guessed the cause of Mary's silence on the subject of Regan's misdemeanour, and he had too much about him not to know that the expression of triumph at the defeat of a rival in the hearing of the woman for whom the rivalry existed would only lower him in her opinion.

Thus the concluding event of the preceding chapter, though it occupied the mind of each, yet, from the causes assigned, all, by common consent, forbore to speak of it; therefore, as the predominant impression on their minds was one that might not be manifested in words, they pursued their way in comparative silence.

The moon was rising when they reached the end of the boreen that led to O'More's cottage, and there Conolly parted company. When he was gone, Rory told Mary to say nothing to his mother about the fight. ''Twould only trouble her,' said he, 'and there would be no use in it. Indeed, we won't spake of it at home at all—even to Mr. De Lacy.'

'I'd rather myself it was so,' said Mary; 'but, Rory dear, won't the mother see the marks on you and suspect?'

'Oh! I've no marks on me that she can know of: the sulky thief never put the sign of his fist on my face.'

'Oh! but I'm glad o' that Rory dear,' said Mary; 'for it looks so ugly and disrespectable to have the marks of fighting on a man's face.'

'Well, sure I couldn't help it if I had itself. You know, Mary, 'twasn't my fault.'

'No, in throth, Rory; and sure my heart sunk within me when I seen you stand up, for I dhreaded that horrid fellow was more than your match; and sure 'twas brave and bowld o' you, Rory, *ma chree*, to put yourself forninst him.'

'I'm not afraid of him, the best day he ever stept,' said Rory; 'but as for to-day, he was too full a' dhrink to give me any throuble, and it went agin my heart to sthreck a man that was in liquor, only you seen yourself he *would* have it.'

'Throth, Rory, you've nothing to blame yourself with,' said Mary, 'you showed the hoighth a' good temper.'

Having reached the house, their conversation ended. They found De Lacy and Phelim at supper, which Rory and Mary helped to finish; and after a desultory conversation about the 'humours of the fair' to give the widow some idea of their day's amusement, they separated for the night.

It was a night of repose to all under the widow's roof except Rory. The excitement of the day, and his anxious anticipation of the morrow, banished slumber, and he rose at an early hour the following morning, unrefreshed and feverish. He appealed to that unfailing friend of a hot head,—namely spring water,—and by a plentiful deluge from the well, he made himself as comfortable as he could during the day, that to him seemed interminable. At length evening arrived, and Rory hastened to the appointed place, where he hoped to meet Kathleen, and clear himself from the charges which had been made against him. The place he named for their rendezvous was a rath, that stood near a bridge which crossed the river about half-way between their respective residences. Rath is the name given in Ireland to certain large circular mounds of earth, by some called Danish forts. That they were intended for purposes of defence, there is no doubt; but they are more likely the works of the ancient Irish than the Danes.

The rath which Rory named stood near the bank of the river, and probably was intended to defend the passage of the stream, which in later days had been traversed by a bridge of low small arches, such as remain in great numbers in Ireland to this day, and present specimens of early architecture more curious, perhaps, than anything else in the same way remaining in Europe. To the inexperienced stranger it would appear that a great deal of masonry had been thrown away on the bridge in question, for there were many arches which were quite dry at some seasons; but by those who know how rapidly the streams in the vicinity of hills expand after heavy rains, the knowledge of our forefathers in providing against such an exigency can be appreciated.

Rory arrived at the place of appointment earlier than Kathleen, of course;—there needs no master of the ceremonies to tell that a lady must not be kept waiting on such occasions. But as time wore on, he began to feel impatience; and then he ascended the rath, and looked from its summit in the direction he expected Kathleen to approach. Here he lingered, in hope, till evening was closing, and the yellow disc of the moon began to rise above the broad belt of clouds which skirted the horizon; then he began to fear Kathleen had promised him only to be rid of his importunity—or that some fresh influence had been exercised against him—or that she believed the calumny;—this was worst of all And so great was his anxiety to remove such a fatal impression from Kathleen's mind, that even in defiance of all reasonable expectation of seeing her, he remained on the rath and strained his sight, through the increasing gloom, to catch the first glimpse of her he wished so much to meet. Still, she came not; and now the moon, emerging from the vapour by which she had been enshrouded, rose above it in all her purity, no longer dim by the yellow mist which had tarnished her silvery brightness. Still Rory remained, although he had given up the

'Last pale hope that trembled at his heart.'

But, as the moonlight became so bright, and as he knew the danger of being abroad at such an hour, he crouched in the trench on the summit of the rath, and watched with his eyes above the embankment.

He had just arrived at the conclusion, in his own mind, it was no use to wait any longer, when he fancied he caught the outline of a figure moving towards him;—it became mere distinct—it was a woman's; a moment more, and his heart told him it was Kathleen.

He sprang to his feet, and running down the rath, he reached the ditch that bordered the field in time to offer his hand to Kathleen, and assist her over the fence. They stood in bright moonlight; and Rory could see that an aspect of care was over Kathleen's brow, which even his fervent welcome, and thanks, and blessings, could not dispel.

'Let us get under the shadow of the bridge,' said Rory.

'No,' said Kathleen with an air of reserve.

'Don't let us stand here, however,' said Rory, 'so near the road, and the moon so bright.'

'We can stand inside the rath,' said Kathleen, leading the way. They soon stood in the trench of the fort, completely shadowed by the embankment, while the moonlight fell brightly on the mound that rose within.

'God bless you, Kathleen, for keeping your promise!' said Rory fervently.

'Whatever you've to say, say quickly, Rory, for I must not stay here long,' replied Kathleen.

'Then tell me openly, Kathleen, what is it you *think* you have to accuse me of; and I will explain it all to your satisfaction.'

'You left home for a day about three weeks ago?' said Kathleen.

'I did,' said Rory.

'You went to the town beyant?'

'I did,' said Rory.

'You were in a cellar there?'

'I was.'

'And not in the best of company, Rory,' said Kathleen, reproachfully.

'Worse than, I hope, I'll ever be in agin,' said Rory.

'You own to that, thin?'

'I'll own to all that's thrue,' said Rory.

'Thin what have you to say about the girl that you were so much in love with?'

'In love with?' said Rory indignantly. 'Kathleen, there is but one girl on this earth I love, and that's yourself. I swear it by this blessed light!'

Just as he spoke, as if the light which he adjured had evoked a spirit to condemn him, a dark shadow was cast on the mound before them; and on their both looking round, a figure enveloped in a cloak stood on the embankment behind them.

Kathleen could not suppress a scream, and even Rory started.

'Is that what I hear you say?' said this mysterious apparition. 'Kathleen! Kathleen! he said the same to me.'

Kathleen could not speak, but stood with clasped hands, in trembling astonishment, gazing with the fascination of fear upon the figure that stood on the bank above them.

'Who are you?' said Rory.

The figure was about to turn, when Rory caught hold of the cloak in which it was enveloped, and dragged the intruder within the trench of the rath.

'Who are you?' said Rory again, turning round the person to face the light.

'Don't you know me, Rory O'More?' said the unknown, who threw back the hood of her cloak at the words, and the pale moonbeam fell on the face of the frail one of the cellar.

XVIII

Containing a council of love and a council of war.

To account for the occurrence which concludes the foregoing chapter, it becomes necessary to revert to Kathleen after her return from the fair. She had spent as restless a night as Rory, and after considering for a long time the fitness of meeting him clandestinely, after all she had heard, was still at a loss how to act, and determined therefore to tell her mother how matters stood, and ask her advice. Between the daughter and mother affection and good understanding had always existed; but of late there had an increasing confidence in and leaning towards each other, resulting from the unruly conduct of the son, against whose aggression and waywardness Kathleen and her mother were obliged to combine, and endeavour by union in the weaker party to make better defence against the tyranny of the stronger.

Regan had not got up the morning succeeding the fair, in consequence of the punishment he had received from Rory, and was lying under so herbal treatment of his mother's, in a room that was partitioned off the principal apartment of the farmhouse, which served not only for the kitchen, but for all the daily purposes of the family. Kathleen had just come from her brother's room, whither she had gone to offer any attendance he might require, and gently closed the door after her, thinking that he had fallen asleep, while in fact he had only indulged in a dogged silence to her kind inquiries, and feigned slumber to be rid of her.

Taking advantage of this opportunity, Kathleen drew a seat near her mother, who was knitting, and settling herself down to her spinning-wheel, she began to work very industriously for some time in silence. The hum of the wheel was interrupted in a minute or two by a short cough; and as Kathleen's fingers were kept busy, and her eyes fixed upon them, so that she need not have the necessity of meeting those of her mother, there could not be a more favourable moment for the opening of the delicate affair she had in hand; and so, after one or two more little coughs, she ventured to say, 'Mother.'

It may be remarked, that when people have any delicate subject to discuss, more particularly all affairs of the heart, there is something in the mere sound of their voices that gives you to understand what they are about, before a word relating to the subject is said.

Now, Kathleen's mother was as wise as mothers in general are about such matters, seeing that they have had such affairs of their own on their hands; and so, the very minute Kathleen said 'Mother,' that respectable individual knew what was coming just as well as if she were a witch.

'Well, *alanna?*' said the mother softly, coaxing her child's heart out of its secrecy by the encouraging tone of her voice, as a bird chirps its young for the first time from the security of its nest.

'There's something I wish to tell you,' said Kathleen.

'Well, darlin', I dare say it's nothing but what I'll be glad to hear.'

'I'm afeard you'll think me foolish, mother.'

'Throth, I never seen the sign iv a fool an you yet, *alanna bawn.*'

Here there was a pause, filled up only by the buzz of the spinning-wheel. The mother thought she had best break the ice; so, with a tone of gentle pleasantry in her manner, to deprive the subject of its sternness—to 'take the cold out of it,' as it were— she said, 'I suppose some o' the boys has been talking to you?'

'Yis, ma'am,' said Kathleen faintly, blushing up to her ears at the same time, while the wheel went round at a desperate rate and the thread was broken.

While Kathleen mended the thread of her spinning, her mother took up that of the conversation.

'Well, dear—well and good—and why not? Sure, it's only raysonable and what's before us all in our time, when it's God's will. And who's the boy, Kathleen dear?'

Kathleen, after swallowing her breath three or four times, said:

'Rory O'More, mother.'

'Sure, thin, but you're the happy girl! God bless you, child, and mark you to grace, to have the very pick o' the counthry axin' you!'

'Indeed I thought so myself, mother; but—'

'But what, dear?'

'Why, Shan, you know, mother.'

'Yis, yis, dear;' and the mother sighed heavily. It was some time before she could resume the conversation, and in the interim she raised her apron to dry a tear that trickled down her cheek.'

How deep is the guilt of the child who causes the tears of a parent!

'If Shan couldn't get Mary O'More, (and more is his loss, indeed!) there is no rayson, darlin', that you wouldn't have Rory.'

'But Shan is very much agin it, mother.'

'How do you know, dear?'

'He suspects, somehow, that I had a liking for him.'

'*Had* a liking?' said the mother. 'Why *haven't* you a liking, Kathleen?'

'Why, you see, mother, he towld me things of him; and if the things was thrue, Rory wouldn't be as good as I thought him.'

'How do you mane, darlin'?'

Here Kathleen entered into an explanation of how Regan had poisoned her mind against Rory, and told her mother all she had heard about the adventures of the cellar;—how, subsequently, she had met Rory at the fair—of her coolness, of his disavowal of guilt, and request that she would meet him to explain everything.

'He said, "This evening, at the rath, beside the bridge—"'

'Whisht!' said the mother, pointing to Regan's room; '*he's* awake.'

And so he was, and heard the principal part of the conversation between his mother and his sister; and it was in raising himself in the bed, the better to catch the latter part of the discourse, that he had alarmed the watchful ear of his mother: for poor Kathleen was so absorbed in her subject, that she quite forgot her proximity to her brother.

Regan now called for some one to attend him and on his mother appearing, he said he was much refreshed by the last sleep he had, and would get up.

'Indeed, you're betther where you are, Shan, for to-day,' said his mother.

'No, no, bed kills me; it's not fit for a man; I'll be the betther of some fresh air.'

'Sure, you wouldn't go out, Shan, and your face in that condition?' said his mother.

'Thim who doesn't like my face,' said he, 'needn't look at it;' and despite of his mother's entreaties, he proceeded to dress himself, which when he had accomplished, he sallied forth.

'Why, thin, where can Shan be goin'?' said Kathleen.

'Oh, musha, how should I know!' said the mother. 'He's never aisy at home, God help him!'

'Well, mother, what do you think about my goin' to the rath?'

'I think you'd betther go there, darlin': I don't think myself that Rory O'More would be as bad as you wor made to b'lieve.'

'Indeed, mother, it was agin' my heart I b'lieved anything bad of him.'

'To be sure, darlin', and it's only fair to hear what the boy has to say.'

'Thin you think I may go?'

'Yis, *ma vourneen*; but in case evil tongues would say anything, I'll go along wid you.'

Kathleen, after some hesitation, said, 'But maybe Rory would be shy of seeing you, mother?'

'Sartinly, dear, and I'll only go along with you convaynient to the rath. I'll stay a thrifle behind you, so that he won't see me; but at the same time I'll be near enough, so that no one shall have the occasion to say a light word o' you—for there's no knowing what ill-natured tongues may invint.'

This being settled, the mother and daughter awaited the arrival of the evening—the mother with interest, the daughter with impatience.

In the meantime, Shan Dhu was not idle. He had heard enough of the conversation between Kathleen and his mother to find that Rory's interest was as strong with the latter as the former, and the thought was poison to him. When he found the appointment with Rory was to be kept, he determined to frustrate the happy result which must ensue if it were permitted to take place without the intervention of another party, and he determined within his own mind who that party should be. He was no stranger to the damsel whose blandishments had been thrown away upon Rory, and he found that a bitter hatred existed against him in that quarter: nevertheless, though he must have known that this could have arisen but from one cause, he it was who was base enough to insinuate to Kathleen that an attachment existed between the girl and Rory.

It was to find this unfortunate woman Shan Regan left his house. He knew where to seek her, and met in her a ready person to act under to his wishes. He held out the opportunity of gratifying her revenge upon Rory thus: to blast his hopes with the girl of his heart by accusing him of treachery and falsehood, and laying her shame to his charge.

To this the nymph of the cellar assented; and thus is accounted for her startling appearance at the rath, which stunned with surprise our hero and Kathleen, to whom we must now return.

XIX

Showing that mothers in the country contrive to marry their daughters the same as mothers in town.

WHEN KATHLEEN SAW THE HANDSOME features of the woman who had been pointed out to her on the platform at the fair disclosed in the moonlight, she recognised them at once, for they were of that striking character not easily forgotten: and coming, as she did, to the rath in the hope of having her doubts of Rory's truth dispelled, and instead of that, finding them thus strengthened by such terrible evidence, she shuddered with a faint scream and sank to the earth.

'Look what you've done!' said Rory, stooping to raise the fainting girl, which he did, and supported her in his arms, as he turned to the ill-omened intruder, and said reproachfully, 'What did I ever do to deserve this?'

'Do!' said she, and her eyes glared on him with the expression of a fiend—'Do!—what a woman never forgets nor forgives—and I'll have my revenge o' you, you cowld-blooded thief, I will!—That's your innocent girl, I suppose! Mighty innocent indeed, to meet a man inside a rath, by the pleasant light o' the moon!—How innocent she is!'

'May the tongue o' ye be blisthered in fire,' said Rory with fury, 'that would say the foul word of her! Away wid you, you divil! the ground's not wholesome you thread on. Away wid you!'

She shrunk before the withering words and the indignant tone of the lover, and retired to the top of the embankment; but ere she descended, she stretched forth her arm in the attitude of menace to Rory, and said with a voice in which there was more of hell than earth,

'Make the most o' your *innocent girl* to-night, *Misther* O'More, for it's the last you'll ever see of her! You think to have her, you do,—but she'll never be yours; for if I pay my sowl for the purchase-money, I'll have my revenge o' you!—ha! ha!—remember my words—never! never!—ha! ha! ha!' and with something between the laugh of a maniac and the howl of a hyena, she rushed down the hill, leaving Rory horrified at such a fearful exhibition of depravity.

When Rory proposed to Kathleen, on their meeting, that they should stand within the shadow of the bridge, it may be remembered that she refused to do so; for her mother, who had accompanied her, decided on remaining out of sight in that very spot, while Kahleen should enter the rath for her conference with Rory.

She had seen her daughter and our hero ascend to the top of the mound, and in a very short time after was surprised to observe a third person taking the same course. This excited her curiosity, and she watched anxiously; and it was not long until she saw the figure descending the mound rapidly, and running towards the very point where she stood. The mother immediately crouched under some bushes to escape observation, and the sound of hurried steps having approached close to her place of ambush, suddenly stopped, and she heard, in a somewhat low, but perfectly clear tone, the name of 'Shan' pronounced, and soon after it was repeated. 'Shan Dhu,' said this unexpected intruder.

'Here I am,' was answered to the summons.

The name 'Shan Dhu,' being that of her own son, Kathleen's mother had her attention still more aroused; and the voice in which the response was made induced her to believe that it was Regan who answered. Peering forth from the bushes as well as she might, she saw the figure of a man emerge from under one of the dry arches of the bridge, and then there was no longer a doubt on the subject; it was Shan Regan who came forth to meet the woman who had just run down the hill.

'Well?' said Regan.

'I've done it!' said the woman.

'What did he say?'

'Oh, they were both knocked all of a heap.'

'But, did you make her sinsible that the sneaking thief was a black-hearted desaiver?'

'Throth I did. Didn't you hear her screech?'

'No.'

'Thin in throth she did. I towld her that he had promised me before her; and she dhropt down in a fit.'

'That'll do.' said Regan. 'And now we may as well be joggin' since the business is done; we mustn't be seen near the place.' And he, with his hardened accomplice, hastened from the spot.

Kathleen's mother remained for some time in her place of concealment, that Regan and his abandoned companion might not be aware of her presence.

During the few minutes she felt it necessary to remain in concealment, her mind became fully impressed with the conviction that some deception had been practised upon Kathleen, and manifestly through the instrumentality of her brother.

When the mother thought she might emerge from her ambuscade in safety, she hastened up the side of the rath, as her fears for her daughter had been excited when she heard that 'she had dropt down in a fit.'

On reaching the interior of the fort, she heard Rory expostulating with Kathleen on the improbability of the accusation made against him; for, before the mother had arrived, Rory had contrived, by brushing the dew from the grass with his hand, and sprinkling the moisture over Kathleen's face, to recover her from the state of insensibility into which the sudden appearance and fearful accusation of Rory's enemy had thrown her.

'Oh, why did you bring me here at all?' said Kathleen in a tone of agony.

'To clear myself to you, Kathleen,' said Rory.

'Clear yourself! Oh, Rory! that dreadful woman!'

'By all that's sacred, Kathleen, I know no more about her than the child unborn.'

'Oh, can I b'lieve it, afther all I've heard and seen, Rory? Can I b'lieve it?'

'Kathleen, as I hope to see heaven, I'm innocent of what she accuses me.'

'Oh, I wish I could b'lieve it!' said Kathleen, sobbing.

'Thin you may b'lieve it, my darlin',' said her mother, who now joined them.

This fresh surprise made Kathleen scream again; but, recognising her mother, she sprang into her arms.

'Oh, mother dear! mother dear! but I'm glad to see you,' said the excited girl, who had not caught the meaning of the words her mother uttered.

'Oh, mother! mother! you are thrue to me, at all events you'll never desaive me.'

'Nor I either, Kathleen,' said Rory; 'and sure, here's your mother to bear witness for me. Don't you hear what she says?'

'What? what?' said Kathleen, bewildered.

'Compose yourself, dear!' said the mother.' Don't b'lieve the bad things you've heard of Rory; 'they're not thrue—I'm sure they're not thrue.'

'Bad luck to the word!' said Rory, plucking up his courage.

'But that woman— —' said Kathleen, 'where is she?' and she looked round in alarm.

'She's gone, dear,' said the mother, soothingly; and Rory, in less gentle accents, made no scruple of saying, '*Where?*'

'Rory,' said Kathleen's mother, with a serious tenderness in her manner. 'I b'lieve that you love my child, and that you mane to be thrue to her.'

'May I never see glory if I don't!' said Rory fervently.

The mother took their hands, and joining them, said, 'Then I give her to you, Rory, with all the veins o' my heart; and may my blessing be on you!'

Rory took the yielding girl tenderly in his arms and kissed her unresistingly, alternately blessing her and her mother for making him 'the happiest fellow in Ireland,' as he said himself.

How all this sudden revolution of affairs in his favour had occurred, Rory gave himself no trouble to inquire,—he was content vith the knowledge of the fact; and after escorting Kathleen and her mother within sight of their house, he turned his steps homeward, and re-entered his cottage a happier man than he had left it.

XX

In which Rory O'More proves himself to be a man of letters.

THE NEXT MORNING RORY AROSE in high spirits, and determined on amusing himself with a piece of sarcastic waggery that he intended executing upon Sweeny, the reformed Papist attorney, whose apostasy was a source of great indignation to Rory.

It is happened that the tombstone of old Sweeny, the apothecary, bearing the Popish phrase, 'Pray for the soul of Denis Sweeny,' stood most provokingly close to the pathway leading to the church-door; so that every Sunday, when his son the attorney was going to attend divine service *as by law established*, his Church-of-Englandism was much scandalised by having this damning (and damnable) proof of his apostasy staring him in the face. Not that he cared for it *himself:* he was one of those callous-hearted people who could 'have botanised on his mother's grave,' therefore this proof of his former creed on the grave of his father could have given him no trouble; but he did not like the evidence to remain there in the sight of other people, and he had asked Rory O'More how the nuisance could be abated.

Our hero was indignant with the petty-minded pettifogger, and wished to retaliate upon him for the renunciation of his old creed; for the Roman Catholics have the same bitter feeling against the man who secedes from their profession of faith, as those of the Church of England entertain against the dissenters from them. And why not? If

the Church of England is right in condemning step number two, the
Church of Rome has rather better cause to object to step number one;
for '*c'est le premier pas qui coûte.*'

So Rory, after hearing the attorney's complaint, said he thought he
could rectify the objectionable passage on the tomb-stone. How he
accomplished this will be seen.

After breakfast he asked De Lacy, would he go over to see 'the
churches,' as the old burial-place in the neighbourhood was called,
where the ruins of some monastic buildings stood, one of which had
been repaired and roofed in for the parish church. De Lacy assented
to the proposal, and Rory suggested that they should endeavour to get
Phelim O'Flanagan to accompany them.

'His school lies in our way,' said Rory, 'and we may as well ax him
to come; for there is a power of owld anshint tombstones in it, in owld
Irish and he can explain them to you, sir.'

True it was, that here many an ancient grave-stone stood, mingled
with those of later days;—the former bearing the old Irish

oη δo

the latter, the

PRAY FOR—

showing, that though conquest had driven the aboriginal Irish from
the spot, the religion, though not the language of the people, had
survived their downfall.

And here what a striking evidence is given of the inutility of
penal laws!—nay, worse than inutility; for prohibition seems to act
on human nature rather as a productive than a preventive cause of
the thing forbidden, and the religion of the Irish, like their native
shamrock, by being trampled on, becomes prolific.

Their language is passing away, though it was not penal to speak it;
but their religion has lasted because penalty attended its profession
and the faith of a persecuted people is still recorded in the language
of the oppressor.

Thanks to God! the days of persecution are past; and fair fame to England in cancelling from her statutes the unjust and unholy penalties that man, in his bigoted profanity, had dared to interpose between the worship of the creature to the Creator!

And Fortune never dispensed a brighter honour on her favourite, than in over the name of Wellington the glory of being the agent of this blessing to his native land. This mingling of the olive with his laurels increases their brightness, as it will their endurance: for when many a victory he has won shall cease to be remembered, the emancipation of his country from the bondage of bigotry will never be forgotten; and soothing be the thought in the hero's last hour, that though many of his achievements have evoked the curses of a foreign land, this greatest triumph of his life will be remembered with blessings by his countrymen!

When Phelim was asked to bear De Lacy and our hero company, he was immersed in the mysteries of his school, and could not immediately accompany them; but he promised to follow soon, and for that purpose gave his scholars half a holiday, for which beneficence on his part they threw up their hats,—that is, such of them as had any; while those of them who had not, made up the deficiency by extra shouting; and Phelim, his school being dismissed, followed De Lacy and Rory to 'the churches.'

This burial-ground was not more than a quarter of a mile from the village; yet, though in the neighbourhood of man's habitation, it was particularly lonely; for, except on Sunday, when the small Protestant congregation went to divine service, or that the occasion of a funeral called the peasantry to the spot, it was little frequented.

Indeed, a churchyard is generally avoided; nor can it be wondered at that the resting-place of the dead should have an appalling influence on the ignorant and superstitious, when even to the most enlightened there is a chastened and solemn tone of feeling produced on entering a place of sepulture.

Much of this feeling is lessened, or at least the indulgence of it is in a more elevated tone, when we walk through the range of magnificent monuments lining the vaulted aisle of some noble abbey. Here the vanity of our nature is indirectly flattered by witnessing the tribute that posterity pays to greatness, and Glory more than half divides the triumph with Death. But in the lonely country churchyard, where some plain head-stone or nameless mound of earth is all that is left to tell that *there* rests, a being once instinct with life as ourselves, and where, instead of vaulted roof and clustered columns, the ruins of some lowly chapel stand, they, like all around, telling of decay,—there it is that the contemplation of mortality exercises its most depressing influence, and the thought of death strikes coldly on the heart.'

De Lacy accompanied Rory to the burial-place, which stood on a small mound, the grave-stones rising in bare relief against the sky, which here and there peeped through the shattered mullions of some window in the ruined wall of one of the little churches, giving an air of peculiar desolation to the place, which was increased, perhaps, by the slated roof of one of them, which was repaired and employed as the Protestant parish church. A pathway led to this building, and Rory came to a stand where, on one side of the path, stood a rather conspicuous tombstone with this inscription:

> Pray for the soul of
> DENIS SWEENY,
> who departed, etc.

'Do you see that?' said Rory to De Lacy.

'Yes.'

'Well, that's what brings me here to-day.'

'How?' said De Lacy.

'Why, that's owld Denny Sweeny's tombstone; and you see the poor owld fellow axes every one to pray for his sowl—and why not?—and indeed I hope he's in glory. Well, you see by that he was a good Catholic, and a dacent man he was; and when he died he ordhered the same tombstone to be put over him, and paid my own father for cuttin' the same.'

'Is it after he died?' said De Lacy.

'Oh, no—you know what I mane; but sure a slip o' the tongue doesn't matther. Well, as I was sayin', my father cut the same tombstone—and a nate bit o' work it is; see the iligant crass an it, and cut so deep that the divil wouldn't get it out of it,—God forgi' me for sayin' divil to the crass!'

'It's enough, indeed,' said De Lacy.

'Ay, and so I towld that dirty brat, Sweeny—the 'turney, I mane—when he axed me about it. What do you think he wants me to do?' said Rory.

'To take it back for half-price, perhaps,' said De Lacy.

''Faith he hasn't that much fun in him to think of sitch a thing.'

'What was it, then?'

'Why, he wants me to alther it,' said Rory.

'For himself, I hope?' said De Lacy.

'No,' said Rory; 'though in throth I'd do *that* with pleasure, for he'd be no loss to king or counthry. But, as I was tellin' you, he comes to me the other day, and towld me it was disgraceful to see sitch a thing as "pray for the sowl" on his father's tombstone in sitch enlightened times as these, when people knew betther than to pray for people's sowls.

'"They might do worse," says I.

'"It might do for the dark ages," says he, "but it won't do now;" laying it all on the dark ages, *by the way*, jist as if people didn't know that it was bekaze when he goes to church every Sunday his poor honest father's tombstone stares him in the face, the same as if the voice out of the grave called to him and said, "Oh, thin, Dinny, my boy, is it goin' to church you are?" Not that he'd mind that, for the cowld-hearted thief hasn't the feelin' to think of it; but it's the dirty pride of the little animal;—he doesn't like the *rale* Prodestants to see the thing stan'in' in evidence agin him. So I thought I'd divart myself a bit with him, and says I, "Sure the tombstone doesn't do you nor anybody else any harm."—"Yes, it does," says he; "it stands in evidence agin father's common sinse, and I'm ashamed of it."

'Oh!' said Rory feelingly, 'what luck can the man have that says he's ashamed of his father's grave!'

The feeling and touching appeal reached De Lacy's heart.

Rory continued 'Ashamed, indeed!—Throth, an' well he may say he's ashamed!—not for his father, though—no—but well may he be ashamed to change his creed!'

'You shouldn't blame any man for his religious belief, Rory,' said De Lacy.

'No more I would, sir, if it was his belief that he was reared in; but—'

'Oh!' said De Lacy, interrupting him, 'if a man feels that he has been instructed in a belief which his conscience will not permit him to follow—'

'Sure, sir,' said Rory, interrupting in his turn, 'I wouldn't blame him for that neither: but is it Sweeny you think does it for that? not he, in throth,—it's jist for the lucre, and nothin' else. And sure if he had the feeling in him to love his father, sure it's not altherin' his tombstone he'd be, that was made by his father's own directions; and suppose he thinks that he ought to be a Prodestant ever so much, sure isn't it bad of him to intherfare with his poor father's dyin' request that they would pray for his sowl?'

'That I grant you,' said De Lacy.

'And so he comes to me to ask me to alther it. "For what?" says I. "Bekaze I'm ashamed of it," says he. "Why?" says I. "Bekaze it's only Popery," says he. "Well," says I, "if it's Popery ever so much, sure it's your father's doin',—and any shame there is in it, it is to him, and not to you, and so you needn't care about it; and if your father did wish people to pray for his sowl, I think it very bad o' you to wish to prevent it."—"It can do him no good," says he. "It can do him no harm, anyhow," says I.

'So he couldn't get over that very well, and made no answer about the good or the harm of it and said he didn't want to argue the point with me, but that he wanted it althered, and as my father done the job, he thought I was the person to alther it. "And how do you want it changed?" says I. "Take out 'Pray for the sowl:" says he, "that's nothing but Popery." "My father always cut the sowl very deep," says I, "and to take it out is impossible; but if it's only the Popery you object to, I can alther it if you like, so that you can have nothing to say agin it."—'How ? says he. "Oh, let me alone," says I. "You're no *sculpture*," says I, "and I don't know how I'll do it; but you'll see yourself when it's done."—"You won't charge me much?" says he. "I'll charge you nothing," says I; "I'm not a mason by thrade, and I'll do the job for love."—"But how do you mane to do it?" says he agin. "Oh, never mind," says I, "go your ways, I'll do the job complate, and next Sunday, when you go to church, you'll see the divil a bit o' Popery will be in the same tombstone."—"That's all I want," says he. "Thin we'll be both plazed," says I—'And now I'm come here to-day to do the very thing.'

'And how do you mean to effect the alteration, Rory?' said De Lacy.

'As aisy as kiss hand,' said Rory. 'Jist do you amuse yourself with looking into the churches; there's some quare carvings round the windows and doors, and a mighty curious owld stone crass up there beyant. Or, if you like, sir, sit down beside me here with your book, and you can read while I work.'

De Lacy had not been long engaged in reading, when old Phelim made his appearance; and with so amusing a cicerone, De Lacy passed a couple of hours pleasantly enough in looking over the antiquities of the place.

After the lapse of that period Rory had completed his task, and sought his friends to show them how thoroughly he had neutralised the Popery that had so much distressed Sweeny.

'How could you have done it so soon?' said De Lacy.

'Oh, I won't tell you—you must see it yourself,' said Rory. 'It is the simplest thing in life—four letthers did it all.'

Rory now conducted De Lacy and Phelim to the tombstone, and the moment they stood before it they both indulged in hearty laughter.

Rory had carved over the objectionable request the phrase 'DON'T' so that the inscription ran thus:

DON'T
Pray for the soul of
DENIS SWEENY.

'Isn't that the thing?' said Rory.

'Capital!' said De Lacy.

'Isn't that sarving the little viper right? You see he daren't say at wanst, out honest, that he was ashamed *for his own sake*, bekaze he was a turncoat; but he lays the blame *on the Popery*. Oh, in throth, there's many a dirty turn and many a cruel thing done on us: and thim that does the thing is ashamed to own to the right cause, and so they lay the blame on the Popery. By my sowl! they ought to be obleeged to Popery for giving them sitch a convenient excuse for not havin' things called by their right names.'

'But won't Sweeny be very angry about this?' said De Lacy.

'Faith, to be sure he will,' said Phelim, shaking his head. 'Rory, *ma bouchal*, though I can't deny your wit, I cannot compliment you with an epithalamium upon your prudence: you have made that little bitther attorney your inimy to the ind o' time.'

'I know that,' said Rory; 'but what do I care?'

'Rory, my boy, Prudence, *Prudentia*, as the Latins had it,—Prudence, my boy, is one of the cardinal virtues.'

'Well, to expose humbuggin' is as cardinal as ever it was.'

'So you won't listen to me?—*Magister docet, sed vos verb neglitis.*'

'Well, who's sayin' it's prudent?—But all I stand up for is the altheration; and isn't *that* complate?'

'That there's no denyin',' said Phelim.

'And all with four letthers.'

'You have demonstherated it as complate wid four,' said Phelim, 'as I do my mattamatics wid three—Q.E.D'

'By dad! I have a great mind to put Q.E.D. at the end of it all,' said Rory.

'For what?' said De Lacy.

'Bekase it is *what was to be demonstherated*,' said Rory.

''Faith, I'm glad to see you remember your mattamatics still,' said Phelim.

'Wouldn't it be grate fun?' said Rory.

'It's bad enough as it is,' said De Lacy, 'without making matters worse. I am afraid, Rory, this was very unwise.'

'Yet you can't help laughin' at it,' said Rory.

'Indeed I can't,' said De Lacy.

'Well, and so will the Prodestants laugh at that contimptible little upstart when they see it, and that's all I want. There's nothing an upstart feels half so much as a laugh against him,' said Rory, making a sagacious comment upon his own imprudent act.

'Quite true,' said De Lacy, 'and therefore the attorney will never forgive you.'

'The beauty of it is,' said Rory, still enjoying his joke, 'that he can't complain openly about it; for all he said, was that he was ashamed about the *Popery* of it. Now, I've taken the Popery out of it at all events.'

'Certainly,' said De Lacy, 'but at the same time, you have increased Sweeny's cause of inquietude by making the offensive phrase more obnoxious.'

'That's what I meant to do,' said Rory, boldly. 'I've caught him in his own thrap. The little schemin' 'turney complained only about the *Popery*; now, with four letthers I've desthroyed more Popery than the parson could do with twice as many.'

'Upon my word, Rory,' said De Lacy, smiling, 'many men of *letters* have failed with the whole alphabet to alter a text so completely as you have done with *four*.'

XXI

In which Shan Regan and Soldering Solomon give a touch of their quality,
and Rory undergoes a trial of temper.

A LTHOUGH REGAN'S MOTHER HAD DISCOVERED his perfidy towards
his sister and Rory, and relieved them from the consequences
that might have ensued from it, she did not reveal to Rory the
treachery of which her son had been guilty,—for still he *was* her son,
and with a mother's tenderness she sought to screen him, in the eyes
of our hero, from the contempt which so base a means of indulging
his dislike must have produced.

But she saw how deep the hatred to Rory must be on Regan's part,
to urge him to such practices as he had exercised against him, and until
matters were riper for a disclosure,—in fact, until Kathleen and he should
be just going to be married,—she begged of Rory to say nothing about
what had passed; for if it came to Shan's knowledge, he would be 'showing
his temper' at home, and it was as well not to vex him until the time came
when the definitive step could be taken which would render his anger
of no avail; for though she would not betray to Rory the baseness of her
son, she had no hesitation in owning that he was not his friend.

It was with this understanding that Rory and Kathleen parted
the night of their meeting at the rath. But though Mrs. Regan kept
the means of her knowledge a secret from Rory, she revealed to her
daughter how she became possessed of the knowledge that exposed
the treacherous influence that had been employed to ruin the hopes

of two innocent people, not only to satisfy Kathleen's inquiries of how her mother could vouch for Rory's conduct, but in order to put Kathleen on her guard against betraying to her brother any symptom of his plot having failed.

'For what would we do if he thought we found him out?' said she.

Miserable mother! whose only hope of domestic quiet lay in seeming to be ignorant of the ruffianism of her child.

With all her caution, however, though Kathleen did not betray any symptoms of happiness in her brother's presence, and subdued her looks and manner as much as possible, still Regan was not quite satisfied with the apparent state of things at home: not that he suspected his plot had been discovered, but he feared that it had not been sufficiently effective, or that Kathleen would exhibit more distress. He, therefore, went further in endeavouring to depreciate Rory O'More in everything he could say and do, not only at home, but abroad.

There are some natures so essentially vile that they can never forgive another's success. Such was Regan's. But to this habitual baseness of mind, was added the stimulus of dislike in Rory's affair: and that his sister's attachment to him seemed still to survive the threats and falsehoods and machinations urged against it, increased that dislike. But it was Rory's triumph over him at the fair that completed the sum of his hatred. This, Regan looked upon as a personal disgrace, and the remembrance of it sank deep in his heart; and deeper and deeper it sank every day, and the depth of the remembrance called for a greater measure of revenge. Until this could be satisfied, he in the meantime got up a piece of slander against Rory, by falsifying all the circumstances of the visit to the fair.

This he did with the most thorough malevolence and injurious perversion of all the facts, he spoke amongst his fellows, openly in the public-houses, where most of his time was spent, in a spirit of jeering slightingness of Mary O'More being 'gallivanted round the fair by that omadhaun Conolly,—and thrated Misther Rory, too, I hear. Well, people's changed! I thought, wanst, that Rory had more sperit than to be takin' thrates from another man on account of his sisther's purty face.'

Now, though he got hearers who were base enough to listen to this, he did not find one to believe him, for they were well aware of the secret and real cause of the spleen. But this disparagement did not satisfy him:—there was another and a viler misrepresentation of which he was guilty. The business of the ducks, which, if truly told, he knew would only raise a laugh against him, he twisted with the true serpent spirit that actuated him, into a crime, and, with the expression of *regret* which is so often the outward sign of the secret *rejoicing* of the bad man's heart, he declared he was sorry that Rory 'let himself down so much, or he thought he was above *stalin'* a poor pitiful pair o' ducks: throth, it wasn't worth while bein' a *thief* for such a *thrifle.*'

All this, in the course of a few days, travelled to the next parish, where Rory lived; for even in sylvan scenes the Dryads have it not all to themselves,—there be evil geniuses in the country as well as in town, and 'd—d good-natured friends are to be found everywhere; and some of these same good-natured folk told Rory what was said of him.

The first bearer of the disagreeable intelligence was Old Solomon, the tinker, who delighted to have it in his power to say bitter things of everybody—or even to them, when he could do it by innuendo, which was a favourite weapon of his, and one he used like a master.

It happened, during the day Rory and De Lacy went to 'the churches,' that Old Solomon paid the Widow O'More a visit. In doing this he had two objects: in the first place, he enacted guide to De Welskein, who wanted to see De Lacy; and in the next, he was sure of 'entertainment,' as the signboards have it, for himself and his ass.

Now Sol was kindly received at the cottage of the widow, and had some fresh buttermilk and good potatoes given him, with a seat in the chimney corner into the bargain, where he roasted his shins, and smoked his pipe, and said sour things of half the country,—and, in short, made himself perfectly happy. But after spending a couple of hours thus, he began to exhibit symptoms of impatience at Rory's absence; for he wanted to proceed further, and yet did not like to go without giving to Rory the pleasant intimation that he was gaining the reputation of being a very ingenious purloiner of other people's property:—waiting to wound the man, the hospitable shelter of whose roof he had enjoyed, not only then, but at all times. And this, he must have been conscious, arose from pure good-heartedness; for his habitual influence through the motive of fear did not exist there, as in other places, Rory being too sharp a fellow to let Solomon exercise such a power over him: and it was partly this fact that made the old scoundrel the more anxious to gall, at least, where he could not govern.

De Welskein waited patiently enough the return of De Lacy, as he consoled himself with making compliments to Mary O'More, and doing the agreeable, as Frenchmen generally do: but Solomon from time to time went from the fireplace to the door to look out for Rory, whom, at last, he saw approaching.

When Rory entered the cottage, he welcomed De Welskein, who seemed rather constrained in his manner towards him, and asked for De Lacy; Rory informed him he would soon return,—that he left him and Phelim behind in the churchyard, looking over some old tombstones, but that they would not be long absent.

'And how are you, Sol?' said Rory.

'Oh, as well as any one wishes me,' replied Solomon bitterly.

'What are you in sitch a hurry for?' asked Rory; 'sure you're not goin' yet?' This was said in pure hospitality, for Rory did not like the old cynic.

'Yis, yis,—you've had enough of me.'

'Well,' said Rory, 'plaze yourself and you'll live the longer.'

'Throth, thin, the more one lives, the more one wondhers,' said Solomon. 'Rory *avic,*' added he, 'will you go and get me the ass?'

'To be sure,' said Rory, who went to the outhouse, where the ass had been enjoying a good feed, as well as his master. Reloading him with his panniers, containing Solomon's

'Nippers, twisters, sand, and resin,'

as well as the three ancient pots and pans, Rory led the animal forth to where Solomon stood awaiting his approach, before the door to the cottage; and when Rory halted the beast before him, the old tinker began very carefully to examine every particular of his ass's furniture and appendages, not forgetting the three old rusty kettles that dangled from the straddle.

Rory inquired if anything was wrong?

'Oh, it's no harm to see if all's right,' said Solomon.

'Why wouldn't it be right?' said Rory. 'Haven't I put on this sthraddle and panniers, and kittles, often enough before?'

'Oh, yis,—but I was only seein'—one, two, three,—I was only seein' if all was safe; one can't be too sure these times;—one, two, three;' and he very carefully repeated his scrutiny of the three old kettles as he leisurely pronounced 'one, two, three.'

Rory's attention was aroused by this repetition of the words which were the signal to the smuggler; and fancying for a moment that Solomon might have discovered his agency in the affair, he became very uneasy, and said,

'What do you mane by reckoning over one, two, three, so often?'

'Oh these is quare times,' said Solomon.

This increased Rory's uneasiness. 'How do you mane?' said he.

'And a quare world, so it is—one, two, three.'

'What the dickins are you at, with your "one, two, three?"' said Rory, whose anxiety increased.

'Only jist seein' that my property's safe,' said Solomon, giving a look at Rory, which our hero could not understand, for, his mind still reverting to the signals, could not reach the meaning which Solomon wished to convey, and he was yet unsatisfied what Solomon's reckoning the kettles meant. However, as the tinker went through that process again, and still repeated, 'one, two, three,' Rory said impatiently,

'Tare an' ouns! is it thim owld kittles you're reckonin' agin?'

'Just countin' them,—is there any harm in that?' said the tinker 'it's betther be sure than sorry.'

'Countin' thim!' said Rory, looking at him with all his eyes. 'Why, sure you never had more nor three owld rusty kittles in your life; and they're so well known over the counthry, that no one would think to make their own of them, supposin' they wor worth stalin'.'

'Oh, some people has quare tastes for what belongs to other people,' said Solomon significantly,—'one, two, three,—and a kittle might tickle some people's fancy.'

'The divil tickle you and your fancy!' said Rory, waxing angry. 'Why, barrin' one wanted to hunt a mad dog with it, bad luck to the use any one would have with your owld kittles!'

'Maybe so,' said Solomon, with great composure; 'but you see,' he added, 'some people is so handy at staling a pair o' ducks, that no one knows but my poor kittles might go asthray:' and he cast a most provoking glance at Rory.

As quick as lightning, the truth flashed upon O'More's mind, that the frolic at the fair had been misrepresented; and though glad to find his fears regarding the discovery of the signals were unfounded, yet, with flushed cheek and dilated eye, he said, in a tone in which wounded pride more than anger was predominant, 'What do you mane?'

'Oh, laste said is soonest mended,' said the tinker;—'one, two, three;—I see they're all safe. Good evenin' to you, Rory.'

'Stop!' said Rory, confronting him; 'explain to me your dark meaning, and don't lave an affront at the door you were always welkini at?'

'How have I affronted you?' said Solomon, whose frigid coolness of age was in startling relief to the excited fervour of the young man who stood before him.

'You made a dark hint jist now,' said Rory.

'Make *light* of it, Rory, *ma bouchal*,' said the tinker, taking the halter of his ass in token of departure.

'You shan't go that way,' said Rory, beginning to lose his temper; and he laid his hand on the old man's shoulder in the action of detention, but at the same time with a proper degree of deference to his age.

'And is it stoppin' a man on the road you are now?' said the tinker, with a low, spiteful chuckle: 'throth, you're improvin' fast!' and he attempted to pass Rory, who now, losing all control of himself, said:

'Bad luck to you, you cruked, spiteful, sawdhering owld thief! how dar you say the like to an honest man's son!—Stop on the road, indeed!—stale ducks! Is it Regan that has the black heart to say I stole his ducks?'

'Oh, you know it, thin!' said old Solomon, becoming provoked in turn.

'Know it!' said Rory, seeing his drift; 'it's well for you you're past bating, you owld cracked bottle o' vinegar that you are! Or I'd thrash you within an inch o' your life. Away wid you, you owld sarpent!' and he flung him from him.

The old tinker staggered back, and made a great clatter as he reeled against his old kettles; but, recovering himself, he led away his ass, saying to Rory, however, before he went, 'I hear they wor uncommon fine ducks!'

Rory was startled by this last expression,—the second part of the signal given to De Welskein.—Was it chance? or did the old tinker mix up the slander of Regan, and imply his knowledge of Rory' s mission, in the same breath, to puzzle him? While he was standing in this state of perplexity and vexation, De Lacy came up to him unperceived,—for Rory was looking after the tinker whose last words De Lacy had heard, and was attracted by, and accosting Rory, who was taken by surprise, said:

'Does that old rascal know anything about our affairs?'

''Faith, I dunna if he does,' said Rory, with an air of abstraction that struck De Lacy as peculiar.

'Is it not strange, that he should use the words of our private signal?'

'Faix, an' it is, and it bothered myself at first,' said Rory, 'when he said it; but I think, afther all, he knows nothing about it, and that he only spoke it by chance, and meant something else intirely.'

'What else could he allude to?' said De Lacy.

'I'll tell you about it, sir, another time,' answered Rory; 'for it's long story, and you'd betther not wait for it now, as Mr. De Welskein is in the house waitin' for you.'

'De Welskein!' said De Lacy, who entered the cottage as he uttered the name.

'*Bon jour, citoyen capitaine,*' was the address of the smuggler to De Lacy, who welcomed him in return; the smuggler continuing to address him in French, desired a private interview; De Lacy pointed to his bed-room, and the Frenchman entered the apartment. De Lacy followed, and as soon as they were within the room, De Welskein pointed to the lock.

'There is no necessity,' said De Lacy.

'Don't be too sure of that,' said De Welskein, with a very significant shake of the head, and one of the keen and cunning glances of his dark eye.

'What do you mean?' said De Lacy.

The Frenchman laid his finger on his lip, to impress the necessity of silence; and though still speaking in his own language, which was sufficient guarantee for secrecy in an Irish cabin, yet the importance of what he had to communicate was so great, that he placed his mouth close to De Lacy's ear, and said in the most cautious tone,

'There is a traitor!'

'A traitor!' echoed De Lacy. The Frenchman nodded assent, and added, 'We are betrayed.'

De Lacy thought of the words he heard Solomon utter, and said quickly,

'That rascally old tinker?'

'*Vieux chaudronnier de campagne?*—No, no.'

'Who then?' asked De Lacy.

De Welskein subdued his voice to the lowest whisper, and said,

'Rory O'More!'

XXII

A trial of temper, and a trial by battle.

WHEN DE LACY ENTERED THE house, he left Rory standing without, looking after the spiteful old tinker, with his teeth set and his hand clenched; and could he at the moment have encountered Regan, and had his blow been gifted with death, he would have struck him— so fearfully are generous natures excited on the sudden by insult; for, that the malicious story emanated from Regan, he had no doubt.

But a few minutes calmed the fierceness of his passion, though he changed not his belief as to the promulgator of the scandal and when he reflected that it was the brother of the girl he loved, who was the offender, it perplexed him how to act under the circumstances. Should he tamely submit to such an insinuation against his character? Against this his nature rebelled yet to make a wider breach with Regan, was what he could wish to escape, for Kathleen's sake. To balance these considerations quietly in his own mind, he walked down to the river, where, undisturbed, he might take a ruminating ramble.

In the meanwhile, De Welskein was closeted with De Lacy, who when he heard the charge against Rory, connected with the singularity of the words he had overheard the tinker utter, and Rory's seeming confusion at the time, was shaken for a moment by the suddenness and distinctness of the accusation against him; but as soon as he had time to recover from the surprise, his better judgment acquitted Rory of the guilt with which he was charged.

He told De Welskein it was impossible; that he knew Rory well that he was of a chivalrous nature, above the taint of so foul a thing as treachery, and he would stake his life on his fidelity.

'You've done that already,' said De Welskein.

'And would do it again,' replied De Lacy.

'You don't know these Irish,' said the smuggler.

'Better than you do,' answered De Lacy warmly.

'They are full of finesse,' said the other.

'They are driven to it by ages of misrule and oppression,' said De Lacy; 'it is their only protection against the heartless persecution they are open to on every side; and if the strong, by their tyranny, force the weak into the last retreat left open to them, on then be the guilt of the habits they have engendered! Blind as they are cruel, their rulers, while they have made them crafty, will not see the noble traits that are still left them—generosity, courage, devotion to those whom they can respect and trust, and a high sense of honour, which even yet survives all that has been done to crush it in their natures, and resists even the contrary example in their oppressors.'

Thus spoke De Lacy, who could not contain his indignation when such a fellow as De Welskein, whose nature was only sensitive to the faults with which he could sympathise, dared to undervalue a people whose finer traits, were above his comprehension.

'Believe me, they are cunning as foxes,' said De Welskein.

'I know they are,' replied De Lacy, 'and they have every need of their cunning, as the fox has amongst his hunters. But say no more against the Irish—you forget that I am an Irishman myself.'

'But *monsieur* has had the advantage of a French education,' said the smuggler, smirking.

'So much the worse for me,' De Lacy was *going* to to say; but, checking himself when he remembered the nature of the rascal to whom he spoke, he contented himself by saying, 'Don't flatter yourself I'm the better of that. In short,' added he, 'you speak in vain to me if you seek to disparage the Irish as a nation'; but in the particular case of Rory O'More, I would sooner depend on his faith and honour than many a king I could name.'

'A *king!*' said De Welskein, in a tone of contempt: 'I believe so indeed!'

'Or the French Directory either,' added De Lacy.

'*Sacre!*' exclaimed the smuggler.

'Say no more, De Welskein: it is as impossible that Rory O'More could be a traitor as that Hoche could be a coward.'

De Welskein seized on the name of Hoche, and repeating it, said, with his eyes fixed *into* De Lacy,—

'*À propos* of General Hoche: I sent you a letter from him—did you get it?'

'No,' said De Lacy calmly.

The manifest composure of De Lacy's manner under the circumstances of such a piece of intelligence being communicated, puzzled the Frenchman, who, after a moment's pause, however, continued, 'You did not get that letter?'

De Lacy repeated his negative.

'Then,' said De Welskein, assuming a triumphant manner, 'I sent you such a letter by that immaculate friend of yours (*votre ami sans tache*).'

'I know you did,' said De Lacy.

This utterly confounded the Frenchman, who, after a short pause, said, 'And why have you not seen it?'

'Because O'More destroyed it.'

'Ha!ha!' said the Frenchman exultingly: 'he tells you so';—*are you sure of that?*'

'Quite sure,' said De Lacy.

'Do you know that he gave private information to the colonel of the town, to save himself from being flogged?'

'I do.'

De Welskein seemed quite crestfallen that all his intelligence, which he expected to swamp De Lacy, seemed to run off him as freely as water from a duck's feathers.

It was now the smuggler's turn to wonder; and in reply to his numerous questions, De Lacy informed him of all the circumstances necessary to the explanation of Rory's closet scene with the colonel.

'But,' said the Frenchman, with the hope of having one startling fact to advance of which he fancied De Lacy was ignorant, 'do you know that the colonel *gave him a pass?*'

'Ye,' said De Lacy.

This last monosyllable '*annihilated*' the Frenchman, as he would have said himself; or, as Rory O'More would have exemplified it, 'he hadn't a word to throw to a dog.'

Now it is necessary to explain how all this suspicion of Rory's conduct arose; 'and, to do everybody justice, or, as some polite people say, 'to give the d——l his due,' De Welskein was not to blame in the matter.

Let it be remembered, that when Rory was brought up for examination before the colonel, there was another prisoner present, who was one of the visitors to De Welskein's cellar, and that mutual recognition had taken place between him and our hero in the guard-house.

This man was aware also of what occurred at Rory's examination;—the threat of flogging,—of the room being cleared when Rory said he had something to communicate to the colonel *in private*,—of the fact of Rory being pronounced free as soon as the room was re-opened—and not only *free*, but favoured with *a pass*—enough to damn his fair fame with all the rebels in Ireland.

All this had been communicated to De Welskein through the friend of this fellow, Betty's husband, who was a very knowing hand in assisting De Welskein's smuggling schemes, and was a United man to boot; and from certain circumstances coming within the knowledge of Scrubbs, he was detained in prison to be prosecuted for his smuggling offences by the Collector. Now, I believe all fellows who get into gaol while others are at large who have as good a right as themselves (in their opinion) to be there too, entertain a grudge against the parties luckier than they; but if they suspect any foul play has been used to keep the aforesaid uncaged parties out of limbo, they take good care the fact shall be transmitted from the gaol 'to those whom it may concern.' Now, circumstances, in their outward form, bore strongly against Rory; and neither the prisoner nor De Welskein could be blamed for looking with a suspicious eye upon the unexplained liberation of our hero.

However, De Welskein was made quite easy by the explanation of De Lacy, who charged him particularly to remove from the minds of all those who were impressed with the belief of Rory's treachery every trace of doubt as to his fidelity.

This being done, De Welskein left the cottage before Rory's return, which did not take place until late,—for Rory was so undecided, after all his deliberation, how he should act with respect to Regan, that it was only the deepening shades of evening which warned him homewards.

On his return, he heard he had been inquired for by the scholar, so he tapped at his apartment, and announced his presence to De Lacy, who invited him to enter, and bidding him close the door, communicated all that had occurred between him and De Welskein.

Rory was indignant that any one should suppose *him* so base as to be guilty of the crime of treachery; and even when De Lacy pointed out to him the strong circumstantial evidence against him, Rory only exclaimed, 'To the divil with their evidence! I never knew evidence of any good, but to ruin a man's charácter.' And indeed Rory's opinion of evidence is but too often borne out by fact.

'But,' said he, 'that they should think me guilty of such a dirty turn! *me*—the rale blood o' the O'Mores! Bad luck to thim, the slandherers! Oh, I only wish I had thim to bate the lives out o' thim! Throth, I'd fight the whole country on sitch a charge, "one down and another come on."'

De Lacy endeavoured to calm him, but it was with much difficulty he at last succeeded. Then Rory, in answer to De Lacy's questions about Solomon's allusion to the 'uncommon fine ducks,' told him the circumstances of the frolic at the fair, which he and Mary, for prudential motives, had previously agreed to say nothing about; and further, communicated Regan's baseness in saying that he had *stolen* the ducks:—'And I wouldn't wondher,' said Rory, 'if the black-hearted villain was at the bottom o' *this* too.'

De Lacy assured him Regan's name had never been mentioned in the business; but Rory declared, that as he found people were goin' about to 'take away his châraccther, he would not let it pass with Regan what he had said; for how could he know the beginnin' or end of sitch things? and so the safest way was to make Regan ate his words first.'

To do Rory justice, his walk by the river had tended to cool his anger a good deal, and he was rather inclined to trust to the public for a proper estimation of his character, and to leave the slander of Regan unnoticed, when the fresh information he received from De Lacy added fuel to the fire which had been reduced to embers, and all Rory's indignation blazed up afresh, and confirmed him in the determination to ascertain if Regan had been traducing him,—and if he had, to shame him, by confronting him openly and giving a public contradiction to the private slander with which he had sought to blast him.

Rory's unsatisfied cravings to be justified sent him to bed in a fever. He was tortured by a night of dreaming, in which fancy played the tormentor. Alternately the grin of Old Solomon, or the penetrating eye of De Welskein, confronted him; and guard-rooms and cellars, empty streets, crowded fairs, old rusty kettles, and roasting ducks, were huddled together in strange confusion. The ducks were the favourites of his dream: he was haunted by a pair all night;—twirl they went before him, till he twirled and twisted in his sleep as if he were roasting too; and his mind, with the ingenious art of tormenting which dreaming bestows upon it, easily converted dangling ducks into hanging criminals, who by a sudden transition were condensed into one, and that *one* became identified with himself, whom he imagined condemned to be hanged for robbery, and brought out to execution, with all the eyes of his friends and acquaintances staring upon him, until the overwhelming sense of degradation and shame awoke him. In vain he strove to sleep; night brought no rest to poor Rory, and the dawn saw him an early and unrefreshed riser.

Immediately after quitting his bed, he started on his tour of discovery, and finding his suspicion as to the author of the calumny against him not unfounded, at once determined on the course he should pursue.— Waiting until the following Sunday, he proceeded to the chapel at the side of the country where Regan resided, which he knew to be the most likely place to meet him, and certainly the most public. For Regan, though a disorderly person, attended mass with punctuality indeed, so

strict is the observance of attendance at public worship on the part of
the Irish peasantry, that the man must be very far gone in crime who
disregards it. There was an additional reason too for Rory selecting the
day and the place for his purpose; after the celebration of the mass,
the congregation do not immediately dispere; but assemble round the
building outside, forming a sort of social 'change,' where those who
have not seen each other for the bygone week barter civilities, and the
current gossip of the day is passed about.

To the chapel, therefore, Rory repaired on the Sunday after his meeting
with the tinker, in company with three or four companions, whom he
wished to be witnesses of his reproval of Regan for his unhandsome
conduct towards him; and when the mass was ended, he and his friends
sought about in the crowd, as they stood in detached groups over the
road about the chapel, and at length he perceived Regan talking and
laughing, the loudest of a noisy cluster of rollicking young fellows, who
were cracking jokes on the old men, and saying half-complimentary half-
impudent things to the young women who passed by them.

Rory walked directly up to Regan; and there was so close a
sympathy between Regan's conscience and Rory's look, that the
former changed colour as the latter made a dead stand before him,
and looked him straight in the face with the bright and open eye that
bears evidence of an honest heart. There was a moment's silence; after
which, Rory was the first to speak.

'Regan,' said he, 'you have not used me well—and you know it.'

'I know little of anything consarning you, and I wish to know less,'
replied Regan, as he turned on his heel, and was going away; but Rory
laid his hand upon him, and said firmly,

'Regan, that won't do! You've said things of me behind backs, thay
I come to contradict before faces; and them that knows both of us is
here to the fore, to judge between us.'

'What are you talkin' about, man?' said Regan, with a swaggering
air that but ill concealed his uneasiness.

'You know well what I'm talkin' about,' answered Rory; 'and so do
them that hears me. Was it good, Regan, to put an ugly turn on an
innocent thrick at a fair, and say I stole your ducks?—I—your owld

playmate, and the son of dacent people, and that never disgraced them, nor never will, plaze God!'

'And didn't you take them?' said Regan with savage effrontery.

'Ay, *take*,' said Rory: 'but, was *take* the word you used behind my back?'

'I'm not to pick my words for sitch as you,' said Regan, who began to recover the faint twinge of shame that abashed him at appearance, and seemed now determined to brazen out the affair.

'Well, I neither pick, nor *stale* either,' said Rory; 'and who ever says to the conthrairy hasn't the truth in them. Aud here I have come this blessed day, and am after hearin' the blessed mass; and it's not at this time, and in this place, I would lay the weight of a lie on my sowl; and yiz are all here round me and hears me, and let them deny me who can; and I say to your face, Regan, that what you've been givin' out on me is not the thruth. I wouldn't use a harder word to an owld friend—though we're cooler of late.'

'What do you mane by harder words?' said Regan, with a menacing air.

'Don't look so angry, Regan. I didn't come here, this quiet and blessed day, to fight; I only kem to clear myself in the face o' the world;—and having done that, I have no more to say,—and so let me go my ways in pace and quietness.' And Rory was turning away but Regan prevented him; and now all his bad passions gaining the ascendency, he said,

'If you mane, by "harder words," to say that you come here to give me the lie, it's what I won't let you or any man do, and if that's your plan, I can tell you I'll thrust your impudent words down your throat with my fist!' and he clenched his hand fiercely in Rory's face.

'Regan,' said Rory, commanding himself, 'I towld you I didn't come here to fight, but to clear myself. Them that knows us both hears me clear myself, and that's enough for me.'

''Faith, you're like your sisther, my buck!' said Regan: 'both o' yiz will go jist half-ways with a man.'

'Regan!' exclaimed Rory, with an honest vehemence that forced him to hear him till he finished his sentence, 'the black dhrop is in you, or you wouldn't say an ill word of a dacent girl that never wronged you! She never liked you, Regan—and you know it. She never wint half-ways with you—and you know it; and now to your teeth I tell you, you're a slandherous liar, and you know it!'

The word had hardly passed Rory's lips, when a tremendous blow from Regan was aimed at him, which Rory avoided by nimbly springing beyond its reach; and Regan left himself so open by his wild attack, that our hero put in a hit so well directed that his ruffianly foe was felled to the earth. He rose immediately, however, foaming with rage, and was rushing on Rory with tremendous fury, when the bystanders closed in between the combatants, and it was suggested by some that hostilities should proceed no further; while others proposed that if the men were bent on fighting, it would be best to adjourn to some adjacent field and strip for the encounter. Regan's friends were for the latter course; while the better-disposed endeavoured to dissuade Rory from exchanging any more blows. But Rory was high mettled: he said they all could bear witness he strove as far as he could to prevent matters going to such extremities; but, as the case stood, he'd never let it be said that an O'More refused to fight. 'I'd rather 'twas any day but Sunday, to be sure,' said Rory: 'but I heer'd mass; so, having done my duty to God, I'm ready to do my duty to man—and in throth I'll do my best to plaze him,' said he, throwing off the upper part of his dress, lightly, and laughing. 'I've the good cause on my side, anyhow; so see fair play, boys, and let him do his worst.'

Great interest was excited by the approaching contest. Regan had the reputation of a bruiser, and was rather inclined to take advantage of it when he had to deal with those who permitted such a practice; and the report having gone abroad that he had been worsted by Rory in the trifling turn-up at the fair, gave rise to various opinions on the subject.

Let not this surprise the reader—it was an *event* amongst a village population: to those who are beyond the reach of more exciting objects, the fall of a favourite fighter is of as much importance as the fall of a minister.

The companions of Regan protested the impossibility of Rory's conquest over their champion, but for the chance of his being in liquor at the time; and the friends of Rory—that is to say, the bulk of the community—looked forward to the approaching fight with a degree of dread that there might be but too much truth in the assertion and that Rory was about to lose his newly-acquired laurel which they had been flourishing in the teeth of Regan's party with that sort of second-hand triumph people always indulge in when some 'cock of the walk' has bean well plucked. They feared the moment was to come which should rob them of the opportunity of saying, 'Phoo! Regan indeed! Arrah, sure Rory O'More leathered him!'

I will not attempt to describe a boxing-match: it has been often better done than I could do it; and the better it has been done, the more I have always wished it had been left undone. The public have had enough of entertainment in that line; and I have sometimes thought that as in Cookery-books they give you a sort of diagram setting forth the various good things constituting a feast, you may lay down a plan, making a glorious set-out—or one should rather say, a *set-to*, to tickle the palate of a gourmand in the Fancy line. What a bill of fare might be produced with a little rubbing up of the memory! At a venture, here goes for a catalogue of items.

Breadbasket.
Buttock.
Gammon.
Fowl.
Game;—in high condition.
Pepper.
Pickle.

So much might content a *glutton*. Then if you want to be *groggy*, there's a

Bottleholder and
Claret.

What more need you wish?—so, make out the fight to please yourself. Of the result, all need be said is, that Regan was savage, and Rory, knowing the power of his adversary, cautious. This, and his activity, did wonders for him; and after some furious hitting from Regan, which Rory sometimes guarded and sometimes broke away beyond reach of, Regan began to breathe hard, of which our hero took advantage: the tide soon turned in his favour; and doubtless, the conscience of either of the combatants had no insignificant influence upon the fight. The ultimate consequence, however, was that Rory again triumphed over his malignant adversary; and a sullen silence on the part of a disappointed few, with a hearty shout from the exulting many, declared that Regan had given in, and Rory O'More was the victor.

XXIII

Containing De Lacy's letter,—contrasting the conditions of Ireland and England.

'Look here upon this picture—and on this.'

THE GLORIOUS NEWS TO BRITAIN of the victory of the 11th of October had now spread rejoicing over England, but caused aching to many a heart in Ireland. The Texel fleet was conquered, and its admiral a prisoner in England. No more chance of aid might be looked for from that quarter, and for a short time the hopes of the United Irishmen were blighted.

But in a few days other news arrived to temper the severity of this blow to their designs, and made them yet more confident of assistance from France.

Other triumphs than Duncan's filled the ear of Europe; for just now the rapid and brilliant succession of Bonaparte's victories in Italy more than outweighed the naval conquest of Duncan; and Austria saw, one after another, her experienced generals beaten by the young Corsican, and her veteran armies overwhelmed by the raw levies of impetuous France. The 18th of October witnessed the failure of the Bourbon plot in the assemblies of Paris; the Clichy Club was suppressed; Pichegru and Carnot fled; the republic again triumphed over the attempts of the Royalists, and was once more secured under a new Directory; Austria was forced to sign a peace dictated by the enemy and France was more free than ever to pursue her hostility against England. Then came that tremendous assembling of her victorious troops, which soon after were gathered on her northern shore, under the denomination of the 'Army of England'; and then was threatened the memorable 'invasion' that occupied all the attention of Great Britain.

This was the period of all others most favourable to the views of the Irish republican party; and De Lacy, seizing the occasion, despatched a letter to France, urging immediate aid to Ireland, which was ripe for revolt.

His report ran as follows:

'My last letter was written against the grain; I had to tell of many unexpected truths, evincing England's security: but now my words flow from my heart, and I say, Strike for Ireland, and it will be an easy victory. Here all is ripe for revolution. The besotted and cruel intolerance of the party in power, and the deplorable wretchedness and long-suffering of the neglected and oppressed people, cannot go any farther.

'The former cannot be greater tyrants, nor the latter greater slaves; the one party cannot add greater weight to their chain, nor the other ever have greater cause to wish it broken. Come, then, and strike the manacles from the bondsmen!'

'This is indeed the land of misery and misrule! How the sister island, as she is called, of Great Britain, can be in so degraded a state, while England revels in prosperity, is one of those enigmas which baffles all attempt at solution. In contrast to the state of England, listen to a rough sketch of the condition of this lovely but wretched country.

'One striking difference between the two islands is, that while in England society consists of many grades, sinking slightly the one beneath the other, but presenting no startling difference in the descent; in Ireland there are but two,—the upper and the lower. There is a sort of mongrel middle rank, but consisting of too few to constitute anything like a class, in comparison with the others. In England there are many degrees between the peer and the peasant—but not so here: the *cementing* portions of society are wanting; the wholesome links that bind it together exist not here; in short, Ireland may be comprised under two great heads—those who inflict, and those who suffer.

'In Ireland the aristocracy seem to live wholly for themselves: the poor they seem to consider utterly unworthy of being thought of. Look at the English tenantry,—lived amongst by their landlords, and their comforts cared for; while the poor Irish are left to take what care they can of themselves. If the fever visit an English village, there is the manor-house to apply to, whence the hand of affluence can be stretched forth to afford the comforts which the hour of sickness demand. If the typhus rage in Ireland, there is not for miles, perhaps, the hall of a proprietor to look to; and where there is, it is vacant; grass grows before its doors, and closed shutters say to the destitute, "No help have you here. My lord spends elsewhere the gold you have paid to his agent, and his wine-cellar is not to be invaded by a pauper." His claret flows freely midst the laugh of revelry, but may not retard the expiring sigh of some dying father of a helpless offspring. "Drain the cask dry for riot!" cries the bacchanal, "and let the call of charity be echoed back by the empty barrel!"

'What can such a landlord hope for from his neglected serf? Is it to be expected that his name will be heard with blessings, and his person looked upon with attachment, or that the wholesome link between landlord and tenant can exist under such a state of things? No: they are not beings of the same community—man and the beast of the field are not more distinct than these two classes of people, and the time will come when the Irish landlord shall bitterly lament that the only bond which held the peasant to his master, was his chain.

'Be it yours to hasten this epoch, for all is ripe for change, because any change must he better for them;—at least, no change can make them worse. Therefore are they brands ready for the lighting.

'I told you of the comforts of a village in England. What is such a thing in Ireland?—an irregular jumble of mud-hovels, whose thatch has been so long without repair that its decomposition produces vegetation; and you may see ragged cocks and hens feeding on the roof; a pig wallows on a dunghill before the door (lucky when they have one!), until a starved cur, roused by some half (or whole) naked children, disturbs him from his place of enjoyment, and drives him for shelter into the house, whose mistress protects "the gintleman that pays the rint." I heard the saying of a "fool" or "natural," as they call idiots in this country, which amused me much for its graphic truth: his definition of a village was admirably given in four words—"Pigs, dogs, dunghills, and blackguards!"

'The hovels of the Irish peasantry are not by any means so good as the stables of their masters' horses. The lord of the soil would not let his hunter sleep in the wretched place he suffers his tenantry to dwell in, and for which he receives the rent that supports *him* in his wastefulness. Nor does he seek to better their condition; and if a murmur of discontent escape these ill-used people, they are branded with the foulest names, and the guilty party seeks, by heaping abuse and calumny on those whom he injures, to justify the conduct which has *produced* the very state of things of which he complains.

'I spoke of the English peasant-children playing at cricket, and remarked that the peasantry must be in a state of comfort who can afford to buy the materials of play for their offspring. What is the Irish game amongst the children?—an imitation of the manly exercise of hurling, which they call "commons;" this is nothing more than driving a stone before them with a crooked stick, which is cut from any hedge that may afford it. The English children took off their clothes, to play: not so the Irish, and for the best reason in the world,—because they had no clothes to take off; they are nearly all in a state of nudity, and even when not quite uncovered, their wretched rags are almost worse than nakedness.

'It is impossible to conceive human nature reduced to so great a state of privation in every way as it is here; and even under all this privation they are merry, and I verily believe would be content, only they are goaded by insult and oppression into the bargain. The most active of their prosecutors are the mongrel middle class to whom I alluded;— *Squireens* they are called by the people. These fellows have not an idea beyond a dog, a gun, a home, and the pleasures of the table. They are generally the descendants of Cromwell's or William's troopers, and, of course, are the fiercest upholders of the ascendancy which gives them all they have. But they are not even content with this: they must revile and malign the people whom their forefathers despoiled. They are the toad-eaters of those in power, to whom they bow, aud from whom in return they get the refuse of the sops of which the ascendant party have the dispensing.

'From this class are all the minor fry of government officers selected, and in their bands is the magistracy throughout the country vested. The consequence is, that the people have not the shadow of Justice to shelter under, much less her shield: the law of the land (so called), and as it is administered by this partisan magistracy, is not the poor man's friend, but his foe. So they are all ready to upset such a state of things as soon as they can. Do not delay this epoch;—I repeat it,—strike now, and Ireland shall be free!

'There is everything ready to aid in the enterprise. In the North, the organisation is extensive, and arms and ammunition prepared; and it is there, as Tone has recommended, I would advise the descent to be made.

'The Midland counties have a tolerably well-organised union also, and it has spread to the West. It is where I am at present, in the South, that there is less of preparation for revolt; but the *spirit* to be free is everywhere, and they are all ready to rise the moment they have a force of disciplined troops landed, to form a nucleus round which they may gather.

'Some time it will take, of course, to make them good soldiers; but they are very quick, and in a cause in which their hearts lay would soon make available troops. The great requisites for a soldier they possess in a supereminent degree,—long endurance of fatigue and fasting, and courage not to be surpassed by any nation under heaven.

'In short, never was there a country more ready for revolution, nor more needing it. Everything is antagonised, everything in extremes: it is waste or want, raiment or rags, feasting or starvation. There is no middle to anything. The very column of society is broken—the capital and base alone remain: the shaft is shattered, and the two extremes are in ruinons separation.

'If anything were wanting to complete this fearful state of things, it is this:—with these two parties, religion is a badge, and not a blessing; and they make their creeds, which profess peace, a war-cry.'

This letter De Lacy forwarded to France; and about a fortnight afterwards, he himself made a visit to Dublin, to consult with the chiefs of the revolutionary party on the necessity of having the organisation in a state of readiness for co-operation with the force from France, which, he doubted not, his letter would hasten.

XXIV

Showing how a gentleman might not dress himself as he pleased forty years ago, in Ireland.

> 'Sure, there's some wonder in this handkerchief.'
>
> *Othello.*

> 'For the wearing of the green,
> For the wearing of the green,
> 'Tis a poor distressed country for the wearing of the green!'
>
> *National Ballad.*

ON COMMUNICATING WITH THE CENTRAL Committee in Dublin, De Lacy found all was in readiness to co-operate with a force landing from France. But, sanguine as were their expectations of aid from the republic, their disappointments had been so frequent, that, after some time had elapsed, they urged De Lacy to present himself in person to the Directory, and urge an immediate movement in their favour. 'Impatience,' said they, 'begins to manifest itself in some;—despair in others; and action becomes necessary. How many opportunities have been frustrated!— While there was mutiny to a fearful extent in the English navy, our friends in the Texel could not give us aid, and thus a favourable occasion was lost;—and now, when the recent victories and glorious peace France has achieved leave her free for action—now is the time to cripple Britain!

Should this moment be allowed to pass, we may not find another.'

Thus urged, De Lacy determined on acting in accordance with the views of the leading members of the United men, and return to the South, to make the necessary arrangements with De Welskein for his being conveyed to France.

During De Lacy's absence, the circumstances of the immediate region of our story were ripening into more serious action. 'The plot was thickening,' as the romance readers say, and Rory was getting more and more into hot water.

The affair of the guard-room, and his *private* interview with the colonel, had spread amongst Regan's set; and however De Welskein was answered by De Lacy upon every charge he could bring against O'More, it was not such an easy matter to silence the murmurs of a parcel of prejudiced ruffians, whose personal dislike of our hero (because he was not of their set, and had thrashed their leader) rendered them impervious to every particle of evidence which they did not *choose* to believe.

At this time, too, they dreaded the approaching trial of Darby Daly, the man who had been arrested the same night as Rory. He was not only a smuggler, but a United man; and they feared, in case of a conviction, that he might 'blab' to save himself. So, to prevent such a disagreeable result, and as the gaol where he was confined was too strong to admit any hope of escape, it was determined that the awkward circumstances likely to result from a trial should be avoided, by putting the prosecutor and principal witness out of the way.

This was no less a person than 'the Collector,' Scrubbs; and how he was to be disposed of, was matter of consultation with De Welskein's party, who, being all liable to implication in the smuggling affair, were equally anxious to get rid of the collector. Now, 'Soldering Solomon,' being a long-headed old fellow, and interested in the success of the smuggling might help them in the matter; and as there was an appointment made for the following Sunday, when a certain 'jollification' was to be held, at which most of the 'set' were to be present, it was agreed to postpone the consideration of the collector's fate until that day, when the tinker might assist in their councils.

In the meantime, De Lacy sought De Welskein, who promised to be ready to sail for France within the ensuing week. De Lacy urged an earlier departure; but as the smuggler said his lugger would not be off the coast until that time, his embarkation was of necessity delayed.

But an event soon took place which might have terminated fatally to De Lacy, and prevented any future voyages he projected. He had been in the neighbouring village, and was about to return, when a troop of yeomanry cavalry rode in and halted half way up the street, opposite to M'Garry's, the apothecary's, at whose shop the post-office was established. The troop had been under the inspection of the district general that day, and was then returning when Solomon Slink, Esq., of Slinkstown, captain of the corps, halted his troop, as already stated, to inquire at the post-office if there were any letters for him. The captain was a violent person in his politics; one of those with whom it is not enough to support their own opinions, but to knock down those of everybody who thinks differently from themselves: and in those days, when on the side of authority so much could be done with impunity, such a person was prone to commit outrage on very trivial grounds.

It so happened, that as he rode up to M'Garry's shop, De Lacy was about to leave it, and was just upon the threshold as the captain was going to ask for his letters; but his eye was attracted by the green handkerchief which De Lacy wore, which, being the national colour of Ireland, was offensive to the sight of those who loved oppression better than their country; and so the captain, being at the head of his corps, thought he could exercise a bit of loyal tyranny with safety.

Casting a ferocious look upon De Lacy, he said in the most offensive manner, 'Why do you wear that green handkerchief?'

De Lacy was taken by surprise at the extraordinary insolence of the man, and the ultra intolerance that would interfere with the private right of dressing as one pleased. Before he could answer, the question was repeated with increased offensiveness.

'I believe, sir,' said De Lacy, 'I have as good a right to wear a handkerchief as you.'

'Not a green one,' said the captain.

'I'm not aware of any law against wearing green, sir,' said De Lacy.

'*I'll* show you law for it!' said the other. 'Take it off, sir!'

'I'll do no such thing, sir.'

'Won't you? Then, if *you* don't, by G——d I will!'

'That you may do if you like, sir,' said De Lacy, folding his arms and drawing himself up to his full height.

The captain pressed his spurs to his horse's side, and plunging rudely upon De Lacy, he laid his hand upon the tie of his handkerchief, which he dragged from his neck, and flung upon the ground, saying, 'There's your d——d rebel green for you!'[1]

De Lacy grew as pale and cold, and *firm* too, as marble, at the brutal affront, and said to the yeomanry hero, with a tone of chilling mockery in his voice—

'Thank you!—And now, sir, after your polite attention to my toilet, may I beg the favour of your dismounting and walking into the fields with me! I see your holsters are provided with pistols, and two of your own gentlemen can arrange our ground.'

'Arrange your grandmother!' said the polished captain. 'Fight a rebel, indeed! I'd see you d——d first!'

'Then, sir,' said De Lacy, 'at the head of your own corps, I tell you you're a coward!'

Captain Slink half drew his sword; but his arm was arrested by the Protestant clergyman of the parish, who fortunately was beside him, or perhaps De Lacy's life might have paid the forfeit of his temerity, in daring to object to this loyal aggression, and fling back insult for insult.

Having thus defied the captain without producing the desired result, De Lacy turned on his heel, and left him boiling with indignation at the epithet that had been flung in his teeth.

'Does any one know who the rascal is?' said he.

'I know where the fellow lives,' said the collector, who, as well as Sweeny, was one of the corps.

The captain, having received his letters from the post-office, the troop was again put in motion; and on the road a long conversation took place between Scrubbs, Sweeny, and the commander, relative to De Lacy, on whom they had always looked with a suspicious eye, and after whom they thought it necessary some inquiry should be made.

'Never fear,' said the captain; 'I'll have a sharp eye on the chap.'

While the lord of Slinkstown that evening was drinking his claret, he was seriously considering a letter he had just received, in which there was a passage arrested his attention, in connection with the occurrence between him and De Lacy that day. It mentioned fears being entertained amongst the well-affected to the government, that emissaries from France were at work in Ireland; and the writer (who was an official in Dublin Castle) had heard so rumours of a suspicious person having been lately seen leaving Dublin in one of the southern coaches; and recommending to the captain vigilance about his district, in case questionable people might be observed.

At this period, though government had not any tangible evidence to go upon to prove a conspiracy, yet their fears were awake upon the subject; and some arrests had been made on mere suspicion, even at this time, and their spies were on the alert in all quarters.

It will not, under these circumstances, be wondered at that the captain determined to see more about De Lacy, against whom not only his loyalty urged him to be hostile, but the insult which had bern cast upon him so publicly: he therefore ordered a muster of the corps for the next day, and determined on arresting De Lacy.

That young gentleman pursued his road homewards after leaving the village, muttering desperate speeches all the way, and longing in his inmost soul to have a shot at the captain: but as that was clearly out of the question, he was obliged to be satisfied with calling him fifty thousand 'ruffians' and 'poltroons.' This relieved his mind considerably; and after swearing over about a mile of ground, he began to think that, after what had taken place, it was just as well he was leaving the country, where to have remained without getting 'satisfaction' would have 'stuck in his gizzard,' as Lord Chesterfield says; so he was all impatience for getting to France, to hurry the expedition, that he might return and wreak his vengeance on all the yeomanry in Ireland for the insult he had received from the bully captain.

1. Fact.

XXV

*Showing how a pass may defend a soldier, as well as a soldier defend a pass;
and how a man in authority may order sabres for one, without admiring
pistols for two.*

THE MORNING AFTER THIS UNTOWARD occurrence, De Welskein and
De Lacy were in consultation in Rory O'More's cottage upon the
projected trip to France. The smuggler anticipated that the Monday or
Tuesday following would see the lugger upon the coast, and he appointed
a place where De Lacy should be in readiness to embark. Before they
had finished their conference, De Lacy's ear caught the sound of the
approaching tramp of horses; and looking from the window, he saw the
troop of yeomanry cavalry trotting down the boreen, with his friend the
captain at their head, flanked by Scrubbs and Sweeny.

Scrubbs never had forgiven De Lacy the liberal sentiment he
expressed on the coach the day of his journey downwards; and
Sweeny, whose indignation was great against Rory for the attention
of the tombstone, had a misgiving that this mysterious stranger had
something to do with turning a loyal Protestant into ridicule. Therefore,
both these gentlemen independently of their duty to their captain and
the good of the state, were very willing to join in a domiciliary visit
to Rory O'More, and make an arrest upon his friend.

The moment De Lacy saw the yeomanry, he calculated some
mischief was in the wind; and feeling that the presence of a
foreigner under existing circumstances would bear an unfavourable
interpretation against him, he opened the door to call for Rory, who,

being always on the alert in cases of emergency, had his hand already upon the latch to warn De Lacy of the approach of the armed men.

'*He* must not be seen,' said De Lacy, pointing to De Welskein 'Can you conceal him?'

'In a jiffy,' said Rory. 'Make haste, your sowl' said he to the Frenchman; 'come along here!' and he pulled the smuggler across the floor of the kitchen, to where, in a recess beside the fireplace, a kish used for holding turf stood; and Rory, in an instant emptying the turf from the basket said, 'Down with you, Divilskin, my darlin',—down on your marrow-bones!'

The Frenchman, though he did not understand his language, comprehended his meaning, and dropping on his knees, Rory inverted the kish upon him and covered him completely.

While all this was doing inside the house, the captain had his plans to put in practice outside; he completely surrounded the cottage with his men to prevent an escape, and then he swaggered into the house; with his sword clattering at his heels, followed by Sweeny and Scrubbs.

De Lacy, apprehending that the women might be alarmed, and their agitation be productive of mischief, came forward to meet the captain and his supporters at once, that his presence might call off their attention from the widow and her daughter. Before they who came to seek him had time to ask a question, De Lacy said 'I rather think the honour of this visit is meant for me.'

The captain at the first glance did not recognise him, for De Lacy had a dressing-dress on him at the time, as his coat had been wetted through that morning by a heavy shower of rain, and was hanging to dry at that moment before the kitchen fire; but on a second look, the yeomanry hero perceived it was his man, and said, 'Yes, you are the person I want.'

De Lacy, pointing politely to the door of his bedroom, whence he had stepped, said, 'Will you do me the favour to go into my room?'

'Go on,' said the captain; 'we'll follow you.'

De Lacy, bowing courteously, and still pointing to the door, said, 'After you, if you please.' And there was that influence in his manner which an air of politeness always bestows, that even the brutality of the squireen captain was not insensible to its power, and he and his satellites entered the room, followed by De Lacy, who closed the door.

'Gentlemen, pray be seated,' continued he.

'There's no necessity,—our business here is very short.'

'May I beg to know what is your business, sir?'

'That's just the question I was going to ask *you*.—I want to know who and what you are, and where you come from.'

'I have yet to learn, sir, what authority you have for asking such a question.'

'That's always the answer that people make who can't give a good account of themselves.'

At this moment the door was opened, and Rory, putting in his head, said, 'I beg your pardon, sir,—here's your coat:' and De Lacy saw in the expression of his eye that he had some meaning in his intrusion;—so, going to the door he received the garment from Rory, who said in a whisper as he handed it to him, 'The *pass* is in the pocket.'

De Lacy caught Rory's idea on the instant, and begging pardon of his visitors, he threw off his dressing-gown and resumed his coat.

The moment that Rory had seen the captain enter the house, the thought struck him of the colonel's pass being made an instrument of safety to De Lacy; but how to put it into his possession was the question. Just then his eye caught the coat hanging before the fire; and to get the pass from his box, put it in the pocket, and make De Lacy change his garment, was the work of a moment.

De Lacy felt for the pass, and when his fingers touched the precious slip of paper, he knew he possessed a talisman to paralyse the attempt made against him;—so, assuming the most perfect composure, he muttered some common-place apology about his being found in dishabille, and again requested his visitors to be seated.

'You seem to take this very easy, sir,' said the captain; 'but it won't do,—I arrest you, sir;'—and he was advancing upon De Lacy, who retired rapidly a few paces, and seizing from a corner cupboard a case of pistols, he presented them upon his would-be captor, and said, 'Dare to lay a hand on me, and you are a dead man!'

The captain paused, but said to Scrubbs and Sweeny, 'Advance and seize him!'

But Scrubbs and Sweeny looked at De Lacy's pistols, and then at each other, and seemed to have no greater stomach for being shot than their commander.

'Don't be rash, gentlemen,' said De Lacy; though indeed there seemed no great necessity for his caution, from the moment his pistols made their appearance. He laid down one of the weapons, and putting his hand into his pocket, drew forth the pass, which he presented to the captain, saying, 'I suppose, sir, you know what *that* is?'

The captain was thunderstruck.

'What have you to say for yourself now, sir?' said De Lacy, with cut severity in his voice.

'Is this his writing?' said Slink, showing the pass to Scrubbs, who, he knew, was familiar with the character.

Scrubbs answered in the affirmative.

The captain handed back the pass, and mumbled some lame apology, in which 'very sorry,'—'a thousand pardons,'—'suspicious appearances,'—'strange times,' etc., etc. were huddled together 'but how could he know?'

'You had better wait until you do know next time, sir,' said De Lacy, 'and not pull neckcloths from unoffending persons for the future.'

'For the occurrence of yesterday, I beg to offer you — —'

'Pray say no more on that subject, sir. You affronted *me*, and I insulted *you*: if *you* are content, I am.'

Captain Slink protested he was delighted to find he had been mistaken, and could not think of harbouring any resentment against a loyal gentleman; that he never was more surprised in his life,—'he could not comprehend.'

'I dare say, sir, there are many things above your comprehension,' said De Lacy: 'but, as a word of parting advice, I recommend you in future to abstain from aggressions on better men than yourself.'

'Sir, I don't see,' said the captain, 'why you should insinuate—'

'If you don't like what I say, sir,' said De Lacy, 'there's fair ground at the back of the house; and here's a case of pistols.'

'By no means, sir,' said the captain: 'I didn't mean *that;* these are not times when loyal men should quarrel among themselves,' etc., etc. In short, the bully backed out.

Scrubb and Sweeny were mute witnesses of this scene, which was equally astounding to them as their commander; but just before leaving the room, Sweeny ventured to say in the most obsequious manner to De Lacy, (for the moment he showed the colonel's ass, his high tone overawed the whole three,) that he begged to ask him what his opinion was of Rory O'More.

'He is as worthy of trust as I am,' said De Lacy.

'He has your confidence, then, sir?' said Scrubbs.

'Most implicitly, sir,' said De Lacy.

Captain Slink in the meantime had made his exit, as Rory said, 'like a dog without his tail;' and as soon as Scrubbs and Sweeny were in their saddles, he went to the rightabout rather crest-fallen at his two *subs* having witnessed his poltroonery in shying De Lacy's invitation to 'pistols for two.'

When the corps was fairly gone, Rory lifted the kish under which De Welskein was concealed, who emerged from his wicker ambush covered with the dust of the turf and cutting a comical figure. As he shook himself and slapped the particles of peat from his person, he grimaced, and ejaculated '*Sacré!*' continually, and seemed little satisfied with the place which had been selected for his retreat; but Rory assured him, as he helped him to clean himself, that he had increased his consequence by the transaction.

'How is dat?' said the Frenchman.

'Sure I made you a gintleman of the turf!' said Rory.

'Rory,' said De Lacy, 'you're a capital fellow;—give me your hand. Your presence of mind on this occasion has saved us all.'

'Oh, thin, if Scrubbs only knew how I came by the same pass!' said Rory. 'Faix, it's his own darlin' rib that saved all the bones in our skins this day.'

'It's your ready wit we may thank,' said De Lacy.

'I beg your pardon,' said Rory. 'It isn't my head, but Scrubbs's, you're beholden to.'

'One thing is clear, however,' said De Lacy: 'I mustn't stay here any longer. Should the affair of the pass get wind, they would be back on us immediately.'

'Thrue enough,' said Rory. 'I thought so myself; but I didn't like to say it first;—it would look like wishing to get rid of you.'

'Don't think so unworthily of me, Rory,' said De Lacy, 'as to suppose I could ever believe an ungenerous sentiment might find a place in your heart.'

A council was now held between the parties as to the best mode of proceeding. It was agreed that De Lacy should proceed to the coast without delay; and this being decided on, he set about making his arrangements at once. Any English books he had, he set up as a present for Mary; and calling her to his room, he begged her acceptance of them as a small testimonial of his sense of her care and attention during his dangerous illness. Poor Mary was quite overcome with this proof of his respect for her that she should have *his* books,—*the scholar's books*. It made her proud but her pride was mingled with sorrow, that they were going to lose the society of this cultivated person, whose presence in their cottage they looked upon as an honour, and whose courteous manners had won him their affection.

'Sure it's sorry we are you're goin', sir,' said Mary.

'I regret it myself, Mary,' said De Lacy. 'I have found more pure and disinterested kindness under this roof than ever I met before, may ever meet again in this wide world, and I shall never forget it; and when I come back to Ireland, which I trust will be soon, I shall not be long in the country without coming to see you all. 'Take these few books, Mary: your name is written in them with my own hand.'

With these words he gave the books to the girl, who was so touched by this last little mark of attention that she could not speak, and on receiving the present, a mute curtsey was all she returned as she held down her head to hide the tears that were coming thick and fast; and before she reached the door, De Lacy heard her sobbing.

'Kind and sensitive people!' said he.

To the widow O'More he begged in the most delicate manner to offer some gold, for all the trouble and expense he had caused but she

would not listen to such a proposition. In vain he urged the propriety
and justice of it—the widow was inexorable.

'Sure, sir, a gintleman, as you are;—and it is the *rale* gintleman you
are, for it is the civil word and the kind word is always, and ever was,
readiest with you;—I say, a gintleman to live undher our humble roof,
and be content with our humble ways, and never complain,—sure it is
an honour you done us, and you wouldn't think of affronting us now!'

'Not for the world, my dear Mrs. O'More!' and De Lacy took her
hand and shook it warmly;—'but——'

'Don't say a word more, sir; sure you said *dear* Mrs. O'More to me,
as if I was a lady: and to have that said to me by *you*, sir,—sure is more
than I desarve if I done twice as much for you; sure that's prouder return
to me than all the goold I could tell; and God speed you, wherever you
go, and send you safe! and maybe we'll see you agin,'—and she paused
as she added—'or maybe we won't: they're quare times, and sore times.'
Here she closed the door. 'Don't think me impudent, sir, nor prying,
nor meddling; but sure I can't help seein' what I see;—*it's comin', it's
comin'*,—and it'll be the sore day for poor Ireland! But, sure, if it's God's
will, His blessed will must be done! And there's my darlin' boy, my Rory,
and he in the thick of it! and who knows but his precious life—and sure
my own heart's blood is not as precious!——Oh, God! Oh, God!'

De Lacy spoke soothingly to her and attempted to calm her.

'Don't think me foolish, sir;—don't,—I'm done now; only I
know of course it must be. Rory has the heart of a lion, though the
gentleness of a lamb is in him too; the good son and brother he is, I
won't deny it: but he can't be kept off *that thing*; he thinks it's his duty
to his counthry; and sure that's the manly part, and why wouldn't
he be a man, though the poor mother's heart sinks with fear? And I
know you're great with him, sir: not that I blame you—don't think
the like,—Rory would be jist the same if he never set eyes on you;
and I'm proud in my poor thremblin' heart to think that my boy is
worthy of that depindince.'

'He's a noble fellow!' said De Lacy.

'God bless you for the words!' said she, weeping with contending
emotions. 'And you'll be at the head of it, I know; and it's the brave

and the bowld leader you'll be, *for you're a gintleman.* And it's to France you're goin';—isn't it to France?'

'It is,' said De Lacy, who could not at the moment have refused her the deepest confidence.

'And will they come soon?' said she eagerly.

'I hope so,' said he.

'Oh, I wish it was over! I wish it was over! for my heart thrembles for my boy.'

'Fear not,' said De Lacy: 'the truly brave are in less danger than the coward.'

'Plaze God! plaze God!' said the mother.

'I hope soon to be back again,' said De Lacy—'and at the head of my grenadiers;' added he, catching the enthusiasm of the mother, who gazed on him with an excited eye that gleamed through her tears. 'I go to summon the victorious troops of France to your aid, and Ireland shall soon be free!'

The enthusiastic woman sunk upon her knees, and, with the earnestness of devotion in her manner, she said, 'May the God of heaven speed you, and watch over you and protect you, and guard you, and all thim that fights the cause of the counthry!' Her lips moved for a few seconds, as if in prayer; and marking herself with the sign of the cross, she arose from her knees, calmed by this outpouring of her feelings; then drying her eyes, and taking De Lacy's hands between her own, she raised her eyes to heaven, and saying fervently, 'May God bless you!' left him.

XXVI

A subterranean meeting.—The sudden appearance of an unexpected agent, threatening the imprisonment and death of De Welskein and his party.

THE SUNDAY ARRIVED WHICH HAD been appointed for the meeting of De Welskein and the smugglers in 'The Folly.'

This was the name given to the ruins of an old, unfinished rambling sort of edifice, which seemed to have been begun without a beginning, if one may say so, and never came to an end. The name is common to such sort of absurdities; and this is one of the follies not peculiar to the Emerald Isle,—for the same things, with the same names, exist in England.

In one of the vaults underneath the pile the smugglers used to meet, and the place was peculiarly fitted for such secret purposes, from its extreme loneliness. The ruins stood in a romantic little valley, along whose abrupt declivities old thorn-trees wreathed their branches in fantastic forms, and gave out the perfume of their white blossoms when the year was young. A mountain stream, which had its source about a mile above the valley, tumbled about through the rocks of this wooded gorge with a wildness and frolic, characteristic of its recent birth: lower down its course, where its banks were fairer and flowers were growing, it circled about in eddying pools, as if loath to leave the pleasant places; and its bubbles and froth, and lingering amid beauty, resembled a riper age;—and at last to the plain it went. The dead level of the world reduced it to a quieter pace; and the rollicking stream settled down into a very smooth, deep, easy-going gentleman.

Close beside the building, this stream gave a spreading sweep, forming one of those pools already alluded to: it was one of the stages in the course of its existence, and possibly induced the projector of the Folly to pitch on this spot for his practice, from the beauty it bestowed upon the scene. This stream, however, was liable to sudden and violent floodings, from its mountain birth; and one of the corners of the ruin gave evidence that it reached a height and force sufficient to wear its flood-mark on the masonry. I will not say it had the reputation of being haunted, but from its loneliness, it was a place rather avoided. The valley, perhaps, had been always lonely, but the old Folly made it appear more so;—for what gives so deep an aspect of desolation to any spot as the ruined and deserted tenement of man?

It was a lovely day in October; the sun was bright, and the clouds, in those large masses indicative of the season, were changing their grand and fantastic forms as they sailed across the sky before the fresh crisp breeze that rustled pleasantly among the trees, whose yellow leaves fell in golden showers to the brisker gusts of the wind.

A man with a dark brow, and downcast eyes, and heavy step, appeared on the edge of the hill that looked over into the valley, and paused on the summit. His appearance was in startling contrast to the scene around him; for *there* was the brightness and loveliness of earth, while he seemed overshadowed by the dark and horrible passions of a nether world.—It was Regan.

The second victory that Rory had gained over him had deepened his hatred to our hero to a fearful degree; in fact, had he dared to strike the blow, *murder* was not beyond him: but he had a coward conscience that quailed at the promptings of his bad heart. Still, however, he hatched minor projects of revenge, and thus was he employed as he stood on the acclivity above the valley. He was about to plunge down the side of the hill that led into the glen, when the faint tinkling of the chapel bell from the adjacent village came fitfully upon the wind, and the sound died away again. Regan stopped as if spell-bound, and looked in the direction whence the sound proceeded. The sound to him was as a whisper to his conscience. Bad though he had become, a regular attendance at mass was one of the decencies of behaviour he had observed, and to-day was the first time he had ever neglected the duty. This may seem strange to the general reader, but to those who know how scrupulously the Irish peasantry attend public worship, it will not be deemed singular. Again the sound floated by him on the breeze; and there he stood listening to the bell as it sounded on his ear at intervals, with the shades of contending emotion passing across his countenance, and seemingly in a state of utter indecision, when a tap on the shoulder aroused him from his trance, and looking round, he saw the sharp eyes and sinister expression of old Solomon the tinker fastened upon him.

'How many grains goes to a bushel o' whate?' asked Solomon.

'What do you mane?' replied Regan.

'Can you tell me?' repeated the tinker.

'How should I know?' said Regan, sullenly.

'Why, you appeared to be in sitch a deep study, that I thought you wor makin' the calculation,' said Solomon, dryly.

'Oh, thin, I wasn't,' said Regan with a long-drawn and heavy sigh: 'I was sthrivin' to remember something I forgot.'

Again the chime of the bell visited his ear, and Regan's look involuntarily answered the sound.

The tinker fastened his keen eye on him, and guessing at Regan's startled conscience, he read his thoughts in an instant, and with a backward twitch of his shrivelled thumb over his shoulder towards he village, he said, 'Forgot!—I suppose you forgot *to go to mass!*—ho, ho, ho! What a loss you are to the flock this day!—what'll Father Kinshela do without you?'

'None o' your humbuggin', Sol,' said Regan.

'Is it *me* humbug?' said the tinker with a sneer, as if rejoicing in the power he affected to disclaim. 'Come along, man; we're late enough. Never mind chapel to-day; the chapel will wait till next Sunday. Don't you know what Punch said?—"Divil may care," said Punch when he lost mass; "I'll be in time for church."' And so saying, the tinker led the way to the valley, and Regan followed in silence.

Within the vaults of the Folly the smugglers were assembled for some time, and were sitting round a rude table formed of three or four planks laid across a couple of large stones, whereon some greybeards filled with brandy stood, one of which was making the circle of the board, and lowering fast in spirits while it raised those of the company. Standing beside a large pot which was suspended over a turf fire appeared De Welskein, who was busy in cooking the contents of the cauldron,—and amongst his various avocations it will not be wondered at that a Frenchman enjoyed the mysteries of the cuisine; but at the same time, while he attended to his culinary cares, he took his share of the conversation—and the brandy also.

'Monsieur Reggan not coame yait?' said De Welskein. 'He go to shappel, I sooppose—ha, ha! G—d d—n fool? no philosophe, too fond of prieste. What good for prieste? for nussing, bote demself—to kesh ten peegs.'

'It's not the priest, but the parson gets the pigs,' said one of his companions.

'All de sem,' said De Welskein contemptuously,—'all de sem I one prieste sem as dudder prieste—all homebogue: prettee feeshe in a keetel.'

'A kittle o' fish, you mane, I suppose.'

'Yais— keettel feesh—das it.'

Regan and Solomon now made their appearance, and were questioned as to the cause of their delay, for they were the last of the party.

'Me know ver well wisout ax,' said De Welskein. 'Meester Solsodderman,' which was his version of Sawdering Solomon, 'he not like to laif de 'ouse vere he sleep las nise visows his brekfas dees morneeng—ha, ha!'

'Small blame to me!' said Solomon, while the others laughed at this touch of De Welskein's knowledge of Solomon's character.

'And for Monsieur Reggan,' said the smuggler, 'he go to shappel aud coos not come before.'

'No, I didn't go to *shappel*,' answered Regan.

'He was only thinkin' of it,' said Solomon.

'Ah! you never love libérts while you love de prieste.'

'Maybe he thinks it's betther be off with the owld love before he's on with the new,' said Solomon.

'*Vous avez raison*,' said the Frenchman triumphantly: 'off wid dem, off wid dem all, prieste and prance!—Bote coame—seet down; time to see vaut to do wis Mister Collectere.—Here Darbee,' said he to a red-haired ruffian who was near the fire,—'here! you wash dis paut wile me mek comeetay of poobleek sefty.'

So saying, he handed his ladle to Darby, and joined the council, who were already muttering amongst each other their notions of what was the best means of silencing the collector.

'We must get rid of him somehow,' said Regan.

'Sartinly,' said a fellow called Jack Flannerty.

'But what's the best way of doin' it?' asked a third.

'Send him over the *say* in munseer's ship,' said a fourth.

'Ver good,' said De Welskein. 'He may spik mosh as he like in France!—ha, ha!—safe 'nuff dere!'

'Give him a dog's knock at wanst!' said Jack Flannerty.

'Dead men tell no tales,' said Solomon sententiously, and with a diabolical expression about his eyes and mouth: and immediately after, addressing the man who was in charge of the boiling pot, whose attention had been attracted by the last proposition, he said, 'Darby *avic!* mind the pot, or our dinner will be spylte.'

'Wash de paut, I tell you.'

'Darby's no great cook,' said Solomon: 'but you know the owld saying—God sends mates, but the divil sends cooks.'

'By gar, den, me send Darbee back to him.'

'Afther you is manners, sir,' said Darby.

'But,' said Flannerty, 'what do yiz say to knockin' out his brains?'

'How do you know he has any?' said Solomon.

'He has enough to hang Darby Daly, anyhow.'

'I don't like murdher,' said Regan.

'Don't you?' said Flannerty, looking at him contemptuously. 'Do you think he'd *hant* you?'

'Maybe you wouldn't like to see a ghost yourself,' said Regan, who was not pleased with the tone of Flannerty's address.

'Bah! Nonsense!' exclaimed De Welskein.

'Dead men tell no tales,' croaked Solomon again.

'Ay, but murdher spakes out,' said Regan: 'it's always discovered one way or the other.' That was the *true* cause of Regan's objection to the measure.

'Wouldn't sendin' him over the *say* do as well?' said the former proposer of that measure.

'I think it would,' said Regan: 'and if you'd take my advice, I know another you'd send along wid him.'

'Who?' was asked by all.

'A black thraitor that'll hang every man of us, if we don't take care.'

'Is it Rory O'More you mane?' said one.

'How aisy you hit it,' said Regan, 'without my tellin' you!—it's a sign there's thruth in it.'

'Settle one thing at a time,' said Flannerty. 'I know you hate Rory; but that's no rayson you're to disturb us with it always. Settle about Scrubbs first.'

'*Bon,*' said the Frenchman. And it was soon decided by the majority of opinions that to transport the collector was the safest course to pursue; and that being agreed upon, it next became matter of consideration how he was to be secured.

In the midst of this consultation De Welskein kept a sharp eye to the fire, to see if Darby was minding his business. He caught him still attending more to the matter in debate than the cooking. '*Bête!* vill you mind de paut? or, by gar, you let 'im run over de way.'

'By my sowl, it couldn't do that if it had twice as many legs,' said Darby.

'Mr. New Jane,' said Solomon to De Welskein, whose name of *Eugene* was thus Hibernicised, 'will you take the collecther wid you thin?'

'Certainlee! you kesh him for me, and me mek gentilman of 'im—tek 'im to traavel.'

'The pot is busy bilin',' said Darby, who wished his guard over the culinary department to be ended.

'Well, don't let it *run over the way, avic,*' said Solomon, quizzing De Welskein.

To the low laugh that followed, the Frenchman replied, '*Vieux chaudronnier de campagne,* you mek ghem auf me—old rog! *Sacré!* tek care you get no dinnaire, mebbee,—how you like dat? ha! ha!'

De Welskein now resumed his culinary cares, and the dinner was pronounced ready for discussion. No time was lost in lifting the pot from the fire; and in a few minutes the dinner was placed on the board, and all were preparing to make a vigorous attack upon it, when Solomon said in a tone of mockery, 'Oh, haythens! why thin would you begin to ate without sayin'grace?' and he arose as if to give a benediction.

'*Sacré nom de diable!*' said the Frenchman; 'vaut you do, you old fool?'

'I'm goin' to say grace,' said Solomon, winking at the rest of the party; and raising his eyes, with a sanctimonious air, he said in mock solemnity,

> One word's as good as ten;
> Leather away,—amen!'

The Frenchman joined in the laugh that Solomon's old and brutal joke produced, and exclaimed, 'Old homebogue! *sacré chaudronnier de campagne!*' as he attacked his own stew, which was not long in being demolished, and the table was soon clear of everything but the brandy-bottle, which still continued to make its rounds.

'And now, this bein' Sunday,' said the tinker, 'I brought the good books wid' me for our edification:' and he pulled from his pocket a greasy pack of cards, whose rounded corners and nearly obliterated faces bore testimony to the many contests in which they had been engaged.

This movement of Solomon's was received with welcome by the whole party, and a game was immediately called for. The game they played was one which has long been a favourite in Ireland, and still continues to be so amongst the peasantry. It is called 'five and ten' when played between two persons, or four engaged as partners; but when a larger number is enlisted, it is called 'spoil five,' and a *poule* is played for. The same cards are influential in both games, though a totally different play is required in one from the other; for in the former, the object is to win as many tricks as you can, while in the latter your own hand, if not sufficiently strong to secure triumph, is always sacrificed to the common good of 'spoiling' the endeavours of a more fortunate holder of cards, and thereby increasing the *poule:* —hence its name of '*spoil* five.' But in either form, this game is a great favourite with the peasantry, and is played by them with considerable skill: there is a remote resemblance between it and *écarté,* which is much the inferior game of the two, and though 'spoil five' does not bear the stamp of fashion, it requires more acuteness in playing than many other games I have seen.

'Sol, the dale is yours,—it's only fair, since you brought the cards, my boy,' said Flannerty; 'so let us see who'll play. We're too many for "five and ten," so we must have the "spoil five." There's too many of us for that same to play all at wanst; but we must begin, anyhow, and we can change hands by turns. Come—there's Solomon, and myself, and—'

'—And the munseer, of course,' said Regan.

This proposition was not relished by the company, evidently; for the Frenchman's adroitness with the pack was no secret to them, and they, very naturally, did not wish to engage with such an adversary; though no one liked to speak out his objection, and the foreigner, with great readiness, at once interposed his own denial to such a proposal.

'No, no—muss not play—cars do for me whatever he please me—so my honner is not satisfy; for dough you know *parfaitement* I woos not play my treeck wis my frens, for dat all de same my honner woos not be happy.'

'We're much obleeged to your honour,' said Flannerty: 'to be sure, we know you're a gintleman every inch o' you.'

'*Oui! Oui!*' said the Frenchman proudly.

'Sure enough, 'faith,' said Flannerty, 'it is *we* that are the rale gintlemen, for we have little work and a grate dale o' pleasure. But come, make up the game.' This was soon done, and they commenced play with much spirit.

Now, the Frenchman in relinquishing a part in the game served two purposes. In the first place, it gave his companions the notion that his own sense of propriety forbade his engaging in it; and in the next, it

left him at liberty to go round the board and see all the hands, and
then communicate by concerted signal the best play to Solomon, who
was his confederate in his system of plunder on their associates; the old
saying of 'honour among thieves' holding as good in this instance as
in most others. On went the game. Whenever Solomon held a hand
of sufficient force to need no aid, the Frenchman kept beyond reach
of the gamesters, the better to screen his purpose; and whenever the
tinker's cards were so weak as to render finesse of no avail, he would
stand behind him and say as some card was played, 'Ha! dat is not
goot.'

'How do you know?' the tinker would cry, in affected displeasure.

'Me know ver well.'

'Not you, in throth—go tache your mammy to milk ducks! I know
more o' "spoil five" than all the Frinchmen that ever was born. Play!'
said he to his fellow-gamesters.

'Hillo! the five fingers! by dad I'm done! Well, the game's spylte,
anyhow. Dale, Regan.'

The cards were distributed again, and Solomon having the ace of
trumps, put out a weak card from his hand to take in the trump card
in its place, saying, as is customary, 'I rob.'

'By my sowl you have been doin' that ever since we sat down
a'most!' said Flannerty. 'I dunna how you conthrive to win so often!'

'When you play as long as I have played, *ma bouchal*, you'll not
wondher,' said Solomon, very quietly taking the turned-up trump card
from its place on the pack. 'That's nothing to what I can do. Give me
a dhrop o' brandy, munseer, as you're idle.'

The Frenchman handed him the bottle, saying, at the same time,
'Wat is dat you say about nussing?'

'I say that is nothing to what I can do,' said Solomon, who put the
bottle to his mouth and took a copious swig.

'*Ma foi!* everyting in dis world is nussing,' said the Frenchman—
'nussing at all.'

'Oh, be aisy with your larning, munseer,' said Flannerty. 'Bote I say
dat is true,' repeated the Frenchman: 'all de univer is nussing.

'And am I nothing?' asked Solomon.

'Nussing at all,' said the Frenchman.

'And is this nothing?' he again asked, holding up the jar of brandy.

'Nussing at all: everyting is nussing!

The old tinker put the jar to his mouth, and finishing the remaining spirit that was in it, he withdrew it from his lips, saying, 'Well, take nothing from nothing, and nothing remainss,' and he held up the inverted bottle amid the laughter of his companions. On went the game, and the laughing and drinking, and the cheating, until a dead pause was produced amongst the noisy group by a vivid flash of lightning, followed by a loud peal of thunder, which suddenly interrupted their revelry. The laugh was silenced, the winning card upheld in the suspended hand of the gamester, and the flask arrested in its progress to the lips of the bacchanal; looks of wonder tinged with terror were exchanged amongst the listeners, and while they were yet fear-bound, another flash gleamed through a narrow grating which admitted a small portion of light and air to the vault, and its white and vivid glare made the dull red blaze of the fire they sat near seem more lurid. The gang, to an imaginative mind, might have seemed like a troop of unholy spirits round a watchfire of the nether world.

'God be good to me!' said Regan, dropping the cards from his hand; 'did you ever see anything like that? I'll play no more—it's not good to play on a Sunday;' and he arose.

'Bah! don't be fool,' said the Frenchman, who was the most unconcerned of the party, and who assumed to be more unconcerned than he really was; 'you no phiosophe—tonzer and loightning is nussing but natture. You no frighten at de sun, and de moon, and de star, which is natture as well as de tonzer: you might as well be fright for the water you drink as de tonzer.'

Another tremendous peal silenced the babbling of the Frenchman, who, when the lessening reverberations died away, said in a very altered tone, 'Dere is gret shange in de wedder.'

Regan had ascended from the vault when he left his game, and on gaining the ground story of the building and looking forth, he beheld a great change indeed from the aspect the scene had worn when he descended from the hill-top a short time before. One of those sudden storms peculiar to the season had come on; the heavens were dark, the forked lightning only dispelling the gloom with terrific and momentary brightness, the rain falling in that deluging profuseness characteristic of such elementary commotion, and the frolic stream that ran through the valley becoming a raging torrent. He returned to his companions, and had scarcely descended the ladder which led to the vault, when a crash rang over the vaulted roof: there was no mistaking the sound—it was evident the building had been struck by lightning, and every one who yet held his cards flung them down and sprang to his feet, and looks and exclamations of terror burst from the gang.

'Let us lave the place,' said Regan; 'it's onlooky.'

'We're safer here than anywhere else,' said Solomon, he and De Welskein being the only persons who retained their self-possession though the withered face of the old tinker was paler than ordinary.

'Ver true, *mom ami,*' said the Frenchman: 'come—come round de fire and tek some brandee. Gret change in de wedder, by gar!'

'I never seen sitch rain in all my days,' said Regan, who bore a particularly troubled aspect. 'And to think of sitch terrible thundher bein' so late in the saison! I always heerd it was onlooky to play cards on Sunday; and I never missed mass before!'

'Bah! said the Frenchman; 'mebbee you better go to shappel now.'

'I wish to the Lord I heerd mass to-day!' muttered Regan, whose superstitious nature operated powerfully upon him.

Another peal of thunder followed.

'You hear *that*, don't you?' said Solomon.

Regan marked himself with the sign of the cross, and muttered the formula of the blessing himself. 'Isn't it wondherful, sitch dhreadful claps o' thundher in October?'

'Not at all,' said Solomon: 'the heaviest thundher-storm ever was in my memory fell on a Christmas day.'

'It's a rainin' as if heaven and earth was comin' together,' said Regan.

'Don't you be 'fraid of dat,' said De Welskein; 'de 'eaven and de ert tay where dey are;—tek some brandee.'

Some sods of turf were thrown upon the fire to increase it, and the party stood round the hearth in silence, awed by the increasing storm and the fearful glare of the lightning; but instead of the fire showing symptoms of reviving under the fuel cast upon it, a low hissing sound gave warning it was assailed by moisture, and in a few minutes the whole floor of the vault was covered with water. The river had risen to a fearful height, and a rapid flooding of this subterranean apartment was the consequence. There was no choice left now, and the party simultaneously moved towards the ladder that led to the upper part of the Folly: but a cry of horror burst from the lips of the first man who gained the accustomed opening, when he found it was completely blocked up by the fallen masses of the building the lightning had smitten.

A sense of terror and confusion now arose which no language could describe. Even De Welskein, though hitherto heeding not the elementary commotion, was not proof against such solid evidence of it as the tons of fallen masonry that choked the only passage from the vault; and Solomon shared the fear in common with the rest. Regan was the most furious of the set; and while the amount of terror which the thunder excited only made him pray, the increase of it, which the horrible fate that seemed to await him produced, made him curse.

'May the divil resaive you, you owld villain!' said he to Solomon; 'what made you bring me here at all? I was going to mass, only for *you*.'

'*Me* bring you!' said Solomon; 'no, you chicken-hearted murdherer—for you *would* be if you *dar*—it was the bitther hate brought you here. You kem to get Rory O'More out o' your sight; but you'll get more wather than you like, yourself, before him,—and hell's curse to you!'

'G—d d—n! why do you curse for!' said De Welskein, who now thought of trying to escape at the grated window.

He induced them to come down the ladder, that he might rear it against the aperture; and having done so, he ascended rapidly. But the grating was too narrow to admit a man to pass, and too strong and firm to be shaken in a hurry; in the meantime the water was rising fast, the men being already knee-deep.

'Pull him down out o' that,' said Regan; 'and let us get up the laddher agin to the door! We'll have room enough to stand up there, and not be dhrowned like rats. Pull him down!'

'*Silence, poltroon!*' said De Welskein. 'You poor cow's-heart! G—d d—n! let ladder 'lone; lissen, all you, lissen!'

He desired that the stones on which the planks had rested to form their dinner-table, and those which had served for seats also, should be rolled over near the wall, where, by piling them one on another, a foundation would be formed on which to rest one end of a plank, while the other extremity might be supported higher up on the ladder; that thus they might be preserved from drowning, while they could be at the same time near the window, at which they could work alternately with their knives till the iron grating was loosened, and their egress effected.

This plan was immediately acted upon, though terror still prevailed amongst them. Solomon was one of the first to follow the Frenchman's advice; and as he approached the table of planks, he saw the stakes of the deserted game lying untouched: even in such a moment the ravening appetite for the coin could not be repressed;—he pounced upon the money and made it his own;—daring to play the robber even on the brink of eternity. Regan was the only one who perceived him, and he had not courage enough to speak out; but in his heart he wondered at and cursed the undaunted old miscreant.

The water continued to gain rapidly upon them, and they had no time to spare in making the proposed arrangement for their safety. When it was completed, there was a dispute who should occupy the highest point on the plank; and the terrible example of selfishness and ruffianism exhibited, would only disgust were it recorded.

It was an awful scene! There were those whose lives were in jeopardy to whom an unprepared call to a final account would have been fearful; and yet, amongst them there was less of prayers than curses.

XXVII

De Lacy departs for France.—Rory gives a hint for making good punch;
and Scrubbs proves the fallacy of the saying, that a man finds his warmest
welcome at an inn.

THE SAME DAY THAT WAS appointed for the meeting of the smugglers in the Folly was destined for the departure of De Lacy from the cottage of Rory O'More.

De Lacy had his misgivings whether it would be safe for Rory to remain in the country after what had happened, and feared that his ready and generous conversion of the colonel's pass to his friend's safety might become the means of his being discovered by the colonel and his party, and marked out for their vengeance. This thought weighed heavily upon him, and he expressed to Rory his fears upon the subject, with an offer of making him the companion of his voyage, and so securing his safety: but Rory refused the offer with thankfulness for the kindness and consideration by which it was prompted, and declared his intention to remain.

'Sure, what would the mother and Mary do without me?'

This was his only, and (with him) unanswerable argument against the measure; so, in conclusion, it was agreed that De Lacy should make his voyage without the companionship of our hero.

'I'll go with you to see you off, though,' said Rory.

'No, Rory,' said De Lacy: 'if you will not bear me company altogether, you must not in part. As you are determined on remaining behind, it would be a still further presumptive evidence against you to be absent even for a day or two from your home.'

It was therefore agreed that a couple of horses should be hired in Knockbracken, and Conolly, instead of Rory, become De Lacy's guide to the coast. Knockbracken happened to be the village on Regan's side of the country; for that in the neighbourhood of O'More's was too insignificant to produce a horse for hire.

The parting of De Lacy from the cottage was painful to all parties—they did not know how much so until the moment came. The women cried, and De Lacy was silent—a kindly pressure of the hand of the mother and daughter was the last parting testimonial of friendship he gave them; and as he hurried from the quiet little lane, the widow and Mary sent after him many a fervent blessing.

Rory accompanied him as far as the point whence he was to take horse, and they wended their way thitherward in comparative silence The approach of the parting hour is saddening; and the thoughts which in happier moments we give to the tongue, the heart refuses to part with then.

On reaching the hostel of the 'Black Bull,' the nags of Larry Finnegan were put in requisition and while Conolly went to assist in their preparation for the road, De Lacy kept Rory for the few last words.

'Rory,' said he, 'the kindness I have met under your mother's roof I can never forget, and *your* courage and conduct have been beyond all praise.'

'Don't mintion it, if you plaze, Mr. De Lacy.'

'I should be ungrateful if I did not,' said De Lacy. 'Now, your mother, Rory, would not permit me to make her any acknowledgment; but—'

'Murdher, murdher! don't disthress me!' said Rory.

'Listen to me, Rory,' said De Lacy. 'Though your mother has refused anything in the shape of remuneration, you, I hope—'

'Is it me?' said Rory.

'Now, *do* listen to me!' said De Lacy. 'Surely you won't refuse some trifling gift from your parting friend as a keepsake?'

'Oh! a keepsake,' said Rory, 'is another affair.'

'That's a good fellow!' said De Lacy. 'Here, then—take this, and keep it for my sake,' and he drew forth a gold watch. Rory kept looking at the watch and De Lacy alternately in wonder, and at last said, 'Why, thin, is it a watch?'

'Yes.'

'And a *goold* watch?'

'Yes: what's so wonderful about it?'

'Is it *me* with a goold watch!—By dad! you might as well see a pig with a cocked hat!'

'But at a keepsake, Rory?'

'Oh something less costly than that, if you plaze, Mr. De Lacy sure, that's worth a handful o' guineas. And thin, what's more, sure I've no use for a watch: there's the blessed sun that rises and sets evermore; and if I want to know the time o' day, I've only to cock up my eye at him, and I can tell it a'most as well at if he was a clock—beggin' his pardon for comparin' him to the like—but all as one, I mane, in the regard of the hour.'

'But, Rory, it is not for use, but as a keepsake, I wish you to take it.'

'Sure, anything else will do as well for a keepsake: give me that switch out o' your hand, and I'll value it as much as all the watches ever was made.'

'That's too insignificant, Rory—indeed it is: think of something else.'

'Well, then, sir, since you desire me to say the thing myself and *will* have it so, there's your sleeve buttons; and if you give them to me, it is proud I'll be to wear the same things on me that you yourself wore.'

'There,' said De Lacy, taking them from his wrist—'and I only regret they are so worthless a gift.'

'Ah, sir! it is the giver, and not the gift I think of,' said Rory.

Conolly now led forth the horses saddled; and though neither the beasts nor their furniture were much to be admired, De Lacy was assured the rough hacks would do him good service so, mounting into a very old high-pommelled saddle, he once more shook hands with Rory, and bidding him an affectionate farewell, with the hope of speedy and triumphant return, he took the road towards the coast, and was soon beyond the village.

Rory then went to chapel; and thoughts of the expedition and hopes for his country mingled with his devotions, and a prayer for the safety of the friend from whom he had just parted, rose sincerely from his heart. Mass being over, he returned to the 'Black Bull,' where the host, Larry Finnegan, was serving his customers with tobacco and drink.

'I'm come to ax you for something, Larry,' said Rory.

'And you shall have it with pleasure, my buck,' said Larry. 'What would you like? I've a fresh tap here, and it's iligant.'

'Nothing in that way, Larry, to-day; but I jist came to see if you're done with the crow-bar I lent you some time agon, as I'm in want of it myself to quarry some stones to-morrow.'

'Yis; there it is, standin' over in the corner beyant the hob in the kitchen forninst you: I'm done wid it,—many thanks to you!'

'Why, thin, what would you want wid a crow-bar, Finnegan?' said one of his customers.

'Oh, it's the misthiss you should ax about that,' said Rory.

'Why, is it for batin' her he got it?'

'No,' said Finnegan. 'It's a flail I have for that.'

'It is *Misthiss* Finnegan that wants it,' said Rory; 'and I wondher you never heerd the rayson.'

'Why, thin, what is it, Rory, my boy? I'll be bound it's a quare one you'll give, anyhow.'

'You see,' said Rory, 'she makes the punch so sthrong, that she bent all her spoons sthrivin' to stir it; and so she borrowed the crow-bar.'

'Long life to you, Rory, your sowl!' said Finnegan, who relished this indirect compliment to the character of his establishment. 'Divil be from me, but you won't lave the house this day without takin' a tumbler with the misthiss, afther that!—and she shall mix it herself for you—*and with the crow-bar*, my boy!'

Rory would not refuse the hospitality offered, so, entering the kitchen, he sat by the fire; and Mrs. Finnegan endeavoured to support the character he had given her, by brewing one of her best, and she returned to the kitchen in smiles to present to Rory a 'screeching' tumbler of punch.

While he was sitting there, chatting, and sipping his beverage, the storm noticed in the foregoing chapter began to threaten, and

soon burst in all its violence over the village. The women blessed
themselves; and the mirth and noise of the public-house sank before
the peals of thunder which rolled above them. Rory, remembering he
had some miles to walk before he should reach his home went to the
door to look out, and judge if the storm seemed but a sudden burst,
or threatened a longer duration; and in the angry aspect of the skies
he saw nothing but the alternative of a long wait in the village or a
wet skin before him. As he looked in the street, Scrubbs was riding
down the road at a furious pace to get under shelter; but before
reaching the 'Black Bull,' a vivid flash of lightning made his horse start
violently, and the suddenness of the action brought horse and rider
to the ground.

'God bless us!' exclaimed Rory.

'What's the matter?' said some bystanders within the house, who
had not seen the occurrence.

'I b'lieve the Collecther is kilt with a stroke o' lightning!'

A universal exclamation of 'God bless us!' echoed Rory's first
ejaculation, and the people crowded to the door to look out. Scrubbs,
who was only stunned by the fall, now made an effort to rise; and
Rory in a moment ran to his assistance, and was by his side,

'You're not kilt?' said Rory.

'No,' said Scrubbs.

'Are you scorched itself?'

The fall of Scrubbs rendered him as yet unconscious of the meaning
of the question.

'By dad!' said Rory, 'I thought you wor kilt with the lightning!
Come into the house out o' the rain.' And so saying, he led Scrubbs
to the 'Black Bull.'

Some others went to the assistance of the horse, but it was found the
animal had slipped its shoulder and could not rise without help. This
being afforded, the poor brute limped along to the stable of the hostel.

After a few minutes the Collector was quite recovered, having
escaped with a few bruises; and his own safety left him at liberty
to lament over the mishap of his steed, to whose stable he repaired,
exclaiming, as he went, 'It's very unfortunate!'

''Faith, it is unfortunate,' said Finnegan, 'that your neck wasn't bruk!—I'd like to dhrink at your wake.'

'Oh, God forgive you, Larry!' said the wife; 'why would you be wishin' the man's death?'

'Bekaze there would be a blackguard the less in the world: sure, he got me fined, come Candlemas next a year; and you know it.'

'Throth, he's a dirty blackguard, I know,' said the polite Mrs. Finnegan: 'so lave him to God.'

'To the divil, you mane,' said Finnegan.

'Thrue for you, by my sowl, Larry,' said some of the by standers, who all hated Scrubbs most cordially.

'I wondher he didn't keep a tight hand over the baste!' said one.

'Faix, so do I,' said another; 'for he keeps a mighty tight hand over everybody else.'

'Sure enough,' said a third, 'it's he that's the rale grinder.'

'Whisht! here he comes back, bad cess to him!' said the former speaker, as Scrubbs re-entered the house.

But the man who dubbed him a grinder, though he did not *speak* the word, continued to *sing* the nickname in the Collector's face; and he hummed to a lilting tune—

'Tarry, heigh-ho!
You *know*
Tarry, heigh-ho! the *grinder.*'—

and a low laugh and furtive glances exchanged among the peasants, made Scrubbs feel very uncomfortable, for he suspected they bore some allusion to himself.

There was not one voice to express sorrow for his accident, nor congratulation upon his escape, so disliked had he made himself in the country; and but for Rory O'More, whose generous heart was open to the distress even of a foe, he would not have had a single being to do him a service.

Scrubbs wished to push homewards, and asked Finnegan to let him have a horse on hire.

'I haven't one,' said Finnegan.

'You've two, you mean,' said Scrubbs.

'They're both engaged,' said the landlord.

'I'll pay you whatever you ask,' said Scrubbs.

'I tell you I haven't thim,' said Finnegan gruffly; and he added in an undertone, 'and if I had, you shouldn't have thim.'

'Do you mean they are both engaged?' said Scrubbs.

'Yis,' was the short answer.

The storm continued to rage on. The public-house, whose noisy mirth was quelled by its outbreak, seemed to have gathered an additional gloom from the presence of the Collector. One by one the customers of the 'Black Bull' dropped off: those who lived in the village, first, who could make a run through the storm to their homes; those in the vicinity, next; and, at last, when there seemed no chance of its abatement, even they whose homes were more distant seemed to think there was no use in longer tarrying, and so, wrapping their frieze-coats round them, burying their faces in their collars, and pulling their *caubeens* tightly over their eyes, they one by one made for the door, and balancing themselves for a moment on the threshold between a wait or a wetting, they butted with their heads against the wind, and 'pelted' away through the storm.

Rory and Scrubbs were the only guests left within the walls of the 'Black Bull,' and Rory seemed, at last, inclined to follow the example of those who departed. On expressing this intention, Scrubbs manifested great uneasiness, for he did not like remaining alone in the public-house, whose landlord he had mulcted in a fine on some trivial pretext; and the savage manner of the man, added to the consciousness of the cause he had given him for dislike, made Scrubbs loath to become a solitary lodger in the deserted inn.

When he found Rory determined to go, and that his way was homewards, he expressed a desire to accompany him, for their road lay together, and it was matter of great importance to the Collector to have a companion,—for to travel the country alone *on foot* was what he dreaded too much to venture upon, and considered even more hazardous than remaining where he was.

A few days before, he would not have chosen Rory for a companion; but the circumstances of the intended arrest of De Lacy had mystified him, and made him imagine that perhaps Rory was not the dangerous person he had taken him for; and at all events, under existing circumstances, he could not but be glad of his convoy; so, declaring himself ready to face the road on foot with our hero, and thanking Finnegan, whose care of his horse's shoulder he urged, Rory said 'Good-b'ye!' to the landlord of the 'Black Bull' and his punch-making wife, and, not forgetting his crow-bar, sallied forth from the snug shelter of the warm hostel to buffet the chilling storm, which still raged with unmitigated fury.

They proceeded in silence until they passed the skirts of the village; when Rory, turning from the high road, struck into a path through the fields that lay beside it.

'Where are you going, O'More?' said the Collector.

'A short cut,' said Rory.

'Don't go through the fields,' said Scrubbs 'the road is safer.'

'Why, what danger do you dhread in the fields?' said Rory.

'Only, the road is safer; the fields are so lonely,' said the Collector.

'Maybe you're afeard o' me, Misther Scrubbs?' said Rory.

'No, no, my dear O'More!'

'Bekaze you may go back to the "Black Bull" if you are. I didn't ax your company; and high-road or bye-road is all one to me.'

'Now, O'More, I beg your pardon,—don't be offended—but indeed these bye-paths—'

'Arrah, don't be so frightful!' said Rory, with a tone of contempt in his voice, which he could not control at this exhibition of poltroonery; 'it's a short cut of full two miles to quit the road here and head up the banks of the sthream through the glin of the Folly.'

'Bless my soul!' said Scrubbs, laying his hand on Rory's arm and making a dead stand; 'surely you're not going through that lonely horrid place.'

'In throth I am,' said Rory; 'and if you don't like to come, as I said before, you may go back.'

Scrubbs was in a painful state of doubt; he could not tell which he dreaded most—the Folly or Finnegan; and thus goaded by the horns of the dilemma, or rather the 'Black Bull,' he ventured to go forward with Rory. After getting over about half a mile of broken ground, they topped the hill that commanded the glen of the Folly and when Scrubbs saw the state of swollen turbulence in which the stream swept down the valley, he asked O'More, in one of his coward tones, if he would venture to approach it.

'Sure, it won't bite you,' said Rory.

'But it might drown you,' said Scrubbs.

'Thim that's born for hangin' was never meant for dhrowndin',' said Rory in a questionable tone.

'You say very odd things, O'More,' said Scrubbs, who could not fathom whether Rory meant himself or the Collector in his last speech. 'But isn't the valley dangerous with this dreadful flood in it?'

'Faix, here will be worse than the flood in it when you and I are there!' said Rory, whose contempt for the Collector's pusillanimity had so increased that he deemed it fit subject for mirth, and didn't hesitate to torment the paltry coward with an ambiguity of expression which left, in the vagueness of the allusion, the application of it open to either of them; so that he might endure either offence or fear, as the case might be.

'Are you sure it's safe?' said Scrubbs.

'It's safe enough for me, anyhow,' said Rory: 'I don't know if you be a dangerous person.'

'How do you mean, dangerous?' said Scrubbs.

'Likely for hurt or harm,' said Rory.

'I hope not, O'More,' said the Collector, straining to keep up with Rory vigorous pace as he dashed into the glen; and as they approached the stream, he again asked his guide if he did not consider the valley impassable without much risk.

'Not in the laste,' said Rory: 'it's over an hour yet before the pass up the valley will be flooded.'

So saying, he pressed on, and was drawing near the walls of the Folly, when he suddenly stopped and said to Scrubbs,

'Didn't you hear a shout?'

'Where?' said the Collector, getting as close to him as he could.

'I thought I heerd a holloo,' said Rory: 'listen!'

A burst of thunder followed: the Collector shuddered.

'I suppose 'twas only the storm,' said Rory. 'Let us push on;' and he made a few more vigorous strides, when his course was again arrested by a loud shout which was audible in one of the lapses of the tempest,—and this time even Scrubbs heard it.

The shout proceeded from the grated window of the vault where De Welskein and his companions were imprisoned. They, seeing two men in the valley, had raised their combined voices in one wild chorus of despair, to attract their attention; and observing the successful result of their first effort, they again essayed to arrest their observation in the same manner: and when the men paused the second time, De Welskein took his handkerchief from his neck, and waving it through the bars of his dungeon as a further means of attracting notice, a third tremendous yell issued from the inundated vault.

'Look, look!' said Rory, pointing to the handkerchief he saw waving from the Folly; 'some one is calling for help there!' and he was going forward to the spot, when Scrubbs laid his hand upon him, and said,

'You wouldn't be mad enough to go!'

'Why not?' said Rory.

'You don't know who may be there.'

'What is it to me who they are?—they want help,' said Rory, 'and that's enough.'

'Let me beg of you, O'More!' said Scrubbs, endeavouring to detain him.

Rory shook him off, and said very decidedly, 'Mr. Scrubbs, if *you're* afraid, that's no raison *I* should be; and if you'd lave a fellow-craythur in want o' help, God forbid I'd do the like. There's some accident there beyant, and I'll go see if I can be of any use.'

With these words Rory ran towards the Folly; and Scrubbs followed, because he was afraid to remain alone.

On approaching sufficiently close to recognise persons, the wonder was mutual between those within and those without the vault at the rencounter.

'Murdher! is it you, Mr. Divilskin!' said Rory. 'Why, thin, what brought you there at all?'

It would be vain to attempt to describe the confused and almost unintelligible conversation that ensued: it was rather a volley of vociferation on both sides,—the Frenchman shouting '*Ouvrey vite!*' while the other prisoners were exclaiming, 'Rory, for the love o' God, make haste, or we'll be dhrownded!'

'Wait a minit, and I'll settle the business for you,' said Rory. 'Sure, and wasn't it the hoighth o' good luck I happened to have the crow-bar with me!' And as he spoke, he put the powerful implement between the bars of the grated window, and wrenched the rusted irons from their sockets; then, giving a hand to De Welskein he assisted him in his egress through the newly-made operture and in a few seconds the whole party, so lately incarcerated in a dangerous dungeon, were liberated even by the very man against whose safety one of their party had endeavoured to direct their vengeance! And now a terrible example was given of the facility with which past mercies are forgotten, and of the hardness of the human heart when brutalised by vice: these very men, rescued from a perilous position, and perhaps a horrible death, the moment they were released, gave way to their vengeful feelings, and thought not of extending to a fellow-creature the mercy that heaven had shown towards them.

Flannerty and Regan were the first to notice, with triumph, the presence of Scrubbs, and they pointed it out to the party with an exclamation of blasphemous rejoicing.

'By the holy, we're in luck afther all; for there he is,—the very chap we were waitin' for!'

They pointed to Scrubbs as they spoke; and he, whose fears were sufficiently awake before, now pressed close beside Rory, who could feel his tremor as he leaned for support against him. The meaning of the desperadoes was too evident to be mistaken,—it was manifest their menacing intentions were directed against the Collector; but as Rory did not knew their motive for such a proceeding, he said firmly,

'Why, what do you want with him?'

'We jist want to take a loan of him,' sad Jack Flannerty, who advanced.

'See, Flannerty,' said Rory, who extended his arm as he spoke, in token of his desire to keep a distance between the parties,—'Mr.

Scrubbs was in the village beyant, and his horse fell undher him; and bein' obleeged to walk home, he said he'd go along with me. When I was comin' this way by the short cut,—as you know it is towards my place,—Mr. Scrubbs asked me to go by the high-road; but I towld him this was the best way. Now, boys,' said he, appealing to the whole party, 'you wouldn't like yourselves, if you promised to lade a man safe, that he should come into throuble afther: and when I tell yiz this, I'm sure you'll put no hurt nor harm on the Collecther.'

'By gor, if you go make a bellwether o' yourself to sitch fellows as that over the counthry, it's a busy time you'll have of it, my buck,' answered Flannerty—'and I'd recommend you to let it alone for the futhur: and, indeed, if you've any regard for your own characther, the less you have to do wid sitch cattle the betther, Rory, my boy. So, jist be aisy, and don't be howlin' your head so high.'

'I howld my head no higher than any honest man may howld it,' said Rory: 'and I say that the man who has any honour in his heart wouldn't touch him that's beside me afther what I say.'

'To the divil wid you and your honour!' shouted Regan. 'Will your honour save Darby Daly from bein' hanged when that vagabone swears his life away?—and you wantin' to save the villain! but "birds of a feather flocks together."'

'You're a slandherous scoundhrel, Regan,' cried Rory 'and it's not the first lie you said of me.'

Regan was about to advance on O'More, who, raising his crow-bar in the act of striking, exclaimed fiercely, 'Keep back, or by the mother that bore me I'll brain you!'

Flannerty dragged back Regan and said, 'I'll tell you what it is, Rory, the Collecthor there is *wanted,* and there's no use in your makin' any bones about it, for we are enough to have our will; so do what we plaze, or we'll make you.'

'Don't betray me, O'More,' cried Scrubbs.

'Bethray you!' said Rory, looking with withering contempt on the craven beside him. 'You dirty hound, who *would* run afther my foot,—to say sitch a word to me afther what you've heerd! You're not worth saving, you poor-sperited cur!—but it's for my own sake that I won't have the man undher my protection harmed.—Boys, let us pass.'

'No, we won't,' said Flannerty; 'we'll have him;' and he was advancing with some others.

'Boys!' cried Rory, in an appealing tone, 'I saved *your* lives five minutes ago, and all I ask is that you'll let us go quietly out o' this.'

There was a shout of 'No!' from the group. The trembling Collector laid hold of Rory.

'Don't grip me that way, or I can't fight!' said Rory: 'mind ourself, you'd betther.' Turning to the group, he then added, 'I towld you I considher I'm bound in honour to this man to see him safe, and if you haven't the heart to feel it, more shame to you! But if it goes to that, by the seven blessed candles you'll walk over my body before you git him!' And he threw himself into a posture of defence and, with the weapon he held, he was a formidable adversary.

'Didn't I tell yiz all he was a thraitor?' said Regan. 'If he wasn't, would he do what he's doin'?—Do you believe me now?'

At the moment, and under the peculiar circumstances, joined to foregone suspicions of Rory's fidelity, the words of Regan were like sparks on gunpowder: there was a shout from the group and a rush on Rory, who felled two of his assailants to the earth as they advanced upon him, while the wretched Scrubbs struck not a blow in his own defence. While Rory was keeping up an unequal fight against numbers, his vindictive enemy Shan Dhu came behind him, and giving him a severe blow under the ear, for the first time had the satisfaction of seeing Rory stagger beneath his stroke. In a moment Rory was overpowered and secured; and he and Scrubbs, the latter of whom prayed in the most abject manner for mercy, were dragged within the walls of the Folly and their limbs secured by strong cords; for until this measure was put in practice, Rory continued to struggle for his liberty.

When he was rendered quite powerless, he and the Collector were placed in an upper apartment of the ruin, with one man to watch over them; while the others remained on the ground story, to consult what should be done with the prisoners. Jack Flannerty still recommended the 'dog's knock,' and Solomon chimed in his chorus of evil omen, that 'dead men tell no tales'; but the majority dreaded this extreme measure, and determined on sending Scrubbs and Rory over sea. They were obliged, however, to wait until night should favour their undertaking, as in the daylight to transport their prisoners would be impossible.

While the council were consulting below, Rory and the Collector were engaged with their own thoughts in the apartment above. Rory in his heart cursed the unlucky chance that had thrown Scrubbs in his way, as to his company he very justly attributed his mishap; and yet the generosity of his temper forbade him to reproach the author of his misfortune with being the cause of it, while he saw him trembling for his safety, and heard the moans which escaped from his pale and quivering lips.

As for Scrubbs, such was his grovelling nature, that even after the noble conduct of Rory, he was still suspicious of his having led him into the trap, and that his resistance was only pretence and at last, the base wretch ventured to give his filthy suspicion words.

'Oh, O'More,' faltered he, 'why did you betray me into their hands?'

'Is it to me you have the ingratitude to say the word,' said Rory, 'afther my runnin' the risk o' my life to save you!'

'Oh, they won't hurt you, you know; but they'll murder me!'

'How do you know they won't hurt me? There's thim among them ready enough to belie and wrong me; and my sthriving to save you has made me as bad to thim in their eyes as yourself.'

'Oh, they won't touch you—you *know* they won't; and speak to them for me,—do, O'More!'

'I see the mane suspicions you have, Mr. Scrubbs; and in throth it's a pity an honest man should get into throuble on your account, for you're not worth it. You think I'm collogueing with these vagabones, and that I only *purtinded* to fight, and all that; and if you worn't as bad yourself as to do the like, you wouldn't suspect another of it. Get out wid you, you mane-spirited dog! Throth, your heart is a dunghill, and suspicion is the cock that crows on it!'

Notwithstanding all this abusive outbreak on Rory's part, Scrubbs contrived to writhe himself over nearer to him, (for both men were bound hand and foot, and lying on the ground,) and getting so close as to be able to whisper to him, so that the sentinel over them should not hear, he said,

'If you'll get me out of their power, I'll give you a hundred pounds, and make a man of you.'

'Keep your dirty bribes and thoughts to yourself, if you plaze,—I want neither of thim. Make a man o' me indeed! God made a man of me already, and thanks be to Him for it!—it's more than He done for you, you pitiful coward, who hadn't the heart eyed to sthrike a blow in your defence. Get out! and don't pison my ears with your nasty thoughts.'

Regan soon after entered the apartment, having left the group below, when the consultation was over, with the base desire of enjoying the sight of Rory's prostration. He told the man on guard he came to relieve his watch and take charge of the safety of the prisoners; and as soon as the other had descended he approached O'More, and stood over him with malignant enjoyment. Rory looked up at him and said,

'Dhu, what's this for?'

'For thraitors,' answered Regan.

'I'm no thraitor,' said Rory.

'You lie!' growled the brute.

'If I wasn't tied as I am, you daren't say the word to me,' said Rory.

'Keep a civil tongue in your head, or it'll be worse for you,' said Regan.

'You're no man, Shan, or you wouldn't do this.'

'If you say another uncivil word, I'll kick you till I make you black as a thraitorous dog ought to be kicked.'

'To a black-hearted coward!' cried Rory, as fiercely as if he were at liberty.

The savage who stood over him proved the truth of the words by giving him a fierce kick on the side with his heavy brogue, which took away his breath; and it was only the sound of ascending footsteps that interrupted Regan in his brutality: he withdrew from the prisoners to the door.

'You're wanted below,' said the man who entered the apartment, which Regan quitted.

'O'More,' said the Collector, who was convinced by the fierce real of Regan's conduct that Rory was in the hands of enemies as well as himself, 'I see I was wrong in what I thought about this affair.'

'It's likely to be worse with us too, I'm afeard,' said Rory.

'Do you remember what you said when I asked you if the valley wasn't dangerous, when we came into the glen?'

'You said we should find something more dangerous than the flood in it. You spoke it in fun, O'More:—it has come true, to your sorrow.'

'I found more than I bargained for, 'faith!—But now that you remind me of sayin' that, there's something else it puts me in mind of that I said also—and equally thrue, to our cost.'

'What was that?' asked the Collector.

'I said, "thim that was born to be hanged would never be dhrownded;" and sure enough, I saved the vagabones from the dhrowndin!—and 'pon my sowl I'm much mistaken if the gallows won't be busy wid some o' thim yet.'

'I tell you what it is, Rory O'More,' said the man who was keeping guard over them— 'divil a much harm I wish you, and maybe there's not much harm intindid you; but I'd recommend you to keep a civil tongue in your head, or maybe it's little more you'll ever spake. Now take that as a word to the wise.'

Rory took the hint—for the words were spoken in a tone that implied the speaker had rather a friendly feeling than otherwise, and to advice so given, he attended. Powerless as he lay, however, and in the hands of enemies, as he was, he did not despair: his fertile brain was at work in many a wild conjecture as to what the intention of his captors could be, and in forming contrivances how he might outwit them and make good his escape.

After some hours thus spent, at length he and his fellow-prisoner were raised from their recumbent position; and the ligatures being removed from their legs, they were taken from their place of confinement and desired to walk in silence in the midst of the smugglers. It was night, and still continued to rain and blow violently; so that no time could be more favourable to their purpose of removing Rory and Scrubbs with all speed and secrecy to the coast. After walking some miles, they stopped at a cabin in a very lonely situation; where, having knocked for admittance, the door was opened by a man of ruffianly appearance, whom Rory had never seen before, though the rest of the party were known to him. Here refreshment was called for, and though the fare was coarse, it was acceptable after their walk in the rain. To Rory it was particularly so, for he had been fasting since breakfast, and notwithstanding his questionable position, he had too much courage to let such an occurrence spoil his appetite. But fear had taken such possession of the cowardly Collector, that he could not swallow a morsel, and a glass of spirits was all he could get down.

During the time they were in the house, nothing was spoken in presence of the prisoners which could enlighten them as to the smugglers' intentions. Indeed, there was more silence than usual amongst so many Irishmen and whenever any communication seemed to be desired between any of the parties, they either conversed in low whispers beside the fire, or beckoned towards the door, and preferred making their confidences outside in the rain, to incurring the risk of being overheard by Rory or the Collector.

After some time, a car and horse were provided, and Scrubbs and Rory again bound by the feet and placed on the car. In vain Rory request the privilege of being allowed to walk. 'Tare an 'ouns!' said he, 'whatever you do, don't make a pig or a cawf o' me, and spanshel me up on a car as if you wor dhrivin' me to market!'

'Howld your tongue and do what you're bid!' was the only answer he received.

In this fashion they pushed on some miles further, and then making another halt, two of the men and De Welskein obtained horses, and the prisoners being consigned to their care, the rest of the escort dropped off. They travelled thus all night, and the horse which drew the car was urged to as much speed as he could effect under the draught of so lumbering a vehicle, to the no small cost of poor Rory's ribs; for when at dawn they came to a halt, at a house equal in loneliness to the one they had first entered and loosening Rory's bands, desired him to walk in, it was as much as he could do to command the use of his limbs, so benumbed and bruised had he become in the course of this nocturnal kidnapping journey.

XXVIII

Giving an example of magisterial severity and maternal tenderness.

IN SOME DAYS, THE DISAPPEARANCE of the Collector produced a great sensation in the country. As far as a day went, his absence from home without being accounted for, however it might cause surprise, gave nobody any uneasiness; but when a second day elapsed without his reappearance within his own walls, it caused inquiry, and inquiry seemed only to perplex people more—that is, as long as they inquired where most they expected to find intelligence of him. But in this case, as in most others of the sort, chance did more than intention, and the clue to the disappearance of the Collector was found by the casual visit of a customer to the 'Black Bull.' This person was no other than Sweeny, who was a crony of Scrubbs, and supplied his wife with patent medicine, while her husband gave him pettifogging jobs of various sorts therefore, when his patron was missing, Sweeny offered his services in the endeavour to find him. In so doing, he had overridden his horse one day, and arriving at the 'Black Bull,' he stopped to give the animal some rest and a feed, for it was yet some miles to his own home.

On following his horse into the stable, what was his surprise to see Scrubbs' steed, which still remained under the care of Larry Finnegan, who kept him until he should be sent for, and had not as yet heard of the Collector's disappearance.

'Hillo!' exclaimed the attorney, 'what brings Mr. Scrubbs' horse here?'

'He left him here himself last Sunday,' was the answer.

'And where is Mr. Scrubbs himself?'

'How should I know?'

'Because he was here last!'

'Last Sunday he was, sartinly; but— —'

'Ay, *but*—there's the thing!—what has become of him since?'

'How should I know?'

'Because this is the last place at which I have heard of him: and if you can't give a satisfactory account of the matter, I can tell you it will be a serious business.'

This led at once to an explanation of the circumstances which had occurred at the 'Black Bull;' and the upshot of the business was, that Scrubbs had left the house in company with Rory O'More, and had not since been heard of. The next step to take, of course, was to go to Rory O'More and ask him what had become of the Collector: but Sweeny did not like to make the visit alone, for this bit of mystery, connected with Rory's name, aroused all the latent suspicions of him, which the appearance of the Colonel's pass had somewhat qualified, if not dispelled; and the remembrance of De Lacy's case of pistols, and his manifest promptness to use them, exercised so potent an influence over the attorney, that he determined to visit Rory with *witnesses*. This was his legal reason for the step; but the fact was, that Sweeny's courage was of a very companionable nature.

To the captain of the yeomanry corps, therefore, he hied him, and that noble commander, on Sweeny's detailing the occasion of his application, determined to pay a second visit to Rory's cottage, with all the force of his troop he could muster at a short notice.

In this determination let us leave them for the present, and take a peep at the quiet domicile they threatened with their visit.

Though Rory was expected to return to his home the day he left it with De Lacy, yet his absence created no alarm, though Mary and his mother sat up late in expectation of his coming home. When the next day elapsed without his making his appearance, they concluded he could not prevail on himself to part with De Lacy at the village, and that he had accompanied him all the way to the coast.

In satisfied belief they had indulged up to the period that the yeomanry captain put his plan of making an armed descent on the widow's cottage into execution; and it was with no small surprise and alarm she saw her humble walls again environed by the amateur dragoons. The Captain and Sweeny demanded, on entering the house, to see Rory.

'He's not here, plaze your honour,' said the widow.

'Where is he?' said they.

Now this was rather a poser, for the widow did not like to tell the cause of Rory's absence—or, indeed, it would be fitter to say, did not dare to tell it,—and so she 'beat about the bush' as well as she could for some time, until, from the nature of her answers, the captain had his deepest suspicions strengthened, and he said:

'The fact is, he is afraid to show himself, and is concealed.'

'What should he be afeard of, sir?' said the widow.

'He's concealed!' said the captain, 'and we must search for him.— And where is the gentleman you had living here with you?'

'He's left the place, sir.'

'Ho, ho! the same story of *him*, too! We must look for them, then.'

With these words, they proceeded, with those under their command, to pull to pieces a stack of hay and another of corn that stood in Rory's haggart, much to the dismay of the poor widow. In vain she protested, in vain she besought: they were bent on the work they had set about.

'Sure, if you think they're hid, gintlemen, sarche the house first, at laste, before you go pull my little bit of hay and whate to pieces!'

'Oh, we know better than that! They wouldn't hide in the house;— but they may be here.'

'Well, sure, if they be, you can prod the stacks with your swoords; but, for God's sake, don't pull the stacks to pieces, and it rainin'. Sure, you won't lave them worth a thraneen! and you *wouldn't* ruin the little thrifle of substance the poor widow has left!'

The appeal was unheeded; they searched not within the house nor did they satisfy themselves by prodding the stacks with their blades (which was a common practice in those times), but they pulled down the scanty savings of her little farming, under the pretence of finding those they were in search of; and in doing this, they were not guilty of any extraordinary atrocity, for in those times it was the common practice to destroy as much of the property of suspected people as the slightest pretext would admit. But these merciless fellows did not only bereave the lone woman of the accumulated produce of her little farm, but bragged of their humanity in not burning her haggart before her eyes.

'God help me!' said the distracted woman, wringing her hands. 'Sure, it's all one whether you desthroy me by fire or wather! You've pulled my little hay and corn about the place in the middle of the rain; and what good is it afther that? Oh, how will I ever pay my bit of rint! Oh, weira! weira! Burn it, indeed!' said she, as her wrongs gave her courage to speak more openly; 'throth, you're welcome to burn it, if you're able, afther the wettin' it has got now.'

In the Dublin Castle journals of the day, this circumstance was set forth at great length, with a flourishing encomium on the *Christian* forbearance of the '——Horse, in having merely *searched* the haggart of the person who had murdered (as it is believed) Jonathan Scrubbs, Esq., of — Lodge, in the County of —, without having burnt to the ground (*as they ought to have done*) every stick and *stone* belonging to the papist ruffian.'

The widow, as yet, had not heard of the disappearance of the Collector, nor of his having been last seen in company with Rory; therefore she was unconscious of any cause of uneasiness on the score of her son, and had nothing to lament over but her ruined haggart. Another day, however, had not passed without her hearing of the occurrence, with all the varieties of account that Rumour with her hundred tongues sends far and wide on such occasions.

The 'Black Bull' was the centre whence these reports radiated for from the moment of Sweeny's visit there, and recognition of Scrubbs' horse, curiosity was at work to know 'what in the world could have become of the Collector;' and, when Rory O'More could not be heard of, the anxiety to unravel the mystery increased. In this state of things it was that the crow-bar which Rory O'More had taken with him from the public-house was found in the glen of the Folly:—this led to further investigation; recent foot-marks near the ruin, bearing the appearance of a *struggle*, were observed. The bars wrenched from the grated window, and the evidences of the recent habitation of the vault, gave rise to many conjectures; and a grand field of mystery, with a noble standing crop upon it, was thus opened to the whole community, who began to reap away at it with might and main, and a very noble harvest of wonder was soon gathered; nor were there wanting gleaners to follow up the work and bring in the last precious grains of the incomprehensible.

The widow heeded not the various forms which the story assumed, for every subordinate interest was lost in the one all absorbing consideration to her, that her son was missing; and in this feeling Mary participated. In a few days, however, an additional pang was added to her grief; for the Scrubbs party had no hesitation in saying the Collector had been murdered, and that Rory O'More was guilty of the crime. When the poor woman became possessed of this report, her agony of mind was excessive—an agony relieved only by occasional indignation that her boy should be so maligned but this temporary relief being of an exciting, instead of a soothing character, her mind was kept in a state of tumult almost bordering on distraction.

'Oh that I ever should see the day,' she would exclaim, 'my darlin' boy should be accused of murdher! Oh that my grey hairs should suffer the disgrace! Oh, Rory, Rory! where are you?—where are you? Why don't you come and give them the lie?—for you never done it—never, never, never! *You* murdher?—You that wouldn't hurt a fly? Oh, my boy! my boy!'

'Mother dear!' exclaimed Mary, weeping as she spoke, 'don't take on so—don't, mother dear, or you'll break my heart!'

'Oh Mary, Mary! isn't it bad enough we've lost our darlin', our pride, and our prop—isn't it bad enough he's gone for ever from us, without his name bein' blackened to the world? Sure, when my darlin' was taken from me, the laste they might have left me was the bright remembrance of him without stain or blame! Oh, the hard-hearted crew!—to rob the lone widow of a mother's pride; and when the grave had swallowed her darlin', to put disgrace over him for his tombstone!'

She wrung her hands, and kept rocking in her seat, while Mary in vain attempted to soothe her.

'Don't be talking of his grave, mother dear; sure, we don't know but—'

Here the mother interrupted her with a wild burst of thought caught up from the passing word:

'Thrue, thrue!—we don't know where he lies. Oh, if I did, I'd go there and throw myself on my Rory's grave, and break my heart, and make my last bed there with him! But my heart *is* broke—broke—broke! and the sooner the grave closes over me the betther!'

'Oh! don't talk that way, mother—for God's sake, don't! Sure, you wouldn't lave your poor Mary alone!'

'No, *alanna!*—no, if I could help it:—but how can I live afther him! And you—you won't live afther him either—for you loved him like your life; and soon we'll follow him, and lave the cowld world, for it *is* cowld and blake to us now without him. And the disgrace—the disgrace! *He* a murdherer!—But who'll believe it?—Will thim that knew him believe it?—Never, never!'

'No, mother dear—no, they won't!'

'You don't think they will, Mary? God bless you, child, for the word! No—who could believe it of *him*, that had the kindest heart, and the proudest spirit?—*he* disgrace his name—*he* lave reproach for his sisther's portion, and despair for his mother's closing days!—no, they can't believe it.'

'No, mother dear, they can't!'

'Thim that could scatter the widow's substance to the wind may say it—but they won't be believed; and the fair name of my dead boy will be sthronger than the lies of the living.'

In this belief the forlorn woman was right; and, when she found the peasantry gave no credit to the rumour, and that, however they were unable to account for Rory's disappearance, and the suspicious circumstances attending it, they entertained no doubt of his innocence, the widow became more reconciled, and bore her loss with greater fortitude. The universal sympathy also which she found in her neighbours tended to support her; and, when she heard the accusation against Rory repelled as indignantly in his own class as by herself, she was much soothed, as the exemption of her son's name from disgrace relieved her from more than half of the weight of her affliction.

Foremost in the tender office of condolence was Kathleen Regan— if that might be called condolence which was rather a communion of affliction. The meeting of the two girls in the Widow O'More's cottage was very touching. Without their having ever a spoken on the subject, the love of Rory and Kathleen was perfectly well understood between them; and, when Kathleen crossed the threshold of her lost lover's cottage, she could not speak a word—but both girls looked at each other for a moment in silent agony, and, rushing with open arms into an embrace of sorrowing endearment, they wept upon each other's neck.

The girls had always liked each other, but now a fresh motive of attachment existed between them. Kathleen saw in the sister whom Rory loved so well an object to be additionally fond of for his sake; and Mary, in looking on the girl to whom her brother had given his heart, was similarly influenced; and thus their friendship at once became increased to affection, and a portion of the love that each had borne to Rory they transferred upon each other. They often met, and for hours together would talk over their bereavement, and, after some time, were forced to admit the long-combated belief to their hearts, that Rory was dead; for as Conolly's evidence was conclusive that he did not accompany De Lacy, they knew of no cause short of death for his absence.

It was in one of these conversations Mary O'More told Kathleen that, after all they had heard about the glen of the Folly, and the many times it had been examined, she would very much like to visit the place herself, and search it carefully up and down—but, it being so solitary, she did not like going alone, and asked Kathleen to bear her company. A ready assent was given to the proposal, and the girls spent a whole day in making a careful survey of the valley—from the Folly up to the wild and rocky gorge where the glen was shut in by a bluff barrier of cliff down which the stream tumbled.

Though making no observation tending to clear up the mystery, their visits were often repeated; and, notwithstanding their continued ill-success in every endeavour to elucidate the fatal cause which had bereft them of Rory, yet there was a melancholy pleasure in being on the spot he was last traced to. The frequency of their walks in the glen had so accustomed them to the place, that habit had overcome their fear of its loneliness, and sometimes each girl went there alone.

It was on one of these occasions, when Mary O'More had wandered nearly to the end of the glen, that she was startled by hearing the sound of a coarse voice which made her blood run cold. She paused and listened, and, in the lapse of a few moments, became conscious she heard the voice of Shan Regan, and, with a hasty and cautious step, the terrified girl ran higher up the glen; and, doubling swiftly round a projecting rock, she struck into a small hazel-wood that promised shelter, and, crouching under the bushes and rank grass, sought concealment from the man whose presence she loathed and dreaded. The sound of foot-steps approached; she could scarcely breathe they came nearer; she trembled so violently, as scarcely to prevent the bush which sheltered her from rustling with her tremor—and in another instant Regan was visible a few paces below her, standing at the foot-step of the rock round whose angle she had just passed.

XXIX

Showing how like a gentleman a tinker is when he thinks he is dying.

'When the devil was sick, the devil a monk would be;
When the devil was well, the devil a monk was he.'

To account for the presence of Regan in the glen of the Folly at this time, it becomes necessary to revert to the events of the night the smugglers carried off the Collector.

When the kidnappers and their prisoners made their first halt at the lonely hut where the car was procured, the old tinker determined to remain there for the night, as he felt unable to proceed, being attacked with fits of shivering, probably occasioned by his remaining standing so long nearly up to the knees in water during the imprisonment of the smugglers in the vault. Copious draughts of hot punch failed to relieve him; and as this wretched hovel was unprovided with a bed, a bundle of straw was all the tinker had to lie upon; and this was a share granted to him by Morty Mooney from his own wisp, which served himself for a bed whenever he used the hut as his resting place—the hovel not being meant for a regular domicile, but serving the disorderly set with whom Morty was leagued as a place of rendez-vous or halt, as occasion required; for from its lonely situation it was admirably adapted to the purposes of those with whom secrecy was often an object of importance.

During the night, Solomon's moans sometimes disturbed the sleep of Morty Mooney, who, as morning approached, was besought by the tinker to get 'a spark o' fire', and make some more hot punch, for in the course of the night the fire had become extinguished. The request was complied with; but Solomon's pain remained unalleviated; he continued his moaning protestations that he was 'racked intirely,' and, at length, expressed his fear that he was dying. As this belief became strengthened, the unfortunate old reprobate exhibited considerable apprehensions of the final hour, and showed his dread of approaching judgment by many pious ejaculations that long had been strangers to his withered lips. At last, he said he should like to see the priest, and urged Morty to go for him. But Morty said he could not do his errand until the return of Shan Regan, who had accompanied the party overnight and promised to be back early on the following morning; but that as soon as he arrived, the priest should be sent for.

'Oh, don't lose any time, Morty,—I'm very bad!—Oh, if I should die without seein' the priest!'

'You're not so bad as all that comes to yet,' said Morty.

'Oh, I'm racked inside, and I feel myself growin' wake!'

'Here's more hot dhrink for you.'

'It's no use.'

'It's brave and sthrong, and as hot as the divil.'

'Oh, don't say divil—God be merciful to me!—don't say divil, Morty—don't!—Oh! oh! I'm racked. Gi' me the dhrink, then—is it hot?—is it hot?'

'Yis, brave and hot;' and he handed him the steaming punch in a jug, which trembled in the old tinker's hands and rattled against his teeth as he drank.

'It's no use,' said Solomon; 'it warms my heart no more than if it was cowld wather.—I'm cowld—I'm cowld!—Oh, the rackin' pain!—For the love o' God go for the priest, and don't let me die this a-way!'

'The minit Regan comes.'

'Oh, he can wait, but my poor sowl can't wait! You wouldn't stand between me and the light o' glory, would you?—Oh, go, Morty, go!—you'll be dyin' one day yourself.'

'Well, whenever that may be, I won't be sitch a coward about it, anyhow.'

'You don't know that—you don't know that.—While the life is sthrong the courage is sthrong, but the heart fails you when you feel the life gettin' low.'

'Tut! don't be so afeard; a man ought always to be a man.'

'Oh, you dunno what it is to be hangin' over the pit, and the thread o' life goin' to break! I thought like you wanst, but now it's dreadful to be near it!—Oh, don't let me die out o' salvation! go for the priest if you hope to see glory.'

Morty went outside the cottage to avoid Solomon's importunity; for he did not like complying with his request without seeing Regan, as, under existing circumstances, he dreaded that the tinker should make some discoveries in the course of his confession with his ghostly visitor which might prove inconvenient to is confederates. He walked therefore towards the point whence he expected Regan to approach, and was not long without meeting him. He communicated to him Solomon's precarious state, and his desire to see the priest, and pointed out his apprehensions of the dangerous consequences that might arise from complying with his request. They consulted together on the course to be pursued in this matter, as they walked slowly back to the hut where the tinker still lay groaning and calling unavailingly on Morty to hasten for the confessor.

'It would be well he was dead, the owld thief!' said Morty, 'for he'd be no loss to any one.'

'That's thrue indeed, and by what you tell me it's like he's not long for this world: don't you say he's dyin'?'

'He thinks so himself,' said Marty; 'but that's the cowardly heart of him; for he's as tough as a gad, and I don't think he'll go without a hard struggle. Suppose we lave him there and let him die!'

'How would it be wid us thin?' said Regan, who did not in the smallest degree revolt at the cruelty of the suggestion, but had an eye to the consequences.

'Sure, we wouldn't have a hand in puttin' any harm on him, and who could say a ward to us?'

'That's thrue, sure enough,' said Regan, who walked a few paces in silence while he revolved in his own mind the proposition.

'If he was found dead there, it might lead to inquiry.'

'When he's dead, can't we throw him into a bog-hole?' said Morty: 'who cares enough for him to ax any questions?'

'Do you know where the ass is?' said Regan, still considering.

'No,' said Morty.

'You see that!' said Regan; 'the cunnin' owld rascal always left the ass somewhere else whenever he kem to the Folly, that it might be to the fore to rise a question if anything happened him and he didn't go back to claim it.—Do you mind?'

'Bad luck to his 'cuteness! what a head he has!'

'He's the biggest owld rogue in Ireland!' said Regan.

'Well, what are we to do?' said Morty.

'We'll see how he is first,' said Regan, as they approached the lonely hut. On getting near the door, they paused for a moment, and heard the groans of Solomon, mingled with ejaculations which were uttered aloud:

'Oh, Morty Mooney, are you gone for the priest?—bring him to save my poor sowl!—Oh, if you desaive me, may a dead man's curse be an you, and may you never see the light o' glory at your own dyin' hour!'

'That's a bitther curse he's puttin' an you, Morty—aren't you afeard?' said Regan, whose superstitious nature was worked upon.

'Betther for him pray for himself than curse me,' said Morty.

'Well, it's betther see him agin, anyhow,' said Regan, who entered the hut followed by Morty.

When Solomon heard the approaching footsteps, he turned on his straw, and cried in a voice of anxious earnestness, 'Is that his reverence?'

'Are you betther now?' was the answer he got from Regan.

'Oh, didn't you bring the priest?'

'By an' by, man—by an' by.'

The old tinker groaned in mental and bodily anguish: 'Oh, if I die out o' salvation!'

'Listen to me, man,' said Regan.

A conversation now took place between them, in which Solomon worked upon the superstitious feelings which he knew Regan to be under the control of, and threatened him with the appearance of his unlaid ghost after death if he permitted him to die without seeing the priest. Regan, in turn, made Solomon swear by 'the holy vestments and the seven blessed candles,' that he would not in his confession to the clergyman commit his companions.

This, in his urgency for haste, Solomon promised, and offered, in proof of his sincerity, that Regan might be present while he received absolution from the confessor. This point being carried, the pastor was sent for, and Morty Mooney was urged to use all speed.

'And suppose I go for the docthor?' said Regan.

'No, no,' said Solomon, 'it's no use,—and don't lave me to die alone, for God's sake!—stay wid me,—let me howld you—there, there sure it's comfortin' to have a grip o' somethin' in this life, while you're in it,—not to be left alone in the last minit, to quit the world like a banished sthranger.'

Solomon continued in great pain and was apparently sinking, and his anxiety for ghostly consolation continued to increase in a fearful degree. Nevertheless, Regan, having acquitted his conscience in *sending* for the priest, was in hopes the tinker would die before his arrival, and so put the secrets Solomon was in possession of out of danger. This inhuman desire, however, was not gratified: the approaching tramp of a horse was heard, and Regan, on going to the door, saw Father Frank riding towards the hut at a smart pace. Regan returned to the straw litter where Solomon lay, and said,

'Now, remember your oath,—don't bethray us; for if you do, hell-fire will be your portion!'

'Lord be merciful to me!' said the dying man.

Regan now returned to the door to receive the priest, and with the disgusting words he uttered to the dying sinner yet hot on his lips, he said, 'God save your reverence!' as he made a low bow to the priest, who alighted and entered the hovel, while Regan secured the bridle of the horse to the staple on the door-post and followed fast into the hut.

'Well, my poor man, are you very ill?' said Father Frank. 'Oh, God be praised you're come!' said Solomon. 'I'm dyin', your reverence,—

dyin'!—give me the comforts o' the church, and God bless you. Oh, I'm a poor sinner! give me absolution for my sins, and save my poor sowl!'

'Leave me alone with him,' said the clergyman to Regan: 'he wants to confess.'

'Plaze your reverence, he has nothin' to confess: he says he only wants the comforts o' the Church before he departs.'

'Retire,' said the pastor. 'You ought to know he cannot receive the sacrament without making a confession.'

Solomon declared he had nothing to confess: 'I have no time for confession, more than that I'm a wicked sinner, and repent o' my sins, and hope to see glory, if your reverence will give me absolution.'

'God help you, poor man!' said Father Frank humanely, 'you shall have the consolations of the church in your last moments; but you should make a clean breast, and unburthen your conscience: you have sins to confess.'

'More than I have time for,' said Solomon faintly: 'I'm dyin'. I confess I'm a miserable sinner, and I ax God's pardon, and my blessed Sav'or's pardon; and won't you give me absolution, your reverence, and promise me the light o' glory?—Oh, take pity on my poor sinful sowl, and give me the absolution!—and I have money, money enough, your reverence.'

'Don't think of your money, you poor sinful mortal! but think of saving your soul, and confess yourself before God, who knows your crimes, and is willing to pardon them if you confess them.'

'Oh, I lave *all that* to His *own honour*, your reverence, if you'll only gi' me the absolution, and say masses for my poor sowl when I'm gone;—and I've money to pay for thim—plenty o' money—will you say the masses for me?'

'Let me confess you first.'

'Sure, I've nothin' to confess, more nor I confessed already,—I'm a poor sinner, and ax absolution; and if your reverence goes to the glin o' the Folly—and there at the upper end there's a big rock stands out in the gun, and some hazel-threes near it higher up the hill.' Here he writhed in agony, and gave his accustomed cry that he was racked. He seemed weaker after the spasm, and in a voice more faint than hitherto, besought the priest for absolution, with a look so imploring, that Father Frank could no longer resist the appeal, and fearing he should expire every instant, the extremity of the case induced him to dispense with a confession, and he administered the last rites of the Church.

The poor wretch seemed much soothed by the act, and after a short pause continued:

'Undher that rock, near a big bunch o' dock-laves, if you dig up the ground, you'll find a leather bag with goolden guineas in it,—more—more—than you'd think—the poor tinker—' Here he paused again in apparent pain; but recovering again, he said faintly 'The goold—your reverence—I give the goold to you—for the masses—for my sowl. Oh, say the masses!—the masses!'

He could add no more, and sank back on his heap of straw.

'God be merciful to his soul!' said the priest devoutly, as he joined his hands in prayer over the poor sinner, whose spirit he thought had passed. But Solomon had not yet given up the ghost; he still continued to breathe, but his state of exhaustion seemed to be such, that no hope could be entertained of his recovery, and as there was no apparent likelihood even of returning consciousness, Father Frank prepared to go.

'This should be an awful warning to you,' said he to Regan, who attended him to his horse. 'See how the death-bed of the sinner shakes the heart! I hope you may profit by the lesson. After the poor man's decease, you must accompany me to the place where he said his money is concealed, to witness how much is there, and I will divide it between masses for his soul and offices of charity.'

When the priest had gone, Regan returned to the hut and found Solomon had sunk into a sleep.

'I suppose he'll go off that way,' said he to himself. 'And to think o' the owld vagabone having such a power o' money, all by chatin' and robbin'—the way he robbed the stakes o' the game yesterday in the Folly!'

To every one's surprise, Solomon, instead of dying, awoke the better of his sleep—much exhausted it is true, but manifestly out of danger. While in this state, he was often visited by Father Frank, who endeavoured to impress upon him how sacred the duty became, to thank God for his mercy in granting the time for repentance of his sins, and not hastening him away in the unprepared state in which the pastor found him, when, trembling at the terrors of death, he prayed for absolution, which, under the extreme circumstances of the case, had been given him then 'But now,' added Father Frank, 'I expect you to lead a good life for the remainder of the period Heaven may please to grant you, and I desire you come to your duty regularly.'

Solomon promised fairly; but the moment the priest's back was turned, his thoughts were far from heavenward. To the earth, to the earth they returned again; for he thought of his concealed treasure, and trembled for its safety, as he remembered that Regan was present when he named the spot where it was buried.

For some days he could not rise from the litter whereon he lay and when he was enabled to move, it was but to crawl feebly along. But even in this exhausted state he made his way to the glen of the Folly, to try if his hoard was safe. The appearance of the spot alarmed him, for the place bore marks of being recently disturbed, and he began eagerly to upturn the soil. Wretched was the work of the old miser: digging up the earth that so soon must cover him, to seek that which was dearer to him than life. What was his agony when he found his misgivings at sight of the place were well founded, and that his gold was gone!

At first he stood as stiff and cold as stone; and had he been of a nature sensible to emotion, the shock would have killed him. At length he gave way to groans and wrung his hands in despair—he threw himself on the ground; and tears, that had never since childhood wetted his cheek, now streamed down the furrows that crime and craft had worn there. He cursed his fate in having been spared from the grave only to taste a bitterness beyond that of death, and his wailing was mingled with blaspheming.

The sweet echoes of the quiet glen were startled at the disgusting sounds, and the pure peace of Nature violated!

But the master-spirit of the miser at length came to his aid:—craft rose, phoenix-like, from the ashes of his heart.—Where, a few minutes before, he wept in despair, and wrung his hands, he now sat motionless, with knitted brow and compressed lips, planning within the dark and tortuous labyrinths of his deceitful mind stratagem after stratagem to regain his lost treasure. With the patience and cunning of a spider, thread after thread he spun; and if the breath of doubt shook his fabric and broke his meshes, on he toiled, unwearied, until the web was completed: and now he only wanted to lure his game within his grasp.

Having determined on his plan, he replaced the earth he had dug up; and so carefully did he restore the appearance of the spot as it existed before his visit, that no one would have suspected it had been so recently disturbed.

He then left the place, muttering curses upon Regan,—for that he was the person who purloined the treasure there was no doubt; and the plan he adopted to make him restore it was this:—He contrived an opportunity of speaking to Regan without exciting his suspicions; and after alluding to the circumstances of his sickness, and of the hidden money which he had told the priest of,—'as you heerd me tell him yourself,' said he,—Solomon then proceeded to inform him that he had hid another hoard of money in another place, but that he did not think it was as safe as it would be in the glen of the Folly: 'and as the priest and you knows that place,' said Solomon, 'and as I can't live much longer now, I would wish it to be known where my money is,—for it's a pity it would be lost; and when I'm gone, sure I'd wish to lave somethin' to my friends to remimber me, and some to say masses for my sowl;—for to give it all to the priest, you see, Shan, is more nor I think right or rasonable. But, as I was sayin', it's betther have it all in one place; and so, if you'll go wid me to the glin, I'll put the rest o' what I have there too.' Here he produced a small leather bag, in which he had put some pieces of clipped tin to resemble the chink of coin, and just shaking it to deceive the ears of Regan, as he gave him a glimpse of the purse, he replaced it in his pocket, asking Regan to accompany him the next day to the glen—'For, you see,' said he, 'people sometimes goes there now, to see the Folly, since the night we done the thrick there; and I'm wake and owld, and would be afeard to go by myself wid so much money about me. So, Shan *agra,* come wid me, and thin you'll know where every rap poor owld Solomon has saved is hid—jist yourself and the priest;—and when I'm dyin', I won't forget you, Shan—throth I won't.'

Regan fell into the trap, for the finished deception of Solomon's acting induced the belief that he really had more treasure to hide, and Shan Dhu lost no time in restoring the bag he had stolen to its former place of concealment, intending, when the additional treasure was placed there, to seize it all and decamp. It was the following day he went with the tinker for the purpose of making the second deposit; and it was on this mission he was engaged when Mary O'More heard his voice in the glen and fled at his appearance. Let us now return to her, whom we left trembling in her place of concealment.

XXX

Which will explain itself.

M ARY O'MORE NEARLY FAINTED FROM terror at the sight of Regan, who stood in silence near the rock; and the thought of his discovering her alone in such a deserted place shot a pang of agony through her frame.

Regan at last raised his voice, and cried, 'Are you comin'?'

The words were delightful to Mary's ear, for they implied he had companion, and the sense of her desolation was lessened.

'Come on,' said Regan again; and Solomon soon was visible to Mary. It was the first time in her life she had ever been glad to see the old tinker.

'Let me rest a bit,' said Solomon, seating himself; 'the walkin' tires me: I'm wake yet.'

'No wondher,' said Regan. ''Faith, I thought you wor gone th' other day!'

'Well, I can't stay very long now anyhow? I feel myself goin' fast; and whenever that'll be, you'll know where to get the goold, Shan *agra*—for it's yourself will have the most of it.'

'All of it,' thought Shan in his heart.

'And so,' continued Solomon, who, with admirable presence of mind, did not seem to be in any hurry to look for his money,—'So you tell me that the Frinchman went aboord himself?'

'Yis.'

'And the Collecthor is out o' the way?'

'Snug,' said Regan.

Mary, at the name of the Collector, was breathless, and listened till the anxiety of hearing made her ears tingle again.

'And Rory?' said Solomon.

'D——n his sowl! *he's* out of the way too,' said Regan.

Poor Mary gasped for breath.

'And not one can make head or tail of it through the counthry,' said Solomon.

''Faith, they may look for him long enough before they'll find him!' said Regan.

'Well, we may as well look for what we kem for, now that I'm rested,' said Solomon. 'There's the very spot where it is.'

'Show it to me, jist,' said Regan, 'and I'll turn up the earth for yon, bekaze you are wake yet, and don't fatigue yourself.'

'Thrue for you,' said Solomon, who knew Regan's motive was to prevent the recent removal of the earth being noticed.

Shan Dhu now opened the blade of a large clasp knife, and commenced the act of unearthing the treasure.

Mary was in a state of confused horror all this time. She had heard them say Rory might be looked for a long while before he was found, and she imagined, from these words, that they had concealed his body after he was murdered (for she had given up all hope of Rory's being alive), and perhaps this was the spot where his mangled remains were hid,—perhaps these were his murderers before her;—if she were seen, her life would be forfeited also! She could observe Solomon's face from where she lay, and she saw his eyes fixed with a look of fascination upon the spot where Regan was delving with his knife and turning up the clay u his hands.

Regan said at last, 'I think I am near it now.'

Mary's blood ran cold;—was it her brother's corpse they were uncovering? Solomon's look became more intense, and in a minute more he exclaimed, 'That's it, that's it!' and with his hands outstretched like the claws of a bird of prey, he pounced upon the hole that Regan had made and rooted up the bag. 'I have it, I have it!' said he, unable to contain his transport at the sight of his regained treasure, which he hugged up close to his breast, as a mother would hug her first-born.

Regan looked at him with a mixture of suspicion and ferocity in his countenance: perfectly horrible, and neither of them spoke for some seconds.

Solomon was the first to break silence, and, rising from his seat, he said, 'I b'lieve we may as well go now.'

'Go where?' said Regan.

'Out o' this,' said Solomon: 'we need not stay here any longer.'

'Why, aren't you goin' to bury it again?'

'Yis, in another place.'

'Why, you towld me you had more to put to it!'

'Ay, ay, and so I will put this along wid th'other.'

'But you said you'd put what more you had here!' said Regan, who began to see the trick the tinker meant to play him.

'Well, that's what I *intindid*,' said Solomon; 'but I changed my mind sence, and I think this will be safer along wid th'other; come wid me and we'll put it there;' and he arose to depart as he spoke.

Regan laid his hand on the skirt of the tinker's ragged coat, and dragged him to his seat again as he said, 'You won't go that way, as cunnin' as you think yourself! Don't be catchin' your young birds with chaff that way, Solomon Sly, my darlin': owld sojers are not to be done with ginger-bread!'

'What do you mane, Shan *avic?*' said Solomon, endeavouring to affect composure.

'I tell you what I mane,' said Regan, with decided ferocity in his manner: 'I mane, that the divil and out o' this you take that money so aisy!'

'Why, you wouldn't hendhor me o' puttin' my money where I like, would you, Shan *agra?* said Solomon, still endeavouring to maintain a quiet state of things; but while he assumed so much indifference, he kept an iron grip of his money-bag.

'I'll hendher you takin' it out o' this—by this knife I will!' said Regan, as he clutched the weapon fiercely, and shook it with vehemence in the tinker's face.

Solomon changed countenance a little as he attempted further wheedling.

'Can't you come and see where I put it along wid the rest?' said he.

'*Along wid the rest indeed!* That was a purty humbug you made me b'lieve, you owld villain! Along wid the rest!—go and see where you put it! Yis, you threacherous owld thief! go out on the public road wid you, and then you'll make some fine excuse as 'cute as a leprauchaun, and give me the slip! No, no; I have you now, and I'll make my own o' you! You promised me some of it, and I'll have it, or I'll know why.'

'You wouldn't take the money from a poor owld man, would you, Shan dear?'

'Poor indeed!' said Regan. 'Why, you owld starved 'ottomy, that never had the heart to buy a male's mate or a hearty glass, you have more gold than many a sportin' fellow in the counthry, and more than ever you can want; and I *do* want it, and, what's more—and take one word for all—by the blessed light, I'll have it before you lave this!'

'Why, Regan, it's not robbin' an owld man you'd be?'

'Robbin'!—*you* talk of robbin'! Tell me, you grey owld vagabone, who was it stole the stakes o' the spoil-five in the Folly? You thought no one saw you, did you? but I seen it—I did, and now I'll see who can play the best game here! Gi' me the half o' that bag, and be thankful I don't take it all!—you know you promised me a share of it.'

'Yis, yis, I did,' said Solomon, 'and I'll keep my word, Shan dear—I will but you remember I said it should be afther I die.'

'*Die?*' said Regan with terrible meaning in his voice—'die? Take care how you put me in mind o' *that*!'

Solomon looked ghastly at the implied threat, and said imploringly, 'Oh, Shan, Shan! sure you wouldn't murdher me.'

'Who was it taught me last Sunday three weeks?—who was it said in the Folly, that "*dead men tell no tales?*"—eh?' and his voice assumed a deeper tone.

'Oh, Shan, Shan! you wouldn't, you wouldn't!' And Solomon again attempted to rise and depart; but Regan laid a still fiercer grasp upon him than he had yet done, and said, 'Wouldn't I?' with the scowl of a fiend. 'Give me the half o' that money or I'll make a way to your throat nearer than your mouth—by the 'tarnal I will! Will you give it?'

Solomon did not speak, but clutched his money-bag faster.

'Will you, I say?' said Regan, getting more excited, and gripping his knife with as determined a purpose as the tinker clutched his treasure.

Solomon now gathered all the strength he had left into one desperate effort, and, in the hope of alarming Regan, he raised his voice and shouted, 'Murdher! murdher!'

'You will have it, then!' said Regan, who, step by step, was workd up to desperation, and, rushing on the old man, he caught him by the throat, flung him to the ground, and, with uplifted knife was about to threw himself upon him with a horrible curse, when Mary O'More, whose mind had been wrought to the highest pitch of terror-stricken excitement, could contain her feelings no longer, uttered an appalling shriek; and, as the echoes of the valley rang to the scream, Regan stood petrified with alarm.

Solomon took advantage of his terror, and, looking towards the spot whence the scream proceeded, he saw, as he arose at the same instant, the girl emerge from her place of concealment; and, with an activity surprising for one in his weakened condition, he was at her side in a moment, and, clinging to her, prevented the escape she meditated. 'Save me! save me!' she exclaimed, as he held her with the energy and tenacity of terror.

The consequences of a witness being present at what had taken place flashed upon Regan's mind in an instant; and, once being committed in an act of outrage, desperation urged him onward, and seeing Mary O'More in such a position inflamed his brutal nature with thoughts fitter for hell than earth. To divide Solomon and the girl and dispose of them separately, was his object; so, stimulating Solomon by the hope of saving his gold, he said:

'Go off wid you—be off, you and your money, and lave this young woman with me: I want to have some words with her.'

Mary was now the person to cling to the tinker, who endeavoured to shake her off, while she begged for the love of God, he would not desert her.

'Let him go, I tell you!' said Regan.

'No! no!' screamed the girl.

The vile old miser whose life she had just saved now eagerly endeavoured to loose himself from her hold, and leave her in the hands of the ruffian from whose knife she had delivered him, and, in the desire to save his gold, would have left her in peril of worse than death.

'Let me go, I bid you!' cried the tinker impatiently, and striking as fiercely as he could at the straining hands which held him.

'For the Blessed Virgin, I beseech you, Solomon darlin',' cried the agonised girl, 'don't lave me with that horrid man! Oh, Solomon! afther saving your life, don't lave me this way!'

Solomon seemed for an instant to have a touch of compunction but Regan said, 'If you stay here two minutes longer, the divil a guinea you'll ever lift out o' this! Be off, and lave this spyin' young lady with me.'

The threat roused Solomon to action, and again he endeavoured to shake Mary from him. She threw herself on her knees before him, and, clasping him firmly round his trembling limbs besought him in the most earnest and touching manner not to abandon her.

'Oh sure you wouldn't desert the poor, helpless, innocent girl—sure you wouldn't! God won't forgive you if you do.—Oh sweet Virgin, protect me!'

'Shake her off, I tell you, and save your money, or, by all the devils in hell, I'll have the lives o' both o' yiz!' shouted Regan as he laid hold of Mary O'More and dragged her fiercely from Solomon, who struggled to disengage himself from her; and at last by his striking her heavily on the hands, the unfortunate girl was forced to relinquish her grasp; but at the same moment she made a desperate effort to regain her feet, and, springing from her knees turned with the energy of desperation upon Regan, and cried with vehemence, 'May the God that looks down on us judge and punish you if you wrong me, Shan Regan!'

The moment Solomon found himself free, he exerted what speed he might in getting away; and Regan, holding Mary with a grip of iron, and looking on her with demoniac triumph, said:

'Now I'll tache you, my saucy lady, how you'll gibe and jilt a man!

and you'll larn more in the glin than you came to watch for!'

With these words, he attempted to seize her round the waist but Mary made an active resistance, and maintained a surprising stand against his ruffian assault; but every instant her power to repel became less, her exclamations to heaven grew weaker, and at last her short and gasping shriek gave token that she felt her remaining strength fast failing.

Just at this moment, when she was nearly within the irrecoverable grip of Shan Dhu, the baying of hounds reached her ear, and she screamed with wild joy:

'The hunt! the hunt!'

Regan made a last desperate effort to drag her into the hazel wood, where he might effect concealment and drown her cries, but inspired by the hope of succour, Mary redoubled her efforts, and while she was writhing in the unequal struggle, a fox ran close beside them, and dashed aoross the glen as the cry of the hounds grew louder.

'They're coming! they're coming!' she cried; 'you villain, they're coming! there's the fox! Oh, Blessed Virgin, you've saved me!'

The cheering cry of the dogs again ran up the glen, the pack opened louder and louder every instant, and, in dread of discovery, Regan dashed into the wood and climbed up the cliff.

The moment she was freed from his grasp, Mary O'More ran with wild speed down the glen towards the point whence the sound of the chase proceeded, and soon saw the horsemen urging forward. The moment she beheld them, the certainty of protection produced so violent a revulsion of feeling, that her brain reeled as she rushed onward, and she fell prostrate to the earth.

Among the foremost of the horsemen was Mr. Dixon, a magistrate gentleman of a kinder nature than the generality of his class. He rode beside Squire Ransford, and they both saw the precipitous flight of Mary O'More down the glen. Mr. Dixon remarked the circumstance to the squire, who attributed the headlong speed of the girl to her fear of the hounds. Still Mr. Dixon kept his eyes fixed on Mary; and seeing her fall, he exclaimed:

'Down she goes!'

'Let her pick herself up again!' said the squire, as he dashed forward in the chase.

But the magistrate, though fond of hunting, thought there were other things in this world worth thinking of; he had some heart about him, with which the squire was not troubled, and, despite the alluring notes of 'Sweet-lips' and 'Merry-lass,' who gave tongue ahead in good style, he drew his bridle when we saw the fugitive sink to the earth, and rode up to the prostrate girl, while the rest of the hunt followed the squire, and left the office of charity to him: and well for poor Mary O'More that there was one to pity and protect her

Mr. Dixon alighted, and was some time before he could calm the impatience of his excited horse, which panted with eagerness to continue the chase, and he could not attend to Mary until he had soothed his steed into quietness; then throwing the rein over his arm, he knelt down to raise the fainting girl from the earth, and found her in a state of complete insensibility. Seeing that to restore her would require his undivided attention, he led his horse, which still pulled at his arm with impatience, to a thorn-tree, and fastening the bridle to it, he hastened back to Mary.

Raising her gently from the earth, he carried her close to the river; and there by copiously sprinkling the cool stream over her face, which a deathlike paleness overspread—a paleness rendered more striking by the dark hair that streamed loosely around her head and neck—he gradually restored her to life; but it was some time before consciousness returned. The sound of many waters was in her ears as she opened her eyes and looked vaguely around. When she caught the first glimpse of Mr. Dixon, the sight of a human face seemed to startle her, and she attempted to scream; but her exhausted energies could only give vent to a hard-drawn sigh. The soothing tone in which she was spoken to tended to restore her, and after some time she uttered a few broken sentences; but from previous terror, such was the incoherency of her expressions, that Mr. Dixon could only conjecture she had been in personal danger, and therefore besought him to protect her.

'I will, my poor girl—I will.'

'God bless you, sir! you won't leave me alone?'

'Certainly not; calm yourself.'

'Are they gone?' said she, looking wildly up the glen.

Mr. Dixon thought she might have been frightened by the hounds, as the squire had supposed; and as she looked in the direction they had taken, he said, 'Yes, the dogs are all gone.'

'Oh, it's not thim; sure, they were the salvation o' me: only for the hunt, I was lost—lost for ever.'

The magistrate by degrees, learnt the cause of her alarm, and asked her name. When she told him, he said he supposed that Rory O'Mor was her brother.

'Brother ' said she wildly—'oh, I've no brother now!' and relapsed into tears.

'How do you know?' said Mr. Dixon.

'Oh, I'm afeard they've murdhered him! they confessed it a'most before me.'

This led to further questions on the magistrate's part; and Mary at length told all the particulars of what she had witnessed between Shan Dhu and the tinker.

When she was sufficiently recovered to walk, Mr. Dixon accompanied her from the glen to the village, and there Mary got a friend to escort her to her home; for even on the open road she feared to be alone, so shaken had her nerves become by the terrible scene she had gone through.

Mr. Dixon determined on having Mary's depositions taken and sworn to in regular judicial form, and for that purpose rode over next day, with the squire and Sweeny, to the widow's cottage.

On leaving the house Sweeny suggested that this story of Mary's might be all a stratagem to divert the suspicion which attached to Rory, on the subject of the collector's disappearance, into another channel. Mr. Dixon said she had done more than divert suspicion, for that she had named the guilty parties.

'But how can you tell she speaks truth?' said the spiteful little attorney, whose hatred of Rory for the tombstone affair was so bitter, that all of his name were sharers in it.

'We must have Regan and the tinker arrested,' said Mr. Dixon.

'If you can find them,' said Sweeny.

'Well, if they keep out of the way, it will be strong presumptive evidence of their guilt.'

'Ah! You're not up to them as well as I am: they may be all in the plot for what you know.'

'They're a pack of rebels altogether,' said the squire; 'and until the country is cleared of them; we shall have no peace.'

'You're right, squire,' said Sweeny.

'Well, I have not quite so bad an opinion of them' replied Mr. Dixon; 'nor do I think the girl's story a mere fiction. We must have Regan and the tinker arrested as the next step.'

The proper authorities were despatched for this purpose to Regan's house; but they found him not, and for many days a useless search was prosecuted. As for Solomon, he had no home where to seek him, and the officers had therefore a roving commission to lay hands on him as they might: but he eluded their vigilance; and no one interested in their apprehension could catch the smallest clue to the finding of Shan Dhu and the tinker.

The priest suggested a visit to the lonely hut where he had seen Solomon in his sickness, and a party undertook the search immediately; but the hut was deserted. Traces, however, of the recent visit of man were manifest: the fresh peelings of some boiled potatoes were strewn upon the floor, and the yet warm embers of a turf fire were in the corner of the hovel.

XXXI

In which Rory makes his first trip to sea: a voyage of discovery.

I<small>T WAS IN A LOW</small> and retired fishing-hut De Lacy was housed the evening he reached the sea-coast, there to await the arrival of the lugger off the shore. He felt lonely on his removal from those with whom he had been lately sojourning, and to whom he had in a manner become attached, and the efforts the inmates of the fishing-hut made to entertain him were unavailing; so he retired to rest earlier than usual, wishing to indulge the thoughts in solitude which the presence of others interrupted without dissipating.

When on his bed the influence of rest induced a pleasant state of mind; and leaving the remembrance of those he had parted from, Hope led him onwards to the shores of France, where he trusted soon to land in safety, and gather the materials for a victorious return to his friends and country. Of Adèle, too, he thought, and Love whispered the joys of again beholding and clasping to his heart the girl of his affections. It was with such pleasing promise on his imagination that he closed his eyes; and the downy wings of slumber, waving over his senses, fanned this spark of hopefulness, into flame and all night long he dreamt of his Adèle,—of their joyful meeting,—of her blushes and her smiles,—of her enthusiasm at the prospect of his name yet living amongst the bright ones that should be dear to his country,—of her anticipation of future pleasures on the war being past—when the warrior should subside into the husband, and Love bind the garland of victory on his

brow! Oh, youth! youth!—how dost thou teem with golden visions,—
while the dreamy impressions of age are but cast in lead!

De Lacy arose from his slumbers as though he had fed on ambrosia
overnight—with that elastic feeling of existence which belongs to
the hopeful lover. Influenced through the whole day by his dreamy
intoxication, he revelled in alternate visions of glory and of love. As he
roved along the strand, if he turned to watch the changeful effects of
the sea, he looked upon the noble ocean stretched before him as the
high-road to his glorious aspirations and hope seemed to beckon him
across the deep; while, as the surge thundered at his feet, and was swept
backwards in foam to the main, he heard the voice of victory in the
sound, calling him to enterprise. If he looked upward, and beheld the
seaward clouds sailing towards the land of his Adèle, his musing was in
a soft mood; and as some touch of sunshine tipped their delicate form
it was recognised by his heart as a good omen. He was all excitement,
and while he fed on such sweet fancies he drew forth his pencil to play
with the pleasant thoughts as they arose; and soon imagination bore him
beyond the world in which he breathed. The roar of the booming sea
was lost in the silver sounds of fairy fountains; the whistle of the brisk
wind sweeping across the waves, to which his blood danced as he mused,
was unheard amid the whisper of the breeze through rustling groves;
and the rough shingle of the shore whereon he walked, felt under the
foot of the enthusiast like the golden sands of the classic fountain.

He was in the land of dreams.

THE LAND OF DREAMS

There is a land where Fancy's twining
Her flowers around life's fading tree,—
Where light is ever softly shining,
Like sunset o'er a tranquil sea;
'Tis there thou dwell'st in beauty's brightness,
More fair than aught on earth e'er seems;
'Tis there my heart feels most of lightness,—
There, in the lovely land of dreams!

'Tis there in groves I often meet thee,
And wander through the sylvan shade,
While I in gentlest accents greet thee,
My own, my sweet, my constant maid!
There, by some fountain fair reposing,
Where all around so tranquil seems,
We wait the golden evening's closing,—
There, in the lovely land of dreams!

But when the touch of earthly waking
Hath broken slumber's sweetest spell,
Those fabled joys of Fancy's making
Are in my heart remembered well!
The day, in all its sunshine splendour,
Less fair to me than midnight seems,
When visions shed a light more tender
Around the lovely land of dreams!

But while De Lacy was indulging his poetic mood, inhaling the fresh breeze and treading the open strand, poor Rory was lying captive not many miles distant, confined in a close hovel, almost smothered with smoke, and revolving far other notions in his busy brain. So closely were he and the collector watched, that it was impossible to make an attempt at escape; and Rory, from the character of the fellows who had undertaken the business, looked upon any plan for deliverance within his power to execute as hopeless: they were all up to everything in the way of finesse and expedient; and however he might overreach a booby ensign, a chuckle-headed sergeant, or an amorous colonel, a party of smugglers were as much masters of fence as he was himself; therefore he felt there was nothing left but to meet with fortitude whatever fate awaited him. At the same time, however, he cast many an anxious thought homewards; and the uneasiness he knew his mother and sister would suffer at his absence caused him more anxiety than any other consideration. When the day was over—and to Rory it seemed the longest he had ever passed—another removal of the prisoners took place, and under cover of darkness they were conducted to the sea-coast, and put on board a small fishing-boat that lay at anchor a short way from the shore: they were stowed away in the fore part of the boat, and Rory could hear them making preparations for putting to sea. In vain did he inquire what they were going to do with him; he could not get any answer to his questions, and was desired to 'howld his whist!'

In the meantime De Welskein had gone forward to the fishing hut where De Lacy was remaining, and told him to be in readiness to put to sea that night.

'Is the lugger on the coast, then?' said De Lacy.

'No, monsieur; we shall finds her some leagues to sea. She keeps a good offing; but the smack will run us out to meet her.'

When the night fell, De Lacy was summoned to go aboard, and getting into the punt of the fishing-boat, was rowed alongside, in company with De Welskein.

The punt was hauled up, the sails hoisted, and away bore the smack for the ocean.

Poor Rory soon got wretchedly sea-sick; and never having heard of the nature of that most distressing of all sensations, thought he was going to die, and lamented, in the lapses of his paroxyms of nausea, that he was doomed to suffer so miserable a death. 'Oh, if they'd shoot me itself, or dhrown'd me at wanst!—but to have a man turned inside out this way, like a - - ow!—murdher! my heart 'ill be up next!'

De Welskein lay his course all night towards the point where he expected to find his lugger, and as the morning dawned she was perceptible; signals were exchanged, the two vessels approached each other, and a boat being lowered from the lugger, De Welskein and De Lacy went aboard.

De Lacy had been on the deck of the fishing-smack all night, wrapped in his cloak, for the mingled stench of fish, tobacco, and bilge-water, rendered the little crib, they called cabin, intolerable. When he went up the side of the smuggler, De Welskein said he must want rest after so long and cold a watch, and recommended him to turn in. De Lacy declined doing so immediately, but as De Welskein wanted to make a transfer of the prisoners from the fishing-smack without De Lacy's knowledge, he assumed a sort of laughing consequence as captain of his own vessel, declared he was absolute there, and insisted on De Lacy's going to rest, offering him his own berth for the purpose. The moment De Lacy was below, Rory and Scrubbs were brought on board the lugger, which put on every stitch of canvas she could carry, and stretched away at a spanking rate for France.

But, sick as poor Rory was, his senses were sufficiently about him to observe that they were removed to a larger vessel; and as he passed along the deck, he heard the voice of De Welskein; this was enough for Rory's enlightenment, and he became certain that De Lacy must be on board. When conducted with Scrubbs below, and placed there in confinement, the excitement produced by this last discovery made him rally against the sea-sickness more than he had hitherto done, and in the intervals of the malady his head was at work in planning by what means he could let De Lacy know he was in the same ship.

'Roaring is no use,' thought he, 'for they make sitch a hulla baloo here, that one might roar their heart out and never be heerd: for there is such thumpin' and bumpin', and crashin' and squashin', and rumblin' and tumblin', and first up on one side and then down on th' other, that I don't wondher they are roarin' and bawlin' up there, on the roof over us.' (The roof was the name Rory gave the deck, because it was over his head.) 'By gor! I wondher how they howld on there at all! for here, even in this room—and indeed there's but little room in it—it's as much as I can do to keep my brains from bein' knocked out agin th' other side o' the wall sometimes: and how the dickins can thim chaps keep from bein' thrown off the roof and dhrownded!—only, as I said of thim before, thim that's born to be hanged—'

Here Rory's thoughts were cut short by getting a jerk to the opposite side of his prison and having another qualm of his new malady. The wind had changed, and becoming adverse, De Welskein was obliged to go about very often; and this produced so much delay, that their course, which they were likely to run in twenty hours had the wind held as it promised in the morning, was not completed under two days.

At the close of the first day, the prisoners were visited by a black, who, by order of De Welskein, brought them something to eat; but the sight of food only produced loathing.

'Ou be berry sick now, eh?'

'Oh! I'm kilt!'

'Tak um lilly bit;—do um good.'

'Oh, take it out o' that, for God's sake!'

'Berry nice;—um nice an' fat.'

The name of fat was enough, and poor Rory was set off again.

The negro laughed, as all sailors do at the suffering of a novice to the motion of a ship; and having had his joke he did not offer any more fat, but suggested to Rory to take some brandy.

'Berry good for sea-sick.'

'Oh! Let me die where I am, and don't taze me!' said Rory.

'Nebber be sitch dam fool! Brandy berry good; best ting um can tak for sea-sick. Come, come, poor lan'-lubber! open im mout. Dere, ou darn fool!—brandy berry good.'

The drop of spirit Rory swallowed did him service; and the black, who was a good-natured fellow, before he left the prisoners, gave them both some brandy-and-water; and the dry and parching sensation which poor Rory experienced, as well as his exhaustion, was much relieved by the negro's recipe.

After some hours the negro came again; and though Rory could not eat, he took some more of the diluted spirit; and that night be experienced some sleep, after having had another talk with blackee.

The next morning, when Rory's sable friend made his appearance offering some breakfast, the course of the vessel was far smoother than it had hitherto been, and Rory was better able to listen to the proposal of eating.

'Try lilly bit, man,' said the black.

'I'm afeard a'most,' said Rory.

'Nebber be 'fraid: ou not sick dis day, like oder day; him cheek not so white, him eye not so like dead fish. Try bit, man;—berry good. Me know 'tis good—me make it myself.'

'Why, thin, God bless you! did you make it on purpose for me?' said Rory.

The negro grinned. 'No, no—me not so good to lan'-lubber as dat! Me cook.'

'Well, I'm obleeged to you, anyhow. And would you tell me, sir, if you plaze, is Misther De Lacy well?'

This was Rory's first thrust at his object.

'Massa Lacy—him gen'lman dat come wid cap'n aboord?'

'Yis, sir.'

'Oh, him berry well now; lilly sick first; but now smood water— near de bay now. Me go give him and the cap'n sometin' for brekf's soon. Take nudder lilly bit, man.'

'No, thank you, sir,' said Rory. 'And is it you that is goin' to take the captain and Mr. De Lacy the brequest?'

'Iss. Me wait on um; me de cook—black man always cook.'

'The devil sends cooks,' thought Rory, and he could not help smiling at the thought.

'What um laugh at?'

'Why, I was laughing to think how quare it is that one may find a friend where they laste expect it, and in the gratest sthranger. Give us a dhrop o' brandy, if you plaze.'

'Dere, man;—make um better.'

'That's a grate relief to me!' said Rory.—'But, as I was sayin', how a man may meet a friend in the gratest sthranger! You've been mighty good to me; and I tell you what it is, I'm behowlden to you and obligated to you, and I'm grateful to you; and you must take a present from me, to show you how shisible I am of your tindherness, for——'

Here there was a call for 'Scipion.'

'Massa Cap'n call me,' said Scipio.

'Well, give me your fist before you go,' said Rory, who, when he caught the negro's hand said, 'Gi' me these sleeve-buttons o' yours and I'll give you mine, and it'll be a keepsake between us;' and with the words he unfastened the button from the negro's wrist, and inserting in its place one of the sleeve-buttons De Lacy gave him, the negro ran off hastily to a second and louder summons from the deck.

'Now,' said Rory, 'if Mr. De Lacy has the luck to remark the sleeve-button in the blackey's shirt, all's right yet.'

The negro was ordered to bring De Welskein his breakfast, and De Lacy was sufficiently recovered by their entering smooth water to join in the repast, and was sharpset, as men always are the first time they are able to eat at sea. The negro set out the rough sea-fare to the best advantage; and as he held a dish balanced in one hand on the edge of the table, while he removed some plates that were opposite to De Lacy to make room for it, De Lacy chanced to look at what sort of fare was coming, and his eye caught the sleeve-button, which he recognised as his own, and the same he had given as a parting gift to Rory.

'Where did you get that?' said De Lacy quickly.

'What!' said De Welskein, with a penetrating glance of his dark eye, as he marked the hurried question of De Lacy.

De Lacy was put on his guard by the jealous quickness with which De Welskein noticed his words, and said, 'The beef—where did you get that fine beef?'

'Why, to bee sure, in Ireland: what ees to soorprise you so mosh?'

'I thought you never had any but salted beef on board,' said D Lapy, who turned the conversation directly into another channel, and as soon as the meal was ended, went on the deck. There he saw they were within a short sail of land, and while they were approaching it he mentally turned over the circumstance that had excited his notice, and was lost in conjecture as to the means by which the negro could have become possessed of the sleeve-button. *He* gave it to Rory, at a distance of many miles from the coast, two days before he embarked on board the lugger, which is found at sea many leagues; and there one of these button is in possession of a black man aboard that lugger, and De Lacy did not remember the negro to be on board the fishing-smack.

There was a mystery in this; and any mystery on board De Welskein's boat respecting Rory, in whom he was known to have such confidence, awakened De Lacy's suspicions of some foul play to Rory. But while he was on board the craft of the smuggler whom he knew to be a wily and desperate fellow, he thought it advisable not to breathe a word nor exhibit a sign of his misgiving; and so, having run all this over in his own mind, he walked up and down the deck with seeming unconcern, and spoke to the smuggler as if nothing had ruffled him.

As they doubled a small headland that shut in the bay they were entering, De Lacy saw a frigate lying in the harbour, and De Welskein said, 'There is *La Coquette.*'

'Indeed!' said De Lacy.

'Why does monsieur exclaim?'

'Because if that be the *Coquette*, the captain is a friend of mine, and I will go aboard and see him.'

On nearing the ship De Welskein's notion was found to be correct—it was *La Coquette*. The lugger's boat was lowered, and De Lacy went up the side of the frigate.

The captain was on board, and mutual kind greetings passed botween the two friends. After De Lacy had given a hasty sketch of the state of affairs in Ireland, and the motive of his present visit to France, he told the captain the suspicions he entertained that De Welskein had been playing a trick with a friend of his, and begged his assistance in setting matters right.

'Certainly; but how?'

'I suspect the fellow has secreted a man on board, and I want to ascertain the fact—and if so, to get him out of his power.'

'But why not order the rascal to give him up to you before?'

'*Monsieur le Capitaine* forgets, on the deck of his own ship, that I was only a passenger on board the smuggler's boat; and her captain is a very desperate fellow when he chooses,—so I thought it preferable to say nothing until I could speak to some purpose. Now, under the guns of the *Coquette*, Monsieur De Welskein will be extremely polite when he knows her captain is my friend.'

'Oh ho! is that the sort of gentleman?—we'll soon finish this affair.'

He ordered his boat to be manned directly, and entering it with De Lacy, they pulled into the harbour, where the lugger had already dropped her anchor.

It was not long before De Lacy and the captain were on board the smuggler.

'De Welskein,' said De Lacy, 'I want to see Rory O'More.'

'Rory O'More!' said De Welskein with well-feigned surprise:
'Monsieur must go back to Ireland if he wants to see him.'

'No, no, De Welskein, he's on board.'

'You mistake, sir,' said De Welskein: 'what *can* make you entertain
such a suspicion?'

'No matter what,' said De Lacy, who did not wish to bring the black
man into trouble for being accessory to the seoret having escaped—
'but I know he's here.'

''Pon my honour!' said De Welskein theatrically, and laying his hand
on the place where his heart ought to have been.

'Search the boat!' said the captain sternly to a couple of his men
who were on the deck beside him.

De Welskein took off his hat with a prodigious air to the captain,
and said, 'Monsieur should consider I am commander here'

The captain laughed at his swagger; but seeing that several
desperate-looking fellows crowded round the hatches, as if to prevent
the search the captain ordered,—for he had but half a dozen men
with him, and the lugger was armed and powerfully manned—he
said in a decided tone to De Welskein, 'You are under the guns of
my frigate: give up the man you have concealed, or you shall be sunk
like a nutshell!'

De Welskein saw there was nothing else for it, but told De Lacy
he considered it not treating him with the respect *one gentleman owed
another*, to interfere in such a manner with *his* affairs.

De Lacy could only laugh at his impertinence.

De Welskein fell back from his dignity upon his true resource—
impudence and reviling—and swore he was very sorry he took De
Lacy out of Ireland, and saved his neck, and so cheated the gallows of
its due. 'But the next time you want me, you'll find me—if you can!'
said De Welskein, strutting back to the stern of his boat, while Rory
was walked up the fore-hatchway.

It vould be impossible to describe the scene that followed, for
Rory's wild delight at seeing De Lacy and finding himself out of De
Welskein's power is past description. De Welskein stamped up and

down one end of the deck, while Rory danced on the other. The French captain looked amazed when he remembered that De Lacy called this man his friend; and supposing that none except a gentleman could be De Lacy's friend, he turned to him and said, with the extreme of wonder in the tone of his voice, 'Are all Irish gentlemen like *him?*'

'I wish they were,' said De Lacy.

XXXII

Containing many sapient observations on Frenchmen and frigates, English subjects, foreigners, etc.

WHEN THE CAPTAIN HAD SUFFICIENTLY satisfied his wonder in looking at Rory's vagaries, he ordered a return to the frigate. With what delight did our hero jump into the boat of the *Coquette!*—though he lost his footing when he alighted there, and broke his shins as he stumbled over her thwarts. 'Bad luck to thim, for boats and ships!' said Rory; 'a man ought to have the legs of a cat, to keep his feet in thim.' One of the sailors caught hold of him, as he feared Rory would go overboard from the rocking he caused in the boat, and desired him to sit down.

'What's that you say?' said Rory.

'Asseyez-vous.'

'You say what?'

The sailor again spoke; and Rory called out to De Lacy, who was coming over the side of the lugger, 'Arrah, thin, will you tell me what this fellow is sthriving to say to me? for the divil a word he spakes I can make out; and my heart's broke with my shins, that I cut over thim dirty little sates.'

'He's bidding you sit down,' said De Lacy; 'and do so, or you may go overboard.'

'Oh, that indeed!' said Rory, sitting down. 'Sure, if he towld me that a wanst, I'd ha' done it: but he went jabberin', and mumblin', that I couldn't make him out.'

'You forget he's a Frenchman,' said De Lacy.

'That's thrue indeed, sir,' said Rory; 'and it's wondherful how hard it is for these furriners to make themselves undherstud.'

The boat was now pushed off; and Rory looked up at De Welskein, who stood in an attitude of theatrical defiance frowning over the quarter at the whole boat's crew. Rory took off his hat, and with a mocking salutation to the smuggler, shouted out, 'Good mornin' to you, Mr. Divilskin.'

De Welskein wrapped himself up in the dignity of silence, and scowled after the barge, as she cleft the waters, and cast a silvery ripple behind her, in her course to the frigate, towards which the men pulled swiftly; and every bound she made to the strokes of the bargemen seemed to excite Rory's wonder, until he said to De Lacy, 'What a lively craythur she is!—one ud think she was alive a'most, she jumps so sprightly!'

'Wait till you get on board the frigate, Rory,' said De Lacy 'that's what will surprise, you.'

''Faith, I've been surprised enough where I was, and I don't want any more o' the same. I thought I'd be turned inside out fairly; and I suppose, if I was so bad in a small ship like owld Divilskin's, that a big one would kill me intirely.'

De Lacy assured him to the contrary, and as they approached the ship of war, pointed out to Rory her noble form and fine proportions, her graceful bows, her spreading yards and towering masts, and the beautiful and intricate tracery of her various cordage.—'Is she not a beauty, Rory?'

'Divil a beauty I can see in her, nor in one like her!' said Rory; 'for afther the tattherin' and taarin' I got comin' over the say, I'll never say a good word for a ship as long as I live—and indeed that wouldn't be long if I was to be on boord; and I hope, Mr. De Lacy, it's not goin' you are to take up wid the sayfarin' business.'

'No, no, Rory, don't be afraid: I'm only going to dine on board the frigate with my friend here, who is her captain, and at night we'll go ashore.'

'On the land is it?—Oh, God be praised! but it's I'll be glad.'

'In the meanwhile, Rory, you will have time to tell me how it came to pass that you were on board the lugger.'

'Not with my own will, 'faith, I can tell you!'

'I thought as much: and was it De Welskein's doing?'

'That I don't know—it was among thim all—but you see, I had the misfortune to come across that dirty Scrubbs, and—'

'Stop, Rory,' said De Lacy; 'here we are at the ship's side—you must give me your story in full when we get aboard.'

On reaching the deck of the frigate, Rory's wonder was immense: the height of her masts, the mazes of her rigging, her great size, and her rows of guns, were, successively, objects of wonder to him, and a tap on the shoulder from De Lacy was required to arouse him from his state of entrancement.

'Well, by gor! it *is* wondherful,' said Rory: 'I own it.'

'You shall see all the wonders of a ship of war by and by,' said De Lacy; 'but for the present, follow me to the cabin, and tell me all the details of this strange adventure of yours which has carried you over seas.'

Rory followed him below, and related at length the particulars of his meeting with Scrubbs—his becoming his guide, his freeing De Welskein and his party from the vault, and their capture of the Collector and himself.

'And is Scrubbs a prisoner on board the lugger?'

'Snug,' said Rory.

'And do you know why all this has been done?'

'Not a one o' me knows a word about it more than I towld you.'

'I am sorry all this has occurred—I'm afraid it may do mischief in Ireland;—that such a rascal as the smuggler should dare to interfere in such matters!—'tis too bad:—I'm very, very sorry for this.'

'So am I, 'faith,' said Rory; 'and my heart's breakin' to think what the poor mother and Mary will suffer, not knowin' one word about what's become o' me!'

'This Collector being taken away will make a great noise,' said De Lacy.

'Faix, he made a great noise himself when they wor takin' him away! And what do you intend to do about him, sir?'

'Nothing: it is not for him I care, but for the mischief his disappearance will produce. But since they have taken him away, the matter is as bad as it can be, for his being restored would not mend the matter; so they may do what they please with him.—But I want to consult with my friend here, Rory, about the best way of providing for your removal on shore.'

'Sure you wouldn't send me on shore, sir, without you were comin' too! 'Faith, I'd rather stay at say with you, bad as it is, than be on land without you.'

'I'm not going to make a separation between us, Rory,' said De Lacy 'but remember that we are on the shores of France, and your being a stranger, and particularly an English subject—'

'Is it *me* an English subject?'

'Yes—are you not so?'

'By Jasus I'm not! I'm an Irishman, glory be to God!'

'Well, you're a foreigner, at all events.'

'A furriner! Is it *me* a furriner!—arrah, Misther De Lacy, what do you mane at all? Sure you know I'm an Irishman, and no furriner.'

'You are a foreigner here.'

''Faith, I'm not; it's *thim* that's furriners.'

'Well, you're a stranger, at least.'

'That I'll own to.'

'Well, as a stranger in this country, it is necessary to contrive some means of protection for you.'

'Why, do you think I'm afeard?—is it afeard of a parcel a' little Frinchmin I'd be?'

'Oh, they are not so little, Rory.'

'Well, big or little, I don't value them a *thraneen*.'

'I know you're not afraid of any man, Rory: but the protection of which I speak is regarding your legal safety—for there are such things as laws, Rory.'

'Devil sweep them for laws!—they're always givin' people throuble, sir.'

'That cannot be helped, Rory. The captain and I must consult on the management of this affair, and in the meantime I will put you into the hands of a person who will show you all the wonders of the ship; and as you have never been on board a man-of-war, it will amuse you.'

Rory, accordingly, was entrusted to a person whom the captain ordered to the cabin, and to whose care Rory was especially entrusted.

'You have no notion, Gustave,' said De Lacy to his friend when they were *tête-à-tête,* 'what a fine fellow that is!—full of address, of courage, and fidelity, with a love of country and a devotion to its cause worthy of a hero; and yet he is but a simple Irish peasant.'

'And are they all like him?'

'He is a specimen of the best,' said De Lacy: 'but, take them all in all, they are a very superior people. And yet the Helot of the Spartan was not a more degraded slave than the poor Irish peasant is made by his taskmasters;—worse than the Helot; for he was a slave by the law of the land, and the law which was cruel enough to make him so was at least honest enough to avow it; but the poor Irishman is mocked with the name of freeman—while the laws of the land are not the same for him as for his more favoured fellow-subjects.'

'That will soon be mended,' said the captain, 'when the expedition is ready.'

'I am delighted to hear you say,' said De Lacy, 'that there is some appearance of action going forward.'

'There is a good deal of bustle in the marine, at least,' said Gustave; 'and some of our best line-of-battle are fitting out in other ports, I understand.'

'Good!' said De Lacy. 'I must hasten to Paris to lay before the Directory my report of the state of Ireland, as well as for some more tender affairs than armaments and invasions.'

'Ha, ha! *Pour les beaux yeux de Mademoiselle.*'

'Certainly.'

'Nothing like it!' said Gustave: 'love and war for ever!

'A charming creature, Gustave! Do you remember Adèle Verbigny?'

'Adèle Verbigny?' said the officer, repeating the name in a tone that was not pleasing to De Lacy.

'Why do you echo the name so?' asked the lover.

'Merely from surprise,' said the captain, 'for I did not know you were tender in that quarter.'

De Lacy said no more on the subject of his love, for there was something in the manner of his friend when he spoke of it that he liked not—too slight for words to define, but which the delicate perceptions of the lover are ever alive to as gunpowder to the spark.

Instead therefore of pursuing the tender topic, De Lacy consulted with the naval officer the best means of securing Rory's safety when he should go ashore.

'If he were near my own regiment,' said De Lacy, 'I could manage it well enough, by enrolling him in it: but as it is—'

'Leave that to me,' said the sailor; 'if *you're* not with your regiment, *I'm* on board my ship, and can arrange the matter for you.'

'I can't let him remain here, *mon ami*—thanks to you for your offer of protection, but I know it would grieve him to be parted from me.'

'I don't mean him to be separated from his friend,' said the captain. 'He shall have a sailor's dress, and a discharge from my ship as if he had been one of the crew: and that will be protection sufficient.'

'Good,' said De Lacy; 'nothing can be better.'

And the captain gave orders for a suit of sailor's clothing to be provided for Rory.

He in the meantime was being conducted over the ship by the captain's appointed guide, who spoke some half-dozen words of English, which he made go as far as he could with Rory; but that was not half far enough, for the inquisitive spirit which prompted his numerous questions was an overmatch for the English of his *cicerone*.

Whenever Rory could not get an answer from him, he asked any one else who was near him; and the strange position in which he found himself, for the first time in his life, amongst his own species, yet without means of communing with them, *bothered* Rory excessively: when he found English fail, he tried Irish, vhich was equally unsuccessful; but still Rory did not give up the point—when English and Irish failed, he employed signs, and he and the Frenchmen became mutually pleased with each other's expertness in pantomime.

On Rory's return to the cabin, De Lacy questioned him as to his tour round the ship, with which Rory declared himself to be much delighted.

'Did you ever see anything like it before, Rory?'

'Nothin' sir—barrin' a bee-hive?'

'How the deuce can you liken a frigate to a bee-hive.'

'Bekaze every corner of it is made use of, and there's sitch a power o' *people* in it, and everybody busy.'

'Well done, Rory! you've made out your simile, and you might carry it still farther: they can sting sometimes, and are often killed by the burning of brimstone.'

'Faith, an' you're right enough, sir, about the Frenchmin not being sitch little chaps as I thought they wor.'

'You have seen some good stont fellows on board this ship, then?'

''Pon my conscience, very dacent boys; and the captain, there, is not a ill-lookin' man at all.'

'What does he say of me?' asked the commander, who perceived by Rory's expression of eye that he alluded to him.

De Lacy repeated to him exactly Rory's speech, and the captain enjoyed it extremely.

'Then the French,' continued De Lacy, 'are not exactly what you conceived them to be, Rory?'

'No, in throth: I always thought, and I dunna why, but I always *did* think, that Frinchmin was dirty, starved ottomies—poor little yellow go-the-grounds, not the half of a man, but a sort of a *spidhogue*.'

'And what's a *spidhogue*, Rory?'

'Why, I can't well explain to you: only whenever one comes across a poor ill-begotten starved spidher of a crayther, we call him a *spidhogue*.'

The captain was much amused on hearing of Rory's preconceived notions of Frenchmen, and his surprise at seeing them other than he thought them; and he requested De Lacy to interpret to him the most of his colloquy with the Irishman.

The day was passed pleasantly enough to all parties on board the frigate; and towards evening, De Lacy, accompanied by Rory attired in a sailor's dress, was rowed ashore, where the shelter of a quiet inn was sought for the night, and the next morning De Lacy, obtaining passports for himself and Rory, set out for Paris.

Rory's thousand and one strange observations as they proceeded often raised a smile on the lip of De Lacy, who, nevertheless, fell into trains of musing as he drew nearer to his Adèle and conjured up anticipations of their meeting. But, mingling in all these dreams, was the remembrance of the voice of his friend Gustave as he spoke of her; the tone in which he echoed the name of Adèle dwelt upon his fancy, and seemed of evil omen: it was the hoot of the owl from the turret of his hopes.

XXXIII

Cupid in Paris.

Rochefoucauld lays it down in his Maxims, that—

'On garde long-temps son premier amant quand on n'en prend pas un second.'

Which may be thus freely translated:

'Your first love most precious is reckon'd
Until you have taken a second.'

And the same thing might be said of a glass of claret; the best judges of that cool and gentlemanly beverage declaring you cannot get the taste of it under half a dozen. Whether the comparison holds between fits of love and glasses of claret as far as the half dozen, I leave to persons more conversant with the subject and better able to decide.

The keen and sarcastic Rochefoucauld wrote maxims of which the world has taken great pains to prove the truth. Whether Adèle Verbigny was profound in the 'moral reflections' of the witty Duke, is little matter; but if she were *not*, then with her intuition superseded study.

When Horace De Lacy left Paris for Ireland, pretty little Adèle thought of him a good deal for some time after, and even engaged on a piece of elaborate needlework to enscroll his name; which work, I believe, was then called 'Tambour:' perhaps I am wrong—but, at all events, *tambour*-work would have been very appropriate in any complimentary tribute to a soldier's name. But, whatever it was called, the work was begun; and Adèle used to sit for hours and hours together, surrounded with long skeins of silk of all manner of colours, and beads of all manner of sizes, and gold thread, and Lord knows what else besides; and there was a certain laurel wreath to encompass a scroll of the three letters she valued most in the whole alphabet, namely, H. B. L.—they were the initial letters of her hero's name and, with a nice little bit of French and female ingenuity, she contemplated the interweaving of smaller letters after each initial, to express, as it were, the attributes of her lover; so that the work, when finished, would give to those who would be at the trouble of hunting the involved sentence through all its twistings and twinings these words:

HONNEUR. DEVOTION. L'AMOUR.

She was enchanted at the thought, and worked very industriously for three weeks; but as she got on at the rate of about half a laurel leaf a day, there was a good chance that a real tree might be grown in the time it would take to make the needlework chaplet. Nevertheless, on she went, and though the canvas in the centre of her design was vacant, her imagination filled up the space in the most beautiful colours, and twistings, and curvetings, that needle or fancy had ever worked or conceived, and she leaned forward to the pleasure of interlacing H. B. L. in some months, and having the work ready to exhibit to her lover on his return. As she worked her web she thought of Penelope and Ulysses: but, alas! she and De Lacy were not married *yet;* and moreover, there were no lovers to come and tease her from her fidelity. Now, although the first part of the comparison did not exist between her and Horace, the second part might and Adèle was such a classic creature, that she almost wished to have the temptation of a lover, that she might enjoy the triumph of fidelity.

It was too charming a thought not to he put into execution, and Adèle got herself up in the character of Penelope.

Amongst those who indulged her in her classic whim, was one who was a great admirer of tambour-work; and moreover, he could thread her needles admirably; this saved Adèle time, and drew her nearer to the delightful period when she might commence the initial scroll of H. B. L. Then he sang very pretty *chansonnettes*; and they were so lively, that Adèle's pretty little fingers moved more merrily to the measure and facilitated her work prodigiously. They got on famously. Adèle could not be so ungenerous as not to give a song sometimes in return; but hers were always in the tender line, as they ought to have been, because Horace was away; there was no unbecoming levity about them—something in the simple and tender style of

'Oiseaux, tendre Zéphire,
Voulez-vous bien me dire
La cause de mes soupirs?'

—to say nothing of the politeness of '*Voulez vous bien*' to the birds.

Well, Hippolyte Délier—for that was the name of the needle-threader—thought the tender songs of Adèle far more beautiful than his lively *chansonnettes,* and so he took to the *oiseaux* and tendre *Zéphire* style, and Adèle declared

'She liked him still better in that than his own.'

And a thought occurred to them then, which they both were surprised did not occur to them sooner; which was, that their voices would go so well *together;* and so they took to singing duets—and very nicely they did them. All this time the embroidery went on, and one day the threads got entangled underneath the work, and Hippolyte was asked for a helping hand to assist in disengaging them; and in doing so, their hands came in contact under the frame very often, and Adèle never remarked before what a very soft, nice hand Hippolyte possessed; and somehow or other, the work was in such terrible entanglement, that the hands went on poking and pulling for some minutes without the extrication of either the threads or their fingers, till at last Hiippolyte fairly caught hold of Adèle's hand and gave it a tender pressure *under* the frame, while his eyes met hers over it. And very pretty eyes Hippolyte had—and indeed so had Adèle, to do her justice; and, with a look of the sweetest reproof, she said, '*Fi, donc!*' But it was singular, from that day forth, how provokingly frequent the entanglement of threads became, and how often Hippolyte was called on to assist in disengaging them.

What could come of poor De Lacy having such a *helping hand* given to his piece of embroidery? Why, that Adèle found there was no room for three letters in the centre of her laurel-leaf; and so, instead of H. B. L., she could only entwine H. D. How singular! they were the initials of *Hippolyte Délier.*

They could not help remarking the coincidence, and the singularity, too, of his name *Délier,* and he so clever in unloosing entanglements. '*Hèlas!*' said Adèle sentimentally, 'you have untied more than threads,' as Hippolyte knelt before her and declared himself her adorer.

Madame Verbigny was of the same opinion as her daughter in the busines; for Hippolyte was on the spot, and De Lacy was absent.

'*Les absens ont toujours tort.*'

Besides De Lacy might be killed, and Adèle lose a match in Hippolyte, who, as far as matches were concerned in point of view, was a better one than De Lacy, for he had a strong friend in the Directory, and was looking forward to promotion beyond his present position, which was, even at the moment, one more advantageous than that of a captain of grenadiers.

So Hippolyte was received as a declared lover, and was sitting with the faithful Adèle a few days before their marriage, when, to Adèle's inutterable surprise, the door of the chamber opened, and De Lacy rushed towards her with extended arms.

Adèle screamed and fainted, and the two gentlemen did all gentlemen could do to restore her. While in her state of insensibility (feigned or real), the bearing of Hippolyte was such as to make De Lacy wish he would not take so much trouble; and the sound of his friend Gustave's voice crossed his memory like an echo from the nether world.

The first object that met Adèle's opening eyes, was De Lacy kneeling beside ber.

'Adèle—my own Adèle!' said the soldier.

'How altered you are!' said Adèle, looking coldly on his face.

'Altered!' echoed De Lacy. 'Good heaven! Adèle, are *you* altered?

'What a fright the smallpox has made of you!' said the Parisian.

De Lacy felt as though a bolt of ice had been shot through him, and, gazing upon the woman he adored, with a look that might have made the most callous feel, he was about to speak; but he had only uttered her name, when Adèle thought the safest game to play was another faint, and, screaming as gracefully as she could, she dropped off again into speechlessness. Her mother came to the rescue, and declared the poor child's feelings would be the death of her some time or other.

'Monsieur,' said she to Hippolyte, 'be so good as to take care of her a few minutes, while I speak to this gentleman;' and she beckoned De Lacy from the room.

What their conversation was, it is needless to record; but Rory O'More remarked, on De Lacy's return to the hotel, that his aspect betrayed deep dejection; while, mingling with the sadness, traces of fierce determination were visible. The eye was clouded, and the cheek was pale; but the knitted brow and compressed lips betokened a spirit brooding over more than melancholy thoughts.

Rory could not repress his anxiety, and, when De Lacy had closed the door of his chamber, asked him what was the matter.

De Lacy drew his hand across his forehead, and paced up and down the room.

'I hope there's nothin' found out, sir?' said Rory.

'Found out!' said De Lacy. 'Yes, Rory, I have found out something!' and he shook his head sorrowfully.

'Tare an' 'ouns! I hope they're not angry wid you for bringin' me up here? Sure, if they wor, I'd quit this minit.'

'No, Rory, no. Ask me no more now: 'tis only some private grievance of my own'.

'Bad luck to thim for fretting you, and you comin' all this way to see thim! And won't they come over to help us, afther all?'

'You'll know more to-morrow, Rory leave me for to-night. Be stirring early to-morrow morning, for I shall want you.'

Rory left the room puzzled and unsatisfied.

XXXIV

Showing how new enemies arise out of old loves.

THE LAST CHAPTER BEGAN WITH a maxim; and, for fear one chapter would be jealous of another, this shall be headed with a maxim also:

WHEN A GENTLEMAN IS ROBBED OF HIS HEART'S TREASURE, THE LEAST AND ALSO THE GREATEST SATISFACTION HE CAN ENJOY, IS TO HAVE A SHOT AT THE FELLOW WHO ROBS HIM.

And that is as good a maxim as ever Rochefoucauld wrote.

Now De Lacy could not have a shot at Hippolyte, because pistols were not the fashion in Paris in those days for the settling of such affairs; but he might run him through the body with steel instead of lead and this difference in the exchange of the metallic currency in honourable commerce makes no difference in the satisfaction which gentlemen either give or take in such transactions.

On leaving the house of his false fair one, De Lacy proceeded to find a friend to whom he might entrust the business of inviting Monsieur Hippolyte Délier to take a morning walk in the environs of the *Place Louis Quinze*; and there was little difficulty in the search, for chance threw in his way a brother officer who undertook the duty with alacrity. The meeting was arranged, and the next morning De Lacy's friend called upon him on his way to the place of rendezvous.

'Why have you this strange-looking sailor in attendance on you?' said Captain Sangchaud, as he looked at Rory in wonder when they turned into the street.

De Lacy explained to his friend who Rory was, and why he bore the habit of a sailor. 'And my object in making him accompany us is, that, in case I should fall, I enjoin you, Sanchaud, by our companionship in arms, to take care of him; and, if you cannot get him back to Ireland, have him with you in your own regiment—and a finer fellow you have never known in your experience.'

On getting a view of the Tuileries, Rory, who did not interrupt the conversation hitherto, could not resist asking De Lacy what was the name of the building.

'I beg your pardon, Misther De Lacy, but whose house is that?'

'That was the king's house, Rory,—called the Tuileries: it was a palace.'

'A palace, it is, sir? Dear me! what a pity they stinted it!'

'Stinted, Rory? Why, I think 'tis large enough.'

'Yes, it's mighty big, but, sure, one 'ud think a palace would be stinted in nothing.'

'And in what do you think it stinted?'

'Bekaze, sir, it looks like as if there was a scarcity o' stone when they built it, and a grate plenty o' wood and slates; for it's mostly roof and windows.'

'Come on!' said Sangchaud: 'we must be first on the ground.'

On reaching the appointed place he drew a pair of swords from a case which he had carried under his arm; and on seeing them Rory opened his eyes very wide, and touching De Lacy on the elbow, he said, 'Tare an' 'ouns! sir, what are you goin' to do?'

'To fight a duel, Rory.'

'A jewel is it!—to fight a jewel! and you walkin' as good friends with the man the minit before! Oh, my God!'

De Lacy could not forbear a smile at Rory's idea that it was with his second he was going to fight, and explained the matter to him.

'Well, it was no wondher I thought so, anyhow, when I did not see any one else for you to fight with. And what are you goin' to fight for, sir, if I might be so bowld to ax?'

'I cannot tell you now, Rory;—but I have brought you with me to put you under the care of my friend here, Captain Sangchaud, who will look to you in case anything happens to me.'

'God forbid hurt or harm would come to you, Misther De Lacy!—And to think o' me, too, when your own life's in danger! Oh, God bless you—God bless you!—you've the kind heart and the good heart, and the divil a fear o' you in the fight, for the angels will watch over *you*, that thought of watchin' over *me* in the sthrange place.'

De Lacy turned aside to hide the glistening of his eye at the poor fellow's thought.

'Feel this,' said Sangchaud, handing him one of the swords. 'Do you like it?'

'Yes,' said De Lacy, 'this will do—it is well balanced: the blade is a little more bent than I like.'

'All the better in giving tierce over the arm,' said Sangchaud.

'I know 'tis so considered by your most accomplished swordsmen but I would rather have this,' said De Lacy, handling the other sword and looking along the blade. 'They are both very good tools,—but this for me.'

'You're wrong,' said Sangchaud. 'You fight at a disadvantage with it, in comparison to that which I hold. However, you'll soon be able to judge for yourself of the one you've got, for I see your men are coming. Will you have the blade I recommend?—do.'

'No,' said De Lacy: 'this is handier to me.'

'Well, as you like; but the other is far the more killing of the two.'

Hippolyte and his friend were soon on the ground, and no time was lost in the parties engaging. Rory was on the alert all the time watching every thrust and parry, and making exclamations as the various vicissitudes of the combat suggested. Many a 'whoo!' and 'hurroo!' he uttered whenever he fancied his friend's adversary gave way; and at length, when he saw him manifestly stagger before a lunge from his foe, he shouted, 'By the powers, you're into him!'

Délier had received a smart wound in the sword arm, which rendered further fighting impossible; and De Lacy and his second, making a formal salute to the discomfited party, left the ground.

'Long life to you, sir!' said Rory: 'sure, I knew you'd get no hurt; but, indeed, while you wor poking at each other with them dirty little bits o' swords, I was wishin' it was a taste o' black-thorn you had in your fist; for there's more dipindence in it than in one o' them little skivers.'

'What! wood against steel, Rory?'

'Ay, indeed—I'd never ask to ate another bit, if I wouldn't give a fellow with one o' them toasting-forks as fine a lickin' as ever he got, if I had a choice bit o'timber about me.'

Sangchaud all this time was tying up his swords; and when he had done so, he tucked them under his arm in a very business-like manner, but did not seem half satisfied.

'You've but a poor opinion of my swordsmanship, I see, Sangchaud,' said De Lacy.

'No,' answered the captain. 'You made some very pretty passes and parries; but I wish your adversary had taken a little more away with him.'

'He has only got a flesh wound, 'tis true,' said De Lacy.

'Yes,' said his friend, 'and that's all because you wouldn't fight with the blade I recommended. You put in your thrust very well; but that blade you chose is the least thought too straight: if it had been the other you'd have been under his ribs.'

'Perhaps 'tis better as it is,' said De Lacy: 'I have escaped having a death to answer for.'

'Well, let us go to breakfast now,' said Sangchaud. 'Nothing gives a man a better appetite than a little morning exercise of this description.'

XXXV

Showing how useful old love-letters are in cold weather.

O<small>N RETURNING TO HIS LODGINGS</small> De Lacy found a parcel directed to him lying on his table: on breaking the seal he perceived the contents consisted of his letters to Adèle, under convoy of a note from her mother. That philosophic individual wrote as follows:—

> '*Our affections are not our own.*—'

'No, indeed,' thought De Lacy;—'they are anybody's who asks you for them'.

> '*My child has been influenced by the destinies which rule the affairs of the heart*—'

'When people behave so ill as to have no other excuse, they always lay the blame on destiny,' continued the lover.

> '*Sentiment to a woman is what honour is to a man: without it life would be worthless.*

> '*Permit me to assure you*
> '*of the highest consideration of*
> '*C. Verbigny.*'

'What folly and falsehood!' exclaimed De Lacy, as he crushed the scroll in his feverish hand, and flung it from him. He then sat down, and looked with mingled sorrow and humiliation on the pileof papers which lay before him. There is not perhaps anything in this world produces a more painful feeling than to contemplate the evidences of our former affection returned to us in the moment of indifference: Cupid does not like to eat his words, any more than another gentleman. And in De Lacy's case it was the more galling, for he still clung dearly to the memory of his love, though he loved no more. To dissever the ties that hold the heart, leaves a pang behind long after the blow has fallen; for with one's feelings, as with one's nerves, a morbid action exists after amputation. When a mutual mouldering of affection has taken place, and such tender mementoes as love-letters are returned, then, after the first gulp you make to swallow your annoyance or your shame, you can throw them into the fire or feed other flames than those they were intended for; but where only one party is untrue, bitter are the records of unrequited affection!

Letter after letter De Lacy turned over—and sometimes, as a peculiar phrase, or place named, met his eye, the time and the circumstances connected with them would arise, and his young heart had the bitter experience to see fancy's fond creations crumble before the withering touch of reality. And amongst these papers were some poems. One in particular caught his eye: it was a metrical trifle he had done in some of his first hours of courtship, when, in the light badinage that is employed in the earlier s skirmishes between beaux and belles, Adèle answered a charge of De Lacy's that she was fickle, by her telling him that he was *volage*. 'Do you not know,' said she, 'what the weathercock said to the wind? *Si vous ne changez pas, je suis constante*.'

De Lacy was pleased with the conceit, and presented her with a song derived from the subject; and there it lay before him, the evidence of his first hours of love, surviving the passion whence it sprang.

THE WIND AND THE WEATHERCOCK.

The summer wind lightly was playing
Round the battlement high of the tow'r,
Where a vane, like a lady, was staying,—
A lady vane perch'd in her bow'r,
To peep round the corner the sly wind would try
But vanes, you know, never look in the wind's eye

And so she kept turning shyly away
Thus they kept playing all through the day.

The summer wind said, 'She's coquetting;
But each belle has her points to be found
Before evening, I'll venture on betting,
She will not then *go*, but *come* round.'
So he tried from the east, and he tried from the west
And the north and the south, to try which was best;
But still she kept turning shyly away:—
Thus they kept playing all through the day.

At evening, her hard heart to soften,
He said, 'You're a flirt, I am sure
But if vainly you're changing so often,
No lover you'll ever secure.'
'Sweet sir,' said the vane, 'it is you who begin:
When *you* change so often, in *me* 'tis no sin.
If you cease to flutter, and steadily sigh,
And only be constant—I'm sure so will I.'

'She hath reversed the image,' thought De Lacy, sadly, as he turned over the poem—'a hard reverse for me! Oh, Adèle! thou wert better fitted to play the weathercock, than I the wind for I changed not, and thou hast turned. Thou hast, indeed, been *la girouette*!'

Still he pursued a revision of the papers, and anguish ever sprang most keenly from the word that had formerly given most pleasure:— as the same flower contains poison as well as honey.

He continued to lift letter by letter from the parcel, until one met his eye on whose back the fair recipient had been trying her pen; and it was manifest the experiment was made not in answer to one of his letters; for there stood, in hateful evidence, '*mon cher Hippolyte.*'

De Lacy sprang to his feet, stung to the heart by this proof of worthlessness; and as he clasped his brow with the energy of agony, exclaimed:

'And could no other place be found to write *his* name than on the letter *I* had written! False one!—false one! Cursed be this evidence of my credulity! Let it feed the flames!'

And he flung it fiercely on the fire, and continued one by one to throw others to the blaze, in rapid succession, while he pursued his painful train of thought.

'Who may believe a woman again? She whose love made her eloquent, in whom passion was the parent of poetry; she who seemed to think not after the fashion of ordinary mortals, but whose ideas appeared to flow from an exhaustless fountain of fancy over which purity held guardianship: she—she to prove false! who a thousand times said, she desired no happier fate than to share my lot, whatever it might be; who would follow me to the camp or the battle-field, the prison or the scaffold! Oh! Adèle!—Adèle!'

His hand was arrested in the work of destruction, by seeing the title of some verses he was about to consume.

The Land of the West.

He paused. 'Ay, I remember;—here is what my fond heart poured out when you said so.' And he bit his lip while he read:

THE LAND OF THE WEST.

Oh, come to the West, love,—oh, come there with me;
'Tis a sweet land of verdure that springs from the sea,
Where fair Plenty smiles from her emerald throne;—
Oh, come to the West, and I'll make thee my own!
I'll guard thee, I'll tend thee, I'll love thee the best,
And you'll say there's no land like the land of the West!

The South has its roses and bright skies of blue,
But ours are more sweet with love's own changeful hue,
Half sunshine, half tears, like the girl I love best;—
Oh, what is the South to the beautiful West!

Then come to the West, and the rose on thy mouth
Will be sweeter to me than the flow'rs of the South!

The north has its snow-tow'rs of dazzling array,
All sparkling with gems in the ne'er-setting day:
There the Storm-king may dwell in the halls he loves best
But the soft-breathing Zephyr he plays in the West.
Then come there with me, where no cold wind doth blow,
And thy neck will seem fairer to me than the snow!

The sun in the gorgeous East chaseth the night
When he riseth, refresh'd, in his glory and might!
But where doth he go when he seeks his sweet rest?
Oh! doth he not haste to the beautiful West!
Then come there with me; 'tis the land I love best,
'Tis the land of my sires!—'tis my own darling West!

The love of country expressed in the concluding lines went to De
Lacy's heart, and the sacred sentiment bore balm to the bosom of the
deserted lover.

'Yes,' he said, 'my country, all my love is now yours!—False one!
false one!' and he clutched all the papers that lay before him, and flung
them on the blazing wood upon his hearth. 'There—there perish those
records of my folly and my faith. Worthless woman! thy foot, that I
had hoped should have kept pace with mine until they both tottered
to the grave—thy foot shall never press the green shamrocks of my
native land—the land that shall soon, soon be free—my own sweet
Ireland, my own darling West!' And, with an enthusiasm pardonable
in his excited mood, he kissed the words as he read them; and folding
the paper, he placed it next his heart, and said, 'Ireland! now my love
is all thine own!'

XXXVI

The disappointed enthusiast cools down, and Rory falls into a strange religious error.

DE LACY QUITTED PARIS IN a few days, and hastened to the northern coast, where the army was concentrating in great force, as it was believed, to make a simultaneous invasion of England and Ireland as soon as winter was over.

The troops were often inspected by Napoleon Bonaparte, to whom the Directory were anxious to intrust some important command, to get him out of Paris, for they dreaded the presence of the general so near the seat of government, who, at that moment was the darling of the people, and little short of worshipped, after his wonderful conquest of Italy. They feared his towering temper and popularity might prove inconvenient; for Bonaparte, just then, openly complained of not being employed, and accused the Directory of being desirous of having him forgotten—for no man knew better than he how short-lived is popularity, and that any amount of fame becomes profitless which has not a periodical increase. And then it was, his secret scheme for the conquest of Egypt became engendered, and the gorgeous dream of founding an Eastern Empire opened on his daring and ambitious spirit. So, while he indulged the popular belief that an invasion to the North was in preparation, his views and hopes were all directed to the South. In the meantime, however, his visits to the Army of the North were continued, and the organisation of his forces was conducted on the shores of the British Channel, where he knew their presence would retain the English navy until the proper season arrived for marching them to the coast of the Mediterranean, where the absence of a hostile fleet was so important.

During the entire winter, De Lacy and Tone, and other Irish emissaries looked forward to the opening spring for the realisation of all their hopes and labours in a descent upon Ireland; but bitter was their disappointment and deep their despair when the order for the whole armament to march southward, arrived in the month of April. As yet it was unknown what was the destination of the Army of the North; but it was enough for the Irish refugees to know it was not for Ireland. De Lacy's heart sank, as well as those of others; but sorrow soon gave place to indignation when Tone informed him that he and other Irish delegates had had an interview with Bonaparte, and that every hope for Ireland was gone for the present.

'You saw him, then?' said De Lacy.

'Yes,' answered Tone.

'What did he say?'

'Not much.'

'The Corsican is short of speech,' said De Lacy.

'Yes,' answered Tone 'and I wish I could say, in the idiom o' our country, "short and sweet:" but it was far from that.'

'What was the objection?'

'Not one: there was no direct reason given against the undertaking, but a manifest disinclination to engage in it; and it seemed to me there was some hidden preference to some other enterprise which usurped dominion over his wishes—I may say, his reason, for he had not a shadow of argument to advance for abandoning the Irish project.'

'Did he say nothing?'

'I wish he had said nothing, rather than what he did say. If he had made a downright objection that one could have met and argued out with him, I would have been content—and, I hope, content even though I had been beaten in the argument. But no, not a word of argument, but—*what* do you think?' said Tone, becoming excited as he spoke.

'I can't conceive,' said De Lacy.

'Why, only fancy—only imagine, De Lacy, my indignation, when on my urging Ireland as an object of importance, he replied, "Ireland has done all for us we can expect or want: she has made a diversion in our favour."—By G—d! the very words—*a diversion, in our favour.* Fancy this!—*a diversion!* Oh, my poor country! that he who ought to fight the cause of freedom, and has power to do so, should give such an answer, and so treat a suffering people, and make a *diversion* of you!—Curse him!'

'It is too bad,' said De Lacy: 'but perhaps the Directory——'

'Are in the same cue,' said Tone: 'they handed me over to Bonaparte.'

'Was there no word of argument for the present delay?'

'Not one.'

'Nor of future hope?'

'Not a syllable: the laconic Corsican, after having made his *diversion* of poor Ireland, gave us our *congé.*'

'This is very hard after all the expectations raised.'

'Hard!—it is infamous!' said Tone. 'I cannot forgive him for it—and may just heaven that sees him turn unheedingly from the cry of a suffering nation, throw the crime into the balance against him, and may it weigh heavily! Yes! may he live to remember and curse the hour he refused to make Ireland his friend, and finds her his enemy!'

The words were uttered with the fervour of national indignation and the spirit of prophecy; for on the field of Waterloo, Ireland was his enemy, and her son his conqueror.

The conversation was continued between Tone and De Lacy in this spirit of bitterness and regret until Tone, having exhausted his fury and his lamentations, retired.

When alone, De Lacy went over all the circumstances of his various disappointments since his return to France, in a very disconsolate mood.—'Is there no truth, nor virtue, nor principle in the world?' said he to himself. 'Here are those in power on whose lips the word "freedom" is the very janitor: they open them but to breathe the blessed sound, and yet the word is desecrated by their use of it; they refuse aid to the most injured and suffering people on the

face of the earth. Shame! shame! they forget the cause of freedom
now, and substitute conquest in its place. I fear me, it is not of peace
and freedom they think, but war and dominion: they seek less to
cultivate the olive than the laurel.—Well—I suppose I am not the
only disappointed enthusiast.—And then the new extravagance of the
Directory. When they were in their most formidable position, they
had a small room with bare walls, a few chairs, one table, a writing-
desk, and as much pen, ink, and paper as served them. But now, they
have suites of apartments, splendid hangings, bureaus, fauteuils, etc.
and their banquets, concerts, balls, and assemblies are conducted on a
scale of lavish expenditure, resembling rather the monarchy which has
been overturned, than suited to the moderate measures of republican
resources. I fear me, there is more of talk than reality in the patriotism
and the freedom, the virtue and the fidelity, the sentiment and
sincerity, of this headlong people. And yet they have done glorious
things—deeds never to be forgotten! But I fear success intoxicates
those who rule in their command that the high and noble aspirations
which first achieved and maintained their liberty are about to be lost
in national vanity; and, mayhap, her victories, hitherto won in the fight
of freedom, may engender a thirst of glory, fatal to the cause whence
it sprang, and Liberty may yet perish under the very arms she made
victorious.'

With the same spirit in which he viewed public affairs, he looked
upon his private concerns. When he remembered all the vow and
sentimentality of the girl he loved so truly, and contrastd her falsehood
with his unpretending affection, he felt shame for her unblushing
frivolity and his own sanguine credulity. In every way had his hopes
been deceived; and with the sudden reaction to which enthusiastic
natures are prone, he began to distrust with as much haste as he had
believed, and disgust rapidly succeeded admiration.

'In great things, or in small, they are alike!' thought De Lacy: 'be
it the destiny of a nation or an *affaire du coeur*, 'tis all the same,—you
cannot depend upon them.'

So great did his repugnance become to joining the army when its
destination was not for Ireland, that he determined to relinquish the

profession of arms for the present, rather than march to the South, and preferred returning to Ireland, as best he might, to remaining in the country where all his hopes had been so grievously disappointed.

It was in this spirit a certain letter reached him, announcing the dangerous illness of his only surviving uncle, and requesting his immediate presence.

His relative resided at Bordeaux, and De Lacy lost no time in obeying the request conveyed in the letter, which was, at the particular moment, in accordance with his ulterior views, as Bordeaux was the most likely port whence he could find his way back to Ireland.

De Lacy was well provided with funds; for his uncle was a rich and also (as does not always happen) a sensible man, and knew that a captain of grenadiers. however well he might march, could not make his way from Normandy to Guienne without money, and the letter which demanded his presence also conveyed the means of speedy conveyance thither.

It would be foreign to the main interest of this story to dwell on the journey of De Lacy to Bordeaux, in the course of which the dozens of 'wonders' per day which Rory uttered at everything novel which struck him would amuse, it is true; but as it would retard the direct course of the narrative, it is better to post on to Bordeaux with as little delay as possible.

When De Lacy reached that celebrated environ which is to be for ever venerated as the birthplace of the cool and fragrant wine so well calculated for those who have plenty of money and leisure—for, decidedly, you must not hurry a man with his claret;—when he reached Bordeaux, I say, he hastened to the house of his uncle, with that universal eagerness which young soldiers generally exhibit to indulge the nepotism of elderly gentlemen who have something more than their blessing to leave behind them.

The disease of the uncle, though sure to terminate fatally, was of a character to baffle medical skill in predicting the length of its course, and the old man lingered on with a tenacity of life which surprised his physicians.

While he lay in this uncertain state, the news reached France of the outbreak of the rebellion in Ireland, and De Lacy's impatience to reach the scene of action became extreme; but his uncle's state of health, as well as the old man's advice and requests, forbade it.

He represented that a single arm could not strengthen the cause, and added his fears that without foreign aid the struggle could not terminate favourably to De Lacy's wishes—and in case of failure, how much more prudent to remain absent when the individual aid was so disproportioned to the individual risk.

'Oh, if every one thought of risk, where would all the boldest and noblest achievements of history be?' said De Lacy.

'Were you on the spot, my boy, I would not counsel you to be a dastard: but as chance has so ordered it that you are absent at the time, rush not into such terrible peril. Besides, you are my only living relation—you must not leave me to die alone, with stranger hands to close my eyes in a strange land.'

De Lacy returned the pressure of his uncle's hand, but still he burned to be in Ireland at the moment.

The eagerness was extreme with which he sought for intelligence thence, through every channel ingenuity could suggest or money procure.

Various and uncertain were the rumours received at that distance relating to the struggle, and his life was a state of fever while it remained undecided.

This lasted all through the summer; but in the autumn intelligence arrived of the total overthrow of the insurgents, and his impatience was then changed to despair.

Shortly after his uncle died, and De Lacy became the inheritor of his property. This was not large, for his uncle's income was derived principally from mercantile pursuits, and the realised wealth was not extensive—the principal portion of it consisting of a small property in Ireland, the proceeds of which reached France annually by an agency communicating through a neutral country.

This circumstance decided De Lacy in his course of conduct. He determined to return to Ireland, retire to his little property, form around him a circle of dependants whom he should render faithful and attached by kindness, and as the chance was past of bettering their *political* position, he would at least make their condition less wretched by affording them the protection and relief of which he had witnessed their want. If he could not prove a patriot on a grand scale, he would become a benefactor on a small.

'And, after all,' said De Lacy, 'I have been so disgusted with the show and not the substance of noble feelings here, that I begin to doubt the possible existence of the state of things I have contemplated—or perhaps I had better say, dreamed of: my hopes, like Astraea, must fly back to the heaven whence they came, when the worthlessness of earth has affrighted them; and as I cannot achieve the freedom I desire for my countrymen, I will return amongst them, and at least make their condition more endurable by spreading comfort and kindness as widely as I can round my own immediate centre. And now, when the supremacy of the dominant party is established, perhaps their security may engender a forbearance to their less fortunate fellow-subjects, which will render society not so intolerable as when I left them; and if men cannot enjoy equal rights, they will at least be permitted to live unmolested.'

It was with these moderate expectations De Lacy looked forward to a return to Ireland, which he intended to effect by the Swedish ship (early spoken of in our story) which traded between Dublin and Bordeaux: and having everything in readiness for his departure, he only awaited her putting to sea, to bid an eternal farewell to France.

On the morning of their sailing, Rory, before embarking, went to one of the churches to offer up his prayers for a safe voyage.

The church was prepared for one of those fêtes common at the time, when the conscripts were presented with their arms by their sweethearts, in presence of the assembled people, who chanted the *Marseillaise* all the time at the foot of the statue of Liberty but Rory, never having seen any such piece of business, did not know what the garlands and banners meant, when he entered the aisle early in the morning, long before the celebration of the fête was to take place, and when he was the only person present.

He looked about in wonder for some time, and seeing the statue of Liberty very magnificently decorated, he thought it could represent no other than the Virgin Mary; and so Rory popped down on his knees before the goddess of Liberty, and began to pray devoutly to the holy mother.

While in the act of devotion, a couple of soldiers strolled into the church, to see if all was in proper cue for the approaching military fête; and seeing Rory on his knees before the goddess of Liberty, they thought him some fond enthusiast of the revolution, and exclaimed with delight,

'Ah! que c'est drôle! Ma foi, c'est un brave garçon, qui aime tant la liberté qu'il se met à genoux à la déesse.'

They approached Rory as they spoke; but their admiration was somewhat dashed when they saw him bless himself very devoutly, making sundry crucial flourishes with his hand upon his breast and forehead as he bobbed and ducked before the statue.

The soldiers then advanced in front of Rory, and, looking upon him with great contempt, exclaimed, 'Sacré sot!' and turned from him with disgust.

Rory, having finished his prayers, returned to De Lacy, who immediately proceeded on board the vessel. On asking Rory if he dreaded encountering the sea again, Rory answered, 'Not in the laste, sir, for I seen the Virgin Mary this mornin'.'

'Saw who?' said De Lacy in wonder.

'The Virgin Mary, sir.'

De Lacy could not help laughing at the serious way in which the absurdity was uttered by Rory, who, not relishing his mirth, said:

'Sure, sir, is it laughing at me you'd be for sayin' my prayers?'

'Certainly not; but you tell me you saw the Virgin Mary.'

'And so I did, and said my prayers foreninst her in the big church; and why wouldn't I, and we goin' on the wide say?

De Lacy now laughed more heartily than before, while he told Rory that it was the goddess of Liberty he had been praying to instead of the Virgin.

'You don't tell me so?' said Rory, with horror in his looks.

'Indeed it is true.'

'Oh, God forgive me if it's a sin; but, sure, I thought it was the Queen iv Heaven herself, and I ax her pardon for mistakin' their dirty haythenish goddess for her; but, sure, I hope it's no harm, since it was done undher a mistake.'

'Don't be uneasy, Rory,' said De Lacy, who saw he had distressed him by his laughter; 'I hope the prayer that is offered to heaven in purity of heart, will find its way there, before whatever altar it is breathed.'

With such tolerant sentiment did De Lacy go on board, committing himself to the care of that Providence in whose unlimited mercies and Protection he reposed his faith.

XXXVII

A mysterious meeting.

AND NOW OUR STORY MUST return to Ireland. A period of a year had nearly elapsed since Rory had left its shores; but how fearful was the history those few months left behind!—too fearful to be touched on here—too tempting to the passion of the party, or too forcibly appealing to the gentler feelings of human nature, for mortal pen to be trusted with. It might be a 'recording angel' alone that could write of that period; and oh! how much must she weep over as she recorded, and well if it *could* be blotted out for ever. It was the awful year of 1798, whose acts seemed the work of fiends, and whose records are but of blood.

In the autumn of that year the insurgents were dispersed, with the exception of a few scattered parties of the most desperate, who still kept the fastnesses of the hills, or held out a miserable and hunted existence in the bogs. It was in the dusk of an evening, at this period, that Mary O'More had a message conveyed to her through an old beggar stating, 'that if she would go to a certain place, alone, she would meet a person to give her tidings she would be glad to hear.'

The woman endeavoured to excite Mary's curiosity still further; but, in such unsettled times, to go alone was a service of more danger than she had courage to look calmly upon; for, though a girl of bold and high spirit, she never recovered the shock which her rencontre in the glen of the Folly had produced.

'Could not the person come to her, whoever it was? if he or she wished her well, they would not object to do so.'

'Maybe they can't.'

'An outlaw it is, then?'

'Not that; but mustn't come into the village.'

'They shall suffer neither hurt nor harm, if they come to our place.'

'No; you must meet the person.'

'I'm afeard of some plot.'

'I tell you, child,' said the woman, 'and I swear to you by the blessed vestments, no harm is meant you.'

'Then tell me who it is.'

'I'm bound not.'

'I'm afeard,' said Mary, hesitating.

'Then you *won't* hear of it: maybe you'll be sorry.'

'I can't be sorry for what I don't know.'

'Maybe there's thim you'd like to hear of?'

'Is it poor Conolly?' said Mary, who, though she never loved, felt deep interest in the faithful friend who had assisted her and her mother, however he could, after Rory had disappeared, and who was amongst those who were outstanding with the rebels: not that he had committed any acts of brutal aggression, but some daring deeds he had achieved during the his correction had marked him for vengeance from the other party.

'There's thim you loved better thin you loved Conolly,' said the beggar-woman.

Mary blushed, and thought of De Lacy, and, ashamed of the thought was glad the twilight forbad the mendicant seeing the evidence on her cheek; for all unconsciously had the poor girl dwelt on the remembrance of him (a remembrance rendered doubly dear, by its being associated with recollections of her brother), and had read over and over again his books that he had give her, and recorded in her memory his courtesy and gentle bearing, until, under these influences of heart and mind, an effect was wrought upon her of which she herself knew not half the strength.

'Suppose you could hear something of him?'

'Who?' said Mary.

'Suppose your brother—'

'What!' exclaimed Mary, clasping her hands in wonder.

'Suppose Rory was—'

'Gracious God! Is he alive?' cried the agitated girl, laying hold of the speaker.

'You may hear something about him you'd be glad of: will you go *now?*'

'Anywhere,' said Mary, with courage which the hope of such news inspired; 'but if you deceive me—'

'I'm not deceivin' you.'

'You're a woman, and should not betray one of your own sex.'

'I tell you, Mary O'More, you're safe if you follow me.'

'Then lead on where you like,' said Mary; 'and I'll follow.'

The beggar-woman walked rapidly away from the village; but, instead of going down the street, she struck into a path which lay behind the Widow O'More's cabin, and led to some solitary upland beyond it.

It is necessary here to explain that the Widow O'More and her daughter were not now living in the snug cabin where first the reader knew them. That had been burned during the rebellion, and then its inmates removed to the village. Kathleen Regan, too, and her mother, were driven from their home about the same time, for Shan Regan had been long a defaulter in the payment of his rent; and when the affair in the glen of the Folly obliged him to fly, in consequence of the magisterial search after him, matters got more involved; for his poor mother knew not what to do, and was nearly heart-broken at her son's misconduct; and when the rebellion broke out, and Regan was known to be amongst the most lawless of the insurgents (for in their ranks he found most personal safety), the landlord visited the crimes of the child on the parent, instead of the sins of the fathers being visited on the children, as the Decalogue declares. But this was not the only instance in those terrible times of men's actions being at variance with Holy Writ.

Under such circumstances, when these two suffering families found themselves deprived of their natural homes, and the men who were their natural protectors, they agreed to reside together; and, as the open country was dangerous, they went into the village, and lived, if not in safety, at least in companionship.

On reaching the upland, the mendicant stopped near the edge of a narrow road which led over the hill, and, from its great age and long wear, formed a sort of covered way: here she stopped, and gave a loud cough by way of signal; it was immediately answered and a man emerged through the hedge that fringed the embankment of the road, and approached the spot where Mary stood with her guide. On his getting nearer, she perceived it was the old tinker who approached, and recoiled at the recognition, but her guide assured her she had nothing to fear.

The tinker approached Mary with the greeting that denotes good faith, and expressed his gladness she had come, as he had much to say of consequence to her; he then asked her to remove from her guide a sufficient distance to be out of hearing.

'Can't you say what you have to say before her? I don't like her to leave me.'

'Come away a few steps, my poor *colleen*,' said Solomon, with more gentleness in his voice than Mary had ever heard before. 'Don't be afeard, there's no harm comin' to you.'

'You won't go far from us,' said Mary to the beggar-woman, for even in her whom she had never seen before she felt more of fellowship and protection than in the old tinker, whom she alway disliked; and, since the day she last had seen him at the glen of the Folly, his image was associated with all that was revolting to her feelings.

'We are far enough away now,' said Mary to Solomon; 'I won't go another step, and whatever you have to tell me, tell me at wanst.'

'Well, thin,' said Solomon, 'I brought you here to tell you Rory's alive.'

'Oh, holy Mother!' exclaimed Mary, dropping on her knees, bursting into a flood of tears.

'There, there! now don't be foolish, *colleen*; he's alive, and—'

'Where? tell me where, for the love o' God!'

'Aisy, aisy. Wait and I'll tell you. Now, first and foremost you must know, that it was Shan Dhu was at the beginnin' and end of it all, and I've nothin' to do wid it but havin' had the bad luck to know iv it; and for that same I've been hunted up and down the country ever since, and would have towld you afore, only I darn't show my face. But you see it was lyin' heavy an my conscience all the time; and now I run the risk o' bein' taken up, and hanged maybe, all for the sake o' setting your mind at aise and takin' the weight av my heart.'

'But where is Rory?'

'Indeed, he's in France, I b'lieve,—at laste he was carried off along with the Collecthor; but he wasn't murthered, as you thought.'

'Solomon!' said Mary impressively; 'by your hopes of mercy on your dyin' day!—*and you're not far off the grave, owld man*———'

'Whisht, whisht!' interposed Solomon; 'don't be sayin' that.'

'Oh, sure we're all nigh death every minit, if it's God's will;—but I charge you not to put false hope into a sisther's heart.'

'It's thruth,' said Solomon; 'and more than that I've to tell you. Shan Regan is in the hills hidin', and a few blackguards like himself along wid him; and I hear he intinds makin' an offer for takin' *you* off.'

'May the Lord pity me!' said Mary.

'But don't be afeard,' added the tinker; 'if you'll only do my biddin'. You saved my life beyant in the glen, and I don't forget it to you, *colleen agra*; and so I kem to tell you the thruth about Rory, and make your heart aisy and if you'll only go along wid me to the magisthrit, I'll swear it all agin Regan; and moreover I know where he's hidin', him and his morodin' vagabones, and I'll lade the sojers on thim sly, and have thim all taken and hanged like crows, for indeed the gallows is greedy for thim.'

'Let us go now,' said Mary; 'Misther Dixon's is not over a couple o' miles.'

'Too late to-night, *colleen,* with the martial-law out; we had betther both keep unknownst for to-night; but to-morrow mornin' I'll be wid you, and go to the magisthrit's. So now away wid you home, and plaze God you'll see Rory yet; and yourself will be the safer from harm the sooner Shan Dhu is taken care of. Good-night to you, *colleen!*—Remimber to-morrow mornin' I'll be wid you.' And the old tinker vanished through the hedge while Mary O'More rejoined the mendicant, who had remained near the spot, and in her company returned to the village.

Let it not be supposed it was any compunctious visiting of the old tinker's conscience urged him to the disclosure he made to Mary O'More, or that it was any feeling of tenderness towards the girl, or compassion for her sufferings, which operated upon him. In this, as in all the other actions of his life, Solomon sought his own advantage.

To explain this, it becomes necessary to revert to the period when Solomon fled with his money-bag from the glen of the Folly and left Mary O'More to the tender mercies of Shan Dhu.

Having escaped the observation of the hnntsmen, and got clear of Regan, he concealed his treasure in a new hiding-place, of which none were cognisant but himself and the stars. This being effected, his next object was to keep out of Shan Dhu's way; but, in a day or two, he found another and more extensive cause for concealment in the search the officers of justice were making through the country, after Mary O'More's depositions respecting the scene she had witnessed in the glen.

Solomon continued to effect concealment with success, until the rebellion broke out, and, while that raged, the authorities were engaged in wholesale business, and did not attend to such paltry details as delinquent tinkers; but, when the insurrection was quelled, Solomon had his two sources of apprehension opened upon him afresh; for government was in a very hanging humour for less than what Solomon was suspected of; and he had got a whisper that Regan, who still held out in the hills, had said, 'he wished he could come across the tinker;' and Solomon best knew why.

'If he could lay his hands on me,' said Solomon to himself, 'he'd thry and get the goold out o' me; and if I didn't tell him where it is—*and I wouldn't*—he'd murther me with the rage; and suppose I did—maybe he'd murther me too; but, anyhow, I think it's not good for my health that Regan's alive; and why wouldn't I sthrive to save my own life? so, wid the blessin' o' God, Shan Dhu, my boy, I'll have you in the stone jug¹ as soon as I can, and dancin' on nothin' afther.'

It was with this view he sought Mary O'More, and aroused her fears respecting Regan's intention of carrying her off, and her hopes regarding her brother. He induced her to go with him to the magistrate, and depended on her friendly presence as a protection to him on this occasion; and as he should not only reveal the circumstances of the kidnapping of the Collector, whose disappearance he should represent himself as being au unwilling witness of, but also volunteer to lead the military to the retreat of a party of desperate rebels who still committed many robberies, he trusted thus to procure his own pardon and protection, and at the same time secure the death of the man he dreaded most—Shan Regan. Such was the web the old spider wove.

1.   The jail.

XXXVIII

Containing Solomon's examination and its results.

IT WAS QUITE TRUE, THE intelligence the old tinker had heard respecting Regan's intention towards him. From the day he had escaped out of the glen of the Folly with his money, Regan had in vain endeavoured to find out his places of retreat; but, Shan himself being a refugee at the time, his means of acquiring information on the subject, and putting his wishes into effect, were so circumscribed, that Solomon had escaped all harm from his designs.

Could he have laid hold of the tinker during the period of his hiding himself after the abduction of the Collector, it was his intention to have endeavoured by force to wring some of the hidden gold from old Solomon, and by its means to procure his flight from the country; but the period of the rebellion gave him other hopes, and, trusting to the success of the insurrection for his ultimate safety and plenty of plunder, the tinker was free from his evil intentions; but when total defeat had driven the last desperate remnant of the rebels into the fastnesses of the mountains and their bogs, his thoughts again reverted to Solomon and his hidden treasure; and the same desire of possessing it returned, in the hope of its enabling him to get a passage to America, and he used every means within his power to discover where Solomon might be seized, while the tinker, at the same time, was meditating how to compass the death of Regan.

Thus were they worthily engaged in plotting each other's destruction; one of the thousand examples that, while the friendships of the good strengthen with age, the attachments of the profligate and base have the elements of ruin in their very foundation!

The tinker was true to his appointment with Mary for the following morning; and they proceeded in company to the house of Mr. Dixon, where Solomon made his depositions before that magistrate to the effect stated in the foregoing chapter.

Solomon's disclosure being so long withheld, threw much suspicion on his testimony; the more so as he himself was an accused person by Mary O'More's previous deposition made some months before; yet, even if he were guilty, Mr. Dixon was glad to take him as king's evidence, for the discovery and punishment of others.

On his being questioned why he did not make the disclosure sooner, he said he dreaded the vengeance of those who had accomplished the act, in case he should divulge it.

'Yet,' said Mr. Dixon, 'you let an innocent man suffer under the imputation of having committed a murder for some time. You knew this poor girl's brother was accused of having murdered Mr. Scrubbs.'

'Yis, sir; but sure, when the *colleen* afther that, swore agin me, that I had a hand in makin' away wid Rory O'More, and I was obleeged to hide for my life, sure I was afeard even *thin* to come and clear myself; and it's only now, when yiz have got the fellows undher that was disturbin' the country, that I ventured to come, for my life wouldn't be safe to do it afore.'

'I think it very extraordinary an innocent person should hesitate to give himself up.'

'Sure, I am givin' myself up, now.'

'Yes, after a year; but, if you were free from guilt, you would have done it sooner. Now take care you swear the truth; because, even if you are guilty, you shall have pardon for turning king's evidence and bringing the other guilty parties to justice. So do not, through any fear for your own life, give false evidence.'

'I'll swear the thruth, sir, and nothing else.'

'Do you swear then, positively, the Collector was not murdered ?'

'I do.'

'And that he has been only taken over sea?'

'Yis, sir.'

'And that no other violence was done him?'

'Yis, sir.'

'Then how came you and Regan by the money this girl saw you dig up in the glen?'

'Oh! that was a thrifle I saved, sir, and put there; and Shan Dhu wanted to take it av me.'

'Saved!—you save!—was it much?'

'Oh! how could a poor old craythur like me save much? it was only a few shillin's.'

'And yet this girl says he was going to murder you for that money. Now, would a man murder for a few shillings?'

'There was no more, upon my oath.'

'Are you quite sure?'

'In throth I am.'

'Where is that money at present?'

'Och now! thin and sure Shan Dhu run afther me that same day, and cotch me in the wood, and tuk it all away from me.'

'Will you swear positively that you did not rob the Collector?'

'I will.'

'Nor see him robbed?'

'He was not robbed, I'll give my oath.'

'And Rory O'More, you say, also is gone with him?'

'He is.'

'Was Rory O'More of your party?'

'Oh!' cried Mary; 'no, no, your honour.'

'Silence, girl,' said the magistrate; 'it is not you who are under examination. What do you answer?' added he to Solomon.

'He was not, sir.'

'How came he there, then?'

Solomon described the circumstances of Rory's unfortunate adventure at the Folly, with the liberation of De Welskein and his party; and for once in his life did justice to O'More in relating his gallant defence of the Collector, and his own fate in consequence. As to the tinker's presence there, he told a long rigmarole so involved in parenthesis and digression, that the magistrate could make nothing of it, which was exactly what Solomon wanted; and he concluded by declaring it was 'all along o' that vagabone Regan that inthrapped him into it, by way of goin' to a party.'

Though Mr. Dixon had every suspicion of Solomon as far as the story concerned himself, yet there was an appearance of truth about the tale as it bore on Rory's adventure almost inducing him to give it credence; but his mind, strongly preoccupied with the generally-received false impressions on the subject, now found the truth difficult of belief, and mystery had hung so long over the affair, and made it doubtful whether Rory was a murderer or a murdered man, that this sudden resurrection of him and clearance of his character from stain required more respectable evidence than the tinker's to obtain credit.

'And you say this Shan Regan is the guilty person?'

'Yis, sir; and is in the hills at this present with some vagabones like himself; and I'll swear it all agin him, and show the sojers the way to the place where he is, and he may be nabbed as aisy as kiss hand'.'

'Very well; but you must remain in custody until you prove what you've sworn to.'

'To be sure, your honour's worship; for now I have no business to be seen out afther tellin' all this,—and I'd rather be in the jail for the safety.'

'You shall be taken every care of after you return with the military party from the hills.'

'God bless your worship's honour! sure they'd murdher me if I was cotch; but suppose they did itself, my conscience is aisier than it was for many a day, afther swarin' the thruth agin that black villain Regan.'

No time was lost by Mr. Dixon in summoning a military party from a regiment in the neighbourhood, to make a capture of the rebels. This detachment was commanded by late Ensign, now Captain Daw, for his regiment had been very much cut up during the rebellion; and Death happening to make his choice from among the sensible men of the corps, Daw got promotion. In addition to the soldiers, some of the yeomanry cavalry, under the command of the bold Captain Slink, (De Lacy's acquaintance,) put themselves under arms to assist in cutting off the retreat, if necessary, of any fugitive rebels; and the combined forces marched for the mountain pass, under the distinguished guidance of Sawdherin' Solomon.

XXXIX

The attack; showing how different is the conduct of soldiers and yeomanry, in the battle and after it.

IT WAS ONE OF THE wildest passes of the hills the insurgents selected for their stronghold. It chanced, on the day the military party marched against them, that these fellows had made a larger muster than usual to hold a council on their affairs; for, being hemmed in more than ordinary, they wanted to break away from their present cover, and take up a position in another range of mountains some miles distant. They usually kept together in parties of three or four, the more easily to effect concealment, and had their points of occasional meeting understood among themselves but, in the movement they projected, it was necessary to make a combined effort, and for such a purpose they had met in this pass, which Solomon found out to be the spot Regan had made his place of refuge.

Living the hunted life they did, the outlaws exercised the greatest watchfulness; and on this day, while the majority of the men held their council under the screen of some bold rocks, imbedded in heather, there were scouts posted at such points as commanded a view of the circumjacent hills and the country below, to give the alarm in case of the approach of enemies. They had not been more than half an hour in conclave, when one of the scouts ran in and told them he suspected the approach of the military. Every man was on his legs in an instant, and looking to the priming of his piece; for they were all well armed, and tolerably provided with ammunition, which their friends in the lowlands contrived to procure and leave for them in secret appointed places; in this way also were they provisioned.

Jack Flannerty, one of the heroes of the Folly, as the reader may remember, and Regan, were principal among the outlaws; so they went forth to reconnoitre in the quarter whence the scout announced the hostile approach, and, after some ten minutes' observation, were enabled to discover the nature of their foes, and make a tolerable guess at their number. They then left their sentinel still on the watch, and returned to the main body of the men to communicate the news and arrange a plan of defence.

'Are they yeos[1] or reg'lars?' asked one of the rebels.

''Faith, they're reg'lars, sure enough; but not over twenty, or thereaway.'

'That's as much as we are ourselves.'

'Well,' said Flannerty; 'and who cares? Sure we have the advantage o' the ground, and the knowledge iv it—and that's more than a match for them. Never mind; if we don't lick them, we'll sarve them the same sauce we sarved the Anshint Britons—devil a man o' thim will go home!'

'But Regan says there is cavalthry as well.'

'And what if there is?' said Flannerty; 'supposin' it was *rale* cavalthry, what good are they up here?—but it's not; it's only the yeomanthry, that you might bate if you had nothin' but sticks.'

Silence now ensued for a few minutes, while the men watched the approach of the soldiers as they wound through a little road at the foot of the hills. On their arriving at a certain point, and quitting the road for a path, Regan exclaimed:

'See that! By the 'tarnal, they're comin' up the right way into the pass! Some one must wid 'im that knows.'

'What will we do now?' said Flannerty; 'we can't have a slap at thim over the bank in the deep road below.'

'Thin we must go higher up the pass, Jack, where the cavalthry can't come at us, and murdher the sojers the best way we can.'

'The yeos is sticking to them still.'

'Well, they can't come beyant the grey stones; at laste they *won't*, you may be sure, for they are mighty proud of a whole skin; they'll come as far as they have a road behind them to run back, but divil a taste farther.'

In a few minutes more the horsemen halted, and a seeming consultation ensued between the officers; after which, the infantry advanced up the heights, which became more steep and broken every hundred yards.

'Didn't I tell you the yeos would lave the business to the sojers? Now, boys, do *you* all fall back higher up there in the pass; and, though you lie hid, keep a good open, all o' yiz, for the muzzle of the gun, and a sharp eye on the sojers; and let the man that is farthest up the pass, level at the foremost sojer, and the man that is nighest to them at the hindmost, and so you won't throw away your fire, by two shooting at one man; and *we'll* hide here; just six iv uz: and when they have passed about forty yards, or thereaway, we'll slap at thim in the rear, and that'll make thim turn and the minit you see thim turn, put the fire into thim immediately at th' other side, and you'll see how they'll stagger! Away wid you boys!'

The plan was instantly put in practice: the principal part of the outlaws were perched on each side of an abrupt and very narrow rocky gorge, defying any regular assault of troops, and admirably suited to the purposes of the marksman, besides affording that perfect concealment suited to a surprise; while Regan and Jack Flannerty, with four of the most desperate of their companions, crouched amongst the rocks and heather at the entrance of the pass. Jack Flannerty had his eye fixed on the advancing party with the eager keenness of a hound, and said quickly to Regan, who lay beside him:

'Look for a minit; do you see nothing among the sojers remarkable?'

Regan was not so sharp-sighted as his companion, and answered: 'No.'

'There's a man in the middle o' thim that's not a sojer,' said Flannerty; 'whist!—by the 'tarnal, it's that owld villain Sawdherin' Solomon!'

'Solomon!' said Regan, looking out eagerly; 'so it is—the gallows owld thraitor!'

'I'll shoot him through the grey plottin' head, the villain,' said Flannerty, 'when I fire.'

'No,' said Regan, who thought at the moment of the secret of the tinker's treasure dying with him; 'don't shoot him—we'll ketch him and give him a death fitter for a thraitor like him; don't shoot him, Jack.'

'I won't, thin,' said Flannerty. 'Whisht! lie close, boys; they're comin'.'

The party of soldiers drew near the pass, with Solomon in the centre, who urged Captain Daw not to march his men in a body, but to 'scatther them,' as he said; 'for you don't know how 'cute these chaps is at a *namplush*.'

But the captain thought it would be a very pretty story indeed, if it ever could be said he took instructions from a tinker; so on he went, without even the precaution of a couple of men in advance or in the rear.

The lieutenant ventured to remark to the captain, that the gorge they were going to enter was an ugly-looking place, and asked, should he send a couple of men forward.

'I can command it, sir, if I think it necessary,' said the bold captain.

The words were scarcely out of his mouth, when the discharge of the half-dozen fowling-pieces in their rear knocked over as many soldiers; the men instinctively turned to fire in the direction whence the shots came, but, before they pulled a trigger, the ambushed party in the gorge put in so murderous a volley, that the soldiers were quite staggered, and returned it almost at random.

Daw became bewildered, and the lieutenant suggested falling back, as they were manifestly entrapped into an ambuscade. The captain gave his assent, and the men very willingly went to the right-about; but here they were met by Flaunerty and his desperadoes, who arose from their places of concealment with a wild shout, which was answered by the party in the gorge; Solomon clung closely to the captain when he saw Regan amongst the assailants, and the military party began to retire as fast as they might in tolerable order.

Regan, seeing Solomon so nearly within his grasp, jumped from an overhanging rock, and, rushing upon him, caught hold of part of his dress, and was dragging him back from the captain, of whom Solomon kept an iron grip.

The captain fancied this was an attempt to rescue from his hands the old rascal who had led him into an ambuscade, and, though still in bewilderment from the suddenness of the surprise his party had sustained, his courage would not brook such an insolent attempt at defiance; and, turning boldly on Regan, he ran him through the body with his sword.

Regan fell with a sharp gasping cry, and the soldiers came to a rally in tolerable order when they saw their captain turn and defend himself.

Regan, after a writhing plunge upon the ground, raised himself on his elbow while he drew a pistol from his breast; and, levelling it at Solomon, gasped out, 'H——l to your sowl!' as he fired it; but his aim was untrue, and the ball intended for the old villain entered the head of poor Daw, who measured his length on the heather. Regan grinned like a demon upon the tinker, who stood riveted to the spot in terror; and Shan Dhu, gurgling up the words 'Blast you!' fell back to speak no more.

The outlaws in the meantime had reloaded their pieces, and put in a second volley which committed dreadful havoc. This destructive fire occurring at the moment after their captain fell, the soldiers became panic-struck, and made a hurried retreat.

'Come along, you old scoundrel!' said the lieutenant, laying hold of Solomon by the collar, and dragging him down the hill as he hurried after his men.

The rebels pursued the fugitives for some minutes; but seeing them fall back upon the support of the yeomanry, who were numerous, they returned to their mountain fastness, unwilling to hazard the loss of the success they had already achieved, and which to them, at this moment, was of much importance; for it would enable them, under the alarm which the repulse of the military would produce, to retire unmolested from their present hold to the stronger chain of adjacent mountains.

When the soldiers rallied upon the support of the yeomanry, the lieutenant addressed Captain Slink, and requested his aid in returning to the pass: but this was a matter the yeomanry captain thought worth thinking of twice; as the rush of the men down the hill, their

RORY O'MORE: A NATIONAL ROMANCE

diminished number, their wounds, and the blood of the lieutenant himself, tingeing deeply a handkerchief he bound round his arm as he made his request, appealed strongly to a certain tender Scriptural recollection the captain had about 'his days being long in the land;' for though he had no father nor mother to 'honour,' inasmuch as the former was a small lord of great patronage who quartered his unacknowledged relations on the public purse, and his mother, therefore, *could* not be honoured, yet as the land had something worth remaining in, for him, he thought it would be, in more ways than one, a tempting of Providence to put his life in jeopardy: besides, as the captain had a very exalted idea of the comfort of a whole skin, he considered the proposal of the lieutenant one of those wild and ill-tempered suggestions a beaten man will sometimes make at the moment he is smarting under defeat.

'My dear sir, don't be rash,' said the captain; 'you seem to have had a very warm reception already.'

'Yes, d——n them!' said the lieutenant bitterly; 'but you see they have retired upon seeing your support of us; and if you will return with me and my remaining men, we shall chastise these rebel rascals yet.'

'I really cannot, sir, in conscience, considering the command entrusted to me, risk the lives of so many gentlemen.'

Here one of the corps put in a word

'I'm sure, Captain Slink, if you think it right, we are all very ready.'

'By no means, gentlemen; your courage is too well known to require any proof on this occasion; and I'm sure it would only be making a sort of unhandsome reflection on the conduct of the gallant men who have suffered to-day, if we were to admit even the supposition, that we could succeed where they have failed.'

'Sir,' said the lieutenant, 'our failure was attributable solely to a successful ambuscade prepared for us.'

'An ambuscade!' exclaimed the captain in triumph; 'my dear sir, say no more; that's quite enough: there was one piece of advice which my friend, Captain Skurry, of the Skurry Horse, used to say to me,—"My dear Slink, never go near an ambuscade.—When you see your enemy in an ambuscade, let him alone."'

The lieutenant looked at the captain with mingled feelings of contempt and wonder at his cowardice and ignorance, and only added,

'Well, sir; I sha'n't ask you to pursue the rebels; but at least support me and my men in recovering the body of our captain, who has fallen in the affair.'

'Indeed, upon my word and honour I won't; that's the very place *them* rascally rebels would be waiting for you: don't think I'll help you to run any more risks to-day.'

'Sir, I don't like leaving the body of our late commanding officer on the ground.'

'My dear sir, what harm can he come to, and he dead? if he was alive, indeed.'

'He may be, sir, although he has fallen,' said the lieutenant.

'Not he, indeed: they always pike every body, *them* vagabone rebels, the minit they fall; I know them better than you, sir.'

'Even as a point of honour, sir, I do not like leaving the body of a king's officer in the hands of such miscreants, and I request your support.'

'Oh, if you talk about honour, that's another affair; and upon my honour, if it was a point of honour, I would be as ready as any man to do my *outhermost* in the business; and if we were fighting with regular troops, the real thing, you know,—the Simon Pure,—I'd do all that could be done; but you see, my dear sir, these dirty blackguards is not to be treated like gentlemen, and I would not indulge them by letting them see they gave me any concern.'

The lieutenant, perceiving it was useless to urge his suit any further in this quarter, turned to his men, and said, 'You won't leave your captain behind you, boys?'

The men returned a fierce 'No:' it was not a cheer,—their recent defeat had taken that out of them; but given, as it was, with something between a growl and a bark, there was the tone of determination in it which assured their officer in leading them once more up the pass.

'I leave this old scoundrel in your care,' said he to the yeomanry captain; 'you can take care of him at least:' and, with this contemptuous farewell to the cavalry, he gave the word 'Forward!'

There was no opposition to the soldiers in their backward march, which was conducted with more caution than under the command of the foolish officer whose rashness had caused their defeat, and whose life had paid the forfeit of his indiscretion: he still lay where he had fallen, and *had not been piked*, as the heroic yeomanry captain had prophesied. Nor was there any savage *post mortem* disfigurement on any of the fallen soldiers. 'We cannot remove all our dead comrades at present,' said the lieutenant, 'but let us bear home our captain;' and the remains of their former commander were carried back by the brave fellows, who would not desert him even in death, to where the horsemen still awaited them; and, on rejoining the troop, the lieutenant showed no inclination to hold any further converse with such a pack of poltroons.

But the captain was not to be put off so: he congratulated him on recovering the body of Captain Daw, as they marched homeward; and, in answer to the lieutenant's remark that the rebels had not piked a fallen enemy, he replied it must have been in consequence of their having seen his corps of yeomanry so near, which forced them to a precipitate retreat. 'For I assure you, sir, they dread us exceedingly: we flog and hang the rascals every day we catch them; and I will say, without fear of contradiction, that our corps has done more in the pitch-cap and tar and feathering line than any other in Ireland.'

'Very likely, sir,' said the lieutenant coldly.

'But in this instance,—the affair of to-day, I mean,—you know I would not have been justified in any rash or hasty movement: life, sir,—life is a precious thing,—life is a thing not to be trifled with; particularly by one of his majesty's justices of the peace, who has such matters in charge.'

'As far as *you* are concerned, sir,' said the lieutenant, 'I am sure it will be taken every care of.'

'Certainly, sir: I respect the laws, and life and property; and why shouldn't I? By the by, if you come over to my place any day, nothing would give me greater pleasure: there is always something ready, and soldiers are not particular; pot-luck is always open to you at Slinkstown, and you shall have a skinful of claret at all events.'

All these proffered civilities of the hero, who wanted to court the soldier's favour, were but coldly received by the lieutenant, whose contempt for his cowardice was too great to be so easily overcome; and the captain had the conversation very much to himself as they made their way to the lowlands. There, meeting a peasant driving his horse and car laden with unthrashed corn, the warlike justice of the peace stopped him, and declaring the fatigue of carrying home the captain's body too much for the soldiers, ordered the peasant to back and unload his car, and bear the body to the town, which was the contrary direction to that in which he was going.

'What am I to do with the corn, your honour?' said the peasant timidly.

'Back it down on the road-side there,' was the answer.

The poor peasant scarcely ventured to *look* as if he thought it hard to throw down his corn in the open road, much less dare to *speak* an objection to the order; and unloosing the cords which bound the produce of his toil to his car that was bearing it to market; he was obliged to scatter his little harvest on the highway, and waste that which God had given to the living for the service of the dead.

The lieutenant had remonstrated against this measure, but the *justice* was inexorable. The body of the captain was laid on the car, a sheaf of corn being strown beneath him;—strange association of the sword and the ploughshare!

The car having been thus appropriated, the party moved onward; and the lieutenant's moodiness having increased, the justice addressed him in a cheering tone:

'Come, sir, don't be down-hearted: 'tis a sad sight, to be sure, to see your comrade going home stiff; but at the same time, lieutenant, remember promotion is the life and soul of the army, and this will be a step for you.'

Such a remark, with the dead body of his fallen comrade before him, was so disgusting, that the soldier made no reply, rather than the one which his feelings would have prompted: so the justice proceeded:

'Very natural: of course you'd be sorry for a brother officer, you'll miss him at mess to-day. By the by, the last time I saw him at dinner was at Slinkstown; he had his legs under my mahogany last week, poor fellow! it's oak they'll be under next.'

With a running fire of such sentimental conversation did the noble captain persecute the lieutenant on their march; and, when his sentiment became exhausted, he took a turn on military affairs.

'By the by, in the midst of our engagement, I forgot to ask you exactly how this d—d affair took place to-day. Strange mistake of poor Daw to let himself be trapped: an ambuscade, you say?'

'Yes.'

'Ah, no good military man ever gets into an ambuscade: as my friend Captain Skurry used to say, "The moment you see your enemy in ambush, having nothing to do with him." Poor Daw!— very rash.'

'He certainly was not a coward,' said the lieutenant, in a tone that might have touched a nicer sense of hearing than Captain Slink's; 'and as for his imprudence in this affair, the blame is very much lessened, when we remember he was led into the snare by the very person on whom he relied for guidance.'

'How do you mean?'

'I mean that old scoundrel, in advance there among my men, let us into the trap.'

'You don't mean to say the tinkering vagabon' played false?'

'I do, though.'

'My dear sir, why didn't you tell me this before?' Then, raising his tone to the pitch of military command, he cried 'Halt!' The party obeyed. 'Why didn't you tell me this sooner? and I would have hanged the old villain on the spot: however, we can do it now.—I say, you old scoundrel!' cried he to Solomon 'come here, you d—d rebel! you treacherous tinkering traitor!'

Solomon looked round in much alarm at the tone of this address: and when he saw the menacing actions which accompanied the words, his heart sank within him.

'Get that rope ready,' said the justice, pointing to the one which hac secured the load of corn to the car.

'You don't mean to hang the man now?' said the lieutenant.

'Don't I?' said Captain Slink; 'he's not the first I've hanged at short notice, nor won't be the last, please God!—that's the way to quiet the country.'

'I think it will be better to march him into the town, and give l a court-martial before he is hanged : lie deserves hanging certainly, and I have no doubt will be hanged, but it will be more regular to try him first.'

'Pooh!' said the justice, 'try him indeed! we'll try if he's proof against hemp,—*that's* the way to try rebels.'

All this time Solomon stood trembling and unable to speak; but when two of the yeomanry corps advanced to lay hands on him, he made a gasping cry for mercy, and, having once gained the power of speech, addressed the lieutenant, and appealed to hin for protection. 'Sure, what would you hang me for? didn't I brngi you to the place?'

'The less you say the better,' said the lieutenant: 'you brought us into an ambuscade, and you must answer for it; but you shall have a court-martial.'

'I'll hang him on the spot,' said the captain.

'I request you will not be precipitate, sir,' said the lieutenant.

'Oh Lord! oh Lord!' screamed Solomon; 'and sure, didn't you see that they cotch me, and wanted to murder me for bringin' you on thim?'

'They caught you, certainly,' said the lieutenant, 'to get you out of my hands when you had betrayed us; and it was in preventing your rescue our captain fell, So, say no more about your innocence: but you shall not die here; you shall have a fair trial before a court-martial.'

'I say, he shall die on this spot!' said the justice.

'I would beg to represent to you, sir, that this man is a prisoner of my party; and as you have had no share in the loss, I think you are premature in the punishment. Let the man be tried: I have no doubt he will be condemned to death; but let him have at least a trial.'

'You say yourself he deserves hanging,—and, by the living G—d! I'll hang him up like a dog.'

'Suppose, sir, I don't choose to give him up to you?'

'I tell you what it is, sir!' said Slink, whose savagery increased whenever he could sniff blood with impunity—'you seem to have been taking airs on yourself all day, and forget I am a magistrate, and that it is, in fact, under my authority you are acting at this minute; and I warn you, sir, on pain of my complaint against you to your commanding officer, not to interfere with me in this affair.'

All this time Solomon, whose face was the colour of death, was trembling between the two yeomen, and faintly mumbling, 'Oh, God!—Lord be merciful to me!' and other such ejaculations; and by one of those strange and lightning touches of thought which bring before us the scene we least expect, he reverted to his meeting with Mary O'More the night before, when she adjured him by his grey hairs not to deceive her, and said, '*Old man, you're not far off the grave!*' The remembrance came upon him like the sound of a passing bell, and from that instant he gave himself up for lost, and only begged for the love of God they would not hang him without letting him see a priest.

'Oh, let me have a priest!' cried the trembling old sinner.

'I wish we had one here,' said Slink, 'and I'd hang him beside you with pleasure.'

The lieutenant, as the last argument, represented there was no place whereon to hang the old man, as the justice *would* have it so; but to this Captain Slink replied:

'That's all you know about it ! Now I'll give you a lesson in hanging may be useful to you yet, if you're in a hurry, as I am now, to get rid of a rebel.'

'I'm no rebel! The God that hears me knows I never was a rebel!' faltered the old tinker—and it was one of the few truths he had ever uttered.

'Unyoke that car,' said Justice Slink: 'take the captain's body off, and lay it beside the ditch, till we finish this business. Do your duty, Scroggins,' said he to the trumpeter of his troop, who was a ruffianly dependent of his; and, nothing loth, the gentle Soroggins whipped the noose of the car-rope round the withered neck of old Solomon, who screamed as he felt his head within the loop.

'Turn up the car,' said the justice.

The vehicle was thrown back on its end, and the shafts thus became sufficiently elevated to give a purchase for the fatal rope across the back-band; and as the coward captain cried, 'Away with him!' the unfortunate tinker was dragged screaming to the impromptu gallows, and his cries were only smothered in the writhing twirl with which he swung upwards to his death.

The yeomanry corps gave a shout; but the soldiers looked on in silence, and the lieutenant in disgust.

'It will be soon over,' said Justice Slink, 'and then you can have the car again for the conveyance of the captain.'

'Sir,' said the lieutenant indignantly, '*your gallows* shall never be the resting-place of a soldier! Take up your captain, boys,' added he to his men, who obeyed at the word, and, glad to escape from the scene of atrocity which was enacting, they turned from the yeomanry in the midst of their gibbeting glory, and gladly heard word 'March!' from the lieutenant.

'That fellow's disaffected, though he wears the King's cloth,' said Slink, pointing after the lieutenant when he was out of hearing 'and, by G—d! I'll report him to the commanding officer!'

'It would be only right,' was answered by several of the corps.

'Things are come to a pretty pass indeed, when we are to be left unsupported by the military in the discharge of our duty, and endeavouring to pacify the country!'

'How d—d hard that old rascal's dying; your hand's out, Scroggins, to-day.'

'He's a tough old thief,' said Scroggins.

'Give him another pull, or he'll keep us here all day,' said the justice; 'and it's beginning to rain, and there's no fun in getting wet to see a tinker hanging. D—n him!—he will never die!—better finish him at once, and ride home.—Stand aside, Scroggins,' added the captain, as he drew a pistol from his holster; 'we can't wait till he's dead, and we mustn't leave unfinished work behind us.'

And levelling his pistol as he spoke, he fired at the still writhing body of the old man, whose mortal agonies terminated with the short muscular jerk which the bullet of Justice Slink produced as it passed through a vital part, and down dropped the legs of the suspended victim in the rigidness of death.

'Fall in!' said the captain to his troop, as he returned his pistol to the holster; and the order of march was resumed when those who had dismounted regained their saddles.

The peasant whose car had been thus polluted, and who stood in speechless horror at the merciless act he was forced to witness, now took off his hat, and in the tone of humblest humility, said:

'Plaze your honour, won't your honour be plazed to order the dead man to be taken down?'

'Take him down yourself,' said the justice; 'he won't do you any harm.'

And giving the word to his troop, away they rode, leaving the peasant looking after them in horror-stricken wonder how men could be such monsters.

When a bend of the road had shut out the horsemen from his sight, he turned with a feeling of loathing to where their victim was hanging between the shafts of the car, which industry had dedicated to the offices of peace, and had been laden with the fruits of plenty, but now bore the harvest of death.

The very thought of touching the body was revolting to him, and he stood gazing on the horrid sight motionless as the object that appalled him.

And there hung the old tinker, the end of his wily and worthless life being a violent death; and though many of his deeds were worthy of capital punishment, he died at last on suspicion of one of the few crimes he had never committed.

While the peasant was still undecided as to how he should act, he perceived a traveller approaching—not a traveller of high degree, but one from whom he might expect sympathy and assistance, for his bundle suspended at his back from a stick over his shoulder declared him to be of his own class.

As he approached, the farmer was startled at tracing in his person the outlines of an old acquaintance, and exclaimed:

'God be good to me! but if ever he was alive in this world, it's Rory O'More!'

The traveller still advanced; and as he approached his attention became

riveted by the appalling sight that crossed his path, and he heeded not
the peasant, when he came to a stand before the the body, until his
wonder and horror had been so far recovered as to turn his eyes upon
the living, with an expression of inquiry in their silent gaze which was
met by one of a similar expression on the part of him he looked upon.

For a few seconds the two men stood in silence; the traveller was
the first to speak.

'Why, thin, don't you know me, Coghlan?'

'May the Lord save us, thin and is it you that's in it?' said the
armer.

'Who else would it be?'

'Why, thin, Rory O'More, is that yourself?'

'Don't you see it's myself?'

'By the blessed light! I didn't know whether it was you or your
appearance[2] only: sure we thought you wor dead. Oh, Queen of
Heaven! and where wor you ever sence?'

'Sence when?'

'Sence your disappearance—God bless my soul!'

'Oh, you mane when the vagabones tuk me away.'

'What vagabones?'

'Oh, you don't know about it!—I forgot. But will you tell me—'

'Stop now,' said the farmer. 'Tell me God's thruth, and is it yourself,
Rory, in airnest? for it's as grate a surprise to me as if you kem from
the dead.'

'Give us your fist,' said Rory, advancing to take the farmer's hand,
which was almost withdrawn, in doubt of the mortal identity of the
form that stood before him; but the warm shake of Rory's hand
dispelled his misgivings, and Rory then said:

'In the name o' God, what's this I see?' and he pointed to the
gallows.

'Why, what's so wondherful in it? Sure, they hang any one they
like.'

'Who?' said Rory in wild wonder.

'Ah, I forgot you wor away all this time,' said the farmer; 'and,
indeed, well for you! for they're bad times for poor Ireland.'

'Sure, I heerd they wor throubled times,' said Rory; 'but I thought it was all over now.'

'So it is,' said the farmer despondingly. 'It's all over, sure enough; and we're down intirely.'

'And if it's all over, what's this for?' said Rory, pointing to the dead man.

'Oh: that's nothin',' said the farmer, with a long-drawn sigh.

'Nothing!' exclaimed Rory. 'Is it nothing, you say, to hang a man in the open road and lave him there like a scarecrow?'

'Throth, that's but the *sweepin's o' the barn*, Rory *avic*. Oh, but your heart would bleed if you knew how many is dead and gone sence you wor here!'

From the melancholy tone of the peasant's manner, Rory's apprehension applied to it a meaning touching himself, and clasping his hands, he said, with the urgency of terror in his manner:

'My mother and Mary!—for God's sake tell me thruth!'

'They're safe,' said the peasant.

'And Kathleen Regan?'

'Safe too, Rory.'

'Thank God!' exclaimed Rory, and the tears sprang to his eyes at this sudden transition from alarm to security.

When he recovered his tranquillity, the peasant related the circumstances of Solomon's death, and besought Rory to assist him in taking down the corse from where the hangman had left it.

The revolting task was performed; and as they had no immediate means of sepulture within their reach, all they could do was to lay the body in the adjoining field; and the peasant once more yoked his horse to the car, which he expressed the utmost loathing to use again.

'But what can I do?' said he. 'I'm too poor to give it up; and sure the blame is theirs, and not mine. But, wid all that, I can't help rememberin' it was made a gallows of: and here's the mark o' murdher on it!' added the peasant, with the expression of disgust on his countenance, as he took up a handful of straw and endeavoured to rub from the body of the car a few drops of blood which had trickled from the wound the pistol-shot produced.

After a few more words were exchanged between the peasants, they bade a melancholy farewell to each other; and with a low-toned 'God speed you!' which, however, iniplied, in the fervency with which it was uttered, that they had need of Heaven's special protection, they parted, and each went his separate way.

1.   Yeomen, or regular troops.

2.   Apparition.

XL

In which Rory seeks his home but finds it not.

IT WAS WITH A FEELING of oppression at his heart that Rory parted from his newly-found acquaintance. What he had seen and taken part in was enough to influence the feelings of a less susceptible person; meeting such an incident almost on the threshold of his home chilled the warm tide of anticipation which had borne him onwards in beguilement upon his reurn to his native place. But his mother and sister, and the girl of his heart, he was told, were safe and well: which consoled him in the midst of all else that might grieve; and yet, though knowing this, Rory was not as happy as he had been before he encountered tbe hateful scene he had left—when, only in the hopefulness of his own nature, he felt at the end of a long journey every mile shorter that brought him nearer to his home.

Then, as he remembered the peasant's alarmed wonder at seeing him, and the supposition he implied to be a general one—namely, *that he was dead*, he fell into a train of painful thought at the notion of how much his mother and sister must have suffered at his absence. This made him resolve also to approach the cottage cautiously; and, in case chance did not throw in his way some means of acquainting those he loved with his return, he cast about in his own mind how he might let them know it with the least possible surprise, should he himself be the person to inform them.

'I must purtend to be a beggar, or somethin' that way, and alther my voice, and spake like an owld man, and stoop and hobble, and all to that, and ask thim for charity, and so let thim know by degrees.'

In the revolving such schemes as these did Rory pursue the road homewards, and at last a distant gleam of the river beside his native hills was like sunshine to his heart, and he stretched forward at a brisker pace, to lessen the distance between him and the little *boreen,* and the hazel hedges, and the cottage which had so often appeared to him in his dreams while he was away; and it was not long until the lane and the hedges were in sight, and Rory ran forward, hurried on by the fervour of his feelings. When he turned into the lane, he crept close to the hedge; and while his heart thumped at his side with eagerness, he approached stealthily towards the cottage, lest his sudden appearance might produce alarm; and as he got near the end of the lane, where the view of his native hut should soon be open to him, he paused for a few minutes to endeavour to overcome the choking sensation of anxiety which almost suffocated him, and made him tremble from head to foot.

At last he determined on approaching the house, and making himself known as cautiously as he could; and emerging from the shelter of the hazels, he walked forward the few paces that opened upon him the gable end of his little cottage. A few paces more and its from would be revealed; but what a shock for the heart of the poor wanderer was there! Instead of the warm thatch he had left behind, the naked gable stood staring coldly against the sky, and two or three ragged rafters crossed each other irregularly, their charred blackness too plainly telling the fate that had befallen the spot of his nativity.

He was petrified with horror at the sight, and for a few seconds the very stones on which he gazed were not more senseless than he.

On recovering himself, he approached the murky ruin in hurried and unequal steps, occasionally stopping and exclaiming, in a tone of the deepest agony, 'Oh, God!' He walked round and round it, as if he dreaded to enter the blackened walls; but at length he crossed the threshold, and the aspect of cold loneliness where he had left warmth and companionship, fell like an avalanche upon his heart, and a long-drawn groan was all he could utter.

After the lapse of a few minutes, he turned round with a bewildered eye. His look fell upon the hearth where wet weeds were now growing, and the image of decay in that place of comfort smote him so touchingly that he burst into tears and wept profusely: it relieved the heart which was full nigh to bursting, and speech, hitherto frozen, thawed at the melting touch of tenderness.

'And the fire is not there!—and where are they that sat beside it? Where are they?—Oh, my God! my God! my heart will break! And *he* towld me they were well. Oh, why did he desaive me! Poor fellow, poor fellow! maybe he hadn't the heart to tell me. Och hone! och hone! and is this what I'm come home to! Mother, mother, where are you! Mary dear, where can I find you! or are *you* gone too, and am I alone within my own walls, with nothing but the grass on my threshold! Oh, father, father! the gravestone over *you* is not so bleak as these blackened walls to me! Here, where I was nursed and reared, and grew up in love and tendherness; here, to have worse than a grave to come to!—Oh, well for me if I had died, and had never seen this day!'

He threw himself passionately against the ruins and wept convulsively.

After some moments of this vehement grief, he looked once more upon the roofless walls around him, and an expression of intense agony again passed over his countenance as he exclaimed:

'Oh, my Kathleen, and where are *you!* are you too without a house and home, and a wandherer on the world! And is the heart that adores you only come back to break over your ruined cabin, or, maybe, your grave! Oh, bitther was the day I was forced from you, to lave you, without the heart to love, and the hand to guard you! Och hone! och hone! my life's a load to me if thim I love has come to harm! And where am I to turn?—where am I to find thim? I'm a sthranger on the spot I was born, and the fire o' my own hearth is quenched.'

Again he looked on the ruined cabin, the fragments of charred rafters, and the thick-growing weeds; and though the sight made his blood run cold, yet he could not leave the spot: still he lingered there, making some fresh outpouring of his bitter grief as some new association was stirred within his mind.

At length he left the desolated spot, and returned with a melancholy step up the little *boreen;* and, after some minutes of consideration, determined on seeking Phelim O'Flanagan, to learn from him the extent of misfortune which had befallen all those who were dear to him.

He found old Phelim at home; and the surprise of the poor schoolmaster was extreme at the appearance of Rory. The first moment of alarm (for such his emotion amounted to) being past, he hugged him, and wept, and prayed, and thanked God for the restoration of his own boy, as he called him, over and over again.

Rory's instant inquiries for his mother and sister and Kathleen were answered satisfactorily; and the poor fellow dropped on his knees, in acknowledgment of heaven's mercies.

'Oh, Phelim! a Turk would have pitied me,' said Rory, 'when I got the first sight of the cabin all tatthered to pieces, and the refthers blackened with the fire!'

''Faith, he would be a Turk, for sartin, if he didn't—the barbarian savage of the Arawbian deserts might be enlightened with a tindher touch of pity for your sufferin's: for though he has no house nor home himself, sure, it 'ud be unnatharal if he wouldn't feel the loss of it for another—for though he lives in the sands, by all accounts, and we live in mud, sure it's all as one, barrin' the difference of the material—as a *domus* is a *domus* howsomever it is built. Oh, to see the owld place burnt down was a sore sight! And how did you feel at all, Rory, my poor fellow, when you seen that?'

'I felt as if my own heart was scorched,' said Rory.

''Faith, that is as complate a demonstheration of your feelin's as you could make—Q. E. D.'

'Will you bring me to where *they* are?' said Rory.

'To be sure I will, boy, and that smart.—The Lord keep us, how they'll be surprised!'

'You must brake it to thim, Phelim, for fear they might get a fright.'

'Sartinly, I'll expound it to thim, by degrees; and what with a dark hint, or a bright coruscation of the distant thruth, through the 'newindos I will give thim—'

'Arrah, never mind the windows, man, but go in at the door, at wanst, and don't keep me waitin' long without, for my heart is burstin' till I howld thim to it.'

'I'm neither talkin' of windows 'nor doors, Rory; but I say that it is by distant scintillations, as it were, they must be prepared for the anticipation.'

"Faith, you may well call it an anticipation, for a man to be taken away for a year or betther, and come back safe and sound afther all!'

"Faith, you're a wondherful boy, Rory, sure enough! you are the rale *rara avis in terris.* How they'll be astonished!'

'Make haste, Phelim, *agra*—I think every minit an hour till we go.'

'We're off now,' said the schoolmaster, fastening the door of his little hut and leading the way.

'The sun is low already, Rory, *avic*, and it will be night before we get to Knockbrackin, so we had betther take to the fields—for as the martial law is out still, we must keep off the road as much as we can.'

'Sure, thin, if it's in Knockbraekin they are, I'll go by myself, and don't you be runnin' risks, Phelim.'

'Arrah, Rory, do you think I'd miss seein' the pleasure that'll be in it this night wid the meeting o' yiz all? No, in throth—not for more money than I could count, though Gough and Voshther is familiar to me: so, come along, boy.'

'God bless you, Phelim! the heart is warm in you.'

'Thank God, and so it is,' said Phelim. 'Though I'm owld it's not cowld; so there's rhyme and rayson for you too. Come along, boy;'— and the old man led the way at a brisker pace than usual, the ardour of good nature overcoming the languor of age.

XLI

Joy visits the house of mourning but does not seem to like her quarters.

It was night when phelim and Rory reached the village. A gentle tap, given by Phelim at the door of a cabin standing somewhat apart from the rest, disturbed its inmates from the melancholy occupation in which they were engaged.

Four women who were praying beside a bed of straw whereon the dead body of a man was lying lifted their tearful eyes at the sound, and paused in their orisons.

The tap at the door was repeated; the women did not speak, but exchanged looks of alarm with each other, and more carefully screened the light than it had been before; but to a third knock they arose from their knees and consulted in whispers with each other.

The corpse was that of Shan Regan; the watchers were, his mother and sister, with the Widow O'More and Mary.

The rebels, at nightfall, had borne their fallen companion to the village, that the last offices for the departed might be performed by his family, although much risk attended the doing so but the waking the dead is held so sacred amongst this affectionate people, that they were willing to incur every danger rather than a Christian should be consigned to the ground 'like a dog,' as they said themselves.

After some brief consultation, the women assumed as much composure as they could, and the door was opened with fear and trembling; but the presence of old Phelim restored them to security. On his observing the sad faces around him, he inquired the cause.

The answer was not in words; but Kathleen, taking his hand and leading him over to the far corner of the cabin, withdrew a blanket which hung before a candle burning beside the dead body, and saying 'Look there!' relapsed into tears.

The women caught the infection and renewed theit lamentation, while Phelim stood silently gazing on the remains of Shan Regan.

'There!' said the Widow O'More—'my poor owld neighbour has lost her son as well as me. Oh, aren't we to be pitied! Though she's not so badly off afther all, for she knows the worst at laste, and has him to do the last duties by him; but my darlin' was taken from me unknownst, and I'll never see him agin!'

'Don't be so despairing, Mrs. O'More, my dear; you don't know but you may have your son restored to you yet.'

'Never, never!' cried the widow.

'There's marvillious conjunctions sometimes, my dear ma'am, wherein the Almighty demonstherates His disphisations accordin' to His own blessed will, and in His own good time; and do you know I have certain misgivin's, or I may say lucubrations, that it will turn out your son will turn up.'

The widow looked at the schoolmaster very intently as he proceeded with his speech, and, though not clearly understanding him, yet through the mist of hard words caught at his meaning; and there was something in his manner which implied so much of assurance, that she held her eyes fixed on him with a look of eager inquiry as she said:

'Why, thin, what do you mane, Phelim?'

'I mane that you should not be surprised out o' your life if God was good to you some time or other; and no knowin' the day or the hour that Rory might be promiscuously, as I may say, restored to us in an individual manner, and without that preparation or hallucination requizit for sudden surprises, or—'

'Phelim,' interrupted Mary, 'I'm sure you've heerd something, or you wouldn't talk this way, and come here at this time o' night. For heaven's sake, tell us at wanst if you do know anything of Rory.'

Kathleen had been attracted as well as Mary by Phelim's last words, and was so overcome by agitation as to sink to a seat; and her eyes, being turned towards the door, which stood jar, became suddenly riveted on a figure in the gloom beyond it—for Rory, having drawn as close to the entrance as he could, to hear the sound of the loved voices within, had come within range of Kathleen's eager eye.

Before Phelim could answer Mary's adjuration, a faint scream from Kathleen called Mary's attention upon her, and she beheld her with clasped hands and fascinated gaze looking through the door, as she exclaimed, 'Great God, he's there!' and she buried her face in her hands as she spoke, and fell backwards.

Phelim caught her, or she must have dropped to the ground; while Mary and her mother rushed to the door, whose threshold Rory's foot had just crossed, and the long-lost wanderer was clasped at the same instant in the arms of his mother and sister.

After a long and tender embrace of each, he hastened to Kathleen, who still kept her face covered. Kneeling beside her, Rory besought her to look upon him, and gently endeavoured to withdraw her hands; but the poor girl trembled violently, while she could only breathe in long-drawn sighs—and it was some time before her lover could prevail upon her to behold him.

Tremulously parting her hands, she looked upon Rory for a few moments, and then again screened her eyes, as though the sight of him had been sunshine to them and could not be supported; but in that one look, there was so much of timorous delight, so much of child-like joy, seeming afraid almost to trust its own happiness, that Rory's heart drank full of delight, and clasping her wildly in his arms, he exclaimed:

'She's my own!—she's my own!'

The melting girl dropped into his embrace, and as her arms hung round his neck, she wept as she had wept before for her brother.

But the tears were not from the same source.—How wondrous near do the founts of joy and sorrow lie in the human heart!

After the first burst of welcome and joy was over, Rory's eye fell upon the figure of Kathleen's mother sitting silently and steadfastly in her chair, as if she belonged not to the scene—nor did she:—to her, her dead son was dearer than her daughter's living lover. Her head was turned away, for she looked upon the curse of Regan, which was screened from Rory's observation but he, advancing towards her to claim her welcome, started and stood still when he saw the object of her melancholy contemplation. He turned an inquiring glance to Mary and Kathleen: the former spoke:

'Ah, Rory, you've come back to see sore trouble.'

'He's dead *now*, Rory,' said Kathleen.

The few words were given in a tone which spoke a history: the meaning travelled over the past—it spoke of injuries inflicted, of wrath and wrongs, and implied that Forgiveness was the handmaiden of Death. Rory felt all the meaning, but his generous heart needed not the appeal: he approached the dead body, and kneeling beside it, took the lifeless hand, and said, 'Shan—though you would not be my friend in life, we're friends now.' He laid the hand gently down, and raising his own in the action of prayer, said fervently, 'May his soul rest in glory!' then rising from his knees, he approached Kathleen, who flung herself in a passion of tears on his neck and sobbed forth audibly, 'God bless you—God bless you, Rory!'

It was an exciting scene which that cabin exhibited. There was grief over the dead, and joy over the living; one had been hurried out of life, and another returned as if from the grave. Words are weak in comparison with human passions, and better may such a scene be conceived than related.

But the startling adventures of the day and night were not yet over. Information had been conveyed to the yeomanry corps that the body of a rebel was being waked in the village; and whenever such an event took place, they always sought to find where this observance to the dead was performed, for the purpose of disovering those who respected a rebel so far, and marking them, if not for vengeance, at least for *surveillance*.

It was in the middle of the night, while Rory was recounting to his family the circumstances of his mysterious disappearance, that a loud knocking at the door and fierce demands for immediate entry alarmed

them. Before the door could be unbarred to the summons, it was burst
open by a blow from the butt-end of a carabine, and Justice Slink,
followed by some of his corps, entered the cabin. The scene which
ensued it is impossible to describe—there was insult to the living
and the dead, and Rory was laid violent hands on, as the murderer of
Scrubbs:—to explain at such a moment was impossible; every attempt
he made to do so was met by curses and blows; and he was dragged
from amongst the shrieking women, hurried to the county jail, and
committed to abide his trial as a murderer.

XLII

Containing an explanatory letter.

A S SOON AS DE LACY and Rory arrived in Dublin from Bordeaux, the latter lost not an hour in proceeding southward, to appease the yearnings of his heart after home. But De Lacy remained in the capital to transact various necessary business with his lawyer respecting his newly-acquired property.

It was with surprise and sorrow he received the following letter a few days after Rory's departure; the address ran thus, penned in a round text:

> To his Honour Horat[io]
> De Lacy Esquire to be
> Left at Counsel[r] Casey's
> Dominick S[t] Dublin.

The missive was closed with a wafer, and bore the impression of a thimble by way of seal, and when handed to De Lacy by his lawyer on his entering his study, excited no small surprise.

'Who the deuce can this be from?' said De Lacy, turning the letter over three or four times.

The lawyer pointed to the impression of the thimble, and giving a knowing wink, replied:

'You soldiers are terrible fellows among the girls!'

SAMUEL LOVER

'We'll see what fair correspondent this is from,' said De Lacy, as he broke the seal. These were the contents:

'HONOURED SIR

'Nemo mortalium in omnibus horis sapit as is illigantly remarked by the Classicks which is my own case at this present writin for I know more know whats to be done then the babe unborn in the regard of his life been in danger as they will hang him if posable unless you can sthreck him out sum way to purvint it been surrounded as we are I may say with truth with sarcumvallations more cuteaneous and perplexn then the Walls of Troy or the Labyrynthus of Crete where the miniature was kept and Diddle-us himself could not get out in short we are in the verry centre of a hobble and wishes you to know it knowin youl be plased to do all in your power for the poor boy who they tuk to jail the minit he came home from the poor women who is brakin their harts and they wont blieve the blaggards I mane what he ses about it but wants to make out he murdhered the Killecthr which he never done though God knows it would be no loss and this is to insense you on that same and ax your honours advice which is no good Im afeard in regard of the villains that is thurstin for his blood which they will have barrin it can be saved and knowin none can do that same but yourself seein that you are a gintleman every inch o you and no less and was always our frind and his frind and I know will do all mortial man can do for him and from him and his they offer you their prayrs and blessins as of owld and hopes youl stand to them now and they will ever pray and so will I who respects your honour more than tongs can tell for minshuration could not measure tbe profunditty of my reverence for your honour which will inkrase in jommethrical ratio to the ind of Time.

'From your Honours
'Obagent Sarvent
'To Command
'PHELIM OFLANAGAN
'*Philormath.*'

The mingled senses of the ridiculous and the serious which this letter excited produced an effect upon De Lacy not unnoticed by the lawyer.

'What the deuce *is* that you're reading?'

'Why do you ask?'

'Because your brow and your mouth are playing at cross purposes; for while gloom sits on the one, mirth is twitching at the other.'

'The face is the index of the mind,' said De Lacy: 'it is a true saying. There,—read that, and you'll know more about the matter,' and he handed him the letter.

The young barrister laughed at the extraordinary epistle, and when he concluded the reading of it declared it to be one of the most extraordinary documents which had ever come under his inspection; 'but, in one respect,' added he, 'it does not fulfil your representation of it.'

'How so?' asked De Lacy.

'You said, as you gave it to me, I should know more of the business; and I confess I am as yet as ignorant on that point as when I began. You who are acquainted, I suppose, with the circumstances of the person and case alluded to, may be enabled to make a guess at the matter; but to a stranger it is perfectly hieroglyphic.'

'Don't you see they have taken him to jail on a charge of murder!'

'And who is *him*, pray?'

'Rory O'More, to be sure: does not the letter say so?'

'Indeed, it does not—nor one tangible fact. *You* may *guess* what all this extraordinary composition means; but I defy anyone to arrive at any knowledge from the thing itself: it has neither mention of name (except the magniloquent writer) nor of distinct fact, nor even time nor place specified. Look yourself: there is neither date nor address.'

'It is so, I perceive, now that you remark it; but I know whence it comes and to what it alludes, and it gives me deep concern.'

'Let us see the post-mark,' said the lawyer as he turned to the outside of the letter. 'Ha!—from the South, I see.'

'Yes,' said De Lacy; 'that's the post-town of the district; so far right, but there is no date! However, it matters not much, for 'tis but a few days since the poor fellow left me for home, and now he is in jail on a charge of murder, of which I know he is innocent!'

'Then your evidence can acquit him.'

'Certainly,' said De Lacy. 'But it is too hard an innocent man must lie in jail on a false charge.'

'He will not lie there long, for they make short work of accusations and trials now; so tell me all about it,' said the lawyer, 'and we'll see what can be done.'

De Lacy then entered into an explanation of the circumstances connected with Rory's and the Collector's abduction, together with the nature of his first connection with O'More, and the cause of his being an inmate of his cottage; and when he had concluded, the barrister shook his head and said it was an awkward affair.

'At all events, I will at once go to the South and see him.'

'You must do no such thing. You forget the state this country is in; and after all you have told me, your presence in his behalf would be quite enough to hang him.'

'And must I let the poor fellow lie in prison without hope or comfort?'

'Certainly not. *I* will see him, if you like; and there will be much more hope for him in that, and much more comfort to you and him in having his life *saved* through my intervention than put in jeopardy through yours'

'Thanks to you, my dear friend!' said De Lacy 'There is nothing by which you can oblige me more than by an immediate attention to this affair, and no expense can be incurred which I will not willingly pay for this poor fellow's safety. How soon can you go down? for I wish him to be assured as quickly as possible of every care being taken of him.'

'There is no time to be lost; for special commissions are now holden all over the country.'

'I *must* go with you,' said De Lacy.

'I insist on your not seeing the prisoner.'

'To that I submit; but I would not for worlds be far away from him a such a time!—I cannot tell you how I value him;—I may say, the affection I have for him.'

'Well, you may come down with me to the town, and remain *incog.* at the inn, if you like; but I assure you, if your presence in the country becomes known to the prosecuting parties, it will be all the worse for your friend Rory.'

'I will be as cautious as you can desire—in short, I will put myself quite under your control.'

'Very well, then; we'll start the day after to-morrow.'

XLIII

Rory indulges in gloomy anticipations.

WHEN DE LACY AND HIS friend reached the town where Rory was confined, the lawyer lost not a moment in visiting the prisoner, making himself possessed of the facts of his case, and assuring him of every care being taken of him by De Lacy, 'who would in person have told you all this,' said the barrister, 'but that I recommended him, considering the state the country is in, not to show himself in this business, as it would only do more harm than good; but he is in the town, O'More, as he is most anxious to know the result of the trial the moment it is over.'

'Got bless him,' said Rory; 'he was always good and kind to me; and tell him, if you plaze, sir, that I'm sinsible of all he's done for me, and even if I should die, I won't forget it all the same'

'It would puzzle you to remember it after you die, O'More. But banish such melancholy thoughts, my man,—don't think of dying'

''Faith, I hear it's a bad chance with any poor fellow who comes here of late, since the bad times. I hear they come in at the door, and go out at the window with a balkinny that has a very unsafe bottom to it; and for fear they should hurt themselves in tumblin' through it, they tie a bit o' string to thim to brake the fall.'

The lawyer could not suppress a smile at this ludicrous description of the fatal drop which Rory looked forward to as his new means of exit, but, in a gentle and soothing tone, desired him to be of good cheer and not to let his heart fail him.

'Tut, sir! don't think I fear to die bekaze I spake of it—I don't desarve death, and it won't be my portion if I get fair play; but, livin' or dyin', I'm ready to prove myself a man, and I'm sure my poor mother and sisther will always have a good frind in Misther De Lacy, and so my mind's aisy on that score; and as for dyin', a man must die some time or other, and whenever I'm called I'll not flinch.'

'Right, Rory—that's like the philosophers.'

'I dunno who *thim* wor; but it's like a man anyhow.'

'Good-bye, O'More!—I'll see you soon again,' said the lawyer as he left him.

On his return to De Lacy, he expressed a good deal of fear as to the difficulty of Rory's case, and acknowledged the circumstances bore hardly against him.

'I can prove he was taken away by force.'

'And how will you account for your own disappearance to France? The mere fact of your going there convicts you of doing what your own life might pay the forfeit of.'

'No matter,' said De Lacy, 'if my testimony can benefit Rory.—Do you think I would live at the expense of that fine fellow's life?'

'Certainly not; but you cannot *prove* anything in his favour.'

'Yes, I can: I know the Collector was not murdered, but was alive in De Welskein's lugger when I took Rory out of his hands.'

'Did you see him?'

'No.'

'Then you cannot *prove* anything doing him a pin's point of service—you perceive you can't.'

De Lacy was obliged to admit the truth of this, and by dint of great persuasion on the part of his friend was induced to keep himself *incog.* at the inn; for nothing but the assurance of his presence in the country being detrimental to Rory could have restrained him from visiting his prison, and also going to offer comfort to his mother and sister.

It is needless to dwell on the interval which elapsed between this period and Rory's trial, to which De Lacy looked forward with feverish anxiety scarcely exceeded by those of his own blood or even poor Kathleen; and when the anxious day arrived which was to determine Rory's fate, De Lacy pressed the hand of the friendly lawyer, on his leaving him to go to the court, with a parting appeal to use every exertion, and an aspiration to heaven for his success.

'The one thing in the poor fellow's favour, however,' said the barrister: 'he appears before a merciful judge; Lord A—n—e sits on this commission.'

XLIV

The glorious privilege of trial by jury.

THE COURT WAS CROWDED ON the day of Rory's trial: the galleries were occupied by the gentry for many miles round, and all the magistrates of the district were in attendance; Justice Slink, the most important of the number. Sweeny was beside the counsel for the prosecution, and as busy as his mischievous and meddling nature could desire. Close beside the front of the dock stood three women whose anxious countenances at once proclaimed them to be deeply interested in the prisoner, for at every fresh movement in the court they turned their eyes towards the entrance of the dock in expectation of beholding him. They were Rory's mother, his sister, and Kathleen. At length to the summons of 'Make way there, make way!' the crowd swayed to and fro; the drawing of heavy bolts was heard, the door of the dock opened, and Rory O'More, in custody of the jailer, entered the place of peril.

'Oh, my darlin', my darlin'!' cried his mother in a heartbreaking tone as she rushed to the bar and stretched her hand over it towards her boy, who came forward and clasped it.

'Stand back!' said one of the constables before the bar, restraining the widow.

'Oh, don't be so hard-hearted!' said she.

'You must stand back.'

'Just let me give him one kiss!—I haven't seen him these three weeks.'

'Silence in the court!' thundered the crier; 'hats off—room for my lord the judge!'

Lord A—— now appeared upon the bench, and some of the magistrates took their seats there also. Slink was at his side, and appeared to be more officious than was agreeable. The jury was now sworn; and as no challenges were made, the judge asked, had the prisoner no counsel. Being answered in the affirmative, he ordered the trial to proceed.

While these preliminaries were going forward, Mary O'More and Kathleen were exchanging signs of affection with Rory, who returned to their clasping of hands and upraised and tearful eyes (expressive of their prayers to the Almighty for his safety), a bright look of confidence, and even a smile, not of levity, but of tenderness such as offended, not against the solemnity of the occasion, but was meant to inspire those he loved with hope.

To the indictment the women listened with breathless anxiety; and its various counts, repetitions, and involvement, puzzled them so excessively, that they at last Regan to doubt whether what was going forward was in any way connected with Rory, and their sense of hearing became blunted to the monotonous terms of the rigmarole that was being read, till they were startled from their quiet by a sudden call of 'Prisoner at the bar.' They looked alternately between the clerk and Rory while the formula of asking the prisoner what he pleaded was gone through; and, after Rory's declaration of his innocence in the legal for the trial commenced.

The counsel for the prosecution made a flaming speech. The exordium consisted of the worn-out common-places of the day, about the demon of revolution, the hydra faction—of the times teeming with terror and torrents of blood. He then reminded the jury of the rebellion which had only just been put down, and congratulated himself, and them, and every loyal man, that their throats were left uncut to 'proclaim the proud pre-eminence of their glorious constitution, and to denounce the ruffian rabble that sought its overthrow.' He then came to the facts of the case before them—representing Scrubbs as 'an amiable and worthy gentleman, torn from the bosom of his family, and savagely slaughtered by the prisoner at the bar. The disappearance of Mr. Scrubbs, gentlemen, must be fresh in all your memories but I think it necessary to remind you of the principal points which will appear in evidence, and I feel confident that not a shadow of doubt will remain upon your minds that the prisoner at the bar has been guilty of the most flagrant, flagitious, bloody, and mysterious murder.' He then went over the details very minutely, and wrought such a case out of the circumstances (which were of themselves sufficiently suspicious to put Rory's life in jeopardy in the best of times), that when he sat down, every one in the court gave up poor Rory for lost, and his mother murmured in a low moan, as she wrung her hands, 'he's gone, he's' gone! my darling's gone!—they'll have his life, they will!'

The counsel for the prosecution next commenced his examination of witnesses. Justice Slink, Sweeny, and others who examined the glen of the Folly, swore to the finding of the crow-bar near the ruins, the appearance of a struggle upon the spot, etc., etc. Larry Finnegan was then called to identify the crow-bar as the one he had given to Rory upon the day of Scrubbs' disappearance; he was also questioned as to the previous meeting of Scrubbs and Rory at the 'Black Bull,' and their departure thence in company: but Larry's anxiety was so great to avoid saying anything which would prejudice Rory, that he did more harm than good by his hesitation, and the prosecuting counsel called the attention of the jury to the disinclination the witness had to disclose the truth.

'You see plainly he wants to save the prisoner.'

'Arrah, thin, do you want me to swear away his life?' said Finnegan. "Faith, I'd be sorry to do that!'

'God bless you!' said the poor mother.

'Silence in the court!' roared the crier.

'You hear him, gentlemen?' said the prosecuting counsel.

'For God's sake!' said Rory from the dock, 'tell the whole truth and I'm not afeard.'

'Prisoner, be silent!' said the counsel.

Lord A— cast a searching glance upon Rory, whose demand for the *whole* truth seemed to impress his lordship favourably and his bright and open look also pleaded for him, in the judge's benevolent heart.

The evidence proceeded.

Counsel. You say that the prisoner at the bar and the late Mr. Scrubbs— —

The counsel for the defence here interposed, and said he objected to the term, the *late* Mr. Scrubbs, as it was assuming the fact he was dead, which was not proven. The examination then proceeded.

Counsel. The prisoner, at the bar and the late—I beg pardon—*Mister* Scrubbs were the last to leave the 'Black Bull' on that day?

Witness. Yes, sir.

Counsel. How did they go?

Witness. They wint out o' the door, sir.

Counsel. I don't suppose they went out of the window. I mean, did they, leave about the same time?

Witness. They wint togither, sir.

Counsel. Both out of the door at once?

Witness. No, Mr. Scrubbs wint first.

Counsel. And the prisoner after?

Witness. Yis.

Counsel. Then he followed him?

Witness. Yis.

Counsel. You observe, gentlemen of the jury, Mr. Scrubbs went *first,* and the prisoner *followed* him.

Witness. Why, you wouldn't have him go *before* the gintleman!

Counsel. Silence, sir! Remember *that,* gentlemen—he *followed* Mr. Scrubbs.

There was a good deal more of examination which it would be uninteresting to record; and, after the landlord of the 'Black Bull' had been bullied and tormented as much as the counsel chose, he said, 'You may go down, sir.'

Larry Finnegan, delighted to escape, scrambled from the witnesses' chair, and was rushing off the table, when Rory's counsel interposed and said, 'I beg your pardon—don't go down yet.'

'Oh!' said the counsel for' the crown, '*you* want to cross-examine him, do you?'

'*I believe* I have a *right,* sir,' was the young barrister's reply.

'Why, sure, what crosser examination can you gi' me than the one I got?' said poor Finnegan.

'Sit down, sit down, my man,' said the counsel encouragingly. 'Now, don't be in a hurry, don't be alarmed; take your time, and answer me quietly a few questions I shall ask you. You say some conversation passed between the prisoner and Mr. Scrubbs at your house?'

Witness. Yis, sir—they'wor spakin' togither for some time.

Counsel. I think you mentioned that Mr. Scrubbs asked the prisoner, was he going home?

Witness. He did, sir.

Counsel. And the prisoner *was* going home?

Witness. Yis, sir.

Counsel. Mr. Scrubbs' road home lay the same way I believe?

Witness. It did, sir.

Counsel. Then he and the prisoner *could not help* going the same road?

Witness. They could not, sir.

Counsel. Mr. Scrubbs went out of the door first?

Witness. Yis, sir.

Counsel. And the prisoner after?

Witness. Yis, sir.

Counsel. Immediately?

Witness. That minit.

Counsel. Then, what do you mean by saying he followed him?

Witness. I mane, he folly'd him the way a poor man would folly a gintleman, of coorse.

Counsel. I beg your attention, gentlemen of the jury, to this explanation of the witness's meaning, upon which the opposite counsel has put a false construction.

Was the crow-bar you gave the prisoner his or yours?

Witness. It was his, sir: he lint it to me, and kem that day to ax for it.

Counsel. He *came* to ask for it, did he?—then it was for that particular purpose he went to your house that day?

Witness. It was, sir.

Counsel. Before he saw Mr. Scrubbs at all?

Witness. Yis, sir.

Counsel. I beg you to remember *this* also, gentlemen of the jury. You may go down, witness.

Larry Finnegan again attempted to descend from the table, but was interrupted by the counsel for the prosecution; and the look of despair which the countenance of mine host of the 'Black Bull' assumed was almost ludicrous, 'Is it *more* you want o' me?' said he.

Counsel. A few questions. Sit down.

Larry scratched his head, and squeezed his hat harder than he had done before, and resumed his seat in bitterness of spirit; but his answers having latterly all gone smooth, he felt rather more self-possessed than he had done under his previous examination by the prosecuting counsel, and his native shrewdness was less under the control of the novel situation in which he was placed.

The bullying barrister, as soon as the witness was seated, began in a thundering tone thus:—

Counsel. Now, my fine fellow, you say that it was for the particular purpose of asking for his crow-bar that the prisoner went to your house?

Witness. I do.

Counsel. By virtue of your oath?

Witness. By the varth o' my oath.

Counsel (slapping the table fiercely with his hand).—Now, sir, *how* do you know he came for that purpose? Answer me *that*, sir!

Witness. 'Faith, thin, I'll tell you. When he came into the place that morning, it was the first thing he ax'd for; and by the same token, the way I remimber it is, that when he ax'd for the crow-bar he lint me, some one stan'in' by ax'd what I could want with a crow-bar; and Rory O'More with that said, it wasn't me at all, but the misthriss wanted it (Mrs. Finnegan, I mane). 'And what would Mrs. Finnegan want wid it?' says the man. 'Why,' says Rory, 'she makes the punch so sthrong, that she bent the spoons sthrivin' to stir it, and so she borrowed the crow bar to mix the punch.'

A laugh followed this answer, and even Rory could not help smiling at his own joke thus retailed; but his mother, and Mary, and Kathleen, looked round the court, and turned their pale faces in wonder on those who could laugh while the life of him they adored was at stake, and the sound of mirth at such a moment fell more gratingly on their ears than the fierce manner of the bullying prosecutor.

But the witness was encouraged, for he saw his examiner was annoyed, and he took a hint from the result, and lay in wait for another opportunity of turning the laugh against his tormentor. He was not long in getting such an opening; and the more he was examined in hope of shaking his testimony, the less the prosecutor gained by it.

At length the counsel received a whisper from Sweeny, that the fellow was drunk.

'He has his wits most d——nably about him, for all that,' said the lawyer.

'He has been drinking all the morning—I can prove it,' said Sweeny; 'and you may upset his testimony, if you like, on that score.'

'I'll have a touch at him, then,' said the lawyer.

When the jury perceived the same witness still kept on the table and a re-examination for the prosecution entered upon, they became wearied, and indeed no wonder; for the silk-gowned gentleman became excessively dull; and, had he possessed any tact, must have perceived from the demeanour of the jury that his present course of proceeding was ill-timed: yet he continued and in violation of all custom sought to invalidate the testimony of the man he himself had called as a witness: but Larry's cross examination having favoured the prisoner, the crown counsel became incensed, and abandoned all ceremony and discretion, which at length was noticed by the Bench.

'I beg your pardon, my lord, but I am anxious to *sift* this witness.'

'By gor!' said Finnegan, 'if you wor to sift me from this till to-morrow, the divil a grain more you'll get out o' me!—and indeed you've been gettin' nothin' but chaff for the last half-hour.'

The answer had so much of truth in it, that the counsel became doubly annoyed at the suppressed laugh he heard around him; and then he determined to bring up his heavy artillery, and knock Larry to atoms.

Counsel. Now, sir, I've just a question or two that you'll answer by virtue of your oath.

The Bench. Really, Mr. ——

Counsel. I beg your ludship's pardon—but it is absolutely important. Now, by virtue of your oath, haven't you been drinking this morning?

Witness. To be sure I have.

Counsel. How much did you drink?

Witness. 'Faith, I don't know: I never throubled myself keepin' count, barrin' I'm sarvin' the customers at home.

Counsel. You took a glass of whiskey before breakfast, of course?

Witness. And glad to get it!

Counsel. And another after?

Witness. Av coorse—when it was to be had.

Counsel. When you came into the town, you went to a public house, I hear, and were drinking *there,* too, before you came into court?

Witness. Oh, jist a thrifle among some frinds.

Counsel. What do you call a trifle?

Witness. Four pots o' porther and a quart o' sper'ts.

Counsel. Good God! Gentlemen of the jury, listen to this:—a gallon of porter and a quart of whiskey!

Witness. Oh, but that was betune six iv us!

Counsel. Then, sir, by your own account you're drunk at this moment.

Witness. Not a bit.

Counsel. On your oath—remember your oath, sir—do you think, after drinking all you yourself have owned to, you are in a state to give evidence in a court of justice?

Witness. 'Faith, I think a few glasses only helps to brighten a man!—and, betune ourselves, Counsellor —— ——, I think you'd be a grate dale the better of a glass *yourself* this minit.

The laugh which this rejoinder produced finished 'the counsellor,' and he sat down without roaring, as usual, at the witness, 'Go down, sir.' But Larry kept his seat until the laugh was over; and not receiving the ordinary mandate to retire, he looked at the discomforted barrister with the most provoking affectation of humility, and said, 'Do you want me any more, sir?'

This renewed the laugh, and Finnegan retired from the table under the shadow of his laurels.

After some more stupid examination of other witnesses, and tedious blundering on the part of this legal wiseacre, the case for the prosecution closed, and Rory's counsel commenced his defence.

After some preliminary observations on the manner in which the case had been conducted on the other side, and the disingenuousness exhibited by his 'learned friend' in endeavouring to pervert the meaning of some of the witnesses,—among others, that of the landlord of the 'Black Bull,'—the counsel requested the jury to divest the evidence of the mystery which had been studiously thrown round it, until he had stripped it by cross-examination to its pure and simple state; and in that state he begged of them to look upon it. 'It is the more necessary, gentlemen,' said he, 'because it is a case of circumstantial evidence; and it behoves you to weigh such evidence most scrupulously, when the life of a fellow creature depends upon it. This is doubly necessary in this case, inasmuch as the prisoner stands in a painfully perplexing situation, by having no means of rebutting the charges against him by contrary *living* evidence, all the persons bearing a part in the transaction wherein he was forcibly carried away being dead or beyond our reach: for you know, gentlemen, how many lives have been sacrificed within the brief but terrible period through which we have just passed! I will produce, however, in evidence an examination sworn to before a magistrate who is now in this court, by one Solomon Slevin, since dead.'

'Yes, gentlemen,' said the counsel for the prosecution, 'he is dead indeed, for he has been hanged since he swore it; so you may guess how much his deposition is worth.'

The young barrister thus interrupted turned an indignant and reproachful look on the crown lawyer as he sat down, and said, 'I cannot help remarking, that I never met a more ungenerous observation in the course of my practice.' Then, turning to the jury, he continued, 'You have been told, gentlemen, with a view of prejudicing the evidence I have put in, that the person who deposed to the facts therein contained—facts, gentlemen, that may acquit my client,—I repeat it, that *must* acquit him in the minds of unprejudiced men, as I am sure you will prove yourselves to be;—you have been told, I say, *that* person was since hanged: but I will ask the learned gentleman who has so cruelly endeavoured to destroy the only hope of life my client has left,—I will ask him, since he provokes the question, was that person legally hanged?—He will not answer that, gentlemen,—he cannot—he dare not; and if that person suffered death *illegally,* it is monstrous that the fact should be put forward in a court of justice, to support the course of the law, of which the fact itself was a flagrant violation.'

'He deserved hanging,' interrupted the counsel for the crown.

'You are told he deserved hanging, gentlemen; but before you give a verdict on that assertion, I expect you will ask, did the punishment result from the verdict of a jury and the sentence of a judge? And if it did not, I trust, gentlemen, you will not, by receiving such evidence, violate the sanctuary of justice, by letting a man's life depend on individual opinion, nor take a receipt in full for human blood from the hands of any man, even a justice of the peace or a king's counsel.' And he looked significantly at the guilty magistrate on the bench, and upon the Prosecuting counsel as he spoke.

One of the jury remarked in no very amiable tone, to the barrister:

'You seem to forget, sir, that martial law exists in this country at present.'

'Forget it, sir!' said the young advocate reproachfully; 'G—d forbid I could have a heart so callous as to forget it! Have I not seen the lamp-irons of our streets made the ready gibbet for the readier vengeance of martial law, as if they selected them to enlighten the public by the promptness of their military measures? Forget it, sir!—no I nor you, nor I, nor our children after us, shall forget it! But terrible as the tribunal of a court is,—even when called at the drum-head, I would not venture here to condemn, however I may lament, the punishment which is recognised by the law. But this deponent of whom I speak— this poor old helpless man—had not even a drum-head to look to, the only likeness to it being the emptiness of the head whose ferocious folly condemned him; but without word of evidence, or question of life and death, even amongst his own troop, this captain-magistrate hanged the wretched man!—Yes, gentlemen, he was hanged, untried and unshriven, less like a Christian than a dog! And yet, this is the condemnation which is called in to invalidate the testimony of the condemned man!—Condemned, do I say? Gentlemen, I cannot contain my indignation; I will *not* say the man was condemned, for the term bears with it the seeming of legal punishment: he was not *condemned*—he was *murdered*!'

From the first allusion made to the hanging of Solomon, Justice Slink seemed rather uncomfortable. As the advocate warmed into indignation, the captain seemed to wince under the lash; and though his brow darkened and his face assumed a vengeful expression, yet was he afraid to lift his eye to meet the bright indignant glance of the young barrister: but when at last the atrocious act he had committed was called by its right name, and he was denounced as a murderer in open court, he dared to keep his seat no longer, but hurried from the bench, forgetting in his confusion to to make the customary obeisance to the judge.

Retiring to one of the rooms of the court-house appropriated to the accommodation of the magistracy, he sent for Sweeny, and gave, through him, special instructions to the counsel for the prosecution to animadvert in his speech in reply upon the defendant barrister's 'atrocious attack' upon a loyal magistrate and to represent to the jury how the military party had been entrapped into an ambuscade by the tinker, who therefore '*had every right to be hanged.*'

'And,' added the magisterial captain, 'if any other judge than that milk-and-water Lord A— (who is half a rebel himself) was on the bench, the Jacobite rascal who is prating would not have been permitted to hold such language against a loyal man.'

Sweeny returned to the court on his mission, and found the speech for the defence just about to conclude; the advocate trusting to the documentary evidence put in for the acquittal of his client.

The jury were little more pleased than Justice Slink himself at the boldness of the young lawyer: for hanging made easy was more to their taste than is desirable in gentlemen who sit on capital cases, and they made no scruple of showing by their looks that the speech for the prisoner was far from agreeable.

When the prosecuting counsel rose to reply, they bestowed upon him the most marked attention; and he proceeded to fill up the outline given to him by Sweeny at Captain Slink's desire. After defending the act of hanging the tinker, he asked them, how could they believe the testimony of a rebel, who had suffered death for betraying the king's troops into an ambuscade; and which very testimony was given for the purpose of hoodwinking a magistrate, and very likely with a view to screen the prisoner at the bar, who stood in the awkward predicament of being open to the suspicion of being just as much a rebel as any of them. 'You are told, gentlemen, he was out of the country all the time of the rebellion—that he was in France and what brought him there, I ask? We have not been told what. It was a very suspicious place to be in, at all events.'

In this strain was he proceeding, when his speech was interrupted by a bustle in the court, caused by the fainting of Kathleen Regan, whose fears for Rory's life were wrought to such a pitch that she sunk beneath them, and much disturbance was occasioned by the movement of the dense crowd in the court in endeavouring to make a passage for her to the open air. There at length she was conveyed, and in some time restored to consciousness. Phelim O'Flanagan was at her side, for he had undertaken the care of her, as the Widow O'More and Mary were too dreadfully interested in the trial to leave the court, where they remained, as it were, in a state of fearful fascination; for though they stayed to hear the result, they feared the worst from the nature of the prosecutor's reply, and the manifest relish with which it was received by the jury. When Kathleen was able to speak, the first words she said to Phelim were:

'Where are they all gone?'

'Who, *colleen*—who?' said Phelim.

'All thim people, and they staring so frightfully!'

'Aisy, *colleen* dear! aisy! You'll be betther in a minit.'

Kathleen drew her hand across her forehead, as if in the act of recalling memory; and then bursting into tears, she cried:

'I know it now, I know it,—I remember it all! They'll murder him,—I know they'll have his life! Oh, bring me back there—bring me back! don't take me away from him as long as he's alive! Phelim dear, take me back again!'

'Stay here, my poor *colleen!* it's betther for you,—the hot coort will make you faint again.'

'Oh, it wasn't the hot coort, Phelim, but the cowld fear that came over my heart: but I'll go back again,—I will.'

'Wait a little longer at laste, darlin', until you're more recovered. Indeed, you'll faint agin if you go back so soon.'

The girl heeded him not as he spoke, but he felt her hand grasp his arm with a convulsive pressure; and when he looked upon her he saw her eyes fixed in a gaze of wild eagerness towards the street, as she gasped forth rapidly, 'Look! Look! for God's sake look! There—the?'

'The Collecthor!—the Collecthor! Oh, great God!'

Springing from Phelim's arms, she rushed into the street; and seizing the reins of a horse which a traveller was riding tip the road, she clasped the knees of the horseman, and screamed rather than spoke to him:—'Get off—get off, and save his life! For the love of God, get off, and save him!'

It was Scrubbs whom she addressed. He had escaped from France, and by a singular coincidence arrived at this opportune moment to save the life of the man who had saved his, and was at that moment under trial for his murder.

It would be impossible to describe the sensation produced among the bystanders at the extraordinary occurrence; and it was not without much fear on his part that Scrubbs was almost lifted from his horse, and hurried into the court-house, Kathleen clinging to his side all the time, and uttering hysteric exclamations.

It was just at this moment the prosecutor was winding up his reply. 'You are told, gentlemen, the prisoner was carried away to France by force, and in company with Mr. Scrubbs: but the prisoner returns, and no tidings have we of the other. The prisoner cannot give a satisfactory account of himself. What brought him to France?—who was he with in France?—how did he get back from France?—why does not the

Collector come back too?—Gentlemen, the question is, which you value most, a gentleman's life, or a tinker's testimony,—the testimony of a rebel, who died the death he deserved? Until they can produce Mr. Scrubbs, I remain incredulous. My answer to all they have said is, "Where is the Collector?"'

As he was about to wind up a grand peroration, the distant sound of the murmur of excitement and agitation in the crowd which thronged every avenue to the court interrupted the attention of the audience. The crier was ordered to command silence; but, in defiance of that functionary's mandate, the sound increased, like that of rushing waters, and above it all the hysteric laugh and wail of a woman rang wildly through the court. There was a momentary pause, in which the counsel, repeating inconclusive question, exclaimed, 'Again I say, "Where is the Collector?"'

The lovely girl, with streaming hair and outstretched arms, forced her way into the court, and screamed, 'He's here!—he's here!' And then the wild laugh which forced her flushed face into an expression of terrible mirth, while the tears were streaming down it, again rang round the court, which was absolutely appalled into silence.—'He's here!' she exclaimed again. 'Great God, I thank you! I've saved him, I've saved him!' And then she relapsed into heart-breaking sobs.

'Remove that poor girl from the court,' said Lord A— , whose gentle heart was quite overcome by the scene; 'remove her, and take care of her.'

It would be impossible minutely to detail all which immediately followed; the surprise, the commotion, the impossibility to command order for some minutes. All this can be better imagined than described; and therefore we shall not attempt to paint the startling scene that passed until Kathleen Regan was withdrawn from the court. Then Mr. Scrubbs was produced on the table; and scores of witnesses were on the spot to identify him,—indeed, every man on the jury knew him.

Order was not obtained for many minutes, and it required some interval to restore to Lord A— sufficient tranquillity to command his judicial dignity in addressing the jury, which he did in a few words, nearly as follows:

'Gentlemen of the jury,—Your duties have been terminated in a very singular and affecting manner. By one of those interpositions of the Divine will which the Almighty is sometimes pleased to vouchsafe in evidence of His eternal providence, a human life has been preserved even when it was in the most imminent danger—'

Lord A— paused, for his feelings were yet an overmatch for his power of composure; and in the interval the foreman of the jury said to his brothers, with a nod of assumption,

'He means our friend Scrubbs; wonderful escape indeed!'

Lord A— resumed.—'Gentlemen, it has been the will of heaven to make manifest the innocence of an accused man, when all other hope had failed him save that of the merciful God who has been his protector!'

Lord A— could proceed no further; and many a stifled sob was heard in the court—everywhere but in the jury-box.

'Gentlemen,' resumed Lord A—, 'though the trial is at an end, it becomes necessary, as a matter of form, you should return verdict.'

Singularly contrasting to the subdued voice of the judge, subdued by the operation of his feelings, was the tone in which the foreman of the jury, with a smirk, answered without a moment's hesitation, 'We are all agreed, my lord.' 'Of course,' replied Lord A—, passing a handkerchief across his eyes. 'Return your verdict, if you please, gentlemen.'

'Guilty, my lord,' said the foreman, with an assumed suavity of voice and manner.

'I beg your pardon, sir,' said the judge; 'your feelings have overcome *you* as well as many others present: you said, Guilty— Of course you mean, *Not* guilty.'

'No, my lord—we mean, Guilty.'

The words were now pronounced sufficiently loud to be audible over the court, and a wild scream from the women followed, while the upturned eyes of every one in court at the jury-box stifled their astonishment. Even the common crier was lost in wonder, and forgot, in his surprise, the accustomed call of 'Silence!' in response to the shrieks of the women.

'Good God, sir!' exclaimed Lord A— , addressing the foreman, 'have you eyes and ears, and yet return such a verdict?' The prisoner at the bar is accused of the murder of a certain nan; that very man is produced on the table before you, and identified in your presence—a living evidence of the prisoner's innocence—and yet you return a verdict against him of Guilty!'

'We do, my lord,' said the foreman pertinaciously, and with an offended air, as if he considered it a grievance his verdict should be questioned.

'Will you be good enough, sir,' said Lord A— , changing his tone from that of wonder to irony, 'to tell me upon what count in the indictment he is guilty?—for really I am not lawyer enough to discover.'

'We should be sorry, my lord, to dispnte any point of law with your lordship; but the fact is, my lord, you don't know this country as well as we do, and we can swear upon the oath we have taken this day, that the prisoner *ought to have been hanged long ago*, and we say, Guilty, my lord!'

Lord A— could not withdraw the look of mingled wonder and indignation he fixed on the jury for a moment; and when he did, he transferred his eye to the prisoner—but in its transit the look of asperity was gone, and an eye beaming with benignity met the bright and unflinching look of Rory.

'Prisoner at the bar!' said Lord A— , whose address turned every eye upon the prisoner.

'I beg your pardon, my lord,' said one of the magistrates sitting on the bench, 'your lordship has forgotten to put on your black cap.'

'No, sir, I have not forgotten it.—Prisoner at the bar,' continued the judge, 'I feel it my duty to tell you that, notwithstanding the verdict you have heard pronounced upon you, not a hair of your head shall be harmed!'

A loud 'Hurra!' interrupted the continuation of the address aud the crier's voice, after some time, was heard shouting 'Silence!' After the lapse of about a minute, order was obtained; and, before Lord A— could resume, the foreman said, loud enough to be heard for a considerable distance:

'No wonder the rebels shout!'

Lord A— noticed not this impertinence directly, but ordered the crier again to command silence; and, when that functionary had done so, his lordship added, fixing his eye on the insolent offender, 'And whoever dares again to violate the decency and solemnity of this court, I will commit him.'

The bullying foreman quailed before the dignified rebuke, and his lordship proceeded in a businesslike tone to the whole jury:

'I cannot avoid, gentlemen, receiving and recording your verdict; which neither can I resist stigmatising as disgraceful to yourselves individually and collectively—for you must be either fools, or worse. But I am not bound to pronounce sentence on the prisoner on that verdict—and I will not; neither will I rest this night until I despatch a special messenger to the lord-lieutenant, to represent the case and have your verdict set aside; and I promise here, in open court, to the prisoner, that with all convenient speed he shall be liberated from prison.'

After the admonition of the judge to the jurymen, the assembled multitude had sufficient good taste to repress any tumultuous expression of joy; but a low murmur of pleasure ran round the court, and Kathleen, and Mary, and her mother, embraced Rory across the bar before he was withdrawn under the gaoler's care.

The jury was discharged, the judge left the bench, and the court became gradually deserted when the exciting cause which had crowded its interior to suffocation was over; but there were little knots in its whereabouts, talking over the stirring events of the day under feelings of varied excitement. The jurymen, before they separated, animadverted upon the extraordinary conduct of the judge in no measured terms.

'By G—d! sir,' said the foreman to his brothers, 'there's an end to our glorious constitution if these things are permitted to go on! What's the use of trial by jury, if a jury can't hang any man they think fit? I ask you, what's the use of a jury otherwise? But here's a d—d rebel judge comes down and refuses to hang him; you know, if that's permitted, there's an end to all justice!—'tis the *judge* is the jury in that case, and all the vagabonds in the country may do what they like.'

'I think,' added another, 'that we should send an address to the lord-lieutenant, signed by us all *in person*, protesting against the injustice, and declaring the danger to the Constitution if such a daring proceeding as a judge daring to presume to refuse a verdict is dared to be permitted in such times as these, with popery and slavery, brass money and wooden shoes, staring us in the face! Sir, the lord-lieutenant himself wouldn't *dare* to refuse such an address!'

'I don't think he would, sir,' said a third. 'You know, if property is not represented, what becomes of the country? And he is twelve men of property, and a rebel judge refuses to take their verdict—which is, as I say, not representing the property of the country; and if property is not represented, what becomes of British connection—I should like to know that! What will the lord-lieutenant say to that?'

'He can't do less than suspend the judge *per tumperis*, and we'll address him to that effect *sine die*—that is *my* motto; and when the matter is properly represented to the minister—'

'I think it should go before the bishop,' interrupted a juryman.

'My good friend, when I say "the minister," I don't *mean* the minister—that is, the minister *you* mean—the Protestant minister: *I* mean the *ministerial* minister.'

'Oh! I beg pardon—I see: you mean the big-wigs at th' other side. Very good, capital idea! Suppose we were to sign a deputation to them, and forward it, *paying the postage of course?*'

'That would be only respectful,' said one of them who had not yet spoken.

'What's this you're all talking about?' said Sweeny, who now joined the group.

'About this extraordinary affair.'

'Certainly,' said the apothecary-yeomanry-attorney; 'most infamous! Never witnessed such a decision in all my life—a judge refusing to purge the country! Where's our Constitution if the country's not purged?—I ask any gentleman that. Such conduct in a judge is most extraordinary—I may say, miraculous! It is a sort of premium on rebellion; in fact, *a bonus.*'

'They'll bone us all, sir,' said the foreman, 'if they're not put down; and the only way of putting them down is hanging them up.'

'Hang them, certainly—hang them!' said a bacon-merchant, whose custom of hanging flitches rendered him callous to the practice in general.

'We were just talking, Mr. Sweeny, when you came,' said the foreman, 'of addressing a deputation to the ministerial minister on this matter.'

'An excellent idea!' replied Sweeny.

'We were thinking of drawing up a letter—'

'I would recommend it to be engrossed,' said the attorney.

'Very good suggestion, gentlemen,' added the foreman. 'We must get our friend Sweeny to engross the deputation.'

'It will be more respectful,' said the respectable man who backed the suggestion of paying the postage.

'Now, who'll write it?' inquired the foreman, with a certain conscious air, in asking the question, that he himself was the proper person.

'Oh, you—you, of course,' was answered by more than one.

'Why, really,' said the foreman bashfully, 'I think we ought to club our heads.'

'Sir,' said Sweeny, grinning, thereby giving every one notice he was going to say a good thing, 'the rebels are ready enough to club our heads, without doing it ourselves!—Ha! ha! ha!'

A corresponding grin and 'Ha! ha! ha!' followed Sweeny's witticism: and a running fire of 'Very good! very good!' went the round of the jurymen.

'But I do think,' continued the foreman, 'this deputation thing should be done by a comit-ée.'

'No one can do it better than you, worthy foreman,' said Sweeny, toadying the man who so readily backed his attempt at the engrossing job.

'I think so too,' said the postage-man; 'you have the pen of a ready-writer, sir.'

'True,' said Sweeny; 'or, as *we* say *correcto colomel*.—Then, my dear sir, as it seems to be the general wish of the jury—or, as I may say, *pro con*— that you are to do it, I'll go along with you and take your instructions.'

This terminated the jury consultation; and Sweeny was walking off with the foreman, when, one of the constables addressed him, to say that his honour Justice Slink wanted to speak to him.

'Then I must be off,' said Sweeny. 'You see I *am* so engaged—in short, I'm a *fee-to-tum*,—I might almost say, a *tee*-totum, for I'm going round and round them all.—I'll go over to you, however, to breakfast to-morrow, and take the instructions.'

Sweeny followed the constable, who led him to a room in the court-house where Slink awaited him. The brow of the justice was clouded, and his tone was angry as he addressed the attorney.

'A pretty bungle Scrubbs has made of this business!'

'My dear justice, it is not his fault, after all.'

'Pooh! pooh!—didn't we tell him on no account to appear until the rascal's trial was over?'

'So we did. But, you see, the trial occurred a day later than we calculated, and I told Scrubbs he might go home on Wednesday.'

'Zounds! why didn't you stop him?'

'I endeavoured to do so, my dear justice, by sending over a messenger last night; but he missed him.'

'It's d—d unfortunate! that's all I can say,' said Slink, 'Come home, however, and dine with me;—I'm as hungry as a hawk, kicking my heels here about the court all day, and for no good, since that rebel has escaped. Come along! it can't be helped,—the old saying, you know, "The devil's children have the devil's luck;" and so that rascal Rory O'More has cheated the gallows.'

'We may be down on him yet,' said Sweeny, following the magistrate homewards to eat a good dinner, with a good appetite, notwith-standing the conspiracy he had joined in against a fellow creature's life: for being apprised of Scrubbs' return to Ireland before the trial, he and the justice considered it an ingenious device, to induce the Collector to remain concealed until it was over, for the purpose of hanging an innocent man, whom they considered a dangerous person—but whose life, by the interference of Providence, was preserved from the murderous attempt;—and he, in defence of whose liberty poor Rory had encountered so many perils, and whose trial arose from that very cause,—even he was miscreant enough to join the horrible conspiracy, and consent to the murder of the man who had been his champion.

Yet this atrocious triad were considered eminently useful persons by the Irish executive at that period; and it was of such persons, it was said by the adherents of government, 'that the country would be lost without them.' And, indeed, government seemed to think so too: for Sweeny rapidly rose in law preferment, being made crown-solicitor for the district; Scrubbs was advanced to a place of great emolument in the metropolitan custom-house; and Justice Slink was created a knight, and in due time a baronet.

XLV

*Showing how the verdict for the hanging of one produces
the banishment of many.*

IT WAS WITH FEELINGS OF intense anxiety De Lacy awaited the return of his friend from the court-house; and with open arms he received him, when he saw by the expression of his countenance all was right before he had spoken a word.

'He's safe,' said the lawyer.

'Thanks! thanks! my dear friend!' exclaimed De Lacy, pressing his hand with fervour. 'Have you brought him with you?'

'He is not yet liberated.'

'And why not, after his acquittal?'

'I did not say he was acquitted; I only said he was safe.—There now, don't look so wretchedly anxious;—let me sit down, for I am exhausted, and I will tell you all about it.'

He then hastily gave him a sketch of the trial: and when he repeated the verdict of the jury, De Lacy fancied he was only joking.

'I assure you 'tis true.'

'What! find a man guilty of murder when the person he is accused of murdering is produced before them?'

'True as gospel, I protest.'

'My good fellow, I cannot believe,—you're joking!'

'On my honour, then, since you won't believe less, it is the fact.'

'But, surely they cannot hang him?'

'Fortunately for him, they cannot; but they would if they could. Lord A—n—e, I need not tell you, would not pronounce sentence on such a verdict and even assured the prisoner, before he quitted the bench, that his life was in no danger: however, he could not help allowing the verdict to be recorded.'

'And *what* a record!' exclaimed De Lacy; 'what a brand of infamy and folly upon the men who gave it, and the times in which we live! One might laugh at the absurdity of the act, only for its atrocity: but here, really mirth is reproved by horror, and the smile gives place to a shudder.'

'My dear fellow, don't be so eloquent,—remember 'twas an *Irish* verdict,' said his friend, who smiled at De Lacy's warmth.

'Nay, nay, I cannot trifle on this matter—I cannot!—Good God! what man's life is safe here under such circumstances?'

'Oh, don't mistake me, De Lacy; 'twas only for the sake of rousing your virtuous indignation I said what I did: and remember, my dear fellow, after all, your Rory's safe. But, seriously speaking, it is certainly a most rascally affair, and I quite agree in every word you have uttered.'

'Well,' said De Lacy, after a moment's silence and with a long-drawn sigh, 'I'm doomed to be disappointed in everything! I returned to my country with a desire of being a useful member of society—of becoming a quiet and unoffending subject, even under the system such as it is,—of doing all the good within my power; and, so help me heaven! I had thoroughly renounced all the romantic speculations in which you know I have indulged, and hoped to be permitted at least to live unmolested; and even these humble expectations are dashed to destruction the moment my foot touches my native soil—the life of an innocent man is sought to be sacrificed to the demon of party hate in the face of the very laws: even in her temple! By all that's sacred, I would not live in such a country to be king of it!—Now, Ireland—poor Ireland! farewell! As soon as I can put my foot on the deck of a free country's vessel, I will leave you; an American ship shall bear me to her shores, and I will place the Atlantic between me and the bloodhounds that I see are bent on hunting this poor country to death!'

'Do not be too hasty, De Lacy: you may do much good here by remaining; you may live to be the poor man's friend, and become the protector of the weak against the strong.'

'If I thought so, my friend,' returned De Lacy, whose flushed cheek betrayed the warmth of his emotion, 'I would stay:—but the tide runs too strong to make head against.—*I* the protector of the weak against the strong? What mortal power may interpose when the divine emanation from heaven—when *Truth herself* cannot screen the victim from the destroyer! That verdict has not succeeded, *as it was intended to do*—in murdering an innocent man; but it has banished another, who meant to do all in his power to benefit his country.'

'Well, we'll talk of this another time,' said his friend, who wished to divert him from the theme of his indignation. 'As you desired, I have directed the three poor women who walked all the way from their village to the town this morning, to come to the inn for rest and refreshment.'

'True,' said De Lacy; 'I forgot;—I wish much to see them, now that all is over and my presence in the country need not be kept a secret:—are they here?'

'I left them to follow, wishing to hasten to you with the news.'

At this moment the door was opened by a great hulking fellow, with bristling hair, staring eyes, high cheek-bones, a snub nose, and a great mouth with a voice to match, who enacted the part of waiter; and the aforesaid, protruding his head, and nothing more into the room, said as loudly and as rapidly, and with as great a brogue as it could well be said, 'If you plaze, sir—'

'What do you want?' said the lawyer.

'If you plaze, sir, there's wan a wantin' you.'

'Who is it?'

'Three women, sir.'

'And are three women one?' said the lawyer, smiling.

'Only wan *ax'd* for you, sir,' answered the waiter, grinning, ready with his answer.

'And couldn't you say so?'

'By dad, sir, it was the owld one o' the three ax'd for you; and th' other two is mighty purty, and so I thought they would be a grate help: and that's the rayson.'

'Show them up.'

Off went the waiter, and in a few seconds the sound of ascending footsteps announced the approach of Rory's mother and sister, and Kathleen Regan. The door opened: Mary O'More was the first to enter, and De Lacy, advancing to her with extended hand, said in a voice full of kindness, 'Mary, I am glad to see you.'

The girl could not repress a faint scream, and, notwithstanding a manifest effort to control her feelings, her sudden flushing and subsequent pallor betrayed how powerfully the unexpected appearance of De Lacy acted upon her.

'I did not let you know sooner I was here; but I would not be far from Rory, Mary, in his time of need.'

'God bless you; God bless you!' faltered Mary, almost suffocating with contending emotions, which were too much for her, and the poor girl, falling upon her knees, kissed De Lacy's hand fervently, and with half-uttered blessings, sank insensible to the ground.

De Lacy lifted the fainting girl, and bore her to a sofa near the window, which was immediately thrown open for the admission of fresh air. A few minutes served to revive her, and a glass of water partly restored her to composure; but still she exhibited signs of agitation, and the mother said, 'Sure, 'twas no wondher, after all the craythur had gone through that day.'

'No wonder indeed, Mrs. O'More,' said De Lacy. 'But, after all, my friend Rory is safe.'

'Oh, but *is* he safe, sir, do you think?'

'As safe as I am,' said the lawyer; 'do not entertain the least uneasiness.'

'But sure they *gave in* "Guilty," the villains they did, and my boy is taken back to jail!'

'That cannot be helped, and I cannot explain to you why he must remain in prison for a couple of days; but, take my word, he's in no danger.'

'Oh, I can hardly venture my heart with the belief until I see him out o' jail.'

'Take my word too, Mrs. O'More,' said De Lacy, 'and you too, Kathleen, Rory will be with us in a couple of days.'

Kathleen could not speak, but, clasping her hands and pressing them to her bosom, she looked her thanks more touchingly than language could have told them.

'And you, Mary,' added De Lacy turning again to the sofa, where Mary still sat with her eyes fixed on the ground, ashamed of the emotion which the unexpected presence of De Lacy had caused,—'you too, must cheer up. And how have you been all the time Rory and I have been away? You've had hard times of it, Mary, since the Sunday I left the cottage: but I must have my little room there again, for a few days.'

'Ah, sir!' sighed the widow, 'you'll never see your little room agin! the owld house was burnt in the beginning o' the bad times!'

'Burnt!' exclaimed De Lacy, who had not before heard of the calamity.

'Ay, indeed, sir,—and everything in it, but jist ourselves and the clothes on our backs; and little o' thim, for we wor hunted out of our beds, and not a shred or a scrap did we save barrin' the books you left behind you: and Mary, the craythur, thought o' thim in the middle of it all, for the regard she had for thim,—and no wondher!'

Mary reddened to the very forehead as her mother spoke.

'And, sure, you are the rale and thrue friend, Mr. De Lacy,' continued the widow. 'To think of your bein' here yourself, let alone *that* good gintleman you sent to us in our throuble! Oh, may the Lord reward you!—But tell me, sir, do you think *indeed* my darling boy is safe?'

'Perfectly safe,—rest satisfied on that point. And now, Mrs. O'More, come over here and sit down at the table; we all want some refreshment;—come over.'

'It's time, sir, we should be goin' home; we have a good step to walk, and—'

'You must not leave the town this evening,' said De Lacy. 'I have ordered you all beds here to-night; therefore you may take your dinner in comfort, and we will talk over old times, Mrs. O'More.'

As he spoke, the waiter entered with a hot joint, and slapped down the dish on the table, spilling half the gravy over the tablecloth and upsetting a couple of glasses, which reached the ground with a grand smash.

'Bad luck to thim for glasses—they're always fallin'!' said he, as he picked up the larger pieces of the broken glass and threw it into the fire.

Mrs. O'More protested for some time against dining, declaring it was too much trouble, etc.; all of which meant, on her part, as well as that of the girls, that they felt awkward in sitting down to table with the strange gentleman. De Lacy had often been the companion of their dinner in their own cabin; but now that he was in an hotel, and with the presence of a second person of superior rank, it made all the difference. However, their modest scruples were at length overcome, and the easy and unaffected bearing of the barrister set them soon as much at ease as they could be under such circumstances.

In the course of the evening, the lawyer could not avoid remarking the downcast looks of Mary O'More, and the timid glances she sometimes ventured to cast towards De Lacy; and this, when considered together with the beauty of the girl, raised certain surmises in the mind of the young lawyer which were not justified by any conduct on the part of his friend. The women retired soon after dinner; and, indeed, the fatigues of the day made an early retreat to bed absolutely necessary.

When De Lacy and his friend were alone, the latter remarked, what a lovely specimen Mary O'More presented of a peasant girl.

'They are both handsome girls,' answered De Lacy.

'That's an ingenious escape, my friend,' said the lawyer; 'but, I'm not greatly mistaken, you have been making sad work with that poor girl's heart.'

'Do you imagine I could be such a scoundrel?' answered De Lacy, rather warmly

'My good fellow, I don't mean you would harbour a dishonourable intention to man or woman breathing; but, somehow or other, that poor girl is desperately in love with you, however it has taken place. Did you not observe her emotion at sight of you,—her not daring to meet your eyes? and I could see many a bashful look at you when she thought herself unobserved.'

'My dear Hal,' said De Lacy, 'it is only gratitude for my care of her brother, nothing more—it can be nothing more.'

'Maybe so,' said the lawyer, who saw the subject had better be dropped;

and turning the conversation into another channel, they chatted and sipped their wine until it was time to retire to rest.

The lawyer did retire to rest, but De Lacy only went to bed. He could not rest: his anxiety during the day, his indignation at the verdict, his determination to leave the country, and the dawning projects which opened on his speculative mind with relation to his intended removal to America, kept him in a state of wakefulness. Then the remarks of his friend before they parted for the night had more influence upon him than his answers would have led one to suppose: though he affected to disbelieve the source of Mary O'More's emotion, the evidence had not been unnoticed by himself, and it made him unhappy. Then her mother's little anecdote of *his* books being the only things saved from the ruin of their cottage when it was devoted to the flames: the cause was plain enough to give a libertine pleasure, but a man of principle, pain.

'Poor girl,' thought De Lacy, 'I would not for the world that I should prove the cause of such an innocent and lovely creature's unhappiness! I should never forgive myself. And yet, why should I say, forgive? I never breathed a word, nor made the slightest allusion, to awaken such a sentiment in her heart; but, then, I lived under the same roof for some months, was constantly in her presence, and gave her those unfortunate books: that was unwise—I see it was; but God knows my heart! it was innocently done. What unaccountable things are human feelings! Here is this poor peasant girl betrayed into an attachment of which she must know the hopelessness; for she is a sensible creature, and one who would shudder at the suspicion being entertained of her indulging an unrequited affection, for she is delicate-minded as one more highly born. And yet she does love, I fear me; and reason awakes but to warn her to conceal what it was not strong enough to prevent. Alas! how often feeling triumphs over reason!—how unequal is the struggle between them! How are we to account for this unequal balance? Why is this reason given as a guide if there be insufficiency in its guidance on any occasion, or in any trial?—why? And thus De Lacy fell into a train of metaphysical musing, which sent him to sleep, as it would do the reader were I to recount it.

XLVI

In which Rory follows De Lacy's advice and his own inclinations.

LORD A—N—E WAS AS GOOD as his word: he lost no time in representing Rory's case to the lord-lieutenant, and procuring his discharge from prison. When he was at liberty, De Lacy told him his intention of leaving Ireland, and recommended him to bear him company, as he did not consider his life would be safe if he remained.

'Arrah! how could I lave the mother, and Mary, and—?'

'Kathleen?' added De Lacy.

'Yis,' said Rory, smiling. 'I don't deny it, though you never gave me a hint o' that before.'

'I can see as far into a mill-stone as most people, Rory. Now, I do not want you to leave them: they can bear you company.'

'Sure, they'd feel mighty sthrange in France, sir.'

'I did not say a word about France. What would you think of America?'

'Oh that's another affair! But how could I take them there?—we are not as snug as we were wanst; and that would take a power o' money.'

'Money has nothing to do with the question, Rory. Come with me. I intend selling off everything I am worth, and going to the back settlements of America—there I shall buy a large tract of ground, and shall want many about me; and how much better for me to have those I know and regard than strangers! You shall be my head man there,

Rory, and teach me to farm. And, before you go, set your heart at rest on one project I know it is bent upon: you shall marry Kathleen Regan to-morrow if you like.'

'That's a grate temptation!' said Rory.

'But, whether you come or not, Rory, let not want of money in any way stand between you and your wishes: I will give Kathleen a marriage portion, enough to set you up in comfort again. If you remain here—which, however, I strongly advise you against, after the specimen you have had of Irish justice the other day—what can you expect but persecution in this unfortunate country? You may marry and have a family, and leave them fatherless some day by a sudden and violent death; while, if you come with me, you may live to see them grow up about you, helping you in the cultivation of your farm and becoming the props of your age.'

'Misther De Lacy, I can't thank you, sir—in throth I can't, for all your *heart* to me. I won't spake—I *can't* spake;' and the poor fellow paused, and drew his hand across his eyes: 'but you've made me the happiest fellow in Ireland this day. God bless you!—Oh, thin, but it's I that will marry my darlin' girl the very minit she'll let me spake to the priest; and that'll be *smart*, if I've my own way. So, you see, sir, I'm no churl in refusing your bounty, but take your offer with a heart and a half; and may you get the reward of all your kindness to me, in meeting a girl that's worthy of yourself, and will love you as my own Kathleen loves me; and that you may taste the pleasure yourself you have bestowed on me, in the prospect of hugging to my heart the girl of my bosom Sure, little I thought— —'

'Rory, my dear fellow, say no more,—say no more: you're too grateful.'

'That's what no man *can* be, sir. I wouldn't be mane,—and I'm sure you know it; but, by the powers! I'd take the heart out of my body if I could, and lay it undher the feet of the one that was kind and generous to me.'

'There now Rory, that's enough,—say no more. You're a good fellow, and a kind man—and deserve more than that at my hands: and now tell me, will you come with me? or shall I get you a little farm here?'

'Throth, I'll be said and led by you, that's such a good frind. It goes agin me hard, I don't deny it, to lave the owld counthry, and the places my heart warms to at the sight of. Sure, I used to dhrame of thim when I was with you in France; and could see the river, and the hills, and the cottage, and the owld rath, as plain as if I was on the spot: and won't it be the same when I'm in another strange land?—my heart will be always longing afther my darlin' Ireland, and the owld tunes of her be ringin' in my ears all day. Oh, but *the shamrocks is close at my heart!*'

'Rory, there are many of our countrymen in America; and there you will feel less difference of country, from the use of the same language. But I do not want to force your inclinations: if you wish to remain in Ireland, do so; but I decidedly recommend you not.'

'Thin I'll do what you recommend, sir, I'll follow you: and indeed, I b'lieve you're right enough, for the poor counthry is ground down to powdher, and will be worse, I'm afeard. So, in the Lord's name! poor Ireland, good-bye to you! though, God knows, it cuts me to the heart's core to quit you. I'm foolish, Misther De Lacy,—I know I'm foolish; so I'll bid you good mornin', sir, and set off to Knockbrackin, and ask the girl to have me, and tell her that it's yourself is more than a father to her, and gives her the fortune. And may the angels——'

'There—there now, Rory; no more thanks. But, as you say I am more than Kathleen's father, it reminds me that I must not be less than her father; so I will give her away.'

'Musha! but you're the very sowl of good-nature, Misther De Lacy. By all that's good, your heart is nothing but a honeycomb!'

'Be off, now, Rory: and give Kathleen my compliments, and tell her she must name next Sunday for her wedding; for I perceive, by an advertisement in this paper I've been reading, that a ship sails in ten days from Cork; and I am going there to make arrangements for my passage. Will you say at once, you and yours will come in the same ship?'

'In God's name, sir, yis!' said Rory, reverently. 'I know they'll all do what you think best, with as ready a heart as myself.'

'Farewell, then, Rory! Next Sunday I shall be at Knockbrackin, to give you Kathleen: and I wish you joy with her! There now, be off!

not a word more. Go and get yourself and your pretty wife ready for
Sunday.'

Rory departed, and De Lacy, when he was gone, ordered a
postchaise for Cork. He there made all arrangements requisite for
the passage of himself and his dependants, and was ready to keep
his appointment at Knockbrackin, where, when Rory arrived,
there was overwhelming joy at all the good news he brought
them; news, however, not unmingled with pain; for the thought of
leaving Ireland touched the women's feelings as much as Rory's.
But, admitting the truth of all De Lacy's arguments in favour of
emigration, which Rory detailed to them, they acknowledged it
to be the safest course to pursue, and one that opened to them
an easier life than could be hoped for in their native land. Still it
was their native land, and their hearts clung to it, and every hour
in the day was crossed by some recollection which embittered the
thought of leaving it. One thing, however, helped to dissipate their
melancholy,—the approaching wedding; and the Sunday morning
smiled brightly on the happy family,—happier than they had been
for many a long day. De Lacy arrived before the hour when mass
commenced, and driving up to the door of the little village cabin,
was welcomed and hailed with blessings by all its inmates as he
entered it.

'There are some articles to be removed from the chaise,' said De
Lacy. 'I have brought a wedding-cake from Cork, and some few other
things, for the bridal of the lady I'm to give away;—which is only
right, you know, Mrs. O'More.'

'Oh, thin, but the kindness of you, Misther De Lacy dear,' said the
mother,—'to remember even such little things as that! Throth, now I
think more of it than even the portion. God bless you!—Dear, dear!'
repeated the old woman, as parcel after parcel was taken from the
chaise; 'here's bottles upon bottles!'

'A little wine, Mrs. O'More, which I know you couldn't get in the
village; and his reverence will like a good glass, no doubt.'

'And, oh dear! the illigaut smell!—why, if it isn't tay! Well, Misther
De Lacy, but you *are*—'

'That's not to be had either in the village, you know, Mrs. O'More; but the whisky-punch we can make out here. By the by, is there a public-house that I can manage to get some substantial entertainment from? for you must ask all your friends to the wedding-feast.'

'Oh, but you *are* the darlin' gintleman! Sure, we are happy enough in ourselves.'

'No, no, Mrs. O'More: the lady I give away must have her friends about her, to wish her joy, and drink long life and prosperity to her.'

'Good luck to your kind heart, sir! Well, we'll manage it as you plaze, sir, and I'll ask what friends we may see at the chapel to come to us; and sure they won't stand on a short axin', but will come with a heart and a half to wish the *colleen* joy.'

It is needless to detail the ceremony of the wedding. Suffice it to say that Rory received his pretty blushing Kathleen from the hands of De Lacy; and that, when the nuptial benediction was pronounced over them, Rory lost no time in getting the first kiss from the bride, which was a regular smacker. 'Long life to you, Mrs. O'More!' said Rory, laughing in her crimsoned face, as he lifted her from her knees.

'There's part of her portion, Rory,' said De Lacy, 'for immediate expenses,' as he placed in his hand a green silk purse containing a hundred guineas.

'Long life to you, sir! you're too good!' said Rory. 'The green and goold is mighty purty in a flag;[1] but 'pon my sowl I don't know if it does not look quite as well in a man's hand.'

The invitations were made right and left at the chapel door, and nothing loath, the friends invited returned home with the bride and bridegroom to partake of the hospitality De Lacy had provided for them: and there was a larger company than the house would accommodate, but the good-humoured neighbours sat on the sod outside, while the most *responsible* people were honoured by being smothered within.

The priest and De Lacy, with the bride and bridesmaids, sat at the head of the table, where the wine was circulated, and plenty of whisky-punch was to be had below the salt. After his reverence and

the founder of the feast had had enough, they vacated the house, to
give room for tea being prepared for the female part of the party, and
repaired to the sod outside, where fiddler and piper were ready to set
the boys and girls together by the heels.

De Lacy led out the bride for the first dance, and the example was
followed by many a sporting couple after; and when some cessation
occurred in the dance, notice was given that 'the tay' was ready within,
while more punch was distributed without.

The tea seemed in high favour with the women, to the best of
whom the commonest quality would have proved a luxury, as that
which they had generally drunk had been partly made from the same
hedges which supplied them with brooms; so that the high-flavoured
exotic which De Lacy's kindness had provided was a marvel amongst
them.

'Dear! dear! Mrs. O'More,' said an old neighbour, who had already
taken extensive liberties with the tea-pot, and who, if tea could have
produced the same effects as spirits, must have died of spontaneous
combustion; 'but that is the most beautiful tay!'

'Sure, my dear,' said the widow, 'and Mr. De Lacy brought it
himself,—his own self.'

'Why, does he *dale in tay?*' said the old woman.

'Whish—t!' said Mrs. O'More with a frown; 'he's a gintleman, my
dear, aud wouldn't dale in anything.'

'—But compliments,' said the old woman: 'see how he's talkin' to
Mary over there!'

'My dear woman,' said the widow confidentially, 'this tay he brought
from his own estate, where it grows,—and that's the rayson it's so
fine.'

'Arrah, and where is that, Mrs. O'More, my dear?'

'In France,' said the widow: 'but don't tell anybody.'

'Tut! tut! tut!—sure, I know av coorse we mustn't say a word
about France now, God help uz!' said the old woman, raising her eyes
and eyebrows, and pursing her mouth with a ludicrous expression
of melancholy: 'and, indeed, I'll take another cup o' tay, my dear, to
comfort me.'

'To be sure, agra,' said the widow, bending the tea-pot over the old crone's cup so far beyond a rectangular position, that the lid fell off and broke a piece out of the tea-cup it was over.—'Pooh! pooh!—murdher! there's not a dhrop o' wather in the pot: where's the kittle?'

The attendant spirit of the kettle supplied more of the native element; and after a few minutes to let it draw, Mrs. O'More replenished the old lady's cup.

'I'm afeard it's wake now, ma'am,' said the widow; 'bekaze, you see, I let it stand a good dale at first;—for tay is nothing without you let it stand.'

'Right,' said Phelim O'Flanagan, who was in the neighbourhood and overheard the conversation,—'Right, Mrs. O'More, my dear,—tay is never worth a thraneen unless you let it stand: and the great particularity, or peculiar distinctive property, or denomination, as I may say, of tay, is, that it differs from all other human things; for while other human things grows wake with standin', tay grows sthrong.—Ha, ha, ha!'

'Ah, go 'long with you, Phelim!—you're always comin' in with your larnin' and your quare sayin's.—But, as I was tellin' you, ma'am,' pursued the widow to her neighbour, 'I let the tay stand a long time, to *burst the grain*: for if you don't burst the grain, what good is it?'

'Sartinly,' said her neighbour; 'but you see, if you take the good out of it at wanst, that-a-way, there's no good in it afther. And there's the grate beauty o' this tay. Oh, but it's iligant tay!—it takes sitch a *beautiful grip o' the second wather!*'

'A song! a song!' was echoed round the room so loudly as to drwn the tea discussion; and a universal call was made on the bride to set the example of the favourite national custom.

Kathleen blushed, and felt somewhat shy at being the first to make herself an object of attention, where already, from other causes, she was sufficiently so; but, encouraged by Rory, and feeling on her own part the necessity of helping to make her friends happy, and therefore complying with their wishes, she sang, with exquisite expression, a little song in her own language; which will be more agreeable to the reader in English.

OH! ONCE I HAD LOVERS.

Oh! once I had lovers in plenty,
When a colleen I lived in the glen:
I killed fifty before I was twenty,—
How happy the moments flew then!
Then winter I ne'er could discover,
For Love brighten'd Time's dusky wing;
When every new month brought a lover,
The year, then, seem'd always like spring.

But Cupid's more delicate pinion
Could never keep up with old Time:
So, the grey-beard assumes his dominion,
When the mid-day of life rings its chime.
Then gather, while morning is shining,
Some flower, while the bright moments last
Which, closely around the heart twining,
Will live when the summer is past.

The song bore so strong an allusion to her own immediate position,
that it was peculiarly touching; and, amid the burst of approbation
which followed the lyric, the silent pressure of Rory's hand, and her
own confiding look at her husband, showed he had felt all she wished
to convey by her song.

'That is a most beautiful flight of fancy,' said Phelim, so loud as to
be heard, 'about Cupid and Time! And why shouldn't it be a flight,
when both o' thim has wings, as the potes, anshint and prophane, tells
us?—for, as the classics say, *Tempus fugit.*'

Mary O'More was now requested, as bridesmaid, to favour the
company with a song: and her mother at once asked her 'to sing that
purty song she was always singin'; and that indeed, she hadn't a purtier
song among thim all.'

'What song, mother?' asked Mary, blushing up to the eyes.

'That "Land o' the West." Wherever you got it, sure it's a beautiful song.'

De Lacy, caught by the name of his own song, of which he was not conscious of a copy existing but the one he had rescued from the papers of Adèle Verbigny, fixed his eyes on Mary O'More, who was crimsoned over from her forehead to her shoulder, and had her eyes fixed on the ground.

'Sing it, *alanna,*—sing it!' said her mother.

'I'd rather sing something else, ma'am.'

'Now I'll have no song but that, Mary: and, indeed, there's no song you sing aiqual to it.'

Thus forced, Mary, after a few nervous hems, began, in a voice which was tremulous from emotion:

> Oh, come to the West, love,—oh, come there with me;
> 'Tis a sweet land of verdure that springs from the sea,
> Where fair Plenty smiles from her emerald throne;—
> Oh, come to the West, and I'll make thee my own!
> I'll guard thee, I'll tend thee, I'll love thee the best,
> And you'll say there's no land like the land of the West!

That's Ireland, for sartin!' said Phelim. Mary continued:

> The South has its roses and bright skies of blue,
> But ours are more sweet with love's own changeful hue—
> Half sunshine, half tears, like the girl I love best;—
> Oh, what is the South to the beautiful West!
> Then come to the West, and the rose on thy mouth
> Will be sweeter to me than the flowers of the South!

There were several audible smacks at the conclusion of this verse, and numerous suppressed exclamations of 'Behave yourself!' were heard in coquettish female voices.

The song went on:

> The North has its snow-tow'rs of dazzling array,
> All sparkling with gems in the ne'er-setting day:
> There the Storm-king may dwell in the halls he loves best,

But the soft-breathing Zephyr he plays in the West.
Then come there with me, where no cold wind doth blow,
And thy neck will seem fairer to me than the snow!

De Lacy could not resist admiring the beautiful and snowy bosom of the singer, which heaved with agitation as she sang.

Phelim, before she could resume, thundered in his annotation: 'That's a fine touch about the winds,—Boreas, Austher, Vosther, Eurus, et Zephyrus!'

Again Mary plucked up courage, and finished:

The Sun in the gorgeous East chaseth the night
When he riseth, refresh'd, in his glory and might!
But where doth he go when he seeks his sweet rest?
Oh! doth he not haste to the beautiful West!

'Pars Occidentalis!' shouted Phelim.

Then come there with me; 'tis the land I love best,
'Tis the land of my sires!—'tis my own darling West!

'Owld Ireland for ever!—hurroo!' was shouted from all; and a thunder of applause followed.

When the song was over, De Lacy could not resist the curiosity which prompted him to know how Mary O'More had become possessed of the song; and he approached the girl and asked her.

'It was written on a bit of paper, sir, and between the leaves of one of the books you gave me.'

'But there was no music to it. How did you get that?'

'Oh, sometimes I go about singing, sir, whatever comes into my head; and so I made a tune to it.'

'And a beautiful tune it is!' said De Lacy.

Here the voice of the priest broke in and interrupted further conversation.

'My good people,' said the priest, 'it is time now to go home. You know the martial law is out;—and you mustn't be out when that law is out.'

'Thrue for your reverence, 'faith,' was responded by some of the *responsible* old men.

'So, boys and girls,—and, indeed, my good people of all denominations,—go your ways home in time, aud keep out of harm's way:—it is not like the good owld times, when we could stop till the night was ripe, and we could throw the stocking, and do the thing dacently, as our fathers used to do before us but we must make the best of a bad bargain, and go home before the sun is down. So let us lave the hospitable roof where we have got the bit and sup, and *cead mile fealté*, and wishing the young couple health and happiness, lave them with their mother.'

A universal leave-taking now commenced, and heartfelt good wishes were poured upon the bride and bridegroom, accompanied with a profusion of hand-shaking, and a sprinkling of small jokes from the frisky old men and women, which were laughed at by the young ones; and, laughing and singing, they went their different ways,—the mirth radiating as it were from the focus where it had its birth, and, like circles on a lake, becoming weaker as it grew wide; till the sounds of merriment died away in the distance, and the cabin, so noisy a few minutes before, became silent. De Lacy was the last to take his leave: he offered his best wishes for the happiness of those whose happiness was, in fact, of his making, and was followed, as he left the family group, by their thanks and blessings.

1. The National colours.

XLVII

De Lacy muses like a gentleman, but feels like a man; and the reader is told all the author can tell him, and left to guess the rest.

Silently and thoughtfully he wended his way to the little public-house where he was to be accommodated for the night, the 'Land of the West' still ringing in his ears,—that song which he had written for the accomplished girl who had deceived him, and valued not by her—treasured up and sung by a simple peasant girl, who more and more, he perceived, had become attached to him,—in short, *loved* him—there was no weaker term applicable; and that girl, beautiful, sensitive, pure-minded, modest, and delicate in feeling as a lady. Ay, there was the point—*a lady*— '*if she were a lady.*' This question arose silently in De Lacy's mind, and his answer to it was a sigh. 'No, no,' thought he, 'it cannot be!—those *mésalliances* are terrible things! Could I, from my name and station, descend to wed a country girl?—No; the world would laugh at me, sneer at me;—"*So Horace De Lacy picked up with a country wench!*" would sound well in the mouth of those who know me:—no, no, it must not be! And yet there's no denying I like the girl,—like her well enough even to marry her;—ay, and *if she were but a lady*, a better wife, and truer and fonder companion, would she be, than the fribble Frenchwoman who jilted me; and there is more truth and simple faith and real affection in that poor girl's heart than in many a courtly dame whose quarterings could match my own. And why should I be less liberal in those matters than in questions of equal importance?—should I, a democrat, be the stickler for high birth in a wife?—What fools we are, after all, in such matters! The slavery of custom is upon us, do what we can to shake it off, and the sneer of a fool is too much in perspective for the firmness of the wisest man.—Poor Mary!—poor girl!—I wish the devil had me before I ever came in her way! And that song too—how deliciously she sang it!— sweet enough to charm a drawing-room,—*if she were a gentlewoman.*—Confound that eternal question—how it plagues me! And, after all, why should she not be a gentlewoman? Suppose for an instant she were my wife: Madame De Lacy would be raised to my rank, and in truth she is naturally well-bred,—with the *patois* of her country, and wanting the *manière d'être* of a fashionable belle, 'tis true; but I never heard the girl say, or saw her do, what could be called a rude or vulgar thing; slight care would give her manner, and her own good sense would keep her quiet till she acquired it.

'What folly is this! here am I supposing a case which can never be; all my prejudices rise in arms against it—*I dare not do it!* What should I feel, on entering a drawing-room, to see the searching eye, and hear the whisper running round the room, as I presented my "country wench"? No! no! no!—Horace: that would never do!

'Yet how unjust is all this on my part! Here am I supposing this drawing-room case, and I am quitting Europe, and all who know me, for ever! I am going to the backwoods of America. Who will know there that Mary O'More is not a gentlewoman born, or that Horace De Lacy is the descendant of a Norman line? And when once there, could I repose my faith on a purer spirit, my heart on a truer affection, or my head on a fairer bosom? Could I desire a more lovely or loveable woman for my wife?—My common sense and common manhood answer, No! and yet does the prejudice of De Lacy rebel against the thought.—Mary O'More, I wish to heaven you were of higher birth!'

Such was the working of De Lacy's brain all through the evening, until he retired to bed. Even then, dreams usurped the place of sleep. He imagined himself with his country wife on his arm, in a drawing-room; a row of perfumed puppies lined the walls and occupied the *fauteuils* as he entered; glances of disdain were cast towards Mary's foot (which was a very pretty foot, by the way); he looked down, and instead of a satin shoe, a country brogue was peeping from beneath her velvet robe! He was in a fever: the lady of the mansion approached— she addressed in accents of fashionable ease Madame De Lacy, who answered in a very rich brogue: a titter ran round the circle,—De Lacy started and awoke.

When he next dropped into dozing, the wide-spreading forest of America was before him: there was its girdle of splendid colour circling the clearance which his own hand had helped to make, and where the thriving crops of different sorts were growing: the sunset was tinging all around with its golden light, and he thought Mary was his wife, and, with her arms circling his neck, she was looking up into his eyes with glowing affection, and saying, 'Are we not happy?'

He clasped her to his breast, and kissed her, and said, 'Yes, happier here than in our native land!'

'But still its remembrance is very dear, Horace;' and a tinge of sweet tenderness came over her face.

'So it is, dearest,' answered De Lacy: 'sit down under the shade of this tree and sing me "The Land of the West."'

And in his dream he thought sounds never were so sweet as that song of his own, sung by the woman he loved.

De Lacy awoke unrefreshed and weary. There is nothing so fatiguing as an unsatisfied action of the mind, which we cannot repress nor escape from.

De Lacy knew that business was the surest relief from such annoyance, and he started at an early hour for Cork to finish his arrangement for sailing, and wrote to Rory, desiring him and his family to follow, appointing time and place for their rendezvous.

A few days sufficed to bring them together again, and an immediate embarkation took place, for the wind was fair and the favourable.

Old Phelim O'Flanagan accompanied the O'Mores to the ship; and De Lacy, touched by this proof of attachment, offered to take him with them.

'Thanks to you in bushels, and may blessings in pailfuls be powered upon you! I'll stay in the owld place. We mustn't transplant owld sticks, though the saplin's may thrive the betther of it. But I am obleeged to you all the same;—I could be of no use in a new place.'

'I beg your pardon, Phelim: I'll find use for you if you'll come. Your learning, Phelim, would make you an acquisition in a new place;—it is *there* you *would* be particularly useful.'

'Proud am I of your opinion, Misther De Lacy,' said Phelim, immensely pleased at this compliment to his learning—'proud am I, and plazed: but thin, if you talk of a *new* counthry, sure I must think of the *owld* one; and what would the country here do without me?'

'That's a difficulty, certainly,' answered De Lacy, smiling; 'but you shouldn't sacrifice your own interest too much to your patriotism. Come with me, and I'll be your friend as long as you live, Phelim.'

'Oh! *proh pudor!* and it's ashamed I am not to be more worthy of your honour's frindship: and, indeed, a good frind and a thrue frind you are; or, as the Latins say, *amicus certus:* but, all the same, I'll lave my bones in owld Ireland; and when I'm gone, maybe I'll go see you—that is, if sper'ts is permitted to crass the say.'

'God keep us! Phelim,' said Mrs. O'More; 'don't hant us, if you plaze.'

De Lacy, when he could recover himself sufficiently from the laughter which Phelim's speech produced, said:

'Rum and brandy were the only spirits he ever heard of crossing the sea.'

'Ay—ardent sper'ts,' replied Phelim. 'Throth, thin, my sper't is as ardent as ever it was, and, at all events, wishes you happiness and prosperity; and—'

Here the old man's eyes began to glisten with tears, and his voice failed him. His thin lips essayed to utter a few words, and trembled with the pang of saying 'Farewell:' but the word remained unuttered, and a tremulous pressure of each hand of the friends he was parting from was the last signal of affection which passed between them.

The decks were now cleared of all save the sailors and passengers; the boats of the attendant friends pushed off; and it was not until old Phelim was seated in the skiff which bore him to the shore that he felt something in his hand, which he opened to look at; it was a purse with several gold pieces in it. He remembered De Lacy had been the last to shake hands with him.

'God bless him! he did not forget even the poor owld man he was leaving behind!' and the 'poor old man' dropped his head upon his knees and cried bitterly.

The sails were shaken out, and, swelling to the breeze, bore the vessel from the lovely harbour of Cove. The ship was soon cleaving the waters of the Atlantic, and the tearful eyes of many an emigrant were turned towards the shore they should never see again.

In one close group stood Rory and those who were dear to him. De Lacy was not of their party, but paced up and down the deck alone, and felt a keener pang at quitting his country than he could have imagined; and as her cliffs were lessening to his view, the more they became endeared to his imagination, and associations to which he did not think his heart was open asserted their influence over the exile.

In an hour the deck was clearer; many had gone below, for the evening was closing fast: but still Rory and his group stood in the same spot, and looked towards the land; and still De Lacy paced the deck alone, and felt most solitary.

The wide ocean was before him, and the free wind sweeping him from all he had known, to the land where he knew none. He was a stranger on the sea; he was lonely, and he felt his loneliness.

He looked at Rory O'More, the centre of a group whom he loved, and who loved him, and he envied the resignation which sat on the faces of Kathleen and Mary as they looked towards their lost country, while their arms were entwined round the husband and brother. He approached them, for his solitude became painful, and he spoke.

'We shall soon see the last of old Ireland, Rory.'

'Yes, sir,' answered Rory, in a tone implying tender regret.

'But you have all those with you who are dear to you, and the parting is less sad.'

'Thank God, I have!' said Rory, fervently.

'And you, Mary, are a brave and sensible girl. I am glad to see you have dried your tears.'

'The heart may be sad, sir, without the eye being wet.'

The words entered De Lacy's very soul; and as he looked at the wet face of the girl, whose beauty became the more touching from the tinge of gentle sadness upon it, he thought how many as lovely a cheek had withered under the blight of silent grief.

'How faint the shore is looking now, sir!' said Mary.

'Yes, Mary;' and De Lacy approached her more nearly as he spoke.

After a few minutes' silence, while they still kept their looks upon the rapidly-sinking cliffs, De Lacy asked Mary if she thought it would not be too much for her feelings—would she oblige him by—

'What, sir?' said Mary timidly.

'Will you sing me "The Land of the West"? It is the last time any of us shall ever hear it in sight of its shores.'

A blush suffused Mary's cheek, and a slight quiver passed across her lip at the request.

'Perhaps 'tis too much for you, Mary; if so, do not sing; but I own I am weak at this moment—I did not know how much I loved poor Ireland.'

'I'll sing it for yon, sir: and sure I would sing the song for the dear country itself—the dear country! and though I may cry, maybe 'twill be a pleasure to my heart.'

Summoning all her resolutien, she essayed to sing; and after the first few words, which were faltered in a tremulous tone, her voice became firmer, and the enthusiasm which love of country supplied supporting her through the effort, she gave an expression to the song intensely touching.

As she was concluding the final stanza, the last beams of sunset, splendidly bright, burst through the purple clouds of the horizon, and shed a golden glow on 'the Land of the West,' as the inspired singer apostrophised it.

De Lacy looked upon her, and thought of his dream: it was the sunset and the song, and the same lovely face which beamed through his vision; and when the touching voice of the girl sank in its final cadence into silence, she could support her emotion no longer—she burst into tears, and held out her clasped hands towards the scarcely visible shore.

De Lacy put his arm gently round her waist, and the unresisting girl wept as he supported her.

'Don't weep, Mary, don't weep,' whispered De Lacy, in a gentler tone than she had ever heard him speak before; 'we shall see many a lovely sunset together in the woods of America, and you shall often sing me there "The Land of the West."

THE END